"If you don't believe in yourself, you can't expect anyone else to."

— CHAPTER 1 —
THE SECOND CHANCE

*D*espite growing up in separate corners of the world, the six fishermen who pulled out of Kodiak Bay Harbor on the *Second Chance* that morning all knew the difference between right and wrong. It didn't matter that they spoke foreign languages or came from different countries.

When they spotted an inflatable zodiac drifting about thirty kilometers off the coast, the fishermen didn't hesitate to lend a helping hand.

"Secure the deck!" Captain O'Brian shouted, immediately veering their ship off course. "We got a small boat in distress off the starboard side!"

The captain was stunned to see such a small craft this far from the nearest harbor and presumed something terrible must have transpired. It wouldn't have been the first time a fishing boat had left the harbor only to end up lost at sea (with survivors surfacing in a lifeboat days later, if at all). He struggled to come up with any other plausible explanation given the frequent whitecaps and thick morning fog that routinely blanketed this part of the Canadian coastline. "Surely, this lone seafarer wasn't foolish enough to think an inflatable zodiac could contend with the unforgiving waves of the North Atlantic," he thought.

Captain O'Brian convinced himself that he was rescuing this lucky sailor from certain death. However, he would soon discover that this encounter might not have been as random as he had assumed.

"Get ready to grab that line!" the captain ordered as the *Second Chance* pulled up alongside the flimsy orange boat.

One of the fishermen leaned over the right side of the ship and yelled, "Got it, skipper!" after he caught the mooring line thrown by the stranger. Gripping the rope, he walked toward the back of the fishing boat and slowly reeled in the zodiac using both arms. He was careful to avoid the great white shark thrashing around on the main deck.

The crew just captured the enormous shark and didn't have a chance to put it on ice yet, although the great white welcomed the untimely interruption. The ferocious shark continued snapping his jaws at anyone daring to look its way.

Once the zodiac was secured to the back of the *Second Chance*, the mysterious stranger grabbed the fisherman's hand, climbed aboard, and announced cheerfully, "Ah, bonjour, gentlemen! Merci, merci beaucoup for your gracious hospitality... And just in time too!"

The French stranger appeared to be an older man with a slender yet athletic build. He had striking green eyes, short white hair, and a cleanly shaven face except for a chevron-style mustache that matched his hair color. He was wearing an Irish tweed flat cap made of dark-gray wool, black boots, and a dark-blue mechanic's jumpsuit that was zipped up all the way to the collar. Considering the boat's precarious location, it wasn't surprising to see that this lone sailor was also wearing an orange life vest over his jumpsuit.

The stranger confidently breezed past the great white shark and stuck his hand out to greet the captain while the *Second Chance* swayed with the ocean swells.

Captain O'Brian quickly shook the man's hand with a firm grip and said, "You sure are lucky we crossed paths, eh? That little zodiac is no match for this part of the North Atlantic!" The Russian fisherman standing next to the captain laughed as he patted the stranger on the back. "The sharks will not be making you for dinner tonight! This is problem we fix," he teased, prompting the other men to howl with laughter while the stranger grinned derisively.

When the commotion began to settle down, the French stranger jested, "Well, I guess everyone deserves a... *second chance*, no?" Uproarious laughter erupted once again among the fishermen.

"Please, please... allow me to introduce myself. My name is Monsieur Saint-Clair, and I am so incredibly grateful that I ran into such a hospitable group of shark fishermen. Honestly, I was really starting to worry there for a minute!"

"Now, please," he humbly insisted, "there must be some way that I can thank you for your kindness." Before the crewmen could respond, Saint-Clair blurted, "My cigars!" He swiftly pulled out a pack of stogies from his left pocket and presented them to the fishermen. "Only thing I managed to save... but not to worry, it looks like there is enough for everyone!"

Without the slightest bit of hesitation, Captain O'Brian accepted the generous gift. His eyes lit up with excitement while he passed them out to the other five fishermen onboard.

"They are *Especial Selectados*," Saint-Clair explained merrily. "Unquestionably, one of the finest cigars. The slow burn simply does not compare to anything else out there. And trust me... I have tried them all!"

Enamored by the smell of Volado tobacco and with eager anticipation flickering in the captain's eyes, one of the fishermen inched closer to Saint-Clair to ask for matches. "You have light?"

The Russian fisherman stepped in with his windproof lighter and flipped the flint wheel using his thumb. Like a swarm of moths drawn to a streetlamp, the rest of the men huddled around the flame, each taking turns lighting their cigars.

While the fishermen stood back and happily puffed away, Saint-Clair turned his attention to the great white shark flailing about in front of them. The shark was desperately gasping for water and sporadically snapping his jaws in frustration. "You know, fishing can be quite dangerous if you are using the right kind of bait," he remarked.

"Although I will say... hunting sharks is an interesting choice. Beautiful animals, if you ask me." Admiring the shark's beauty from a safe distance, he carried on enlightening the unsuspecting fisherman. "Truly the greatest hunters on the planet. Forget lions! Most lions rely on the pride. They are all about family and defending their territory."

"But not all sharks are made equal!" Saint-Clair chortled, "No, no, no, the great white is special. Their territory covers *seventy percent* of the planet... and there are no borders. No rules, either. They don't even know what hesitation means... It's that insatiable need to eat pretty much anything that crosses their path once they smell blood in the water."

Captain O'Brian blew out a ring of smoke after taking a puff and responded curiously, "Is that right, eh?"

The six fishermen casually enjoyed their cigars while clouds of smoke began to waft in front of Saint-Clair's face as he stared back at them perspicaciously. "That's right, my friends," he answered with a menacing smirk. "From the minute a great white is born, that shark is on its own. Abandoned at birth by the mother... and the father is gone long before that. This is the moment for every great white shark where they realize hunting is life. There is no time for compassion or empathy. They must hunt to survive from day one. And while the lion cubs are being fed and nurtured by their mothers in the comforts of the den, the baby shark eats only when it learns to kill on its own."

Saint-Clair snickered. "Oui, it sure is a hell of a way to start your first day, but that is why they've been around longer than the dinosaurs!"

"I mean, just look at this guy." He gestured dramatically toward the writhing shark on the deck of the *Second Chance*, boasting, "This magnificent creature has special sensors in his nose, and even right now, he is listening to the electricity from our hearts. He can feel how fast they are beating without even touching us. Can you believe that? It is one of the only animals that can literally *smell fear*."

The gigantic great white continued thrashing as Saint-Clair warned, "Oui, this beautiful shark probably wishes he could show us how sharp those serrated teeth really are. All *three hundred* of them!"

One of the fishermen chimed in, gloating with a thick New York accent, "Not fuh nuthin', but I wouldn't worry about this one, buddy. He'll be a bowl of shark fin soup by this time tomorrow... just like his friends below deck!" The six fishermen burst into laughter. They gawked callously at the great white shark, which was still frantically gasping for water.

Saint-Clair shook his head in disappointment and smiled while he watched the men puffing away on their cigars arrogantly. He glanced at his watch and quipped, "I guess we better hope he doesn't make it back into the water then."

A split second later, one of the fishermen shouted something in Russian after the cigar he was smoking suddenly burst into flames; it caught fire like a road flare, with unrelenting sparks shooting out of the tip. The unexpected burns on his hand shocked him, and he hastily tossed the cigar away.

The rest of the fishermen were speechless at first—they could only watch in bewilderment as the burning cigar rolled across the deck while the boat rocked back and forth.

Everything changed in an instant once the cigar found its way to a small puddle of water near the wheelhouse. Instead of fizzling out, the opposite happened. It was as if someone had just poured a bucket of gasoline on a smoldering campfire. Raging flames spewed uncontrollably, catching everyone by surprise (everyone except Saint-Clair).

Beyond perplexed, the fishermen soon realized this was only the beginning of their problems—one by one, the rest of the cigars began to burst into flames as well. Two of the men managed to throw their cigars overboard, but it didn't matter. They still had to grapple with the other four cigars now burning on the deck of the *Second Chance*.

A blinding cloud of white smoke consumed the surrounding area while the fishermen scrambled to fill buckets of water. The captain yelled hysterically, "Get the hose! Right now!" prompting two of the men to race across the deck as the fire grew larger.

The fishermen connected the emergency firehose in a panicked frenzy and directed the gushing water coming out of the nozzle toward the four blazing hotspots on the deck. To their surprise, this only exacerbated the flames. What seemed like small but manageable fires were now quickly spreading, engulfing the middle section of the ship in a relentless inferno. It was absolute chaos by any measure.

Extinguishing one fire was hard enough; trying to put out four at the same time would prove to be near impossible, especially when everything they threw at the flames only made them grow larger. The men watched in disbelief as the uncontrollable firestorm continued raging near the wheelhouse.

While the fishermen tried feverishly to contain the fire, Saint-Clair calmly walked toward the aft of the ship as if nothing were wrong. He climbed into his inflatable zodiac after grabbing a large white bucket from the back of the *Second Chance*. Nobody even seemed to notice—they were all distracted by the blaze.

Saint-Clair chuckled as he untied the mooring line and started up the outboard motor. He quickly pulled away from the fishing vessel, giving himself a better vantage point to watch the mayhem unfold from a safe distance.

Unbeknownst to the fishermen, only the tips of those gifted cigars had pure tobacco in them. Everything below the first half inch contained tobacco leaves that had been meticulously soaked in a special compound of magnesium and sodium. Much to the surprise of the crew, this particular mixture of chemicals would prove to be nearly impossible to put out once ignited.

Despite their best efforts to extinguish the blaze, it was already too late—at least one of the cigars had burned a hole directly through the main deck, eventually rupturing the hull of the fishing vessel. An unstoppable surge of ocean water flooded the lower compartments, permeating every crevice of the engine room. The ship's lights started to flicker as the saltwater infiltrated the onboard electrical system.

Things weren't faring any better on the top deck either. The fire continued to grow with terrifying speed while the crew scrambled about in their blundered attempts to bring it under control.

Jumping through the flames, Captain O'Brian raced to the wheelhouse and barged in. He lunged for the radio but didn't get there fast enough. As he pushed the call button to send out a distress signal to the Coast Guard, the entire boat went completely dark. Desperately shouting into the radio, the captain's heart dropped to his stomach when he realized no one could hear the mayday call—help wasn't coming.

The electricity had finally failed under the sabotage of the unabating seawater, which only added to the growing number of setbacks encumbering the distressed ship. Crippled from the complete power failure, thick black smoke started billowing from the

Second Chance.

With the situation quickly spiraling out of control, Captain O'Brian feared the worst when he suddenly felt the ship listing at an alarming rate. "Get your vests on now!" he shouted. "All of ya! Right now!"

Saint-Clair beamed at the sight of the turmoil, clearly in no rush to help the embattled fishermen. In fact, he actually appeared to be thoroughly enjoying the show. The crewmen could hear the haunting sound of his cackling in the distance as they struggled to maintain their balance on the top deck of the doomed vessel. Saint-Clair just carried on circling the *Second Chance* in the orange zodiac as if nothing was wrong.

Fortunately for the shark, the ship's list was increasing at an untenable rate, and cold water from the North Atlantic rushed beneath his tail, prompting another bout of thrashing. It was a familiar feeling that the great white had been craving. Especially since the shark had spent the last ten minutes thinking about the dreaded thought of slowly dying without an ounce of dignity.

It didn't take long for the stern of the *Second Chance* to become fully submerged, sending the bow of the ship straight up into the air.

The shark didn't question the serendipitous turn of events; he quickly wriggled off the deck and back into the ocean. Liberated and eager to escape, the massive great white rushed to get far away from the humans that had nearly taken everything from him.

Saint-Clair watched from the inflatable zodiac and shouted cheerfully, "Au revoir, *mon ami*!" just before the shark disappeared into the darkness of the North Atlantic.

Without any further delay, the six fishermen jumped overboard as the *Second Chance* bobbed up and down. Clinging to the burning vessel was simply no longer an option. The ship was now fully vertical, with the bottom half entirely submerged beneath the water line.

It only took about ninety seconds for the *Second Chance* to finish sinking, never to be seen again as it plummeted toward the depths of the ocean floor.

Saint-Clair slowed the zodiac and eventually brought it to a full stop; he wanted to devote his full attention to savoring every last detail. Everything from the absence of hope in their eyes to the panicked shrieks for help—it was all priceless. Watching people deal with the consequences of their actions in real time was something he truly relished.

Floating amongst the debris left behind by the *Second Chance*, the fishermen immediately pleaded with Saint-Clair to rescue them, "Over here! Over here! Come help us!"

Grinning back at them menacingly, Saint-Clair had something else in mind and pushed the throttle forward. Keeping a firm grip on the wheel, he began to circle the distraught fishermen at a slow speed. "Gentlemen, gentlemen... I would caution you to conserve your energy," he warned. "The primary cause of most drownings is rooted in exhaustion!"

Unamused, Captain O'Brian shouted back, "What the hell was in those cigars? This is all your fault... You maniac!" Confused and growing more resentful with each passing second, the captain demanded, "Bring that boat over here and hurry it up... These waters are filled with sharks!"

Saint-Clair continued circling them. "Humans are so very predictable, no?" He laughed, as if he had planned this entire series of unfortunate events.

"What? What are you talking about, eh?" Captain O'Brian screeched in frustration. One of the Russian fishermen bellowed, "The boat, you bring here!"

"Now that your lives are in danger... now that your hopes and dreams are in jeopardy... this is what I was waiting for! *Finally*, you have a real appreciation for the shark's ability to smell fear!" Saint-Clair replied merrily. Glaring at the fishermen in disgust, he added, "Anybody can admire the shark's natural gifts from afar, but to really feel it in the water... oui, now that is something you should be thanking me for! *All of you!*"

"What? Are you crazy?" Captain O'Brian cried out. "Stop messing around and get over here right now!"

Even though the riotous laughter that ensued sounded quite sinister, most of the fishermen assumed this obnoxious little charade was coming to an end once Saint-Clair pulled the throttle back and brought the zodiac to an abrupt stop. They couldn't have been more wrong. He was far from finished toying with the puzzled fishermen and became infuriated that they would dare ask for assistance.

Saint-Clair sprang to his feet, berating them in the most contemptuous manner, "Help? You want my help? You want me to help six cowards that came out here to kill dozens of sharks?" His smile had vanished almost as quickly as the last flicker of hope in the fishermen's eyes. "Say it out loud then!" he demanded furiously. "Tell me how many sharks you slaughtered today! How about yesterday... or the day before that? Come on now! Say it like you mean it!"

Astonished by the pure vitriol in Saint-Clair's tone, the fishermen were starting to regret having ever left the docks this morning. They nervously looked around for any sharks circling nearby, while the enraged stranger asked, "What is it? Did you lose count? Too busy selling them by the piece on the docks?" He screamed, "And for what? For money... for a bowl of soup?"

The bewilderment of it all was turning into inescapable terror for the six fishermen bobbing up and down with the passing ocean swells of the North Atlantic.

"No, no, no. I am sorry, but that is not how the jungle works," Saint-Clair explained. "Nobody forced you to come out here. You did that on your own. Every last one of you!" Smirking, he continued scolding them, "But now you have a big problem... You see, sharks don't care about excuses. They don't care about regrets or mistakes. Respect is the only currency that matters out here."

Saint-Clair's demeanor turned more cheerful. "Not to worry, though... The sharks have a special way of dealing with trespassers. Oui, I suspect there are at least a few out there listening to your hearts beating right now. Taking their time to decide which one of you is the most terrified... which one will be the easiest prey."

Captain O'Brian desperately shouted back, "We're sorry, alright? We're sorry! We were wrong! Just help us!"

"*The jungle owes you nothing*!" Saint-Clair screamed wrathfully at the top of his lungs. "And that is exactly what you will get from me! Nothing! No help, no assistance, no rescue!" All of a sudden, a shark fin breached the waterline near the orange zodiac and sent the six fishermen into a panic as they continued to tread water.

"Don't worry, my friends! You don't need my help!" Saint-Clair announced. He saw the shark fin disappear under the water and carried on explaining, "You see, the average Olympic swimmer can cover over ninety-six kilometers in just one day. *Ninety-six kilometers*!"

The thought of being dragged under the water at any moment made it hard for the dismayed fishermen to focus on the French stranger's incessant prattling. And it didn't help matters when he resumed circling them; they feared the noise from the small zodiac would only attract more sharks to the area.

"Now, while it is clear that none of you are professional athletes, I have got some good news here. You only have to swim thirty kilometers to make it to the nearest shore," Saint-Clair added snidely. Sensing that the fishermen were in need of some encouragement, he advised, "So, when your arms start getting tired and your legs are exhausted from kicking, just pretend like your life depends on it...

Maybe that will be enough to help you make it back to shore in one piece."

After circling the fishermen one more time, Saint-Clair pulled the throttle back again and brought the orange zodiac to a standstill. He glanced at his watch and exclaimed, "I would love to stick around to see how it all turns out... Unfortunately, I must be going now. Oui, I have some unfinished business to take care of in Kodiak Bay."

"But I hope this encounter was educational!" Saint-Clair said with a smug wink, "We really covered it all, no? Lessons about picking up strangers, smoking things that will kill you, and, most importantly... an education on the hazards that can arise when hunting the world's most experienced predator. Killing sharks to make soup can be a complicated profession, it would seem, oui?"

The French stranger laughed to himself and murmured, "Honestly, I should start calling myself *Le Professeur*!"

A scowl washed over Saint-Clair's face. He suddenly snapped at the stunned fishermen, "Don't make me come back out here... Or next time, it will be *fifty kilometers* from the coast. Remember that, and remember my face, because if you see me again, I guarantee you will gain a newfound appreciation for the definition of regret."

Without uttering another word, Saint-Clair slammed the throttle all the way forward—in the blink of an eye, the zodiac zoomed off toward Kodiak Bay, leaving the fishermen stranded in the notoriously shark-infested waters of the North Atlantic.

It only took a minute before the small inflatable boat had completely disappeared from sight.

Captain O'Brian tried to remain optimistic. He knew panicking wouldn't help anyone, and the safety of the crew was still his responsibility until they all made it back to shore. "Take it easy, men," he ordered. "I promise we'll find a way out of this mess. Everyone just stay calm, eh?" The shaky apprehension in his voice implied otherwise, but the fishermen didn't have much of a choice.

Not with the *Second Chance* gone and an untold number of great white sharks swimming in the vicinity. Truth be told, the captain was terrified; the others could see it in his eyes, and they felt the same way.

Ten minutes quickly passed. But it seemed like hours to the inconsolable survivors floating amid the debris.

After waiting for the fear of imminent death to really set in, Saint-Clair turned the inflatable zodiac around and steered the boat back toward the fishermen.

When Captain O'Brian spotted the orange zodiac headed back their way, he was beyond relieved. "Ah, you see... It was all just a big prank, fellas. He's coming back for us now, eh?"

As the inflatable craft approached the six fishermen clinging to their life vests, the captain hollered, "Wooooooo! Saint-Clair, you really put on one hell of a show! I really thought you were gonna leave us all out here, eh?" Saint-Clair howled with amusement while the fishermen erupted in laughter and cheerful celebration.

Despite the French stranger's questionable sense of humor, the survivors of the *Second Chance* were happy to look past it—especially if it meant getting out of this dangerous predicament. The weary fishermen had seen at least one other shark fin breach the water in what must have been the most harrowing ten minutes of their lives.

Once the zodiac got closer to the band of sailors bobbing around, Saint-Clair brought the boat to an unexpected stop. It was just close enough to keep their last sliver of hope alive, giving him an opportunity to confess, "Come on guys, that would not be fair! I couldn't leave you out here like this!"

"The shark got a *second chance* today," he admitted. "It's only right that you all get a *second chance* too, no?"

As the fear in their eyes dissipated, Saint-Clair gazed at the fishermen and added, "How can I expect you to learn from your poor decisions without giving you another chance to prove it, oui?"

There was a hint of skepticism among the six men, but Captain O'Brian refused to believe that it was anything more than a misbegotten joke gone wrong. The first mate of the *Second Chance* was thinking the same thing. "Why would Saint-Clair come back if he were truly intent on marooning them this whole time?"

Not all the fishermen were so forgiving. One of them was still enraged and muttered something under his breath in a foreign language.

Growing tired of treading water, they started swimming toward the zodiac while Saint-Clair walked toward the back of the boat to grab the white bucket he had taken from the *Second Chance*. None of them seemed to notice when he placed the bucket near the center console, although they were absolutely befuddled when he slowly resumed circling the fishermen like he had done before.

"But then I realized, you cannot come out of this on the other side without first changing your beliefs," Saint-Clair warned. "And of course, if you know anything about change, it can only materialize with the proper incentive. So, I have returned to give you the greatest gift one could hope for... *Desperation*."

With his right hand on the wheel, Saint-Clair removed the lid from the top of the white bucket. He pushed the bucket to the edge of the zodiac and carefully spilled its contents into the water while circling the confused fishermen. When they realized what was happening, Captain O'Brian screamed frantically, "Hey! Stop! What the hell are you doing? Are you out of your mind?"

It didn't take long before the fishermen found themselves surrounded by a circle of red blood and chopped-up pieces of dead fish. Like an oil sheen, it all floated on the surface, but in a vastly more terrifying fashion.

Nearly getting burned alive on the *Second Chance* paled in comparison to the heart-stopping sight of bloody water in every direction. The sharks loved the irresistible fish carcasses, and it would only be a matter of time until more of them arrived.

Saint-Clair crowed with delight after he finished emptying the chum bucket—the same bait the fishermen were using to attract sharks. He shook it vigorously to make sure every last drop had been emptied out into the North Atlantic and then tossed the bucket toward the back of the boat.

Bringing the zodiac to a full stop once again, Saint-Clair was overcome with uncontrollable laughter; he stared in amusement as the fishermen desperately floundered in the water. He found the whole ordeal to be justifiably ironic.

The more the fishermen thrashed, the easier it would be for the sharks to find them. They were facing a rather precarious dilemma indeed. The tables had turned quite precipitously, and Saint-Clair was proud to be the one to level the playing field. "Careful, careful gentlemen," he announced enthusiastically. "The great white shark is a very curious animal." He laughed when he saw a dorsal fin breach the waterline just past the pair of Russian fishermen waving their arms in distress.

Still not convinced the men were frightened enough, Saint-Clair's tone changed and became more serious. "Oui, the great white spends a lifetime alone, navigating endless oceans of darkness as he hunts for his next meal. The other fish, the sea lions, everyone... they cross the street when they see the great white shark coming. They run for their lives when they see that shark on the move!"

"Believe me, nothing else matters... Because when that shark smells blood, it's already too late," he cautioned. "The great white just loses all control! Eats everything in his path without the slightest trace of reluctance or empathy."

"You see, the shark can never stop being a shark." Saint-Clair taunted, "*The real king of the jungle*, oui?" He locked eyes with Captain O'Brian and advised, "So, if I were you, I would stop crying about what you don't have and start swimming while you still have the opportunity to do so!"

Saint-Clair couldn't help but wonder how many of the fishermen would actually make it out alive. Much to his chagrin, the aspiring French educator didn't have time to stick around and find out. The sheer terror in the fishermen's eyes would have to suffice for now, though he was looking forward to eventually reading about it in the news.

Forcing the throttle all the way forward, Saint-Clair waved as the inflatable zodiac zoomed away toward Kodiak Bay. "Au revoir!"

"Get back here, you lunatic! You can't leave us here!" Captain O'Brian screamed, slamming his fists down in a panicked rage. It didn't matter, though—Saint-Clair was already gone and wasn't coming back this time.

With nothing but endless ocean as far as the eye could see, the fishermen started swimming toward Kodiak Bay in a hurry. They knew better than most that these waters were overrun by sharks; waiting around to see how many would be enticed by all the fish blood floating nearby seemed like a bad idea.

At least half of them feared it wouldn't matter how fast they swam. The great white was faster. Much faster. Between the ocean swells and the unrelenting threat of being eaten alive, making it back to shore in one piece felt insurmountable.

Proud of the lessons he had taught the unsuspecting crew of the *Second Chance*, the mysterious French stranger raced toward the coastline in the orange zodiac.

Meanwhile, in Kodiak Bay, the harbormaster sat in his office reading yesterday's top headlines in the newspaper with mounting concern. It was the front-page story that he found most unsettling.

— CHAPTER 2 —
KODIAK BAY

*C*aptain William Fulbright served as the harbormaster of Kodiak Bay, a bustling Canadian town on the east side of Prince Edward Island. The captain's presence was unmistakable. The former Royal Canadian Navy officer towered over everyone—some would say he was the tallest man in all of Kodiak Bay. Despite his older age, he still had a muscular physique and a reputation in town for being as tough as nails. He retired from the Navy almost ten years ago, but that hadn't slowed him down one bit.

His handsome face was accentuated by short white hair and a neatly trimmed beard with a mustache that matched. The seasoned mariner routinely wore a plain black necktie over a white button-down collared shirt. On top of that was a black double-breasted peacoat with matching pants, black shoes, and his old officer's cap.

Even though it had endured years of weathering over the span of his career (stripping the original luster like faded paint on an old car), Captain Fulbright proudly wore his Royal Canadian Navy cap wherever he went. The golden anchor embroidery, maple leaf stitching, and St. Edward's red crown seal on the front served as a welcome reminder of the sacrifices he made in service to his country.

Everyone in town loved celebrating Canada Day, and Captain Fulbright was no exception—but on the eve of this year's celebration, he wasn't in a very festive mood after reading today's front-page story in the Kodiak Bay Gazette.

A newspaper article alone wasn't enough to rattle this old sailor, although he was admittedly concerned about the unusual ship that dropped anchor right outside the harbor this morning. The timing of the mysterious ship's arrival combined with today's front-page story left him feeling a bit anxious. He knew it couldn't be an innocent coincidence.

The captain noticed the peculiar vessel when he arrived at work earlier that morning. Due to the angle of the ship's position and the blinding sunrise in his eyes, he could only see part of the name painted on the bow. The letters *OOM* weren't enough to confirm his suspicions, but the captain was convinced he recognized the unique hull design. He had seen this ship before, many years ago, and knew its presence could only mean one thing.

Following a long afternoon, Captain Fulbright folded up the newspaper on his desk and grabbed the binoculars hanging from the wall next to the door. As he stepped out of the harbormaster's office, he glanced over at Regent Street, which ran parallel with the harbor. There were hundreds of red maple leaf flags as far as the eye could see, decorating store windows, billowing from lampposts lining the street, and fluttering on flagpoles atop every building in town.

The people of Kodiak Bay loved Canada. They weren't shy about showing their patriotism around this time of year, and even though the country's most popular holiday was just one day, the town celebrated all week long. The abundance of red flags was impossible to miss against the sea of dark-green spruce trees that surrounded Kodiak Bay in every direction.

Captain Fulbright couldn't help but smile when he spotted the largest Canadian flag in town; it was gigantic and hung above the *Kodiak Bay Central Station* entrance as a magnificent display of national pride. The central station was only a few blocks down at the end of Regent Street and served as the international passenger terminal for trains and transatlantic ships.

With the evening hours fast approaching, he shifted his gaze toward the bay and spotted dozens of small fishing boats steadily making their way back into the harbor for the night. It was a familiar sight at this time of the day. However, the fishing boats paled in comparison to the size of the mighty RMS *Queen Charlotte*.

At nearly twenty stories high, the enormous transatlantic ocean liner was docked next to the passenger terminal at the *Kodiak Bay Central Station*. Its looming presence was a welcome sight, even if the shadow cast by the vessel was enough to cover what seemed like half the town in darkness on a sunny day.

As a blanket of thick fog started to slowly consume the harbor, Captain Fulbright squinted anxiously toward the expedition ship that was anchored off the coast. He lifted his binoculars and looked past the harbor channel toward the North Atlantic. The mysterious vessel that arrived this morning was now barely visible.

It wasn't unusual for the town to be engulfed in fog once the sun set, and the visibility around the harbor was already diminishing. Only seconds before his view of the ship would be blocked, the captain finally saw the full name painted on the bow once he managed to focus the binoculars. He gasped in disbelief—it was indeed the legendary *Arthur Broome*.

Captain Fulbright hadn't seen this ship in years. The last time was back during his days serving in the Royal Canadian Navy, almost a lifetime ago. He lowered his binoculars, mumbling under his breath, "The *Broome!*" The old memories that resurfaced instantly captivated him.

Suddenly, the approaching sound of a horse trotting down Regent Street commandeered his attention. When Captain Fulbright spun around, he spotted Constable Oliver Hamilton (and his equine partner, Rusty) of the Royal Canadian Mounted Police.

Constable Oliver Hamilton recently graduated from cadet training and was a typical young hotshot that carried the naive feeling of being invincible everywhere he went. Despite his youthful arrogance, he took the job quite seriously and had wanted to be a Mountie ever since he could remember. The constable was in peak physical condition from his weightlifting days at the academy; he had short brown hair and a cleanly shaven face.

Dressed in the customary Red Serge garb, Constable Hamilton wore the RCMP uniform with immense pride. He was rarely seen without his scarlet tunic, dark blue trousers, and the traditional broad-brimmed campaign-style hat.

His loyal partner, Rusty, was a beautiful black thoroughbred horse with a flowing black mane and a long black tail. Although well trained, Rusty was still young and could be rather brazen at times, not unlike his human partner.

"Ah, captain, my captain. Bonjour, bonjour," Constable Hamilton said with a smirk.

"I trust you saw what my Grizzlies did to your beloved Maple Barons last night in the playoffs," the constable gloated. "At this rate, I should probably sign up as a reserve player just to make it a fair game, eh?"

Captain Fulbright chuckled. "I'm thinking your dentist would advise you to stick to being one of the town's best Mounties."

Constable Hamilton interjected fervently, "*One of the best*? The town only has four Mounties... and the Chief Inspector is about to retire!" Grinning, the captain quipped, "Like I said, pal, you're one of the best, eh?"

"Fair enough, Captain," the rookie officer laughed. "So, how's our harbor faring this evening?"

Captain Fulbright peered through the fog and noticed most of the fishing vessels pulling into the harbor had now found their boat slips. Amid the fishermen trudging in, he also spotted the young dock attendant scuttling down the pier. The kid was racing to secure as many mooring lines as possible.

"Looks like they're all trying to beat the fog," the captain remarked, "or maybe it's just happy hour. I suspect these boys will be ready for some two-fours on account of the holiday tomorrow."

The constable shrugged with a chuckle as Captain Fulbright put two fingers up to his mouth and whistled loudly. The sound echoed throughout the harbor and immediately caught the attention of the teenage dock attendant.

Constable Hamilton took a deep breath and said, "Well, I guess it's going to be a long night ahead, my friend... But nothing Rusty and I can't handle, eh?"

"I'm not too worried about it," Captain Fulbright replied. "Rusty looks like he's ready."

The overly confident rookie laughed and shook his head at the playful teasing. He then repositioned Rusty by gently tugging on the reins.

While the banter continued, the young dock attendant rushed past the fishing boats up the pier, carefully dodging chum buckets, crab traps, and a slew of salty fishermen unloading after a long day. He would always jump at any opportunity to see Rusty. The small dog at his side felt the same way, and she mirrored his every step, scampering closely behind.

Breezing past Captain Fulbright, the energetic teenager greeted the equine officer before anyone else. The majestic horse loved the attention and happily leaned into the boy's hand to express his appreciation. Not surprised in the slightest, the captain laughed when he saw Rusty devour a green apple the dock attendant pulled out of his pocket.

"Good afternoon, Constable Hamilton!" the boy exclaimed.

"Did you see today's front-page story in the Kodiak Bay Gazette? Another fishing boat has gone missing... They're saying it's the *Amity Jane* this time!" Clearly amused, Captain Fulbright smirked.

The constable answered reluctantly, "Ah, yes, Mr. Henry Halifax and his faithful sidekick, Penny."

Henry Halifax was a clever young man with short blond hair and sapphire blue eyes, which were common in the Halifax family. Those who knew him would swear he looked just like his late father and grandfather. He wasn't particularly muscular, but he was in excellent physical shape and stayed lean with regular exercise. He was taller than most kids his age, but not quite old enough to be burdened with adolescent stubble on his face.

Despite his skinny arms, Henry never missed a chance to compete in Kodiak Bay's annual axe-throwing competition and never missed a day of work helping Captain Fulbright on the docks either.

Henry routinely wore an oatmeal-colored sweater with dark brown trousers and brown shoes. He would rarely leave home without his yellow raincoat, which was always unbuttoned unless it was actually raining. The raincoat once belonged to his late father, and even though it was a little big on him, Henry didn't care. It gave him confidence and was the only thing he had to remember his father by, aside from a few old photographs.

The small companion at his side was named Penny, a black wirehaired dachshund with tan coloring around her paws and snout. Captain Fulbright brought Penny home for Henry's fourteenth birthday last year, and the two have been inseparable ever since. She was fiercely loyal to Henry and followed him everywhere.

Penny usually rode in the front basket of Henry's bicycle or in the bespoke brown leather rucksack he wore on his back. She was known to be a bit dramatic (as most dachshunds are), but incredibly well behaved when it mattered most. She enjoyed privileges not often extended to other dogs and was mindful of acting decorously.

Constable Hamilton brushed off Henry's concerns. "Yes, yes... of course, I heard about the *Amity Jane*. They probably just decided to head out further for a longer haul, eh? Fishermen around here can be quite stubborn after all. I can't even remember the last time one of these fishing boats actually called for help."

Not worried in the slightest, the constable was more interested in last night's hockey game. "You should be more worried about the playoffs! My Grizzlies mopped the floor with Fulbright's Maple Barons last night... and I'm betting they're going to take the Cup home in four this year!" he boasted. "Bobby Lemieux can't be stopped, eh? It was an absolute barnburner last night!"

Undeterred, Henry responded confidently, "Yes, I know, Constable. I'm sure the whole town watched last night's game, and I could sense the captain's disappointment with the outcome this morning at breakfast." The constable snickered. "You see, the thing about the Maple Barons is..."

Henry interrupted him, hoping to avoid one of the rookie's long-winded rants about how the Grizzlies could beat any team on the ice. "But what about the *Amity Jane*?" He blurted, "Do you think it's related to the Frenchman? Do you think he's back?"

"Don't worry so much, my young friend!" Constable Hamilton tutted. "I'm sure those boys on the *Amity Jane* are doing just fine. They would have made a distress call if there was any trouble." He sighed in frustration and explained, "I'm guessing the reporters down in the newsroom didn't have anything juicy enough to write about today, sensationalizing something out of nothing just so they can sell more papers. But the truth is... deep-sea fishermen stay out longer than expected all the time. You would know that better than most!"

Dissatisfied with the lack of privileged information he was getting from the constable, Henry exclaimed, "But nobody has seen the Frenchmen in over a year! Now the papers are reporting that bear cubs have vanished from zoos in Sydney and Paris over the past few weeks... plus we've got two local fishing boats out there that might be missing. And if that wasn't suspicious enough, the *Kodiak Bay Zoo* just opened their new polar bear exhibit a few days ago!"

"Every time the Frenchman breaks into a zoo, the newspapers are overrun with stories about missing fishing boats in the days that follow," he warned impatiently, hoping to weaken the constable's skepticism. "And not just any fishing boats, Constable!"

Constable Hamilton rolled his eyes with indifference. Seeing Henry all riled up was mildly entertaining, or at least it had been in the past when the legend of *THE MYSTERIOUS FRENCHMAN* first splashed across the front page of the Kodiak Bay Gazette last year. The novelty of the teenager's enthusiasm had long since dissipated for the constable.

"They're all shark fishermen! Different cities, but the pattern is the same!" Henry shrieked, trying to persuade him further. "I'm telling you, that must be his calling card. And if I'm right about the *Amity Jane*, the Frenchman could be planning to hit the *Kodiak Bay Zoo* next!" Growing tired of the boy's wild conspiracy theories, the constable clicked his tongue in annoyance, as if he were waiting for a wound-up toddler to tire out.

"Just look at the docks... The *Second Chance* is missing!" Henry gestured emphatically toward the harbor. "That's the only other boat out here fishing for sharks around these waters."

The constable's eyes flickered with a hint of curiosity as Henry added swiftly, "Those guys are almost always in by four o'clock every afternoon... Just ask the captain!" Before he could finish, Captain Fulbright chimed in, "Henry, Henry... you worry too much, my boy."

Henry stammered disappointingly, "But, but the..."

"The Mounties have the watch, my boy!" Captain Fulbright interrupted. "And I'm sure they're staying in close contact with the

Coast Guard, eh?" Henry nodded his head respectfully and abandoned his spirited line of questioning.

Even though the captain was often short and curt when giving orders, Henry had tremendous respect for the man (more so than anyone he had ever met).

Captain Fulbright had served with Henry's father in the Royal Canadian Navy for years; they were best friends until the very end. After his father's patrol ship was lost at sea during an unexpected Nor'easter over ten years ago, Captain Fulbright and his wife graciously offered to look after Henry. If the captain and his wife had not been so kind, Henry would have undoubtedly been sent to an orphanage since his mother tragically passed away on the day he was born.

Henry looked at Captain Fulbright as a beloved uncle figure and admired that he was far more than your typical harbormaster.

Ever since Henry could remember, the captain would always regale them at the dinner table with astonishing tales of his adventures over the years. There was the time he delivered cargo and supplies to remote scientific research outposts in the Arctic after sailing through the treacherous Northwest Passage. And Henry could never forget Captain Fulbright's skirmish with a particularly dangerous group of pirates near the coast of Madagascar while serving in the Royal Canadian Navy. The captain even navigated through a hurricane in the Caribbean to rescue a group of stranded sailors when their ship started taking on water.

Henry had heard countless stories of all the times Captain Fulbright had managed to escape unscathed—each one seemingly more harrowing than he could imagine. The one where he tussled with a pack of vicious crocodiles on the Nile was probably Henry's favorite. The captain was tougher than most, and he commanded respect from all the local sailors that docked their boats in Kodiak Bay.

Constable Hamilton agreed with Captain Fulbright and chimed in, "Exactly, my young friend. Stick to the local animal cases... Like the time you helped track down Mrs. Wilson's golden retriever when he ran off into the woods. Or the time you stopped traffic in both directions to help that family of geese cross Baker Street a few months ago."

The defeated expression that washed over Henry's face gave the constable pause, as did the guilt that followed.

"Look, I'm sorry. I know you love animals." The constable sighed, regretting that this friendly exchange had turned into somewhat of a scolding. "There's only one police force in this town, though. So, please... do me a favor and leave the detective work to the real Mounties, eh? It's for your own good, son."

Henry conceded, "Yes, sir, constable." His tone was peppered with just enough respect to mask the underlying disappointment. He gave Rusty some parting nuzzles with his head and stepped back next to Captain Fulbright.

"That's a good lad!" the constable replied. "Alright, gentlemen. I must get back to the station for supper. Rusty gobbled up that apple faster than usual. He's got to be getting hungry."

Constable Oliver Hamilton tipped his hat politely. "Have a good night, fellas," and he headed down Regent Street without any further delay.

As they watched the constable and Rusty trot down the street, all of a sudden, Penny erupted into a fit of vociferous barking. While Henry and Captain Fulbright were all too familiar with her histrionic temperament, they both found it strange to hear the rascally dachshund start yapping without any provocation. Everything made sense when they turned around, though.

Penny had picked up on the scent of an unfamiliar seafarer pulling furtively into the marina—it was an orange zodiac, which seemed rather odd given the hour.

— CHAPTER 3 —
THE FRENCH STRANGER

*C*aptain Fulbright peered through his binoculars and surmised, "Looks like we've got another tender coming into town to pick up supplies. Probably from one of the big yachts anchored out there for tomorrow's fireworks show." As Henry stared curiously at the orange zodiac cruising through the rocky jetty channel, the captain added, "Can you run over there and help 'em tie up? Give 'em the end slip on row twelve, eh? I'm heading out to take a quick pass of the harbor before nightfall."

"Roger that, Captain," Henry eagerly responded. He dashed past the harbormaster's office and hurried down the wooden dock while Penny scurried right behind him.

After Henry and Penny reached the end of the pier, they watched as the orange zodiac slowly entered the harbor. Most of the fishing boats had beaten the fog and were already docked. It was peculiar to see such a small vessel headed into the marina at this late hour. Nevertheless, he waved both his hands high above his head to signal the person driving the boat. The man behind the wheel eventually locked eyes with him and steered the zodiac toward the docks accordingly.

Once the small boat got close enough, the man turned off the engine and tossed out a mooring line. Henry caught it with ease and used both arms to pull the inflatable zodiac into the nearest dock slip. As Henry finished securing the line to the cast iron cleat, he heard a loud thud hit the wooden planks. He sprang to his feet and noticed the stranger was standing next to a large black duffle bag. The bag seemed out of place for a man traveling by inflatable zodiac, yet that would hardly prove to be the only curious thing about this mysterious stranger.

"Bonsoir!" the man said exuberantly. He spoke with a heavy French accent that couldn't be confused with anything else, but it gave Henry pause. Penny just cautiously peered between his legs, sniffing from a safe distance.

Henry was surprised by the jovial tone of the man's voice, hesitating, "Uh... good evening, sir. Can I help you with anything? Do you need a dock slip for the night... or fuel for your boat?"

The French stranger appeared to be an older gentleman with a white mustache and short white hair that was covered by a dark gray Irish tweed flat cap. He was wearing black boots and a dark blue jumpsuit that was zipped up to the collar, leading Henry to believe the man was a mechanic for one of the big yachts anchored nearby (the subtle traces of oil stains and dirt on his clothing were a dead giveaway).

That alone certainly wasn't out of the ordinary for a harbor town like Kodiak Bay, although the unusual protrusions around the ankles of the stranger's jumpsuit struck Henry as odd. It appeared the man was wearing another set of clothes underneath the mechanic's outfit. Penny noticed too and glared at the duffle bag with her tail wagging.

The unassuming gentleman casually replied, "Oui, please fill it up. I'm just passing through town to pick up a few things. Should only take me a couple hours."

"No problem, sir!" Henry answered promptly. "I'll get the gas caddy and take care of this right away."

The stranger picked up the black duffle bag with ease (almost as if it were empty) and reached into his pocket to pull out a few coins for the fuel. Henry held out his hand to collect the loose change, and, to his surprise, it was the exact amount owed. "Merci, merci," the French stranger murmured, breezing past Henry.

Somewhat befuddled, Henry spun around and scrupulously eyed the man sauntering down the dock.

The sound of Penny's whining eventually interrupted his confused gawking. She was growing quite hungry, even though it had been no more than an hour since her last treat.

Quickly shoving the coins into his pocket, Henry dashed over to the fuel pump and filled the gas caddy. He hastily lugged it to the stranger's orange zodiac once the container was half full. Penny supervised, keeping her paws planted firmly on the pier; she wasn't particularly fond of the stench coming from the gasoline and trusted that he could manage on his own.

Anyone else would have probably missed it, but not Henry. In the midst of removing the cap on the fuel tank, he froze after noticing something lying at the back of the zodiac. It was a large white bucket. Suspecting things weren't adding up as they should, he lunged for the bucket to get a closer look. He flipped it around and blurted, "*Sweet maple syrup!*" The young dock attendant was so startled by what he saw written on the side of the bucket that he lost his balance and nearly fell overboard into the cold waters of the marina.

Henry was absolutely stunned; he immediately recognized it as one of the chum buckets used by the *Second Chance*. The unmistakable initials *SC* were scribbled in black marker on the side. He knew he'd seen those initials before. He often helped clean equipment and other gear used by the fishermen when they came in for the night. The fishermen of Kodiak Bay always marked their buckets to ensure they didn't end up on the wrong boat—it was sort of like an unspoken rule of the harbor.

"This bucket must be from the *Second Chance*, Penny! *SC*! Just look at those initials!" Henry announced impetuously, glancing at the confused wirehaired dachshund.

Henry's heart leapt with exhilaration. His first thought was to storm down the pier, demanding that the stranger explain himself in front of everybody. The disapproving look gleaming in Penny's eyes made him reconsider, though. Henry knew he had to be cautious.

The last thing he needed was trouble with the Mounties, and there was no way Constable Hamilton would believe him without ironclad proof. A chum bucket by itself didn't necessarily prove anything, nefarious or otherwise. It surely didn't measure up to the level of evidence warranting a full-fledged RCMP investigation.

Penny wasn't convinced and just stared at Henry as he mumbled in speculation, "Or maybe the bucket got knocked overboard... and this gentleman picked it up as a courtesy when he saw it floating out there?" Admittedly, he would have done the same thing if he spotted some garbage littering the harbor. Sensing that he was on the verge of spiraling into a rambling tizzy, Penny let out a muffled yet playful bark. Any further delay in leaving work wouldn't bode well for her insatiable appetite, which had been building since lunchtime.

"There's something off with this guy, eh?" Henry carried on, oblivious to Penny's subtle dinnertime reminder. "Too many irregularities to be a coincidence. And he can't be from Quebec. Not with that accent. It sounded more Parisian to me... sort of similar to that new deckhand from Paris who works on the *Debbie Sue*."

"And did you see his face?" Henry asked, looking at Penny with a furrowed brow. "No wrinkles for a mechanic over the age of sixty?" The wirehaired dachshund growled with skepticism while he screwed the gas cap back on the fuel tank.

Wrestling with an infinite number of theories, Henry stepped off the boat onto the dock and wheeled the gas caddy over to the fuel pump. He scooped the coins out of his pocket and dropped them in the locked box next to the pump, laying out the most compelling supposition that came to mind in the process. "Nobody has even seen the Frenchman in over a year, Penny! The *Amity Jane* has been missing since yesterday, and now a French stranger shows up the next day with a chum bucket from the *Second Chance*?"

Penny let out a sharp bark, to which Henry responded, "Let's follow him and find out what he's really up to, eh?" They watched intently as the stranger walked past the harbormaster's office and headed for Regent Street.

After hesitating, Henry took off running down the pier in the same direction while Penny mirrored his every step. The winded dock attendant took a minute to catch his breath once he reached the harbormaster's office; Penny did as well, gulping down the remaining water in the bowl that Captain Fulbright always kept next to the stairs.

Frantically looking at Regent Street in both directions, Henry caught a glimpse of the unsuspecting stranger ambling into town. If he had gotten there a second later, he would have missed it entirely— the stranger quickly disappeared out of sight, turning the corner on Cambridge Lane and heading toward Prince Street.

Prince Street would be filled with people at this hour, especially since Canada Day was tomorrow. If he didn't hurry, he would surely lose the man in the crowds. With little time to spare, Henry darted up the stairs into the harbormaster's office and grabbed his dark brown leather rucksack. He rushed out of the office, slamming the door behind him with a heart-pounding sense of exhilaration.

Penny was happily sitting at the bottom of the steps, waiting patiently with her tongue hanging out.

"Alright, Penny," Henry said, kneeling down and holding the rucksack open with both hands, "hop in, girl. Let's go, eh?" The scrappy dachshund scurried into the leather bag headfirst and quickly turned her body around so that her face was sticking out of the top.

There was special cushioning sewn into the bottom of the rucksack, and the interior was lined with soft cashmere, which offered extra warmth and comfort during the cold Canadian winters. This was no ordinary bag—Penny had Mrs. Fulbright to thank for that.

Henry grabbed his forest-green bicycle from the usual spot next to the harbormaster's office and threw his leg over to hop on. He pushed off with his right foot and raced uphill on Regent Street with Penny in the rucksack.

Now on the move and pedaling as fast as he could, Henry's thoughts were consumed with nefarious conjecture about how this French stranger ended up in a small town like Kodiak Bay. Peering out of the rucksack, Penny was equally intrigued—more so by the buffet of smells whisking past her nose, though. She loved a good bicycle ride and smiled with delight as he pedaled feverishly toward Prince Street.

Henry gradually slowed his bicycle, finally coming to a stop when he rounded the corner on Prince Street. He anxiously searched up and down the sidewalks; his eyes moved rapidly from one person to the next, scouring the crowds for any sign of the mechanic's outfit. The dark-blue jumpsuit had been etched into his memory, and he was keen on seeing it again. However, it wouldn't be easy with the sea of people crowding the sidewalks in front of the restaurants and taverns that lined the street.

Just as the embarrassing feeling of defeat started to set in, Henry fortuitously spotted the mechanic's outfit a couple hundred meters uphill on the opposite side of the street. The man turned down the narrow alley next to *Paddy O'Connor's Tavern* and vanished out of sight again.

"We've got him now, Penny!" Henry announced confidently. "That alleyway leads nowhere. It's a dead end!" He was mindful to keep a low profile, so he walked his bicycle up Prince Street and used the crowds of people as camouflage to conceal his clandestine pursuit.

Henry wanted to dart across the street into the alley, but he managed to stop himself before causing an unnecessary ruckus. If he was wrong about his suspicions, it could land him in quite a predicament with both Captain Fulbright and the Mounties. He didn't want to get caught following a seemingly innocent stranger.

As far as he could tell, there was no proof the man did anything wrong. Picking up a chum bucket out of the water certainly wasn't a crime; some folks around the harbor probably would have even thanked the man for his kindness. Henry couldn't ignore the unwavering notion that there were one too many coincidences happening at once, though.

With his eyes laser-focused on the alley next to *Paddy O'Connor's*, Henry stopped in front of *Don Ciccio's Pizza Window* directly across the street.

Penny thought it was the perfect place to rest, while Henry immediately started to reconsider. The sound of fierce sniffing began to reverberate in his ear—it was the type of incessant noise that only made it harder to concentrate on the hordes of people walking past the alleyway.

The dachshund's frantic infatuation soon turned into a familiar combination of muffled growling and whimpering. As Don Ciccio pulled another freshly made pizza from the oven, Penny nearly leaped out of the rucksack in excitement. Despite the precarious nature of Henry's investigation, she was much more interested in the special mixture of bread, tomatoes, mozzarella cheese (*Fior di Latte*, of course), and basil that was glinting back at her.

"Don't worry, Penny," Henry chuckled, grabbing a small

handful of dog treats from his pocket. "I'll get you some supper soon. I promise!" She devoured the treats in his hand, assuming they were merely an appetizer.

Penny rested her head on Henry's shoulder begrudgingly, disappointed he didn't have some of that delicious pizza in his pocket as well. The sight and smell of that wonderful Italian creation would have to suffice for now. Henry was too busy vigilantly watching the dark alley on the other side of the street.

A few minutes passed, and Henry became increasingly worried. He feared the French stranger might have already slipped away unnoticed; there were at least a few opportunities to do so with him distracted by Penny and Don Ciccio prattling in the background. The thought of simply going home for dinner crossed his mind more than a couple times. But his patience finally paid off when someone emerged from the shadows and snuck into the throngs of people walking by.

Bewildered, Henry tried to make sense of what he just witnessed. He had seen someone wander discreetly from the alleyway (of which he was absolutely certain), yet there was no sight of the mechanic's blue jumpsuit anywhere.

Henry walked his bicycle up Prince Street at a brisk pace, hoping to find the elusive stranger amid the revelers. More determined than ever to get to the bottom of this detour, he was beginning to realize the man was no ordinary mechanic. Despite dozens of people casually strolling down the sidewalk, the blue jumpsuit was still nowhere to be found. He desperately looked in both directions as his impatience began to turn into panic.

The young dock attendant came to an abrupt halt after something serendipitously caught his attention. "That's him, Penny!" Henry quietly exclaimed. He had spotted a man moving through the crowds carrying a large black duffle bag.

It appeared to be the same French stranger from the harbor, except there was something undeniably different about him—the mechanic's outfit was gone. The man was now wearing black trousers, a white collared shirt with a black tie, and a red sweater that had black epaulettes on the top of each shoulder.

Henry felt a stomach-dropping sense of alarm wash over his body. He recognized that unique combination of attire from a place he had visited many times in the past, a place only ten blocks up Prince Street, in the same direction that the stranger was presently headed.

While Henry followed the man on Prince Street, his heartbeat continued to race faster and faster. The red sweater alone was certainly not unusual for this town (especially on the eve of Canada Day). In fact, most people on Prince Street tonight were wearing red to show their patriotism—but it was the unique black epaulettes that gave it away. Henry was certain the stranger had changed into the exact same uniform worn by the maintenance staff at the *Kodiak Bay Zoo*.

"Penny, did you see that? It's gotta be him! It's the Frenchman!" Henry affirmed, overcome with nervous excitement. "He switched his clothes, and now he's dressed just like the *Kodiak Bay Zoo* maintenance staff!"

Henry was convinced they were witnessing the infamous Frenchman embarking on his next caper. He knew the crowds of people on Prince Street would start thinning out as they got further away from the harbor district, so he jumped on his bicycle and headed toward the zoo. He pedaled vigorously downhill, zipping past the seemingly oblivious stranger tramping on the sidewalk.

There was no guarantee that any of Henry's presumptions were true, but he couldn't stop now—he had to see it for himself. The sweet taste of vindication was too tempting to pass up. If this mysterious mechanic turned out to be the same man mentioned on the front page of today's Kodiak Bay Gazette, Henry might actually get a genuine apology from Constable Hamilton, one that he would be delighted to collect.

There'd be plenty of time to gloat later. He needed proof first and figured the zoo was the best place to catch the Frenchman red-handed.

As Henry rode his bicycle down the street at breakneck speeds, he remembered that the zoo had closed early on the night preceding Canada Day. That had been the case for the past five years, and he assumed tonight would be no different.

With the *Kodiak Bay Zoo* coming up on his left at the corner of Prince Street and Windsor Avenue, Henry noticed the main lights outside the front entrance were turned off. Just as he anticipated, the zoo was indeed closed for the night.

Henry came to a stop before parking his bicycle on the rack at the corner of Windsor Avenue, near the zoo. He looked up Prince Street toward *Paddy O'Connor's* and saw fewer people walking around this part of town. The Frenchman and the Mounties were nowhere to be found. Things felt eerily quiet compared to the hustle and bustle of the harbor district.

Sparse crowds meant Henry was liable to be noticed by anyone walking by—the yellow raincoat he had on wasn't exactly conducive to maintaining an inconspicuous presence, nor was the unpredictable wirehaired dachshund riding on his back. Penny could be quite loud, and any impulsive barking would certainly scare away an evasive outlaw that was wanted for questioning in at least four different countries.

Gawking from the sidewalk simply wasn't an option. Henry had to find a better location nearby, one that was across the street from where he could keep a watchful eye on the zoo's front entrance. He ultimately settled on the narrow, gloomy alley next to the *Crown &*

Anchor Tavern. It was a popular watering hole among the local fishermen, and he knew it would be relatively quiet around this time of night.

Once the traffic light turned red, Henry hurried across to the other side of Prince Street.

Nothing appeared out of the ordinary at first, until he glanced through the dimly lit *Crown & Anchor Tavern*'s window. The man standing alone at the bar seemed out of place. Unlike the other patrons watching tonight's hockey game on the tavern's only television, the dapper gentleman who caught Henry's attention was staring intensely at the zoo's front entrance.

Growing up in Kodiak Bay, Henry had seen plenty of tourists come and go over the years; the town was a thriving transit hub for international rail and transatlantic ship crossings. Not a single thing about this peculiar man in the tavern gave Henry the impression he was on vacation, though. The inquisitive dock attendant found it rather unusual to see anyone wearing a black cloak over a fine wool suit (especially for a place like the *Crown & Anchor Tavern*). He was certain nobody would ever confuse the stylish man for someone who worked on a fishing boat—not dressed like that.

Keeping track of all these innocuous coincidences kept Henry's mind racing. This latest one left him feeling particularly puzzled.

Henry did have a tendency to overthink things, and he started to wonder if maybe his suspicions were becoming grossly exaggerated, inflamed, and embellished by his limitless imagination. He thought, "The Frenchman? And now this man in the black cloak?" Constable Hamilton would undoubtedly never let him hear the end of it if he was wrong about either one.

Unfounded accusations were no longer tolerated. Not since he tried to persuade the Mounties last year that Kodiak Bay could be the Frenchman's next target. They had wasted a generous amount of time following up on Henry's hunches in the past with nothing to show for it.

Nevertheless, Henry tried to shake off his lingering doubts and proceeded into the unlit alley on the side of the tavern. He promised Penny they'd head straight home for dinner if the Frenchman in the red sweater didn't show up soon.

Finally situated with an ideal vantage point, Henry carefully kneeled down to let Penny out of her bag—she was growing tireless and let him know by playfully licking his ear. He swung the rucksack back over his shoulder and pulled a monocular scope from his jacket pocket as he stood up.

"Let's take a closer look at the zoo, eh, girl?" Henry said, raising the scope to his eye. "I've got a feeling this could be the night we prove them all wrong."

— CHAPTER 4 —
EMPLOYEES ONLY ENTRANCE

*T*he *Kodiak Bay Zoo* was unequivocally the most beautiful building in town. The classic Italian Renaissance façade with six Corinthian columns routinely captured the attention of practically everyone that walked by. A pair of magnificent bronze lion statues flanked the entrance, and a grand staircase with over fifty steps extended all the way down to Prince Street. It was like a little slice of Rome right in the middle of Kodiak Bay.

As Henry adjusted the focus wheel at the base of his monocular, he pointed it at the zoo's front entrance and quickly scanned the area from left to right. "Nothing yet, girl," he whispered. "Still no sign of the red sweater."

Penny growled tenaciously. She could smell things Henry couldn't and suspected it would only be a matter of time until the Frenchman reappeared.

After a few minutes had passed, Henry began to wonder if the French stranger had spotted him riding up Prince Street. "Maybe the man got spooked and decided to flee in light of the unwanted attention?" The Frenchman did have a reputation for being quite meticulous, according to the newspapers. It seemed he always strived to avoid confrontation, frequently breaking into zoos undetected.

This wasn't Sydney or Paris, though. Kodiak Bay was just a small harbor town on the east coast of Canada, and there was hardly ever any crime outside of the occasional pickpocket or tussle amongst drunken bar patrons—nothing the local Mounties couldn't handle.

Henry couldn't shake his lingering doubts. Ignoring the most plausible explanation was becoming harder with each passing minute; the chance that this was anything other than a good Samaritan picking up litter left behind by the *Second Chance* felt like pure fantasy at this point. After all, the fishermen that worked on that boat could be quite clumsy at times.

Fortunately, those poisonous thoughts proved to be fleeting once Henry raised the monocular scope to his eye again. A wave of optimism instantly drowned out the remnants of cynicism undermining his natural intuition. The French stranger was approaching the zoo, still wearing the maintenance employee uniform. "That's him, Penny! That's him!" Henry quietly exclaimed under his breath.

Peering from across the street, Henry watched curiously as the man bent down to tie his boot laces (presumably to see if the coast was clear). All of a sudden, the French stranger dashed up the grand staircase toward the zoo's front entrance.

Henry's mouth gaped open, astounded and feeling somewhat vindicated at the same time. Unable to take his eyes off the man, he knew this hunch was different from the moment that black duffle bag hit the dock.

There were four oversized glass doors at the top of the stairs that stood over fifteen feet tall for the general admission entrance. In the far-right corner, there was also a gray, nondescript door that had painted letters at the top with the words: *KODIAK BAY ZOO EMPLOYEES ONLY.*

Henry eagerly moved to the edge of the alley to get a better view, enthralled by the French stranger heading straight for the gray door.

His heart was racing, and his palms were visibly sweaty. While nobody else seemed to be aware of the man's brazen plan as it unfolded, Henry was completely transfixed. He eventually surmised that the small tools the man pulled out of his pocket were an instrumental part of that plan.

Within seconds of beginning his attempt to pick the lock, the stranger had opened the door and entered in one swift, acrobatic motion. The door promptly closed behind him, and just like that, the Frenchman had vanished once again.

Standing there, an incomparable sense of adrenaline flowed through Henry's body. His first instinct was to rush into the *Crown & Anchor Tavern* to phone Constable Hamilton and the Mounties. He hesitated, though, not out of fear. It was the outright surprise of what happened next that gave him pause—the tavern door unexpectedly burst open after the Frenchman disappeared, leaving Henry frozen with bewilderment.

Henry stared in astonishment as the gentleman in the black cloak ran across Prince Street and darted up the grand staircase toward the *EMPLOYEES ONLY* entrance. With a wide-eyed look of concern, he was more confused than ever.

"Did you see that, Penny?" Henry murmured after the gentleman in the black cloak walked through the same door that was unlocked by the Frenchman. He had no idea what was going on behind that gray door but was convinced he'd just witnessed two people breaking into the zoo.

"Who was that guy?" he asked, glancing at his furry companion. "And what's with the cloak?"

Penny raised her tail with suspicion and began sniffing fervently. She had the same questions as Henry and was inclined to bolt across the street to collect some answers. The wirehaired dachshund managed to restrain herself from chasing the pair of nocturnal zoo enthusiasts nonetheless.

Overcome with exhilaration, Henry ignored his initial compulsion to call the Mounties from the tavern. Despite being fairly certain that a crime was in progress, a part of him wanted to get a closer look before calling for help, just to be absolutely sure.

Henry could only imagine the vitriolic expression on Constable Hamilton's face if he was wrong. As improbable as it may have seemed, these guys could merely be working the late-night shift to help an understaffed skeleton crew. There was no way to know for sure without further investigation. It's not like he was privy to the official employee schedule for maintenance staff or administrators.

"Let's get after them, Penny!" Henry asserted boldly. Penny instantly barked once to announce she was ready. He looked both ways on Prince Street to confirm there were no cars coming, then sprinted across the road and raced up the grand staircase to the front entrance of the zoo. Penny ran next to him the whole time; she had no trouble keeping up as her little legs moved at a rapid pace.

When they reached the *EMPLOYEES ONLY* door at the top of the stairs, Henry and Penny paused for a minute to catch their breath. There was a moment of reluctance as he gazed down at the *Crown & Anchor Tavern* across the street. He was admittedly worried that he might be putting Penny in real danger by walking through the door. He considered whether he should abandon this risky endeavor entirely. It still wasn't too late to back out. He could stop everything right now and simply call the Mounties using the phone at the tavern across the street.

Following a short but frantic deliberation, Henry soon realized the decision had already been made the second he left the alley. There was no time to call the Mounties, and even if he did, they would never arrive in time. The police station was on the other side of town. He assumed the pair of strangers inside the zoo would be gone before the Mounties actually showed up.

Henry took one last glimpse at the *Crown & Anchor Tavern*, and in that moment, he decided he wasn't going to let fear be the reason these trespassers got away. Fear was a choice, just like anything else. He reached into his rucksack and pulled out a homemade bola, which he had crafted months ago out of some rope and two old tennis balls.

Even though he had never practiced his throwing skills on a moving target, Henry figured something was better than nothing if he was going to try and stop these people from getting away. Looking at the bola, Penny had her doubts; she had seen Henry practice on some fence posts last month, and his aim certainly left room for improvement. However, that wasn't going to stop her. Penny's boundless supply of temerity overshadowed any potential dangers awaiting them inside.

Henry took a deep breath as he grabbed the handle on the door and gently opened it. Holding the homemade bola tightly in his hand, he glanced down at Penny and ordered, "Stick close to me, Penny!"

Staring into the dimly lit foyer, Henry cautiously entered the zoo while Penny mirrored his every step. To his surprise, the zoo was eerily quiet inside—all he could hear was the sound of his heart beating. He had been to the *Kodiak Bay Zoo* dozens of times and knew the building very well. Nevertheless, this occasion was different. If the zoo's security guard spotted him, he'd be in just as much trouble as the pair of trespassers. The thought of confronting the Frenchman was terrifying, but that would be the least of his concerns if he landed in hot water with Captain Fulbright.

The captain always did things by the book, and he'd be furious if he knew what Henry was up to right now. It would undoubtedly lead to a proper scolding if Henry got caught on the wrong side of this little escapade (which likely meant he'd be grounded for two weeks at a minimum, plus extra chores). Truth be told, it'd be nothing compared to what Mrs. Fulbright might do if she learned that Henry was breaking the law. Good intentions or not, he would be in *big* trouble if his adopted parents knew he broke into the zoo after hours.

The looming dread of scathing reprimands dissipated the second Henry heard a loud thud echo from the other side of the zoo. It sure seemed like the perfect time to run away and call for help in the tavern across the street, yet he couldn't move. His insatiable curiosity outweighed the fear clouding his thoughts; he just stood there and kept both feet firmly planted on the ground.

Despite his clammy palms, Henry clutched the bola tighter and mustered the courage to keep moving forward. Penny stayed at his side with her nose raised in the air, rapidly analyzing the plethora of scents wafting in their direction.

As Henry vigilantly approached the main atrium area, he peered over at the entrance to the *Aviary Wing* exhibit and saw someone lying motionless on the ground. He rushed over and immediately recognized the man as Thomas Callahan, a jovial security guard who had worked at the zoo for years. Penny instinctively sniffed the guard up and down, from his shoes to the peculiar dart sticking out of his neck.

Henry looked closer and noticed what appeared to be a throwing dart. He was no stranger to dartboard games, but he had never seen anything like this before. He carefully removed the unusual object from Mr. Callahan's neck and thoroughly inspected it while Penny observed. Wherever the dart came from, it was clear this was no accident—the incapacitated security guard in front of him made that worrisomely evident. He mumbled under his breath, "It must be laced with some sort of poison."

"No, Penny, stop!" Henry whispered urgently, fearing the worst as the curious dachshund almost touched the tip of the dart with her nose. Rattled by his stern command, Penny obediently heeded the warning after taking another look at the security guard's lifeless body. He placed the dart on the floor next to Mr. Callahan and quickly checked the guard's wrist for a pulse.

"He appears to be alive, Penny," Henry declared. "Looks like he's just knocked out."

Captain Fulbright had taught him the techniques of cardiopulmonary resuscitation in case there was ever an emergency at the docks, although pounding away on Mr. Callahan's chest didn't seem like it was the appropriate remedy here. The security guard was in need of proper medical attention.

Henry sprang to his feet, announcing emphatically, "We need to call the Mounties! Right now!" As he stood near the corner of the rotunda that led to the *Aviary Wing*, his head swiveled back and forth in an anxious search for the nearest telephone. Calling for help was no longer the backup plan—it was the only plan now.

A flood of noises suddenly whooshed past Henry's head, interrupting his concentrated efforts in a most disruptive and startling manner; the shock of it all instantly sent him ducking for cover. Penny was beyond startled and yapped nervously in response.

Overcome with bemusement, Henry looked up and saw more than two dozen exotic birds circling the glass dome of the atrium above. He watched in awe as parrots, blue macaws, and toucans flew above him in a colorful display of aerial agility. It didn't take long for the wonder to be eclipsed by the consequences of their presence, though. The Frenchman had already started releasing some of the wild animals in the zoo, and this was probably just a foretaste of what could be coming next if the stories in the newspaper were true.

Henry was floored by panicked thoughts as he hunched over the motionless body of Mr. Callahan. Fortunately, he noticed a payphone by the front entrance. That sliver of hope was vanquished when he squinted to read the inauspicious sign taped to the side: *OUT OF ORDER*.

He remembered there might be another telephone near the maintenance office through the *Panthera Wing* that housed the big cat exhibit—actually getting there was a different matter entirely. He was worried that if the birds were a harbinger of what was to follow, the path would be quite treacherous.

Henry could handle dodging a few exotic birds. But running for his life from a pair of African lions experiencing freedom for the first time in years was something he preferred to avoid.

Before Henry could take another step, he froze upon hearing the sounds of hissing and growling coming from the *Reptilia Wing* of the zoo. When he spun around to look in that direction, it felt like his heart had stopped beating. A renewed sense of panic sent him stumbling to the floor as he tripped over Mr. Callahan's legs in a frightened scramble to back away.

"Good grief!" Henry yelled, beyond stunned at the sight of two huge saltwater crocodiles shuffling across the marble floors. They were snapping their jaws, looking at him and Penny in an appetizing manner. Despite the hungry reptiles' menacing approach, he was too shocked to get up off the ground.

Henry never anticipated coming face-to-face with a pair of angry crocodiles when he got up for breakfast this morning, and he couldn't believe they were coming straight for him at this very moment. Anyone else probably would have screamed in terror, but the sheer adrenaline running through his body easily eclipsed the stomach-dropping fear that should have sent him running for the exits. He knew better than most that crocodiles had the strongest bite of any animal in the world (ten times more powerful than a great white shark), eliminating the possibility of escape if he got caught between their jaws.

Fueled by an unwavering sense of moxie, Penny leaped out in front of Henry without hesitation and tried her best to intimidate the reptiles with a threatening snarl. Things quickly escalated when she erupted in a vociferous fit of defiant barking. There must have been at least seven or eight hostile barks in rapid succession, followed by her most vicious-sounding growl. She didn't have as many teeth as the saltwater crocodiles, yet she proudly put her sharp fangs on full display for good measure.

Penny wasn't going down without a fight, emboldened by her everlasting disdain for badgers and instinctive hunting skills. She came prepared to run circles around these crocodiles to defend Henry. The wirehaired dachshund couldn't speak the same language as the massive reptiles in front of her, but that didn't matter. She made it clear in her own way that they would have to go through her to get to Henry.

The crocodiles stopped in their tracks, shocked by the scrappy dachshund's steadfast resolve and her thunderous bark (which could have been mistaken for a German Shepherd or even a Siberian Husky). The pair of reptiles continued to hiss and growl, although they were both somewhat concerned with the ferocious dog that was in their path.

After a few moments of consideration, the crocodiles decided the scent of freedom was more attractive than a fight with an irritable wirehaired dachshund. They changed course abruptly and scuttled off toward the front entrance of the zoo.

Henry lunged for the walkie-talkie clipped to the security guard's belt. He scrambled to change the frequency to the same channel used by the RCMP and desperately shouted, "Calling all Mounties! Calling all Mounties! Get everyone down to the *Kodiak Bay Zoo* right away! The Frenchman is here! He broke into the zoo, and he's letting the animals loose!"

Almost immediately after Henry released the talk button, he

heard a scornful voice that sounded like Constable Hamilton. "Halifax? Is that you? You know this channel is for RCMP personnel only. Over."

"Constable, you need to get down to the zoo right now!" Henry replied with a profound sense of distress in his voice. "Thomas Callahan is knocked out, there are crocodiles running loose, we've got broken glass in the *Aviary Wing*... and I saw the Frenchman break into the zoo with my own eyes. Send the whole police force down here now! Please, sir!"

Constable Hamilton knew Henry since he was a young boy and had never heard the kid sound so panicked. Even though Henry had pestered him with unsubstantiated theories about the Frenchmen over the past year, there was something different this time.

The constable suspected that Henry might not be exaggerating and responded, "Alright, son. We're on the way now. Just get out of there, eh? Wait for me at the tavern across the street. Over."

Henry dropped the radio next to Mr. Callahan, grabbed the podgy man by the legs, and dragged him a few feet across the marble floor from the grand atrium to the front entrance of the *Aviary Wing* exhibit. He felt exhausted and out of breath from lugging the heavyset Irishman all by himself, but he managed to trudge back out past the entrance.

Standing in the atrium, Henry grabbed the red lever on the wall near the exhibit entryway and pulled it with all his might. The vertical security gate dropped down from the ceiling, and within seconds, the entire *Aviary Wing* was completely sealed off from the rest of the zoo. Mr. Callahan might have been safe from the wandering zoo animals on the loose, but the danger was far from over for Henry and his faithful sidekick.

The pair of African crocodiles were now halfway between him and the front exits. Henry shrugged with exasperation—he was hoping for an easy way out and wasn't too keen on tussling with the pair of hungry crocodiles standing in his way. Picking up the bola in his hand, he glanced down at Penny and said, "Let's make a run for the door, alright girl?"

Penny took two steps forward but suddenly stopped after pointing her nose up into the air. She lifted her right front paw and sniffed feverishly while looking toward the other wings of the zoo.

Henry spun around and asked anxiously, "What is it, Penny?" A moment later, he heard the sound of footsteps coming from the wing that housed the big cat exhibit. Based on the irregular cadence of the approaching clatter, it sounded like there were at least two people running down the hallway.

Gripping the homemade bola in his hand, Henry stared at the entrance as the noise from the footsteps got louder. His intuition was confirmed. Two men emerged from the *Panthera Wing* and entered the atrium in a rumbustious way. The Frenchman raced toward the exit with the duffle bag around his shoulder as the other guy in the black cloak from the tavern frantically chased after him.

Henry thought about throwing his bola, but he was overcome with an unsettling combination of apprehension and bewilderment while observing from a distance. He would have completely missed what happened next if he had blinked; it all unfolded so quickly. The guy in the cloak managed to grab the Frenchman's sweater by the collar in what would prove to be a poorly executed attempt to bring the chase to an end.

The Frenchman immediately dropped the duffle bag while grabbing the assailant's arm and doing a somersault flip forward, using their momentum to his advantage as he flung the cloaked man through the air toward the main entrance. It was like something out of a karate film—the man was sent crashing to the floor, directly in front of the two African crocodiles.

With the gigantic reptiles snapping at his feet, the man in the cloak regained his footing almost instantly and got back up with his hands in a defensive position.

As if Henry didn't already have enough to deal with, the cloaked man had become another unwelcome impediment to his impromptu exit, right behind the crocodiles. He decided right then and there that he was done watching from the sidelines. Even though he wasn't sure what was going on, he figured it couldn't hurt to try and slow these people down before the Mounties arrived.

Henry eventually found the courage to blurt, "I'm sorry to interrupt, but it's all over! The police are already on the way... Just drop the bag and give it up!" Penny chimed in with a few clamorous barks to reinforce his warning.

Confounded by the boy's brazen warning, the man in the black cloak exhaled and retorted, "Probably best you stay out of this one, mate! Just leave this with me and get lost!" The derogatory rebuke, wrapped in a thick Australian accent, left Henry speechless.

While the Australian was distracted by the daring teenager, his pint-sized dachshund, and the pair of hissing crocodiles inching forward, the Frenchman pulled a stick of dynamite from the black duffle bag. It only took him a split-second to ignite the fuse with the lighter that was conveniently waiting in his other hand.

Before they realized what was going on, the Frenchman suddenly tossed the burning stick of dynamite in the Australian's direction. Henry, Penny, and the man in the cloak watched helplessly as the dynamite bounced off the front entrance and came to rest directly next to the oversized glass doors.

Sparks emanating from the fuse caused the flustered crocodiles to retreat in the opposite direction, while Henry immediately grabbed Penny with both hands and crouched down in the corner to shield her from the impending blast. The Australian attempted to run away, but the explosion from the dynamite quickly knocked him off his feet and launched him forward. The sound of glass shattering reverberated throughout the atrium, while thick smoke and debris started to cover everything in sight.

Disoriented and unable to hear much of anything since his ears were still ringing from the explosion, Henry slowly stood up after checking on Penny. Thankfully, neither of them had been injured. Shaken up by the chaotic turmoil that left the surrounding area in shambles, his jaw dropped when he spotted a huge, gaping hole in the zoo's entrance. All the glass doors were completely destroyed. He watched incredulously as the exotic birds that were circling the dome above swooped down and escaped excitedly out the front.

Without the slightest trace of regret, the Frenchman picked up the black duffle bag and walked calmly over to the Australian. The man in the cloak appeared to be alive, although he was struggling to get up.

The Frenchman smiled as he stood over the sharply dressed man and smugly dropped a pair of throwing darts from his hand. The darts bounced off the floor and landed directly in front of the weakened man's face.

Henry wasn't sure if these two knew each other, but he'd been teased enough at school to recognize taunting when he saw it.

Using the Australian's back as a stepping stone, the Frenchman strutted over to the front entrance, wearing a sinister grin on his face. He glanced back at the cloaked man, cackling with unbridled exuberance. Undoubtedly, he took a moment to savor the outcome of their most recent scuffle.

Henry still didn't know what the other gentleman was doing there, although it was clear the Australian was after the Frenchman's duffle bag. He presumed the man had to be law enforcement from out of town or maybe an amateur bounty hunter. Either way, the trouncing the cloaked Australian just endured looked quite painful.

The questions kept piling up, almost as fast as Henry's heart was pounding. Whoever these people were, he could only be sure of one thing. There was far more going on here than just a simple case of trespassing. Nonetheless, Henry was more concerned about the stolen zoo animals he suspected were in that black duffle bag. As the ringing in his ears subsided, he raced to the center of the atrium and launched the bola with all his might just as the Frenchman stepped through the front entrance.

Henry gazed at the bola wrapping perfectly around the Frenchman's legs, which instantly sent the fake zoo employee tumbling into the hard stone near the top of the grand staircase. The spirited dock attendant was overcome with amazement and immense pride. He couldn't believe that it actually worked. Penny was just as surprised, and she let out two cheerful barks to congratulate him.

However, their premature celebration ended the second Henry rushed past the gaping hole where the front doors had previously stood. By the time he got outside and reached the grand staircase, only his bola remained. Much to his chagrin, the homemade contraption had done little to impede the Frenchman, who was already halfway down the grand staircase.

If this was indeed the same French bandit that had been stealing bear cubs from zoos all over the world, Henry knew he couldn't let that bag out of his sight.

With the Frenchman on the cusp of getting away, Henry and Penny hurried down the steps to chase after the duffle bag. Just as they were catching up, everything came to a screeching halt. About halfway down the grand staircase, the man carrying the large black bag had stopped, leaving Henry wondering if the elusive Frenchman was finally about to give up.

It didn't take long for Henry to realize he wasn't as intimidating as he thought. The booming sound of four horses galloping down Prince Street was the real reason the Frenchman had hesitated near the bottom of the staircase. Henry knew hearing that noise on Prince Street at this time of night could only mean one thing in this town, and it commanded the attention of everyone within earshot.

Four black horses suddenly charged into view and surrounded the bottom of the grand staircase. Atop the horses sat the town's four Mounties, which included Constable Hamilton and the Chief Inspector, all wearing their scarlet-red tunics and brown campaign hats. The Royal Canadian Mounted Police wasted no time in creating an equine barrier that separated the French bandit from Prince Street.

Stuck between the four horses at the bottom of the staircase and an overconfident dachshund standing a few steps above, the Frenchman's cavalier demeanor turned into pure panic.

"Hold it right there, sir!" Constable Hamilton demanded fiercely, pointing at the Frenchman. "I need you to drop the bag and get down on the ground right now!" From the tone of the constable's voice alone, Henry had a feeling there would be serious ramifications in the absence of immediate compliance. He had never seen Constable Hamilton so angry.

As the Frenchman silently weighed his options (including and especially the ones that involved him escaping unscathed), the Australian in the black cloak came dashing down the staircase, oblivious to the Mounties' arrival. It seemed like the man was gripped by a fit of rage. Although, when he realized what was happening, he came to an abrupt stop next to Henry and Penny.

Clearly stunned to find the Frenchman in the middle of a tense standoff with the Mounties, the Australian slowly raised his hands to show he was not a threat. Distracted and confused by the cloaked newcomer, Constable Hamilton's attention shifted. "Hey, you! Stop right there!" the constable shouted, fuming with hostility. "Nobody move!"

Henry gulped, too dismayed to say anything of consequence. His hands were trembling, and the adrenaline coursing through his body only made the danger more apparent. It was a far cry from playing detective in the alley across the street ten minutes ago. This was as real as it got, and he could tell the constable was in no mood for games or friendly banter.

A part of him wanted to speak up boldly and explain every last detail of what transpired, but he never got the chance. Everyone, except for the Frenchman, gasped in disbelief upon hearing what sounded like a ferocious growl coming from the top of the staircase. Henry nearly fainted when he turned around.

Three full-grown lions had escaped from the big cat exhibit. They emerged from the front entrance of the zoo, slowly walking side by side.

Constable Hamilton and the other Mounties gawked in utter astonishment. "What in the Sam Steele?" the constable mumbled, while his three colleagues gaped at the enormous lions. The bewildered looks painted on their faces sharply contrasted with the sinister smile that suddenly caught Henry's attention. The Frenchman couldn't have been happier to see the lions arrive in such a breathtaking manner.

Glaring back at them from the top of the staircase, the biggest lion in the middle let out a deafening roar, exposing his sharp white fangs in the process. The testosterone fueled display of authority caused the other two lions to follow with a pair of equally terrifying roars that reverberated throughout the entire town.

These lions were either angry, hungry, or both, and Henry shuddered in fear, knowing these majestic jungle cats might leap down the stairs at any moment.

The four horses were startled by the massive predators at the top of the staircase, and they weren't shy about letting the Mounties know. They neighed with high-pitched shrieks of distress and kicked their front legs high into the air unexpectedly, hurtling the RCMP officers onto the ground.

The Frenchman relished the sight of how quickly the tables had turned; cackling in delight, he bolted past the befuddled Mounties as their horses continued to panic. His timing proved to be all too perfect.

A young man had just pulled up to the stoplight at the corner of Windsor Avenue on a lime-green dirt bike, and he never expected his evening ride would be cut short.

— CHAPTER 5 —
SWEET MAPLE SYRUP

*R*ight as the young man on the dirt bike noticed the commotion unfolding in front of the zoo, he felt a sharp tingling pain in his arm; it carried the semblance of a bee sting but had immensely different repercussions. The sight of the Frenchman sprinting toward him and horses panicking in the background would be all he remembered after collapsing onto the street.

Fearing the Frenchman was on the verge of getting away, the Australian in the black cloak rushed down the grand staircase as Henry just stood there in astonishment. The man made it to the bottom of the steps and climbed atop Rusty's saddle without the slightest bit of hesitation. "Sorry, mate," he remarked in a soothing manner, gently tugging on the reins while stroking the horse's neck. "Afraid I'm gonna need your help."

Sensing the Mounties could benefit from some assistance, the Australian reached into his suit jacket. He pulled two thin, stainless steel cases out of the holster on his suspenders.

Henry squinted from the steps as the man removed a handful of what appeared to be throwing darts—the same ones he'd seen in the zoo earlier.

Constable Hamilton was still disoriented after being thrown from his horse and looked up in confusion when the man tossed the darts on the sidewalk. "Use these on the lions, fellas!" the Australian advised reassuringly. "They'll put those cats to sleep without hurting 'em."

Befuddled by the man in the black cloak absconding with Rusty, the constable and his fellow Mounties didn't have a chance to utter a word of protest. They suddenly became distracted after hearing the Frenchman rev the motorcycle's engine tauntingly.

The police watched helplessly as the French stranger turned right onto Prince Street and raced uphill toward *Paddy O'Connor's* on the lime-green dirt bike.

The Australian instructed Rusty to commence pursuit by pulling confidently on the reins and giving him a gentle nudge. Happy to get as far away as possible from the trio of lions sauntering down the grand staircase, the horse took off galloping after the Frenchman.

"Halifax, behind you!" Constable Hamilton shouted, standing at the bottom of the stairs. "Move it, son! Run!" He saw the pride of lions eyeing Henry and Penny like they were a pair of turkeys on Thanksgiving Day.

Mesmerized by the Australian's improvised pursuit of the Frenchman in what felt like a New York minute, Henry's gaze finally broke once he heard the desperation in the constable's voice. It was impossible to ignore.

Henry bolted down the steps while Penny scurried beside him. They brushed past Constable Hamilton as he distributed the throwing darts to the Mounties.

The pack of lions weren't discouraged and continued their slow, menacing descent on the grand staircase. Feeling somewhat annoyed that the Mounties hadn't scattered yet, the *two hundred twenty-five kilogram* lion in the center roared with authority as he crossed the step where Henry and Penny were standing only moments ago. It was a clear reminder to everyone that this jungle belonged to him, and there could only be one king around here.

The thunderous roar, which could be heard for kilometers, and the pair of feline companions at his side were enough to send the remaining RCMP horses frantically running away in the opposite direction.

Despite the human obstacles in their path, the lions were quite keen on exploring the town, one way or another.

Undeterred, the four Mounties assumed defensive positions at the bottom of the stairs. They clutched the throwing darts with trepidation while preparing to challenge the approaching lions. As the RCMP horses fled down Prince Street, the Mounties were left with the terrifying task of stopping a pack of vicious jungle cats from wreaking havoc on the normally quiet harbor town.

The man in the cloak, barreling toward *Paddy O'Connor's* in pursuit of the Frenchman, wanted to help the beleaguered officers, but he knew that's exactly what his French adversary was counting on. Catching the Frenchman had become an obsession after several failed attempts in the weeks leading up to today's encounter, and the Australian refused to let him get away scot-free again.

Henry was more concerned about the presumably stolen polar bear cubs and dashed over to the bike rack near the zoo as Penny followed closely behind. He scooped her up into the leather rucksack and yanked his bicycle free, riding off in one swift motion.

Penny could barely contain her excitement. She had picked up on a hint of fresh pizza wafting by and assumed they were heading back to *Don Ciccio's*. Pointing her nose up into the air, Penny sat in the cashmere-lined rucksack strapped to Henry's back.

Convinced the Mounties had their hands full trying to capture dozens of wild zoo animals on the loose, Henry decided it was up to him to chase after the Frenchman (and the stolen polar bear cubs) on their behalf. The temerarious dock attendant zoomed up Prince Street toward the harbor, pedaling frantically to catch up to the man in the cloak.

Even though the Australian had a considerable head start, Henry was rapidly gaining ground. He could see the brightly colored dirt bike in the distance, ahead of Rusty, and the black cloak billowing in the wind.

Henry zipped past the crowds of revelers lining Prince Street. Nobody even seemed to be aware of the heart-pounding pursuit tearing through town, but that all changed once they heard the dirt bike screeching to a sliding stop near *Paddy O'Connor's Tavern*.

The collision appeared to be a consequence of the Frenchman's failure to apply the brakes, just as a maple syrup delivery truck unexpectedly turned left onto Prince Street. Surprisingly, the Frenchman and his black duffle bag were relatively unharmed, but the lime-green dirt bike didn't fare as well; it became wedged under the back wheel of the delivery truck.

Assuming the Frenchman's escape plan had surely been foiled now that a huge maple syrup truck was blocking Prince Street, Henry eagerly pedaled uphill in anticipation of a guaranteed surrender. Rusty and the Australian were only slightly ahead of him. "We've got him now, Penny!" he declared arrogantly. "This guy has nowhere to run!"

The Frenchman was growing tired of the Australian and the meddlesome boy interfering with his escape. He rushed over to the back of the delivery truck and impulsively pulled the side-gate release lever. Howling in amusement, the Frenchman cut the straps holding the barrels in place, and in a matter of seconds, the first barrel of maple syrup rolled off the truck's flatbed onto the street below.

One by one, the barrels careened down the hill on Prince Street toward the Australian, Henry, and Penny.

Henry slammed on his brakes when he spotted the calamity on the horizon; the bicycle skidded to a halt as the Frenchman's wicked laughter echoed down the street. He gasped at the sight of nearly two dozen maple syrup barrels tumbling chaotically in his direction.

The Australian in the cloak pulled back on the reins to bring Rusty to a complete stop the moment he saw the first barrel roll off the delivery truck.

Nearby, there were countless innocent bystanders, and sheer panic ensued. They all started frantically running away to avoid the *two hundred seventy-five kilogram* barrels picking up speed down Prince Street. Outright mayhem consumed the surrounding area.

The Frenchman stood next to the empty flatbed truck, reveling in the pandemonium unleashed on Prince Street. He was genuinely proud of this latest caper, but not proud enough to stick around and wait for the man in the black cloak to thwart his escape. In that instant, the French bandit spun around and took off running downhill toward the *Kodiak Bay Central Station*.

Henry watched frustratedly as the Frenchman vanished over the other side of the hill. He couldn't believe the audacity on display and never imagined anything this crazy would happen in his hometown. This was definitely no ordinary Saturday night.

"Shhh... it's okay, it's okay, mate," the Australian whispered into Rusty's ear. The RCMP horse kept kicking his front legs into the air while the man in the cloak tried to hold on. The swarms of people running by, combined with the barrels of maple syrup hurtling down the street, clearly spooked Rusty.

Uncontrollably prancing and neighing in distress, Rusty had enough of this pursuit. He was gravely concerned after a few barrels collided with some of the parked cars nearby; they practically disintegrated on impact. The thick wave of pure maple syrup rushing down Prince Street only inflamed his reluctance to carry on with the chase.

The Australian knew it would be too dangerous for Rusty to proceed and jumped off the horse as his cloak billowed in the wind.

THE TUTORI'S CLOAK   61

He stroked Rusty's neck, properly thanked his new equine friend, and said, "Much appreciated for the ride, mate. I got it from here, though! Go and help the constable!"

Rusty kicked his front legs up into the air once more and let out a farewell neigh, quickly galloping away at full speed in the opposite direction, back toward the *Kodiak Bay Zoo.*

Henry knew there was little time to waste and instinctively followed suit in abandoning his mode of transportation. The bicycle would be useless against a flood of sticky maple syrup covering everything in its path, so he decided to continue the pursuit on foot.

The man in the cloak charged forward up Prince Street toward the maple syrup delivery truck and dodged the dangerous obstacles careening his way like a footballer dribbling down the pitch.

Not ready to give up just yet, Henry chased after the man with Penny on his back; he welcomed the adrenaline that propelled him forward and navigated around the *two hundred seventy-five kilogram* barrels that were headed straight for him.

Uninterested in seeing his recently polished oxfords ruined by the wave of maple syrup ahead, the Australian leaped from the last dry spot of pavement onto the hood of the nearest parked car. He avoided the syrup but stumbled onto the sidewalk before continuing his pursuit.

Even though Henry followed the man's exact footsteps, he underestimated the speed at which the maple syrup was flooding down the street and accidentally stepped into the sugary substance right as he jumped onto the car hood. Impressively, he maintained his balance without falling and landed on the sidewalk in front of where the first barrel broke open. One step too late or too early, and he might not have been so lucky.

Henry watched as the remaining barrels carried on with their erratic freefall down Prince Street while the wave of pure Canadian maple syrup gradually covered everything it touched. He looked back toward the delivery truck, and a renewed sense of urgency set in after he saw the Australian disappear from sight.

Time was running out. Henry knew he could only run so fast with Penny on his back and decided to let her down. She rushed out of the rucksack. The mischievous dachshund was immediately enamored with the sweet aroma of Canadian liquid gold surrounding them and lunged for a little taste. "No! Not now, Penny!" he ordered. "We can get some flapjacks later, I promise! Now, follow me!"

Penny whined and snorted in protest. She had become distracted by the sight and smell of fresh maple syrup blanketing the sidewalk. The urge to dive headfirst into the sweet mixture of sugar and maple was enticing, to say the least. Nevertheless, she complied with his request begrudgingly, and they both raced to the top of Prince Street without further delay. Her legs were short, but this small dog was born to run, and she loved a good chase.

Henry took a moment to catch his breath once they reached the delivery truck. Panting heavily, he scanned the area for any sign of the Australian or the black duffle bag. Fortunately, it didn't take long for him to spot the Australian's cloak swirling in the wind.

"That's him!" Henry exclaimed after catching a glimpse of the Frenchman in the red sweater. The man was approaching the entrance to the *Kodiak Bay Central Station*. The Australian in the black cloak wasn't far behind; he was clearly seething but appeared more determined than ever to recover the black duffle bag.

Galvanized by the pair of elusive visitors departing Kodiak Bay in a hastened manner, Henry and Penny raced down the street past the harbor to chase after them. He didn't care that the Frenchman had already disappeared into the train station. He only ran faster as a result, convinced the cloaked man would lead him to the red sweater.

The frazzled dock attendant burst through the front door when he reached the entrance of the *Kodiak Bay Central Station*. Henry was in such a panicked rush that he inadvertently knocked over the Australian in the black cloak. It was the same man who was desperate to stop the Frenchman from escaping with the black duffle bag.

"Oops! Sorry! I'm so sorry, sir!" Henry apologized before realizing he had toppled into the same person he'd been chasing this whole time. He blurted, "It's you!" as Penny instantly barked twice to confirm (she never forgot a smell).

Tired of the boy following him like a shadow, the Australian got up and responded snidely, "Crikey! Not you again! Listen kid, I don't have time for this right now."

"But wait!" Henry pleaded. The man ignored his request as if he were speaking a foreign language. Before he could utter another word, the Australian suddenly took off running.

Manners aside, the cloaked man had just spotted his French advisory wearing the red sweater between train platforms *#9* and *#10*; he didn't have time for apologies and couldn't care less about why the boy was following him.

As the Australian approached the platform where the Frenchman was standing, a train from Toronto pulled into the station on track *#10*. Henry remained near the front entrance. He was anxious to see where the pursuit would lead next.

"All aboard!" the conductor yelled, stepping off the train that was preparing to depart from track *#9*, "*Empire Express Number 8814* with nonstop service to New York City. Last call!"

The Frenchman tried to hide among the travelers boarding the train to New York, hoping the crowds would serve as camouflage. Right as he thought nobody was following him any longer, the Frenchman froze when he spotted the man in the black cloak pushing his way through the unsuspecting masses.

The Australian stopped abruptly when their eyes met a second later. He slowly put one hand on the collapsible cattle prod attached to his belt and squared off with the Frenchman. The sea of passengers continued to part around the two stationary adversaries as they just stared at each other.

Henry watched nervously from afar as the standoff unfolded. He couldn't believe it; the Frenchman was about to be captured in Kodiak Bay of all places, and he had a front-row ticket to the show.

Despite the hostile implications subtly conveyed by the man in the cloak, the Frenchman didn't appear to be intimidated in the slightest. In fact, it was quite the opposite. A sinister grin swiftly replaced the shocked expression on his face. The Frenchman winked at his cloaked nemesis before glancing over at track *#10*.

The Australian was caught by surprise when hundreds of travelers got off the train that had just arrived from Toronto.

Throngs of people flooded the middle platform, and within seconds, the surrounding area was filled with dozens of men, all dressed exactly like the Frenchman. They were carrying the same black duffle bags and wearing identical *Kodiak Bay Zoo* employee uniforms; the red sweaters were unmistakable. The men even wore wigs and mustaches with the same white hair color to bolster their disguises.

Henry and Penny stood by the front entrance and marveled as the zoo employees poured into the station in the most fascinating way.

It must have only been a minute or so before the Australian lost sight of the *real* Frenchman amid all the madness. His French adversary slipped into the droves of travelers while dozens of people wearing red sweaters spread throughout the terminal. Some boarded the departing train to New York City on track *#9*, and the rest walked off in different directions.

The exasperated Australian pushed his way through the crowds and grabbed the nearest person wearing a zoo employee uniform. He threw the impostor up against a concrete column and yelled, "Got ya now, mate!" as he searched through the stranger's black duffle bag.

"Bloody hell!" he muttered in disbelief, pulling out a stuffed polar bear toy from the bag.

The impostor in the red sweater burst into laughter when he saw the puzzled look on the Australian's face. He was apparently quite amused by the preplanned snafu and wasn't shy about gloating.

The Australian suddenly lost his temper like a belligerent rhino that had been roused from a delightful afternoon nap. Enraged by this whole charade and the charlatan laughing in his face, he yanked down on the strap slung across the guy's shoulder, instantly sending the phony zoo employee and the duffle bag crashing to the tile floor. The man in the cloak picked up the bag, turned it upside down, and violently shook it to confirm his suspicions.

Completely baffled, Henry gawked as a pile of plush polar bear toys emptied out onto the ground below. He was somewhat entertained, watching from a distance, though it soon became irritatingly obvious that he'd been duped by the same distraction. He had lost sight of the real Frenchman as well.

Incensed at the thought of the Frenchman escaping once again, the Australian forced his way through the swarms of travelers, snatching the closest person wearing a red sweater that he could get his hands on. One at a time, he grabbed nearly a dozen guys; none of them were shown any mercy. The brazen Australian ripped each duffle bag from their clutches, shaking them empty in frustration.

It didn't matter how many guys he roughed up, because the outcome was always the same—nothing but stuffed polar bear toys piling up at his feet. He was flustered at the never-ending number of impostors and started to worry that the *real* Frenchman had already disappeared.

There was much more hanging in the balance than just a pair of stolen polar bear cubs. Even though Henry wasn't aware of the high stakes involved, he could tell the man in the cloak had a lot riding on recovering that duffle bag. Underneath all the anger, a look of desperation flickered in the man's eyes.

The Australian quickly turned around after hearing the doors close on the *Empire Express Number 8814*. Once the train started pulling out of the station, the man ran alongside it for as long as he could while frantically looking for any trace of the Frenchman through the railcar windows.

Feeling defeated, he ultimately gave up when the train passed the end of the platform and sped away toward New York City. The embarrassment of it all was maddening—ensnared in another one of the Frenchman's elaborate traps, catching him now seemed utterly hopeless. There were too many red sweaters to follow. They were in virtually every corner of the *Kodiak Bay Central Station*.

Still fuming as he walked back up the platform, the man in the black cloak kicked the stuffed polar bears on the tile floor out of his way. He was facing an untold number of consequences if the Frenchman managed to escape. Running short on time, the Australian continued harassing anyone wearing a red sweater who crossed his path.

In spite of the cloaked man running amok, Henry had stayed put the entire time; that was until he noticed something highly suspicious near the ocean liner terminal. It was barely visible, yet at the same time, the promising clue instantly stood out as he squinted in that direction. The sleeve of a red sweater appeared to be hanging over the side of a rubbish bin. He raced over to the bin with a propitious feeling that it had to be the same sweater the Frenchman was wearing.

When Henry pulled it out of the trash, he was completely stunned to discover the red sweater wasn't the only thing discarded—he also found a fake mustache and a wig that matched the same white hair color of the man they had been chasing. Kneeling so that Penny could pick up on the scent, he remarked, "This guy is really cooking up a little scheme here, Penny."

Looking around the terminal, Henry glanced over at the hallway toward the boarding area for the RMS *Queen Charlotte*. His heart sank to his stomach once he saw that it was empty of people. The boarding process had already concluded, and he presumed the Frenchman had likely gotten away on the ocean liner.

Henry turned toward the train platforms and spotted the Australian manhandling another impostor. The man in the cloak was rifling through another black duffle bag in search of the missing polar bear cubs.

With the red sweater raised above his head, Henry shouted, "Hey! Outback Jack! He went this way!" A boisterous wave of loud barks ensued, courtesy of Penny.

After the dachshund's raucous barking captured his attention, the Australian dashed over when he spotted Henry holding the red sweater and the wig. "Oh, great!" the man in the cloak bemoaned, sighing in frustration. "This is just bloody beautiful, isn't it?"

Somewhat annoyed that the young kid managed to find the real Frenchman's disguise before he did, the Australian just sprinted down the transatlantic passenger terminal without saying another word. Henry glanced at the clock on the wall and shouted, "Wait a minute! It's too late!" which did nothing to slow the man in the black cloak down.

Hell-bent on getting to the bottom of what was really going on here, Henry chased after the Australian as Penny followed curiously.

Upon rounding the corner near the gangway boarding area, they all came to a halt. The sound of the *Queen Charlotte*'s horn underscored the gift of defeat that awaited them. The booming noise echoed throughout the picturesque harbor town with two resounding blasts. The majestic ocean liner was right there, but it was too late. The gangway ramp had already been retracted back into the passenger terminal building, and the ship was slowly moving away from the dock.

Penny, Henry, and the Australian in the black cloak stood there, watching in silence. They had all lost in their own way; for Penny, it was *Don Ciccio's* pizza.

Nobody was madder than the Australian. Even though they all suffered the same agony of staring at the *Queen Charlotte* steadily pulling away from Kodiak Bay, he was downright furious.

What happened next left Henry feeling more bewildered than ever. On the aft deck of the ship, they saw a woman waving her arms back and forth. "Au revoir!" she shouted triumphantly, gloating with elation. "Au revoir, *Barnabas*!"

Illuminated by the ship's bright deck lights, the woman appeared to be in her mid-thirties and had a petite, yet athletic build with striking red hair that came down just past her shoulders. However, it was the black duffle bag hanging off her shoulder that gave Henry pause.

"I'm coming for ya, Saint-Clair!" The Australian man in the black cloak pointed at the woman and screamed furiously. "This ain't ovah! Ya hear me?"

The sound of the woman's cackling carried across the harbor as the *Queen Charlotte* drifted further and further away.

— CHAPTER 6 —
THE AUSTRALIAN

*T*here were so many questions racing through Henry's mind. "Who was that woman holding the black duffle bag? How did she know the Australian man in the cloak? And more importantly, was the Frenchman actually a French *woman* this whole time?" He could barely comprehend any of it. The newspapers, Constable Hamilton, and even Captain Fulbright were all wrong. The disguises had deceived everyone, including Henry.

As the *Queen Charlotte* disappeared beyond the thick white fog, Henry felt the Australian owed him some answers. He couldn't resist the urge to collect on that debt and blurted, "*Barnabas?*"

The man in the cloak looked at Henry disdainfully, too annoyed to answer. He just sighed and walked away, grumbling. Henry chased after him, badgering the man, "Barnabas? Is that your name... Barnabas?" Penny trotted close behind, equally curious to learn more about this sharply dressed visitor.

Growing tired of his new shadow and in no mood for questions, the Australian stopped abruptly to confront the pesky young kid. "You know, I really had everything under control until you showed up at the zoo." He snapped in a snarky tone, "You're the reason she got away tonight!"

The man shook his head and quipped, "Good on ya, mate. Hope

you're happy!" Uninterested in spending another second talking to the zealous teenager, he stormed over to the central station exit without saying another word.

Henry scoffed in disbelief, shocked to hear the man in the cloak blame *him* for the Frenchman's escape. After all, he was the one who saw the discarded disguise while the Australian fumbled about with the other impostors. "Do you believe this guy, Penny?" he said with a hint of amusement in his voice, glancing down at the smiling dachshund. It was going to take more than that to discourage him. He just dodged massive barrels of maple syrup and narrowly escaped a pack of ferocious lions. Contending with a grouchy Australian seemed like no trouble at all in comparison. Henry dashed across the station, brushing past the crowds of travelers, while Penny followed at his side.

Upon exiting the station, it only took a few moments for Penny's nose to point them in the right direction. He spotted the man's black cloak billowing in the wind beyond the long line of queued taxicabs as the man walked briskly toward the harbor. "There he goes, Penny!" Henry exclaimed, racing down Regent Street, chasing after the man.

"Barnabas! Wait up a minute!" he shouted eagerly. "Who was that lady?"

Once he finally caught up to the man in the cloak, Henry added, "I was only trying to help, Barnabas!" The Australian stopped unexpectedly in front of the harbormaster's office and spun around, wearing an exasperated expression on his face. "Look, mate, the name is *Barnaby*! Barnaby Murdoch. Ya got that? Only my mum calls me Barnabas."

Still panting after sprinting down Regent Street, Henry said in a winded tone, "I'm, uh... my apologies, Mr. Murdoch."

"Great! Good riddance!" Barnaby replied irritably before

marching off toward the docks. Henry darted ahead and blocked the man's path, nervously demanding, "Wait a minute! I'm not sure where you're rushing off to, but we deserve some answers!"

"Is that right, mate?" Barnaby sneered.

"Well, for starters," Henry said in a quavered voice, "you can tell us what you were doing at the zoo tonight."

"Not sure that concerns you... and quite frankly, I don't reckon your parents would want you asking," Barnaby answered pompously. "Look a bit young to be working at the zoo after hours, kid."

Henry stammered, "Uh, well, um... I was following the Frenchman, of course."

Barnaby snickered and breezed past the young kid as he walked off without saying anything else. Visibly aggrieved, Penny bolted in front of the burly man, stopping him in his tracks with a pair of loud barks.

Hoping to persuade the man to tell him more about the Frenchman, Henry remarked enthusiastically, "Guess it sounds like we both were! I saw you in the tavern earlier... How'd you know she would be in town tonight anyway?"

"Alright, let me stop ya right there, mate," Barnaby interrupted. "Looks like we were after the same French menace tonight, but that don't make us partnahs, and I ain't got the time to hold your hand while you learn how to cross the street."

Henry scrunched his face in bemusement as Barnaby explained snidely, "I came here for one reason and one reason only... To stop that maniac from stealing those polar bear cubs. She's got 'em now, thanks to you, and I've got nothing to show for it except a bad headache. So do us all a favor and bugger off, will ya kid?"

Huffing with a flustered, crimson-faced expression, Henry didn't agree with that assessment one bit. If anyone was to blame, it certainly wasn't him, and he was tempted to refute the man's accusations in a less than polite manner. Fortunately, a familiar voice shouted from behind them before he said anything that might have enraged the Australian.

"*Barnaby   Banjo   Murdoch*!" Captain   Fulbright   yelled nostalgically, smiling from ear to ear. "You know... When I saw the *Arthur Broome* this morning, I was hoping it would be you, old friend."

Beaming with delight, Barnaby turned around and stuck his hand out to greet Captain Fulbright. "Ah yes, Kodiak Bay's salty harbormaster. Nice to see that retirement hasn't slowed you down, old-timer."

Henry was completely stunned. The astute dock attendant couldn't fathom how the captain somehow knew the cranky Australian he'd been chasing all night. Overcome with bewilderment, he cried out, "Captain! You know this guy?"

"Barnaby?" the captain chortled. "Oh, I most certainly do... And it looks like he still has the softest hands in the business, eh?" Barnaby burst into laughter despite being annoyed with the young boy's persistent questions.

While most men his age endured calluses and sandpaper-like roughness on their palms, Mr. Murdoch looked after his hands with great care. Some say it was the special moisturizer he used each night; others assume he had never worked a day in his life. In either case, he became used to the jesting and ridicule that usually ensued upon shaking hands with old friends.

It was dark out, but the harbor lights made it easy to see that Barnaby was in excellent physical shape and maintained a muscular build that could only come from routine weightlifting. He had a chiseled jawline, brown eyes, and short dirty-blonde hair.

The clothing worn by the Australian was equally intriguing. Fashionably attired would be putting it lightly. The man wore a stylish, dark-gray Italian suit made from the finest wool and a forest-green cashmere tie with a crisp white dress shirt. His suit jacket was unbuttoned, and Henry noticed what appeared to be a collapsible, electric cattle prod attached to his belt. Henry could also see suspenders that had empty holsters on both sides right below his chest.

A unique black cloak rested on Barnaby's shoulders. Henry thought it must have been a cape at first, but it wasn't long enough—the cloak only came down to the man's waist. It was secured in the front by a small silver medallion with a very distinct emblem. The pendant had an anchor symbol in the center, two crossed swords positioned above it, and tiny lettering written around the edges.

Between the chaos at the zoo and the frantic pursuit that followed, Henry hadn't even noticed the medallion until now. When it finally caught his attention, he gasped as if the whole world had been turned upside down. "It couldn't be true," he thought to himself. Those were only myths and tall tales he had heard when he was a young boy.

Surprisingly, Captain Fulbright's cheerful demeanor turned more somber. "Yeah, it's been a long time since I've seen my old Australian friend, and if it weren't for the six traumatized fishermen that just got pulled out of the North Atlantic, I'd say it was nice to see him. Although I reckon Mr. Murdoch has come to Kodiak Bay on official *APA* business, eh?"

"I'm afraid so, mate," Barnaby replied. "I've been chasing the Frenchman for weeks. Three continents later, and still nothing to show for it. Always two steps behind... and now I know why."

The man recounted his failed pursuit. "Thought I had 'em tonight. She nicked two polar bear cubs from the zoo, set the rest of the animals loose, and then figured it would be hilarious to send a few dozen barrels of maple syrup hurtling my way."

"*She?*" the captain remarked, tilting his head dubiously. "You mean the Frenchman is a woman?"

Right as Barnaby was about to answer, Henry chimed in energetically, "That's right, Captain! I saw the whole thing! She got away on the *Queen Charlotte* headed for London, and she apparently knows Mr. Murdoch. I think her name is Saint-Clair!"

Barnaby's tetchiness could be felt in the sigh that ensued, but he was amused by Henry's temerity (if only slightly). The flicker of levity in his eyes suggested he was starting to see a bit of himself in the tenacious young boy.

Grinning derisively, the cloaked man asked, "Who *is* this kid? He a friend of yours?" Captain Fulbright laughed. "Ah yes, I see you have met the illustrious Mr. Henry Halifax... and his invariably vociferous sidekick, Penny."

"Mrs. Fulbright and I have looked after him since before he could walk. He and his furry companion are the finest dock attendants in all of Kodiak Bay. They're also keen on helping the animals, eh?" The captain added, gesturing toward Barnaby, "Sort of like your lot, I suppose."

Captain Fulbright patted Henry on the back and boasted, "Gifted lad too, eh? Graduated last year from high school by the time he was fourteen... top of his class with honors to boot." He smiled and continued proudly, "And when Henry's not helping this old sailor on the docks, he's developed a bit of a reputation in town as an incipient detective... specializing in animal-related quandaries." Penny let out two cheerful barks to remind the captain that Henry didn't work alone—in fact, her nose often led the investigations.

Glancing at Henry with a chuckle, Barnaby jested, "Yeah, that enthusiasm of his is certainly an acquired taste." Captain Fulbright knew exactly what he meant and instantly laughed.

After wiping the smile off his face, Barnaby offered Henry some genuine gratitude for the first time. "But good on ya for looking after the animals, mate. They can always use another person in their cornah." He shook Henry's hand and advised reassuringly, "And don't worry about Saint-Clair, kid. I'll eventually catch her and get those bear cubs sorted out in no time at all."

"Good to see you again, Captain!" Barnaby announced cheerfully, taking a step back. "I should be back around these parts soon... So keep a few stubbies on ice for me, will ya, mate?"

The captain looked off in the distance toward the anchored ship that was partially concealed by the thick white fog and asked, "Do you need a ride back?" Barnaby replied, "No worries, sir. I got it... Appreciate the offer though, and always good seeing ya again, pal!"

Henry stood there in astonishment, still wondering how Captain Fulbright knew the mysterious man in the black cloak. As Barnaby started walking away, Henry blurted, "But, Mr. Murdoch! Wait!"

Barnaby stopped, exhaling in frustration as he turned around. Clearly exhausted, his patience was running out. He put his hands on his hips and looked insolently at Henry in the eyes—it was the kind of silent stare that demanded a timely response.

Perplexed, Captain Fulbright just stepped off to the side; he also wanted to know what was so important and listened with immense curiosity. The tension was palpable. With all eyes on Henry, the young dock attendant took a deep breath and announced nervously, "Pardon me, sir, but I can't let you leave..."

The man in the black cloak was absolutely baffled. He interrupted in an overtly sneering manner, "*Let me leave*?"

Even though there was a part of Henry that regretted opening his mouth, he mustered the courage to carry on nonetheless, explaining, "Sorry, I didn't mean it like that. You see, I'm technically the designated government official responsible for the pair of polar bear cubs that went missing tonight. And since I take my duties quite seriously, I respectfully request that you allow me to join your expedition to retrieve the bears in question... Temporarily, of course."

Barnaby hooted with blatant skepticism, "Government official? Are you putting me on? You're a little young to be a Mountie, mate."

Henry answered confidently as he effused, "Well, you probably didn't know this... But as an official volunteer of the Kodiak Bay Fire Brigade, it's my duty by law to make sure those bears are safely returned to Canadian soil. I was the first responding officer on the scene tonight, and seeing how one of my equine colleagues gave you a lift earlier, I think Rusty and the Mounties would agree that this is a perfect opportunity for you to reciprocate in kind."

The incredulous look on Barnaby's face was priceless. He thought the young dock attendant was joking at first, although it became clear his presumption was way off when Henry continued, "For that reason, I'm obliged to tell you... *I am a stranger, traveling by land, seeking assistance to protect those who cannot protect themselves.*"

It had been many years since Barnaby had heard someone utter those words. He couldn't believe that Henry, of all people, had just said the last thing he wanted to hear right now. Forcing a contemptuous smile, he mumbled in response, "Well, well, well. Clever boy, indeed."

Barnaby's jovial attitude turned more serious, and he begrudgingly declared, "Alright. You got me, mate. Well done. *Barnaby Banjo Murdoch* is certainly a man of his word, with the greatest respect for a sworn oath. So, I guess I would have to reply... *I am a stranger, traveling by sea, and I am the guardian you seek.*"

"It's true! The legend is true," Henry shouted with a look of excitement beaming from his face—he was beyond elated. The thought of leaving Kodiak Bay for the first time ever sent a wave of excitement through his body.

Henry never imagined the *APA* was actually real. As far as he knew, the legendary organization was just old folklore. For years, he believed they were nothing more than stories, tall tales that were told to young children at bedtime. That all changed in an instant after Barnaby confirmed what Captain Fulbright knew all along. Henry had been in the presence of a *real* Tutori this entire time.

His celebration was tempered as Barnaby warned curtly, "Listen, I ain't no babysittah, kid. You're gonna have to pull your own weight and look out for yourself. Just because you're temporarily riding with me... and I do want to emphasize the *temporary* part... that don't make you a Tutori, and we still ain't partnahs. So, stay out of my way and stick to taking notes in the cornah, got it?"

"Yes, sir, Mr. Murdoch. I'll stay out of your way," Henry replied, immediately wiping the smile off his face. He turned to Captain Fulbright and asked anxiously, "Of course, only with your permission, Captain?"

Captain Fulbright took a moment to consider and then responded reluctantly, "I'm probably gonna catch hell when I tell Mrs. Fulbright tonight... But, I guess you gotta grow up sometime, my boy. Suppose you're old enough to make your own decisions now, eh?"

It was exactly what Henry was hoping he would say—although the subtly cracking emotional tone in the captain's voice brought on a bout of guilty feelings. In the midst of his exuberance, Henry forgot all about his promise to Mrs. Fulbright. Only a few days ago, they were discussing his plans for attending university; he vowed to pick one close to Kodiak Bay so that routine visits back home wouldn't be a problem.

Despite some of the finest schools across North America offering full scholarships, he still wasn't old enough to accept any of them. The minimum age for new admissions was sixteen, which meant he had to wait another fourteen months until next fall to attend as a freshman.

The captain knew Henry would never get another chance like this again. Most people go their whole lives without ever encountering the Tutori, and even fewer get the opportunity to work alongside one. If he didn't let Henry go now, it would only be a matter of time before the resentment and blame started to surface; the inescapable regret would likely follow Henry around for the rest of his life.

"Thank you, Captain! Thank you!" Henry proclaimed, rushing forward to wrap his arms around the sentimental old harbormaster. It was a bittersweet moment for both of them.

Henry promised he would write Mrs. Fulbright a letter as soon as possible, prompting two loud barks from Penny. The wirehaired dachshund wasn't quite sure what was happening, yet she could sense his elation and assumed it must have been good news.

Captain Fulbright could tell Henry was excited and offered some parting advice. "Now, you be sure to listen to everything Mr. Murdoch says. The *APA* is serious business. This is not a game to them. The work they do can be very dangerous... So, if Mr. Murdoch tells you to jump, just do it and don't waste time asking questions, eh?"

Henry tried to hide his excitement as he nodded respectfully and replied, "Yes, sir, Captain. Whatever Mr. Murdoch says, I will follow his lead at all times. I promise!"

"Good lad... Make sure to be careful out there, ok? And look after Penny!" the captain said as he pulled Henry in to give him one last hug. He stepped back and turned toward Barnaby to announce, "Just bring 'em back in one piece, eh?"

"No worries, mate," Barnaby snickered, winking at the captain. "Think I can manage that... at least for the bear cubs, right?" Captain Fulbright crossed his arms dismissively and smiled in silence.

The man in the cloak reached behind his back and retrieved a small red stick with a white string hanging from the bottom. It kind of resembled a road flare. He pointed the red tube toward the sky and was about to yank on the string, but stopped himself at the last second.

Barnaby inspected the small writing on the side of the tube. He shrugged as if he had just fortuitously avoided pouring tomato juice on a bowl of cornflakes instead of milk. After tossing the stick in a nearby rubbish bin, he pulled another seemingly identical one from behind his back and yanked on the white string without hesitation. A green-colored firework launched into the air and illuminated the harbor as soon as it exploded a few hundred meters above them.

The captain marveled at the fireworks display. It had been years since he had seen a real Tutori, and he could never forget how the *APA* came to his rescue all those years ago. Seeing that familiar signal reminded him that Henry was in good hands.

Standing next to his office, Captain Fulbright gazed at Barnaby's cloak billowing in the wind as the man walked down the wooden dock, Henry and Penny following closely behind. He thought about calling the whole thing off when Henry turned around to look back, although he resisted the fatherly urge and simply nodded his head with reassuring approval. It was time for Henry to step out into the world on his own.

Like a father teaching his kid how to ride a bicycle, Captain Fulbright became overwhelmed with emotion. There was a real sense of pride that came with watching Henry grow up over the years. Knowing that he had helped shape the young boy's life up to this point nearly brought the old sailor to tears. He knew this moment would eventually come and felt a bit sad that today was the day. It's an inevitability that every parent faces (something most will never be truly prepared for), but the captain could feel in his heart that it was time to let go, training wheels or not.

Once Barnaby, Henry, and Penny reached the end of the boat slips, they saw a black zodiac entering the harbor.

The small inflatable boat quickly pulled up to the side of the dock near the fuel pumps. Barnaby greeted the woman behind the wheel as he jumped aboard, "Ciao, Valentina!" He looked back at the young boy standing on the docks. "Well... are you coming or not, kid?"

Despite the earlier spell of courage that gave him the confidence to recite the Tutori Creed in front of a real Tutori, Henry was nervous about leaving Kodiak Bay for the first time. It wasn't too late to turn around and go home right now—Penny certainly wouldn't protest, especially if there were stacks of warm flapjacks covered in delicious maple syrup waiting for them. Mr. Murdoch wasn't too keen on partners anyway, so he'd probably be doing him a favor.

Henry peered at the vessel anchored outside of the harbor; the thick white fog had started to dissipate, faintly revealing the curved bow. That brief glimpse was all it took to assuage his fears. It was a moment that would change Henry's life forever. The young dock attendant suddenly scooped up Penny and finally replied, "Let's get after those bear cubs, eh?" before hopping onto the small boat.

"I assume this is not the Frenchman we came here for?" Valentina smirked. "Coming back empty-handed again, Barnabas?"

Barnaby exhaled in frustration and responded with a forced smile, "Don't you worry, Valentina. I know exactly when and where that maniac will be next."

"Sì, sì, sì, exactly like last time, no?" Valentina jested. As Barnaby's face turned redder than *Don Ciccio's* pizza sauce, she couldn't resist pressing him for more details. "And who's the kid?"

"Him? He's nobody," Barnaby chuckled, "just a professional courtesy who knows one too many creeds for his age. But I'll be rid of 'em soon enough... right after I catch up to that French menace!"

"Well, nice to meet you, Mr. Nobody," Valentina chortled.

"Actually, ma'am... It's Henry. Henry Halifax!" he answered enthusiastically. She winked at him and cheerfully warned, "Well, you better hold on, Henry Halifax!"

Slamming the throttle forward without warning, she sent Henry and Penny tumbling to the back of the zodiac as it zoomed away from the docks.

Henry carefully picked up Penny and planted his feet firmly on the boat deck while Barnaby stood next to Valentina. The black zodiac zipped past the harbor entrance and turned left toward the mysterious ship anchored outside the breakwall. He looked back at the docks and saw Captain Fulbright wave one last time, right before the zodiac disappeared into the thick white fog.

The sea breeze whisked past Henry's face, and he wondered what to expect as they approached the ship. He still couldn't believe that he was only moments away from boarding the legendary *Arthur Broome*. His mind raced with curiosity.

Henry had an endless number of unanswered questions, and the story behind Valentina's highly unusual uniform was at the top of the list.

Ms. Valentina Vinciguerra was the first officer of the *Arthur Broome* and second in command. She wore tall black boots and black trousers that had two vertical red stripes lining the outer sides of both legs. Her black necktie and white button-down shirt were accentuated by the matching jacket, complete with red piping around the black epaulettes on the shoulders. With a white cross-belt bandolier and aiguillette, this wasn't an ordinary uniform by any measure. The dark-blue cap atop her head was equally interesting; it had a silver medal emblem on the front that appeared to be the symbol of the Carabinieri.

Henry had seen old photos of a younger Captain Fulbright from his days with the Royal Canadian Navy; he immediately recognized the uniform from the photographs of the captain and some of his Italian Navy pals. "What are the Carabinieri doing here?" he mumbled under his breath to Penny.

Whatever the reason might be, it would have to wait. Henry quickly became distracted once the *Arthur Broome* entered into view. Towering above the tiny inflatable boat, the mighty ship was unlike anything he had ever seen. He marveled at the futuristic design and sheer size in comparison to the zodiac. Before today, he never fathomed that he'd find himself boarding the legendary *APA* headquarters.

"Whoa!" Henry whispered in astonishment. The zodiac veered to the left past the front of the massive ship, and his eyes glimmered with excitement the moment he first saw the letters *ARTHUR BROOME* painted on the side.

Valentina turned the wheel abruptly and made a wide circular maneuver in the opposite direction; in no time at all, the front of the zodiac was positioned perpendicular to the starboard side of the ship. Henry was captivated by the majestic vessel. Simply being in its presence only heightened his fascination with the *APA*.

But underneath all the awe and wonder, the treachery that awaited onboard would challenge him in ways that he could never have seen coming.

— CHAPTER 7 —
THE ARTHUR BROOME

*T*he *Arthur Broome* was a polar-class expedition ship unlike any other. It had a strengthened ice-breaking hull and a curved, wave-piercing bow design that could withstand even the harshest arctic conditions. The bottom of the ship was painted black, right up to a thick red stripe of paint running horizontally from the top of the bow all the way to the stern, wrapping around the entire ship. Contrasting sharply, the upper decks above the stripe were all painted white.

At one hundred sixty meters in length by twenty-six meters in width, the *Arthur Broome* spanned ten decks high and made the inflatable zodiac look like a small toy.

Henry had never seen such a modern and futuristic ship in his whole life. The slanted stern design and the dramatic curves shared a strong resemblance to a spaceship on water, at least in comparison to anything else sailing the high seas.

With the anchor already pulled up and the zodiac pointed directly toward the side of the *Arthur Broome*, Henry wondered how they would actually board the ship. He didn't see any rope ladders hanging off the side.

Nonetheless, Valentina gradually pushed the throttle forward, seemingly unconcerned about plowing into the side of the massive ship ahead. Henry shuddered at the sight of the obstacle in their path, worried that they were going to crash straight into it.

A sigh of relief was overshadowed by utter astonishment when Henry gazed toward the waterline at a huge panel in the center of the hull that retracted upwards (effectively like a hidden garage door). Too bewildered to say anything, he found himself completely transfixed by the lights coming from the cavernous hole on the starboard side of the ship.

Once the panel had fully retracted, the black zodiac zoomed through the gaping entrance and slid straight into the *Arthur Broome*'s tender bay as if it were a car pulling into a garage. It turned out to be a tight squeeze with two other boats already tied up inside, but Valentina parked the zodiac without the slightest trace of apprehension.

The tender bay was a floating rubber dock inside the bulkhead of the ship that had enough room for three small boats. In the far corner, a davit held up a yellow compact submarine with *two hundred seventy-degree* spherical windows. It appeared to be able to accommodate six passengers.

Henry marveled at the large retractable door as it started closing behind them and then heard a series of locking mechanisms secure the hull's watertight seal. He looked down curiously, watching as an automatic pump began to force the saltwater inside the tender bay back into the ocean. He was so distracted by the engineering feats on display that he didn't even notice that Valentina and Barnaby had already gotten off the boat and were standing on the rubber dock.

"Let's go, mate!" Barnaby remarked impatiently. "Unless you want to stay down here all night?"

Valentina and Barnaby kept walking as Henry collected Penny and hopped off the boat. Dashing down the platform to catch up, he was awestruck by the hallway in front of them—and it wasn't just the unusually high ceilings or the trio of elevators at the end. Even the extravagant chandeliers hanging from above weren't nearly as fascinating as the men lining each side of the hallway; apparently standing guard, there were a total of ten by Henry's count.

The uniforms worn by the men suggested that these were no ordinary guards. They were all dressed exactly the same, wearing tall black leather boots, white riding pants, and black double-breasted jackets that had silver buttons on the front and red trim piping. They were also sporting white gloves on their hands and black capes on their shoulders. The guards looked stately, and their swords were enough to intimidate even the most formidable adversaries.

Henry stared at the shiny, gold cuirass armor covering their torsos and the dragoon helmets with black horsehair resting atop their heads.

A booming noise surprisingly interrupted his naive gawking. Without warning, all ten guards stomped at the same time while simultaneously raising their swords at attention. It was an unexpected coincidence that happened the instant Valentina and Barnaby entered the hallway.

Barnaby's headache only got worse from the onslaught of questions spewing from the young boy's mouth during their walk down the hallway. He was already regretting not leaving Henry on the docks.

"Who are those guys?" Henry blurted, excitably gesturing toward the guards. "Are they Carabinieri too... from Italy? What are the Italian police doing here, eh?"

Valentina chuckled, while Barnaby just sighed wearily. They both knew what Henry meant, although he butchered the pronunciation in the most egregious fashion.

Barnaby was exhausted from chasing Saint-Clair all over Kodiak Bay, and his tolerance for Henry's enthusiasm has been waning ever since. He pushed the elevator call button and replied, "Look, kid, it's pronounced *Kar-uh-bin-yair-ee...* and I suggest a bit of caution before referring to them as just the police. Now, I know you're from a small town in Canada, and you probably don't know any bettah. So, I'm gonna give you a pass this time."

"But pay attention and listen carefully because those guards might not be as forgiving next time, mate." Even though he was in no mood to give Henry a history lesson, Barnaby still felt he owed it to the Carabinieri to carry on explaining. "You see, the Carabinieri is an institution... an ancient organization founded by the King of Sardinia before Italy was even established as a country. Loyal throughout the centuries, the Carabinieri have always been a friend to the *APA*."

Henry was embarrassed and red in the face after blundering the name so badly, and he listened humbly to Barnaby correct his misapprehensions. "That's right, the Italians share our passion for helping animals, going all the way back to the King of Sardinia. And many years ago, a clandestine Carabinieri regiment was formed and assigned to assist the Tutori in carrying out our duties. Most of the ship's crew are Carabinieri, from the captain on down to the cook."

"They're always first in line to rescue the injured during disastahs. And when that's all over, you can find them at the hospital bringing toys to sick kids or comforting the elderly in times of need." Right as Henry opened his mouth to apologize, Barnaby boasted in the same breath, "You'll never see one hesitate to put their life at risk to save animals in danger either. *They protect those who cannot protect themselves*, no matter the cost. From the tiny hilltop town of Cortona to the bustling streets of Rome and everywhere in between, the Carabinieri are always there. Not because it's their *job*... not because they're *just* the Italian police... *it is their duty as guardians*."

Captivated by Barnaby's remarks, Henry gulped as the long-winded reprimand reached its conclusion. "Respect will be paid!" Immediately, the thunderous sound of ten Carabinieri guards stomping their feet simultaneously followed. The deafening noise was so loud, it caught Henry by surprise, and he lost his balance after stumbling backward inadvertently.

Feeling mortified, he sprang to his feet and replied meekly, "Yes, sir, Mr. Murdoch. My most sincere apologies." Fortunately for Henry, the arriving elevator bell chimed, and the doors on the far right opened moments later. Valentina smiled, winking at the unwitting dock attendant as they all shuffled inside.

Smirking, Valentina turned to Barnaby. "To the council chambers, I assume?" She pushed the corresponding buttons before he could answer. A look of delight replaced the annoyed expression on his face while he teased, "Well, I'd much rather have the honor of taking you to dinnah instead, love... But I suspect the council is keen to know what happened out there tonight."

Valentina tittered and responded in a subtly flirtatious tone, "Oh Barnabas, you know I prefer dinner... and a show. I guess it's a lucky happenstance because there's an urgent matter that I must discuss with the council right away."

"Is that right?" Barnaby snickered. "What happened? Did the kitchen run out of maple syrup?" Despite feeling exhausted from such a long day, he chuckled to himself as he looked down at Henry and Penny.

There was no denying that Henry enjoyed pure maple syrup on his breakfast flapjacks practically every morning. Yet the remark didn't amuse him in the slightest. He tilted his head and smiled derisively as Penny let out a muffled growl; they both didn't take kindly to the sarcastic affront to Canadians.

"Woah!" Henry exclaimed. He lost his balance when the elevator stopped abruptly before changing directions—much to his astonishment, it started moving to the right instead of the usual up or down movement he was accustomed to. He asked confusedly,

"Are we moving... *horizontally*? What kind of elevator is this?"

Henry had only been on an elevator twice in his life. Both times were at Kodiak Bay's tallest hotel and were nothing like this.

Too tired to entertain Henry's boundless curiosity, Barnaby grumbled, "I can already tell this is gonna be a long week... Listen, do me a favor and let me do all the talking when we get off the elevator. I know you have a million questions, but you're just an onlookah here, and this ain't the time nor the place, kid."

If it were any other day, Henry might have felt discouraged; this was no ordinary day, though, and he wasn't going to let Barnaby sully his mood. He could tell the cranky Australian felt a bit anxious and sensed the trepidation in his voice. Nevertheless, he cheerfully replied, "My apologies, Mr. Murdoch. I promise not to say another word, sir."

The elevator soon came to a stop, and the rear doors opened unexpectedly. Henry spun around, following Valentina and Barnaby off the elevator as Penny trotted close behind. He couldn't help but wonder if Barnaby was in serious trouble with the council— based on what Valentina said back at the docks, it sure sounded like this wasn't the first time Saint-Clair managed to get away from him.

"This way, mate," Barnaby instructed. He turned to the left and began walking toward the council chambers.

At the end of the hallway were double doors that must have been twice as tall as the pair of sword-wielding Carabinieri officers standing guard outside. Henry noticed they appeared to be the same type of imposing guards he saw down in the tender bay.

The two guards promptly opened the large doors as they got closer to the entranceway. With Penny at his side, Henry trailed nervously behind Barnaby and Valentina. He didn't have a clue as to what to expect upon entering the council chambers. But judging by the fear flickering in Barnaby's eyes, he assumed a scolding awaited.

Henry had a million questions—the Australian Tutori was right about that.

In spite of the wild pursuit that unfolded in Kodiak Bay earlier, Barnaby still had nothing to show for his efforts. Meanwhile, Saint-Clair was on her way to London, probably sipping champagne and enjoying dinner in the *Queen Charlotte*'s lavish dining room.

As the huge double doors closed behind Henry and Penny, Valentina stepped off to the side near the exit. She couldn't wait to hear what sort of creative excuses Barnaby had concocted this time around. Watching the inevitable spectacle had become something of a pastime for her.

Henry paused a few steps in, glancing back at the exit. Valentina could tell he was concerned and reassuringly directed him down the aisleway, gesturing to keep following Barnaby. He realized in that moment there was no turning back now, and he kept trudging forward accordingly.

The dimly lit room looked very similar to a grand theater. There was a raised, circular center platform in the middle and rows of seats that surrounded the stage. Directly in front of the platform were three high-backed seats that resembled thrones fit for royalty, complete with a front-row view of the center stage.

Henry and Penny followed Barnaby as he walked down the aisleway and onto the raised platform.

Once they actually stepped onto the center stage, Henry was more nervous than ever. He looked timorously around the room and saw nearly two dozen paintings hanging on the walls—they appeared to be portraits of fallen Tutori from years past. More than happy to let Barnaby do all the talking, he stood off to the side as the Australian stepped forward into the spotlight.

They were immediately met with a glaring look of contempt from the trio of women sitting on the ornate thrones. Dressed in ceremonial gold-colored robes, nothing about their demeanor gave him the impression that they were pleased to see Barnaby. Henry wasn't sure who they were, although he found the scowls painted on their faces to be quite intimidating—even more so than the palpable tension in the room.

In the center chair sat Mary MacDougall from Scotland. Older than the other two women, she had a well-known reputation for being tougher than oil rig roughnecks.

Sofia Machado sat in the chair on the right and was originally from Mexico. She was notoriously unapologetic about the passion she brought to the council hearings.

Charlotte Cross, on the other hand, was more reserved yet always prepared to make tough decisions. She sat in the chair on the left and was proud to be the newest member of the council. Madam Cross expected results and had very little patience for excuses or sloppy work.

Standing next to Henry on stage, Penny could smell the increased perspiration wafting past her nose. Surprisingly, Barnaby appeared to be feeling more anxious than anyone else in the room. She wasn't frightened, though. Penny welcomed the torrent of unfamiliar scents and knew at least one person in the audience had tacos for dinner.

Henry peered through the bright stage lighting and saw several people randomly spread out amongst the rows of smaller chairs; he presumed they must have been members of the Tutori. Their matching gray wool suits looked just like Barnaby's.

Gazing at them one by one, Henry first spotted a woman wearing a cowboy hat. She appeared to be around Barnaby's age and was sitting next to a teenage girl. As his eyes wandered, he also noticed a Japanese man by himself, an older British gentleman sitting next to a young boy, and a handsome Indian man seated all alone. Nothing seemed out of place until he saw a familiar face seated in the back row. His heart leapt with exhilaration when he spotted the red hair glinting in the light.

"That's impossible!" Henry mumbled under his breath in disbelief. "She looks exactly like Saint-Clair!" The woman near the back of the council chambers appeared to be the same person he had been chasing through the streets of Kodiak Bay a few hours ago. "It couldn't be true," he thought to himself.

Henry saw Saint-Clair on the deck of the *Queen Charlotte* with his own two eyes. Absolutely baffled, there was a part of him that wanted to impulsively rush off stage, run over, demand she give up the bear cubs, and confess in front of everyone. The only thing more shocking was that Barnaby didn't seem to care. Surely, he must have spotted the woman as well. The uncanny resemblance to Saint-Clair would have been impossible to overlook.

Nonetheless, Henry remained on stage; he was mindful to be on his best behavior in the presence of the legendary Tutori council. He still wasn't sure what was going on, but he listened with bated breath to Barnaby's report of tonight's events.

"Mr. Murdoch, what news do you have to report to this council?" The woman on the ornate center throne inquired with a thick Scottish accent.

The council member sitting on the right, Madam Machado, didn't let him get a word out and interjected, "Forgive me, but before we get to that, did I hear Captain Carlucci say that you launched a green signal into the air this evening?" She scoffed and asked again, "Is that right? Or was the captain mistaken?"

Waywardly grinning, Barnaby quipped, "Right as rain, madam. Although it remains to be seen if it was a mistake." Madam Machado laughed. "Very nice, Señor Murdoch... A little surprising coming from you, no?"

The councilwoman on the opposite side, Madam Cross, chimed in. "Surprising, indeed."

Seated in the middle chair, Madam MacDougall grew impatient and remarked, "Yes, yes, it is... But if you don't mind, I would still like to hear Mr. Murdoch's field report."

"Well then, let's have it, Señor Murdoch." Madam Machado asked sternly, "What happened out there tonight?"

"Honorable council members, it appears that things are not as they seem in the town of Kodiak Bay," Barnaby declared before being interrupted by Madam Cross. "Not as they seem?"

Madam Cross tutted and retorted, "Please do continue, Mr. Murdoch... because I can already tell by the defeated expression on your face that it would seem you were unsuccessful in your attempt to catch this bear thief tonight. For the third consecutive time, if I'm not mistaken?" Her posh, British accent had the innate ability to make even the most antagonizing accusations sound affable.

Barnaby respectfully replied, "That is correct, madam. The Frenchman escaped again. This time with two polar bear cubs from the *Kodiak Bay Zoo.*"

"But no worries," he added boldly, "I know exactly where those cubs are headed next. We just need to get to London before they arrive, and I guarantee this whole mess will finally be sorted!"

Henry was thoroughly confused. He wondered why Barnaby wasn't more forthcoming about what *really* happened tonight. It certainly sounded like the cunning Tutori failed to disclose some rather important details, leaving out the part where he recognized the Frenchman, which would have been at the top of the list.

Barnaby didn't even mention that he knew her real name. At the very least, Henry assumed the Australian would have told them it turned out to be a French *woman* stealing bear cubs from zoos all over the world. And most important, a woman who looked just like the redhead currently sitting in the back row of the council chambers.

"Did he let her escape on purpose?" Henry murmured to himself suspiciously.

The councilwoman on the right responded in a feminine Mexican accent, "And tell us, Señor Barnabas... What will you be doing between now and then? Surely, reacquaint yourself with the art of throwing tranquilizer darts."

"Well, it never hurts to practice, madam, but I can assure this council that my accuracy is mastered." Barnaby snickered arrogantly. "I'm quite certain I managed to hit the Frenchman tonight. Two times, actually... The darts did nothing to slow him down, though. Almost as if he were impervious to the tranquilizer." He threw his hands up dramatically and concluded, "Never seen anything like it before!"

"Well, well, well... I suppose you could have used a wee bit of help out there tonight, Barnabas," the Scottish woman in the center throne remarked. She exhaled sharply. "Perhaps the time has come for you to embrace the idea of working with a partner again?"

Barnaby dismissed the suggestion and shook his head like a child being asked to brush his teeth before bedtime. He loathed the very thought of working with a partner again and rushed to downplay their concerns. "Well, I'm undoubtedly humbled by the idea, madam, and that's certainly warranted given tonight's outcome. Although it's prudent, we avoid making any hasty decisions, right?"

Sensing the council members were unconvinced, Barnaby protested uproariously, "We all know that *Barnaby Banjo Murdoch* works best alone. Ask anyone!" Growing visibly frustrated, his voice creaked as he desperately tried to regain the council's confidence. "Sure, this polar bear thief has given me the slip a few times... and I'm confident I'll have the bruises to prove it after tonight's tussle, but nobody wants to catch this guy more than me." Madam Machado rolled her eyes, like she had heard this song and dance before.

"A partner will only slow me down!" Barnaby warned.

It was no secret that Barnaby had always been stubborn when

confronted with the recurring proposition of partnering up with another Tutori. He hated the idea and preferred to work solo.

The British councilwoman anticipated his resistance and opted to shift the inquiry. "And who is this young boy in the yellow raincoat? Why did you bring him here?"

Barnaby glanced back at the befuddled dock attendant and sighed, almost as if he had forgotten Henry was still there. "This kid right here?"

"No worries. He's a nobody, madam," Barnaby chuckled, slightly amused by the infectious smile on Penny's face, "just a professional courtesy with an interest in getting those two polar bear cubs safely returned to Canadian soil."

Barnaby continued, with a hint of annoyance peppered in his voice. "Afraid I had no choice, madam. You see, this lad found himself caught up in the middle of tonight's commotion. Apparently, he's the youngest member of the Kodiak Bay Fire Brigade and is also vexatiously familiar with the Tutori Creed."

Unimpressed by Barnaby's vague explanation, Madam Machado politely demanded to know more. "Young man, please step forward and tell this council what brought you here before us." Barnaby looked back at Henry with a raised eyebrow, clearly worried about what the young dock attendant might reveal to the council.

Henry was more nervous than he'd ever been in his whole life. It could have been due to the flood of whispers amongst the audience that quietly echoed throughout the room, or maybe it was Barnaby dragging him into this dreadful deceit before the council. Nevertheless, he stepped forward next to Barnaby. Penny seemed to be enjoying the show and insouciantly trotted alongside him.

Standing by the Australian Tutori, Henry tried his best to keep his hands from trembling. After a moment of fidgeting and anxiety-filled glances at Barnaby, he gathered the courage to respond, "I'm truly sorry if I interfered with Mr. Murdoch's investigation tonight."

A deafening silence fell upon the room. Henry knew that a terse statement wasn't going to cut it, and he carried on talking at an almost frantic pace. "Guess I should've started with my name. It's Henry Halifax, by the way, and, uh, my best friend here is Penny."

"You see, I didn't even know Mr. Murdoch was in town. It all started when I was working the docks with Penny at the *Kodiak Bay Harbor* this evening. We were just about to head home for the night when a French stranger in an orange zodiac showed up looking for a boat slip and some fuel. That's certainly not unusual by itself, but we noticed a white bucket in the back of the zodiac. Taking a closer look, I realized this bucket belonged to a local fishing boat, and I found it odd that this same boat never made it back to the docks before sundown. Combined with the mysterious disappearance of the *Amity Jane* yesterday, I surmised this was no coincidence. In fact, I thought the stranger in the zodiac was the same person that had been stealing bear cubs from other zoos around the world."

The sound of murmuring among the half-dozen or so Tutori in the audience permeated the council chambers. Suspecting the council of three was not appeased, Henry took a deep breath and continued with a spirited, long-winded clarification. "I'm talking about the same person that has also established a reputation for sinking local fishing boats in the days preceding the thefts. Presuming this person in question would be headed for the newly opened polar bear exhibit at the *Kodiak Bay Zoo*, we decided to follow the French stranger. Our suspicions were confirmed when we witnessed the stranger change clothes in the alley next to *Paddy O'Connor's Tavern*. Dressed in a *Kodiak Bay Zoo* employee uniform, the Frenchman then broke into the staff entrance at the zoo."

"That's when I saw Mr. Murdoch commence his pursuit and enter the zoo through the same door. Obviously, calling the Mounties right away would have been the proper course of action, but I had to see it for myself. And sure enough, it only took a few minutes before a boatload of animals were set loose," Henry recalled, gesturing with his hands.

"After a bit of a tussle between Mr. Murdoch and the Frenchman, the thief managed to escape with the polar bear cubs. A chase ensued, but we lost sight of the Frenchman at the train station once another pre-planned diversion was initiated. Despite our best efforts, the Frenchman escaped on the *Queen Charlotte*, headed for London."

Madam MacDougall wasn't entirely convinced that the account of tonight's events represented the whole story. She looked at Henry and encouraged him to share more. "Go on, lad. Is that all?"

He glanced over at Barnaby again. The Australian nodded reassuringly, which gave Henry the courage to add, "Well, then we followed Mr. Murdoch back to the harbor. I presumed he was a Tutori after noticing the medallion, and I recited a creed that I remembered from some old bedtime stories. I never imagined the Tutori were actually real, and honestly, I didn't think anything would come of it when I requested his assistance to help recover the stolen polar bears."

"Like all of you, I too have a duty to protect those cubs," Henry announced confidently. "I was the first responding official of the Kodiak Bay Fire Brigade on scene tonight, and I'm sincerely grateful that Mr. Murdoch obliged when called upon. With the greatest respect, I am here to help make sure those polar bear cubs are safely returned to Kodiak Bay."

The council members remained silent after he finished explaining. Henry stood there wondering if they knew he wasn't being completely transparent about his interest in possibly joining the *APA* or the *real* identity of the Frenchman.

Henry was taught to always be honest. However, there was a fine line between truthfully answering a direct question and volunteering additional information. Especially if the latter meant immediately shattering his dreams of serving under the Tutori as a Magari. He was there to help recover those missing bear cubs, and there was no denying that he loved helping animals.

At the same time, Henry also knew you didn't just ask to be a Tutori; you had to first be invited to train as a Magari by a senior member of the *APA*. He couldn't see himself winning over any new friends by making unsubstantiated accusations about the red-haired woman in the back row. Calling out Barnaby for failing to mention the Frenchman's real name was Saint-Clair didn't seem like it would be helpful either.

Even though Henry didn't technically lie to the council, it made him feel dishonest. Barnaby had really put him in an uncomfortable position.

As his mind raced with doubt and suspicion, Henry remembered that Captain Fulbright trusted Barnaby wholeheartedly. He wasn't quite sure what the Australian was up to but decided to follow his lead for now and ask questions later. If Captain Fulbright trusted this man, that was good enough for Henry, and he figured Barnaby would appreciate the discretion on his behalf.

The council members continued deliberating amongst themselves while Henry and Barnaby stood on stage in anticipation of what the three women would say.

Barnaby seemed rather jittery and appeared to be grappling with the fear of what might happen if they knew the Canadian lad wasn't telling the whole truth. He had witnessed the merciless wrath of the council in the past and certainly didn't want to anger them.

Not concerned in the slightest, Penny kept smiling with her tongue hanging out, faithfully waiting at Henry's side. Despite the possibility of the council sending them back to Kodiak Bay at any moment, she just basked in her ignorance and gazed out into the audience.

It all came down to this moment. Either the council believed Henry and he could live out his dream of sailing across the world on a fabled ship he had only heard stories about, or everything would come crashing down on him like a house of cards.

Suddenly, Madam MacDougall shouted, "Officer Vinciguerra!"

After hearing her name, Valentina walked briskly down the aisleway and stood at attention near the center platform. The Scottish councilwoman turned toward her, announcing, "Please tell Captain Carlucci to set a course for London. It's very important that the ship keep pace with the *Queen Charlotte*, headed in the same direction." Valentina responded without hesitation, "Sì, madam," then proceeded up the aisleway toward the exit.

The guards immediately opened the tall double doors as Valentina got closer, then promptly shut them behind her when she headed off to see the captain.

Henry tried to curb his excitement, but anyone could tell the young boy in the yellow raincoat was elated just by looking at his face. The new feelings of relief and excitement smashed his fear of being left behind while the Tutori chased after Saint-Clair on the legendary *Arthur Broome*.

Somewhat grateful that Henry managed to stay within his account of tonight's events, Barnaby patted him on the shoulder and quipped, "So there you have it, ladies and gentlemen. He's just a good Canadian lad with a heart of gold, a taste for the maple syrup, and most importantly... a shared interest in seeing Barnaby Murdoch catch this bear thief without any assistance."

"No worries though," Barnaby smirked, "I'll be sure to lend him my binoculars when we get to London so that he can safely watch the show from the top deck." The three council members began whispering amongst themselves once again.

After a few moments of careful consideration, Madam Cross responded, "Mr. Murdoch, you will take young Henry on as your partner, effective immediately. He will shadow you on a temporary basis, in accordance with the *Professional Courtesy Code*, until this matter is resolved and those bears have been safely returned to Kodiak Bay."

"Hear me when I tell you that this is an official order, Barnabas!" the British councilwoman commanded, in spite of the disapproving expression that had replaced the confident grin on his face. "The boy goes everywhere you go when you step foot off this ship."

Madam Machado chimed in, "And this time there will be no mistakes because you are going with reinforcements. Señorita Sunday and Señor Blackfriar will be accompanying you to apprehend the thief and recover those bears."

"Woah, woah, woah," Barnaby protested, "let's just pump the brakes here for a minute." He was clearly not thrilled about the idea of anyone tagging along for his next encounter with the Frenchman.

Before he could say anything further, Madam MacDougall interjected, "The council has trusted you to resolve this matter on your own, and you have returned empty-handed thrice now."

"We have been pursuing this bear thief across four continents and half a dozen countries," Madam Machado added passionately. "Enough is enough, Señor Murdoch. The *Animal Protection Authority* will not fail those bears again."

"But wait one minute," Barnaby said as Madam MacDougall interrupted and warned him again. "This council has adjudicated."

Henry gawked in amazement, surprised to see the three throne-like chairs descend unexpectedly into a hidden room beneath the floor—as if the council members were riding an unusually wide elevator. Seconds later, the gaping hole in the floor sealed shut automatically, and the trio of mysterious women vanished.

Barnaby sighed as Henry did his best to mask his exhilaration. Henry was absolutely enamored by the idea of working alongside a real Tutori, regardless of whether his new partner felt the same way.

While the remaining Tutori in the room got up and headed for the exits, the woman wearing a cowboy hat pointed two fingers at her eyes and then slowly rotated the same hand, aiming her index finger directly at Barnaby. Despite her provocative smile, the overt taunting didn't seem to be enough to elicit the outburst she had hoped for. Nevertheless, the woman tipped her hat and winked at Barnaby, casually walking out of the council chambers. The teenage girl next to her followed closely behind.

"Alright, the show's ovah, mate," Barnaby declared with a defeated tone. "Let's get outta here." He marched off the center stage and toward the tall doors that the Carabinieri guards were holding open.

Even though Henry was ecstatic to partner up with Barnaby, he could tell the feeling wasn't mutual. Henry didn't care, though. He was just happy to still be onboard the *Arthur Broome* and refused to let anyone or anything damper his mood.

As they walked past the Carabinieri guards into the hallway, Henry kneeled down to give Penny some ear scratches. He was proud that she had managed to keep her barking under control on stage.

With her stomach rumbling, the hungry wirehaired dachshund trotted behind Henry toward the elevators, desperately hoping a visit to the kitchen was imminent. Penny hadn't seen one pizza window since boarding the ship, and she was worried they had made a huge mistake by skipping *Don Ciccio's* earlier.

Just as Barnaby was about to push the call button, the elevator doors opened unexpectedly—a small kangaroo hopped out and landed directly in front of Henry.

— CHAPTER 8 —
OTIS AND OSCAR

*H*enry stood face-to-face with the wild marsupial while Penny peered through his legs in awe. They had never actually seen a real kangaroo, aside from photos in newspapers and encyclopedias. The *Kodiak Bay Zoo* didn't even have one. Equally amazed and startled by the close encounter, he wasn't sure if he was more fascinated by the animal itself or the fact that this kangaroo was riding an elevator on a ship sailing to London.

Utterly flabbergasted, Henry tried to keep still while the adolescent kangaroo curiously inspected his yellow raincoat. Penny immediately let out a muffled growl laced with bitter jealousy; the wirehaired dachshund at his feet didn't trust the strange creature one bit. Despite her apprehension, he eventually lifted his arm to gently pet the kangaroo's fur.

Barnaby knew all too well that this young kangaroo had a funny way of introducing himself to strangers, but he decided to let the boy find out on his own. The Australian watched as the scrappy kangaroo mistook Henry's affection for an invitation to play.

Without warning, the kangaroo simultaneously grabbed ahold of the yellow raincoat, jumped into the air, and thrust his hind legs right into Henry's stomach. The force from the kick sent Henry flying back onto the floor into a somersault tumble while knocking the breath out of him at the same time. Barnaby burst into a boisterous fit of laughter. He thought the whole thing was truly hilarious, especially after such a long day riddled with failure and annoying reprimands.

Penny, on the other hand, didn't find it funny at all. She raced over to check on Henry and frantically licked his face to make sure he was okay. A little flustered and blushing in embarrassment, Henry got back up while Penny took a defensive position in front of him. She erupted with three thunderous barks as her protective instincts took over.

"Don't see too many of those in Canada, eh?" Barnaby sneered.

In a soothing voice, Henry tried to calm Penny down. "It's okay, girl, it's okay."

"This here is Roger." Barnaby snickered as the kangaroo retreated next to him. "Yeah, he loves to play, don't ya, pal?"

"Oh, I picked up on that, *mate*." Henry retorted, "And thanks for the heads up, by the way!"

"Come on now, he's just saying hello... Didn't mean anything by it," Barnaby joked.

"Found him when he was just a little joey near Walkabout Creek in the Northern Territory." Barnaby explained in a more somber tone, "Sorry to say, he lost his mum to the great bushfires last year. Rescued him and a whole mob of 'roos and koalas from those fires, though. Got 'em all safely to the sanctuary in Alice Springs, but this one took a liking to ol' Barnaby here." His face lit up when he recalled how Roger ended up aboard the *Arthur Broome*. "Refused to let go of my leg as I was leaving for the ship, and we've been the best of mates ever since."

Barnaby stroked the back of Roger's neck affectionately and asked, "Ain't that right, pal?" as the young kangaroo nestled up against him. Moments later, the kangaroo hopped past Henry to examine the bright yellow raincoat again.

"Promised myself I would never let anything happen to him after all he'd been through." Barnaby beamed while he boasted, "Yeah, Roger's growing up to be a fine 'roo indeed. In fact, it's his second birthday tomorrow. That's right, I already talked to the chef this morning, and he's got a proper cake in store for my best mate here. Yes, sir, that's one party you won't wanna miss."

Henry remembered that Barnaby still owed him some answers and remarked sternly. "Well, it was certainly nice to meet your kickboxing companion there... But are you gonna tell me why you lied to the council? Why didn't you tell 'em Saint-Clair is the Frenchman? And what is she doing on this ship? I saw her sitting in the back row!"

"Alright, take it easy, kid," Barnaby responded wearily. "It's like I told the council... things aren't always as they seem. I promise I'll tell you everything tomorrow, though. I'm just too tired to get into it right now... been a long day for all of us." He pressed the button to call the elevator and added, "A solid night's rest will do us all some good. Trust me on that, mate."

Without the faintest idea of where he was actually going to get that solid night's rest, Henry replied, "But wait! Where are we supposed to sleep tonight?"

Barnaby hesitated for a moment and then answered, "Righto... you can take cabin *6991* on the sixth floor," as he impatiently pushed the elevator button again.

Suddenly, Henry realized that he wasn't very familiar with the *Arthur Broome*—he didn't even know which floor they were currently on. Concerned he wouldn't be able to find the cabin, Henry blurted, "The sixth floor? Which way is that?"

"Just follow the ottahs, mate," Barnaby answered smugly. Henry asked, absolutely baffled, "Otters? Wait! What otters?"

Amid Henry's befuddlement, two sea otters snuck up from behind and climbed up his legs in a cheeky manner. They came out of nowhere and instantly caught him by surprise; the whole ordeal sent Henry crashing to the floor after he lost his balance in a panic.

Even though Barnaby was exhausted, he couldn't help but howl with laughter at the encounter.

Henry was startled by the sociable pair of mischievous otters crawling all over his body, and Penny was equally stunned. She sniffed them from a safe distance, being careful to maintain a wary stance. The playful otters didn't appear to be a threat, but she wasn't entirely convinced.

The otters raced over to Barnaby when they heard the arriving elevator bell chime. "Otis! Oscar! My two favorite stowaways!" he exclaimed cheerfully, kneeling briefly to greet them. The pair of otters turned their attention back to Henry a few seconds later, once Barnaby stepped into the elevator with Roger.

After Barnaby pushed the buttons for his floor, he hollered, "Now, don't be late for breakfast tomorrow at nine o'clock. And lose the yellow raincoat... You stand out like a Canadian tuxedo at the opera!"

"Hold on! I don't have any other clothes!" Henry yelled anxiously.

As the elevator doors started to close, Barnaby stuck his arm out to hold them open. "Go see the tailor at eight o'clock before breakfast tomorrow. He'll fix ya up good and propah, mate." He lowered his arm despite Henry's persistent question, "*The tailor*? What tailor?"

Barnaby smirked while the elevator doors started to close a second time and shouted, "Like I said, mate... Just follow the ottahs!"

The doors closed, and Henry found himself standing in front of the elevators, more confused than ever. He just stood there with Penny and the pair of sea otters as the *Arthur Broome* traversed the rough Atlantic Ocean toward London.

Looking down at the gregarious animals, Henry mumbled,

"Okay... just follow the otters, eh?" He wondered what that actually meant but figured it couldn't hurt to ask, no matter how bizarre it seemed, "Mr. Otis. Mr. Oscar. Can you please lead us to cabin number *6991* on the sixth floor?" The pair of otter brothers stood up on their hind legs, smiling while nodding their heads puckishly.

Without hesitation, Otis turned and pushed the call button to summon another elevator. Henry marveled at their intelligence, although he wasn't entirely surprised since he knew otters were one of the few animals on earth that used tools in the wild. How they ended up onboard the *Arthur Broome* remained a mystery, but it was clear to him that these two were not to be underestimated.

The elevator doors opened a moment later, and the pair of otters darted inside. Penny followed Henry cautiously as he stepped in after the spirited animals. He glanced at the cluster of buttons and froze.

Before Henry could ask which one to push, Oscar stood four feet tall and used his tiny paws to press a series of buttons in the following order: *6–9–9–1*.

With his feet firmly planted, Henry was careful to mind his balance this time as he felt the elevator change directions. The playful otters didn't seem to mind one bit—they proceeded to run circles around him in a highly entertaining fashion. They loved chasing each other around, and having a new guest onboard wasn't going to interfere with that.

After another eventful ride, the elevator eventually came to a stop, and the two otters raced past the doors the second they opened. Henry stepped off with Penny reluctantly, hoping this was indeed the correct floor. Heeding Barnaby's advice, he wandered over in the same direction, where Otis and Oscar were already busy wrestling with each other.

Walking down the hallway, Henry chuckled at how quickly the otters resumed their tour guide duties. They rushed toward the back of the ship, fearlessly leading the way. Penny and Henry followed them at a brisk pace. They passed a dozen unoccupied cabins before approaching the end of the corridor.

"Are you otters sure this is it?" Henry asked as he stared at the cabin door. The sea otters were standing on their hind legs next to the door, smiling. They both nodded their heads at the same time to confirm, but Henry still had his doubts.

Despite the lights emanating from the paper-thin crack at the bottom of the entrance, Henry opened the door nervously; Penny couldn't control herself and immediately bolted past him into the room. He rushed in after her while Otis and Oscar raced down the hallway in the opposite direction, back toward the elevators.

When the door to the cabin closed behind him, Henry stopped in amazement. "Wow! What a room, Penny!" He was instantly captivated by his new accommodations and gasped. Penny trotted around the room, sniffing everything from the bedsheets to the carpet, familiarizing herself with their new surroundings.

The room itself wasn't huge by any measure; it was only three hundred square feet, yet the cabin felt like a palace to Henry. He had never stayed in a hotel and would have been happy to sleep on bunk beds in a shared room if it meant he could join the Tutori on the *Arthur Broome*.

Henry breezed past the private bathroom on the left and noticed the large queen-sized bed directly in front of him. Beyond the bed, there was a separate sitting area that had a small couch next to a coffee table and a desk mounted against the opposite wall with a digital clock hanging above.

Penny was still adjusting to the discernible rocking motion from the *Arthur Broome* swaying in the choppy Atlantic seas. The perpetual transatlantic swells didn't bother Henry, though. Enthralled by his new surroundings, it was easy to forget that they were currently sailing across the world. However, he welcomed the frequent reminders as the ship sliced through the ocean waves.

Eager to check in on the storm brewing outside, Henry dashed over to the curtains and yanked them open. He was elated to find a small private balcony with a sliding glass door that stretched from the floor to the ceiling; he had only expected to see a tiny porthole window inside the cabin. Pleasantly surprised, he discovered that his room was larger than he had initially assumed.

Peering through the glass door while Penny sat next to him, they watched the raging storm and stared at the endless ocean stretching as far as the eye could see, glimmering from the occasional flashes of lightning.

"Good grief!" Henry shrieked upon hearing the booming noise of thunder pierce throughout the ship. It was so loud, Penny scrambled for cover under the bed in a panicked rush. "It's okay... It's okay, Penny. Don't worry, girl," he calmly said in a reassuring tone, hoping to coax her to come out.

In the end, the promise of a delicious dinner was all it took—she couldn't resist and waddled cautiously over to the coffee table in front of the couch.

The enchantment of cabin *6991* had Henry mesmerized, and he completely overlooked the serving tray sitting atop the coffee table. There were two separate plates covered by stainless steel cloches, two tall glasses of iced water, and a dog bowl filled with water.

"Well, look at this," he said, intrigued. "What do we have here, Penny?"

Frantic sounds of whimpering and snorting immediately ensued. Penny's unwavering excitement was palpable; she knew exactly what was under those cloches and couldn't wait any longer. Henry put the bowl of water on the floor. The impatient dachshund wasted no time gulping down nearly half of it as loud sips echoed throughout the small cabin. Her attention reverted back to the tray of food, and it didn't take long before the muffled cries of anticipation resumed.

"Fettuccine Alfredo for me, and, uh, looks like turkey sticks for you," Henry announced merrily. "Don't mind if we do, eh, girl?" Penny's incessant whining turned into excited squealing as Henry lifted her onto the couch and moved the tray closer so she could reach the plate of pencil-sized turkey sticks. They were both famished after the chaos that unfolded earlier in Kodiak Bay. Even so, Penny's relentless hunger would surface pretty much anytime the scent of food wafted in her direction.

It didn't take long for them to finish the delicious meals prepared by the ship's chef. Relaxing on the couch with their bellies full and Penny fighting to keep her eyes open, they gazed out at the ocean while the rain continued battering the sliding glass door.

Knackered after such a long day, Henry got up and closed the curtains, saying, "We better get some rest, eh? Gotta be up early for our appointment in the morning with the tailor."

Sensing that Penny was replete and relaxed from the generous helping of turkey sticks she just devoured, Henry carefully picked her up and placed the wirehaired dachshund gently on the bed. She wandered over to the center and plopped herself down directly in the middle, curling up into a crescent moon shape.

"Alright, scoot over a bit, eh, Penny?" Henry chuckled as he switched off the lights and climbed into bed.

The rocking motion of the *Arthur Broome* cruising across the Atlantic made it easy for Henry to fall into a deep slumber within minutes.

After a satisfying night of rest, Henry was awoken by Penny licking his face. It had become something of a habit upon waking up; routine or not, the affectionate kisses still caught him by surprise, and today was no exception.

"Good morning to you too!" Henry chortled, giving her a big hug and plenty of ear scratches. Despite the revitalized dachshund showering his face in affection, he noticed the bright sunshine creeping in around the edges of the drapes. He sprang out of bed and eagerly pulled the curtains open. Immediately, he was hit with that indescribable feeling of sailing the high seas.

The magic of falling asleep in one place and waking up somewhere far away gave Henry a humbling taste of perspective. He had just left Canada only a couple hours ago, and now he found himself in the middle of the Atlantic, with Europe somewhere out there on the horizon. Some might say it was no different than flying on an airplane, but Henry would politely disagree. Nothing compares to constantly being at the mercy of the most powerful force on earth. He relished in the adventure of it all, and the feeling of not knowing what might happen next fueled his excitement for the day ahead.

As Henry watched the ocean waves go by, a renewed sense of elation extinguished any lingering remnants of drowsiness. He turned around after gazing out the glass door and began to get ready for his appointment; he showered first and then gave Penny a quick bath, followed by a thorough brushing.

"What do you say we get some fresh air before our appointment, eh, Penny?" Henry asked as he walked over to the balcony door, sliding it open. The passing sea breeze flooded the cabin and sent a barrage of fresh new scents whirling past Penny's nose. She followed him onto the balcony, snout in the air, sniffing rapidly with curiosity.

Henry leaned forward over the balcony railing to get a better look at the *Arthur Broome*. Glancing to the right, he only saw one other cabin—the massive wake trailing behind the ship confirmed his previous assumption that cabin *6991* was indeed located near the stern. When he turned his head to the left, he could easily see the rest of the futuristic ship. There were dozens of other cabin balconies across multiple floors, extending all the way to the main bridge at the front.

At this hour, the *Arthur Broome* seemed eerily quiet, even with the constant noise of waves crashing against the hull. Yet amid the ambient noise, it was hard to miss the only two people standing on the promenade deck one floor below.

Even though they were further down, closer to the bow of the ship, Henry recognized that red hair immediately. It appeared to be Barnaby and the same woman from the back row at the council meeting yesterday—the same woman Henry suspected had eluded them and escaped with the stolen polar bear cubs on the *Queen Charlotte*. They were too far away for him to read their lips or hear what they were saying, but their body language told the real story, and Henry could tell it was a heated discussion.

Judging by the animated nature of his hand gestures, Barnaby sure seemed to be angry or annoyed about something.

Henry checked his pockets and soon realized he must have lost his monocular scope during the pursuit back in Kodiak Bay. Squinting toward the two people arguing on the promenade deck, he desperately wondered if the redhead in his sights was the same person he saw on the deck of the *Queen Charlotte*. Penny growled, prompting Henry to agree, "You're right about that, Penny... Mr. Murdoch owes us some answers, that's for sure."

The red-haired woman shook her head out of frustration while Barnaby threw both his hands into the air and then stormed off. She also appeared to be heading inside but stopped abruptly upon noticing Henry staring. Mortified, the young dock attendant froze; he locked eyes with the woman for a moment before the impulsive urge to stumble backward finally caught up to the panicked expression on his face. Crouching down to comfort Penny behind the balcony wall divider, he waited a minute to get back up.

Henry eventually peered over the balcony railing again, albeit in a more furtive manner this time. The woman was now gone. However, the heavy sigh of relief that followed proved to be fleeting. His heart nearly leapt over the railing into the ocean once he heard the balcony door to cabin *6990* slide open suddenly.

Struggling to decide whether he should quietly slip back into his cabin or boldly introduce himself, Henry's whole body tensed up. The rampant indecision robbed him of the precious seconds he had left to make a choice. Before he could take another step, a girl peeked her head around the divider to peer into his balcony unexpectedly; she appeared to be around Henry's age.

"So, how was your first night away from home?" The girl asked as she chuckled, "You don't get seasick, do ya?"

Henry could tell instantly that she was American; her distinct southern accent was unmistakable. Bemused by the personal and direct nature of the question, he was on the verge of responding when she interrupted, "You're Henry Halifax, right? From Kodiak Bay?" He was stunned. He had never met this girl, and yet she seemed to be quite familiar with his whole life story. It felt somewhat unsettling.

"Yeah, that's me," he answered tersely.

"But how did you know it was my first time leaving Kodiak Bay?" Henry asked with an overt sense of suspicion in his voice. "I didn't mention anything about that during the council meeting yesterday." He knew she was there last night. She was sitting next to the lady wearing the cowboy hat, who winked at Barnaby.

The fearless girl had a slim physique with dark-brown eyes and long black hair, which was fashioned into a braided ponytail. She also had the same dark-gray wool suit as Barnaby, except with a black necktie instead of the forest-green color the Tutori wore. Henry couldn't help but notice the black Tutori cloak was conspicuously absent, though, and she had on black cowboy boots instead of oxfords.

Surprised by the question, the girl stammered, "Oh, uh... I could just tell by the look on your face last night and, um, the tone in your voice... Yeah, it was a dead giveaway."

"It's my job, ya know?" She simpered, carrying on confidently in a more upbeat tone, "Pickin' up on the little details that others miss... That's how we stay ahead of the bad guys."

In an attempt to assuage his reservations and make him feel a bit more welcome, the American girl stuck her hand out around the balcony divider to introduce herself. "June Nakamura from Midland, Texas." While they shook hands, she added, "And that's *West Texas*, if y'all didn't know!"

"Well, it's nice to meet you, June," Henry acknowledged, shaking off his doubts. "Didn't realize any of the Tutori bunked around this part of the ship."

June blushed and replied, "Oh, I'm not a Tutori." She immediately clarified her surprising admission, "Not yet anyway. I only came aboard a few months ago. I'm still just a Magari... That's what they call an apprentice in training around here." Henry's eyebrows rose with intrigue.

"But I'll have my cloak soon enough," June asserted. "You can count on that!"

"Oh, I'm sorry... My mistake," Henry remarked cheerfully. "Either way, I'm happy to be neighbors during my stay onboard."

Beginning to feel left out, Penny directed a loud bark in his direction. "Of course, where are my manners?" He added, "This is Penny, by the way. She can be a bit of a rascal... and is apparently feeling quite sensitive this morning."

"Wonderful to meet you, Miss Penny!" June responded warmly. She loved dogs and would have properly greeted Penny if it weren't for the balcony divider separating them. June had never seen a wirehaired dachshund, especially one with a charming face that reminded her of an old man.

Penny let out a slew of short barks in rapid succession to introduce herself. With her tongue hanging out, the wirehaired dachshund was beaming with delight as she voiced her support for his new acquaintance.

Glancing inside toward the clock, Henry blurted, "Hockey sticks! I forgot, we've got an appointment with the tailor at eight o'clock. We need to leave right now or we're going to be late!"

"The tailor?" June replied. "Y'all best get a move on then. He doesn't take kindly to tardiness."

"Right! Well, hope I see you around the ship later!" Henry exclaimed, rushing back into the cabin. Penny dashed inside behind him, and he hastily pushed the sliding glass door shut.

— CHAPTER 9 —
THE TAILOR

*W*ait a minute, Penny," Henry said, hesitating on the verge of opening the front door. "How are we supposed to find the tailor's shop? Barnaby never told us where it is!"

It would have been all too easy to simply ask June for directions, but that idea was abandoned. And for good reason, Henry had just met June and didn't want to leave her with the impression that he was completely helpless. Pinning his hopes on asking one of the Carabinieri roaming the ship was the only option that made sense.

Henry opened the door, confident he would run into one of the stately guards, and instead, he instantly found himself tumbling backward onto the floor. Penny's nimble reflexes were second to none, and she dashed out of the way, avoiding him just in time. The pair of mischievous otters had been waiting in the hallway, directly in front of Henry's door. They caught him by surprise when Otis crawled up his leg while Oscar leaped into his arms at the same time.

Despite another jolting encounter in the span of only two days, Henry laughed it off. "You rascals! Just the otters I was looking for!"

Startled by the otters' arrival, Penny sniffed them from a distance with a wide-eyed look of alarm. She still wasn't comfortable with their zany personalities and felt a slight tinge of mistrust whenever they were nearby.

Once Henry managed to pick himself up, he pleaded for their help. "Guys, we need you to show us the way to the tailor's shop!" The otters appeared to ignore his request at first; they had become quite distracted by Penny's wagging tail and continued circling her in a playful manner. He glanced at the clock again and implored frantically, "Can you help us? Please! We only have ten minutes to get there, and we can't be late!"

Otis and Oscar ceased their playful antics abruptly. They could sense the desperation in his voice and didn't want him to be late for such an important appointment. Standing on their hind legs, the otter brothers gazed at him, and they both nodded.

Henry exhaled in relief. He wasn't sure if they understood him or the urgent nature of his predicament, but he trusted everything would work out if he just followed the otters. He opened the cabin door again, trudging after Penny and the pair of otters into the hallway. Otis and Oscar bolted straight toward the elevators, while he and Penny chased after them.

The otters had already pushed the call button by the time Henry and Penny rounded the hallway corner, and it only took a few moments for the elevator doors to open. Henry watched Oscar push *1-3-4-0* on the button control panel and remembered to keep his balance as it suddenly started moving sideways (he was still getting used to the elevator's irregular direction changes).

Otis and Oscar were busy chasing each other between Henry's legs, and they didn't seem bothered by his fidgeting.

Henry's forehead was covered with beads of sweat, and his thoughts were consumed by the potential consequences that awaited if he couldn't find the tailor's shop by eight o'clock. The regret over not leaving earlier had been building with each passing second. While Penny was more concerned about what they would be having for breakfast, he hoped there would still be a chance to avoid an embarrassing first impression with the tailor.

He felt the elevator change directions two more times before coming to a stop. As soon as the doors opened, a red parrot and a blue macaw sent him ducking for cover—the birds swooped in unexpectedly, adding a bit of chaos to his morning commute.

Penny bolted past him at the first sight of the exotic psittacines. She wasn't particularly fond of flying animals and maintained a defensive stance in the hallway as Henry shuffled out of the elevator with his back hunched over. Right before the doors closed, he caught a brief glimpse of the birds landing inside, ostensibly greeting Otis and Oscar.

"Good grief, Penny! How many animals do they have on this ship, eh?" Henry remarked, still taken aback by the colorful birds that just whooshed by his head. Instantly, an unfamiliar voice answered, "I'm sure the real number would surprise you."

Henry spun around and saw a tall figure towering over him.

The bald, middle-aged man had a short black beard shaped with precision; he was wearing a black suit, black shirt, and a matching black necktie. He also had a forest-green pocket square tucked neatly into the front chest pocket of his suit jacket. The broad-shouldered gentleman extended his arm and added, "You must be Mr. Halifax from Kodiak Bay."

Henry shook his hand nervously and replied, "Um, yeah... that's me. I'm Henry Halifax, sir. And this here is Penny. We were... uh, just looking for the ship's tailor."

The tall man kneeled and slowly put his hand out in front of Penny's face to properly introduce himself. She sniffed with great interest before eventually nestling her head into the man's palm. The wirehaired dachshund loved the attention and smiled with delight, enjoying the warm welcome.

"Well, you can call off the search," the man chuckled as he stood up, "because he's standing in front of you, my boy. *Rufus Robinson,* from the city of Chicago, at your service." Henry was thoroughly relieved and responded, "Ah, Mr. Robinson. Glad I found you! I hope..."

"Just call me Rufus... Mr. Robinson was my grandfather," the tailor interjected.

"Oh, I'm sorry. My apologies, Rufus," Henry answered humbly. "Well, uh... Barnaby Murdoch told me to be here by eight o'clock. I guess he didn't like my current attire and felt a change of clothing might be in order."

Rufus laughed. "Oh, Mr. Murdoch, huh? Yeah, I'm not surprised. Let's just say he's a complicated fellow." He winked at Penny and led the way toward the tailor's shop. "But don't you worry, my boy... You came to the right place!"

"By the way, that's a beautiful hound you got there," Rufus added swiftly, "the badger dog... Never seen a wirehaired one before." Penny let out two cheerful barks to show her appreciation for the compliment as the three of them entered the tailor's shop. He gazed down at the dachshund in admiration and acknowledged, "Yeah, more stubborn than even Murdoch himself, I'm betting... Although you won't find a breed that's nearly as loyal or stubborn either! They never back down in the face of danger." Penny barked twice in agreement.

"Lot of folks underestimate them... you know, due to their small size and all," Rufus carried on explaining. "Smallest type of hound there is. I'm guessing she's quicker than those little legs would suggest. Yeah, I reckon she can run faster than most of the people onboard this ship... myself included!" The well-informed tailor boasted, "*Sausage Dog*, *Hot Dog*, *Doxie*, *Doxin*, *Dashie*, *Ween*, *Teckel*, *Dackel*... or even *Bassotto* in Italiano. Yes, sir, the mighty dachshund goes by many names... but coward isn't one of 'em, that's for sure."

Henry was astonished; he had never been to a professional tailor before and wasn't sure what to expect. The gentleman standing in front of him didn't appear to be an ordinary tailor, though—far from it indeed. Rufus was clearly a man of scholarly pursuits, and Henry got the feeling that the tailor's role within the *APA* extended well beyond the walls of this shop.

Despite Barnaby's snide comments about his yellow raincoat yesterday, Henry would be thankful for any help that Rufus could provide on that front. Even though the yellow raincoat had served him well over the years, it wasn't exactly inconspicuous, especially on a ship like the *Arthur Broome*. Now that Henry planned to accompany the Tutori in London, he wanted to dress the part. He wanted to blend in.

Henry stood next to the tall gentleman, staring at himself in the mirror, and quickly realized that would be quite difficult in his current clothes. It was a sharp contrast to Rufus' perfectly tailored black suit.

The tailor shop itself had dark walnut wood on the walls, extending to the floor and onto the ceiling. There was a couch on the left, two chairs on the other side, and a triple-panel wardrobe mirror in the center. There were also dark curtains that blocked off the back half of the tailor shop, which made the room feel smaller.

"Alright, my Canadian friend... take that raincoat off and step up onto the platform," Rufus said politely. "Let's have a proper look at you."

Henry set the yellow raincoat on the couch and revealed his lack of experience in these matters. "Well, I'm not sure exactly what my size is. I've never worn a suit before."

"Not to worry, my boy," Rufus affirmed. "I come from a long line of tailors. Ever since my grandfather opened one of the first tailor shops in the city of Chicago, you can always count on the Robinsons to look after haberdashery matters of this type." He whistled loudly and called for assistance, "Come on out here, Shinzo! We got a fitting to tend to. Can't be sleeping on the job all day now."

Henry wondered who the man had summoned. He looked down and chuckled when he saw a small gray koala strolling over from behind the curtains. The tailor's assistant had some measuring tape hanging around his neck and was wearing a tiny black suit similar to the one Rufus wore.

Shinzo was about the same size as Penny, but that didn't stop him from crawling up onto the boy's shoulder. Henry tried to stand still as the curious koala wriggled across his shoulders and shrieked while he grabbed his ears playfully.

"Alright, alright... that's enough, Shinzo," Rufus asserted. The koala slowly climbed down Henry's leg and onto the platform as he added, "You'll have to excuse my colleague here. He's feeling a bit cranky and tends to do that with newcomers."

"No worries," Henry replied while staring at the koala. "It's nice to meet you, Shinzo."

Rufus lifted the measuring tape off Shinzo's neck and then instructed Henry to raise his arms for some measurements. When it came time to measure his legs, Shinzo held the bottom of the measuring tape near Henry's ankles while Rufus lifted the other end near Henry's waist to get the correct inseam size. Throughout the fitting, Rufus never took notes; he memorized everything without batting an eye.

After he finished taking Henry's suit measurements, Rufus announced, "That'll do it, Mr. Halifax. Just take a seat here for now. Shinzo and I will prepare your new attire in the back. Should only take us twenty minutes or so." He walked over toward a panel of light switches near the curtains and added, "In the meantime, I reckon you might be keen to learn more about the Tutori."

Henry's face lit up with excitement while Rufus dimmed the lights. "I know you're just along for the ride as a professional courtesy, yet you look like a young man who understands the value of a proper education."

The tailor flipped four switches upward at the same time before disappearing behind the black curtains. Shinzo rolled clumsily in the same direction; an irregular wave had caused the *Arthur Broome* to pitch backward unexpectedly, thwarting his stride. The small koala finally managed to crawl under the curtains just as the sound of film projectors and speakers turning on captured Henry's attention.

Multiple film projectors located in the ceiling and walls suddenly cast moving hologram projections, filling the room. It instantly transported Henry into a surreal enchantment. The whole experience reminded him of a movie theater, only much better; it felt like he was in the middle of the film, with three-dimensional holographic images projected all around him. He flinched when a small koala riding an ostrich appeared in front of him.

Surprisingly, it wasn't the first koala wearing clothes that he'd seen today. This particular marsupial was dressed in the same gray wool suit, forest-green necktie, and black cloak worn by the Tutori. Presumably the smallest member of the *APA*, the animal glanced at Henry and then carefully dismounted. The koala looked back toward the ostrich, exchanging a brief look of gratitude and nodding with respect.

Henry marveled at the ingenuity on display. He listened intently to the thick British accent as the pint-sized Tutori began a long oration.

"Ahoy there, sailor! The *Animal Protection Authority* welcomes you aboard. Any friend to the animals... is a friend of the *APA*. Now, you might be asking, what is the *APA*, and who are the Tutori? Well, before we get to that, I think some proper introductions are in order.

"My name is Barry Slater, although my friends call me the Koala Prince, or KP for short. I am a scientist, a professor, and above all else, *I am a Tutori of the Animal Protection Authority.*

"You see, humans have always had a complicated relationship with animals. For thousands of years, most people have treated them as inferior. Endlessly trading blood for blood. Putting the comforts of their own existence above everything else. One species exerting its power over the millions of others forced to share this world. Poisoning their air, polluting their oceans, decimating their rainforests... buying and selling animals as if they were property. I'm afraid disgraceful doesn't even begin to describe the atrocities endured on a regular basis.

"Don't worry, friend... Not all humans are bad. Sometimes, there are good people like you. People who recognize the difference between right and wrong transcend species. And long ago, it was because of people like you that the *Animal Protection Authority* emerged from the darkness. A world-class organization tasked with protecting all animals from unjust human interference.

"You're probably thinking... hang on a minute, Barry. How can the *APA* possibly protect billions of animals all over the world? Well, the unfortunate truth is that we can't... and we don't protect animals from other animals. The animal kingdom is complicated. It's messy. And it's true that animals eat other animals to survive. It's the circle of life, and that's just the way things are on this planet. The plankton eat the algae, the krill eat the plankton, the fish eat the krill, the seals eat the fish, and the polar bears eat the seals. All in accordance with the unwritten laws of the jungle.

"But what happens when a human interferes with the natural order of the animal kingdom? Who protects the majestic elephants from being slaughtered for their ivory? Or the mighty whales, hunted senselessly for sport and tradition? What about the fearless lion, forced to sing and dance at the circus?

"For over two hundred years, the Tutori of the *Animal Protection Authority* have dedicated their lives in service to restoring the balance between humans and animals. Working in the shadows to dispense justice and bring peace to animals that suffer under the hand of man... 'Tis a duty that never ends.

"From the Arctic Circle to the Amazon rainforests, *the Tutori of the Animal Protection Authority serve to protect those who cannot protect themselves.* If you think the animals deserve better, then now's your chance to prove it. Not just to yourself, but to everyone who has sacrificed so much in the pursuit of shining a light on the darkness that plagues this world. You might find that things can change when there is someone willing to show the misguided souls a better way.

"Be that change. Go forth and bring honor to those who have worn the black cloak before you. *For the animals... All of them.*"

Henry was mesmerized by the enlightened marsupial. Truly inspired, he felt quite humbled as the hologram of the Koala Prince flickered out. Watching that three-dimensional projection further ignited his desire to become a real Tutori. He was now more determined than ever to join the *APA*.

"So, what's it gonna be? You got what it takes to wear the cloak?" Rufus asked, flipping the lights on unexpectedly. Shocked by the tailor's sudden reemergence, Henry wiped the stunned look off his face and mumbled. "I think we do, sir."

Rufus snickered, emphatically firing back, "Think? You think? That's not gonna cut it around here, my boy. No, sir... You gotta be sure because this ain't no part-time job now... It's not like being the mayor of Chicago." With a new suit in his hand, he stepped closer and continued, "You heard the Koala Prince, didn't you? Becoming a Tutori is a calling, not a job. A duty that *never* ends."

Recognizing the poor choice of words used, Henry corrected himself in a more confident manner, "I know we do, Rufus! And I'll do my best to prove that to you, Barnaby, and every other Tutori on this ship!"

"Whew... you had me worried there for a minute, my young Canadian friend," Rufus replied cheerfully. The wide smile on his face vanished, and he advised, "Well, if that's what you want, don't let anybody tell you anything different. Not 'til you come back to Rufus Robinson's tailor shop here, ready to trade in this blue tie for the official Tutori forest green. Otherwise, you're just making excuses."

"But first things first. Let's have you try this on to see how it fits," Rufus instructed as he handed Henry a finely cut gray suit, a white button-down shirt, and a dark-blue necktie. "Don't worry about the tie. I'll square you away on that part after you change into your new suit."

Rufus added, "In the meantime, Shinzo and I will finish preparing your shoes in the back. I figured oxfords would suit you just fine, so it'll be the same shoes Mr. Murdoch wears." He disappeared behind the curtains once again before Henry could thank him.

Henry changed into the wool suit while Penny managed to keep herself distracted by sniffing the old clothing he tossed on the floor.

Drawn to the familiar scent of Kodiak Bay, the wirehaired dachshund plopped down on the pile of clothes as if it were a makeshift daybed. Penny had a knack for making herself comfortable on just about anything that was soft enough. Bath mats, towels, pillows—even Captain Fulbright's peacoat wasn't safe once she decided to rest her paws.

Henry stared at himself in the mirror and beamed with pride. Not only was this his first time wearing a suit, but dressing like the Tutori gave him a glimpse into what the future might hold.

"Looking sharp, if I do say so myself, Mr. Halifax." Rufus boasted, "Yes, sir, it's all in the tailoring." The bald gentleman was clearly proud of his work. He inspected the suit very much like an artist admiring his latest masterpiece.

Thrilled with his new attire, Henry replied enthusiastically, "I believe it, Rufus. This suit is brilliant! Thank you so much!"

"Shinzo, where you at, pal? Bring those shoes out here, will you?" Rufus hollered. He began to loop the tie under Henry's collar and said, "Now, we just need to take care of the finishing touches here, and I'll have you on your way."

Rufus fastened the dark-blue necktie in a double Windsor knot while Henry observed, trying to remember each step so that he could do it on his own next time.

When Rufus finished adjusting Henry's tie, Shinzo sauntered out from behind the curtains with a pair of black oxfords. The sleepy koala held one shoe in each claw, and Henry could tell he was growing tired after watching him take a lengthy pause to yawn. Smirking, Henry stepped down from the fitting platform and walked over to meet Shinzo halfway to grab the oxfords.

As Henry sat down and slipped the socks on his feet, he remembered that there was a lingering question that still remained unanswered. Too embarrassed to ask anyone else after yesterday's gaffe, he trusted that Rufus would be happy to clarify. "Say, Rufus, if you don't mind me asking," he remarked curiously, "why are the Carabinieri on the ship? The Koala Prince didn't mention anything about them, and I was wondering how they ended up sailing with the Tutori on the *Arthur Broome*."

Rufus chortled, "Oh, the Italians?" He exhaled sharply, thinking back to the time when someone first told him the story. He gave a long-winded answer, carefully recounting the legend with the respect it deserved.

"The Tutori and Carabinieri go way back. You see, it all started the moment a flash flood tore through a small mountain town in what was then the Kingdom of Sardinia, known today as the country of Italy. King Victor Emmanuel and a dozen of his finest Carabinieri were on their horses when they all got swept away by the unrelenting floodwaters. Careening directly toward a steep waterfall where the town's only river came to an end, making it out alive seemed impossible.

"Facing certain death, the Carabinieri and King Emmanuel clung to their horses, fighting desperately to keep their heads above water. Luckily for them, a group of eight Tutori passing through town intervened and changed their fate forever.

"With no time to waste, the Tutori lassoed the horses and pulled them out one by one from the merciless avalanche of water that was decimating the center of town.

"Against all odds, they managed to rescue the whole lot of them... or so it appeared at first. The tide can turn quickly, however, and I'm sorry to say that not every Tutori was able to escape unharmed. Confronted with the unbearable decision of saving one horse over another, an assiduous Tutori in the group tried to lasso two horses at the same time using a single rope. His throw was perfect, but he didn't have the strength to bring them close enough to the riverbank so the horses could get out on their own four legs.

"Unwilling to give up, this lone Tutori refused to let go of the rope as he got dragged into the floodwaters. Sadly, he plunged over the waterfall's edge, along with the pair of horses and the Carabinieri officers he was trying to save.

"King Emmanuel was absolutely distraught over the losses sustained on both sides. His own near-death experience served as a haunting reminder of what really mattered in this life. And in that moment of clarity, the king vowed that the Kingdom of Sardinia would forever be indebted to the *Animal Protection Authority*.

"By royal decree, the king created a secretive Carabinieri regiment tasked with the perpetual duty of supporting the *APA* and Tutori in their mission to help animals. Like the Swiss Guard protects the Pope at the Vatican, the Carabinieri protect the institution of the *Animal Protection Authority*, and that all starts right here on the *Arthur Broome*, the headquarters for the *APA*.

"Roman Empire, Kingdom of Sardinia, Sicily... yeah, I suppose the boot-shaped country of Italy has gone by many different names over the years, but the Carabinieri will always be the real stewards of that land. Steadfast guardians, loyal throughout the centuries."

Henry was blown away. "Wow! I had no idea, Rufus!" At the same time, though, he also felt somewhat ashamed of his ignorant remarks yesterday in Valentina's presence; he now understood why Barnaby was so miffed. The Carabinieri were far more than he had initially assumed.

"Wait a second, Rufus... How did you end up on the *Arthur Broome*?" Henry asked as he finished tying his shoes and stood up. He just couldn't resist the urge to slip in another question.

As much as the tailor appreciated Henry's enthusiasm to learn more about the *APA*, there simply wasn't enough time to appease his insatiable curiosity. Rufus chuckled and patted him on the back. "Well, that's a long story... but I'm afraid it'll have to wait for another time, my friend. My next appointment will be here soon, and I gotta get back to work."

"Of course, I'm sorry," Henry replied modestly. "Well, thanks again for setting me up with this new suit. It's a perfect fit, and I'll take good care of it for sure."

Grinning with delight, Rufus walked him over to the front door. Penny sensed it was time to go and dashed ahead of them.

The dapper tailor saw Henry out and added, "You two should head on down to the dining hall and get some breakfast." Penny snorted in response. She had been eagerly anticipating their next meal and was elated by Mr. Robinson's suggestion. "Just push *1-8-6-4* when you get into the elevator. You'll see the dining hall as you enter the grand atrium... Can't miss it," he advised.

Before Henry could thank him once more, Rufus warned, "And watch your back out there, especially around Mr. Murdoch. He plays by a different set of rules... the Australian kind."

The front door of the tailor's shop closed swiftly, leaving Henry with yet another mystery to unravel. "*Australian rules*?" he mumbled under his breath curiously.

Strolling down the hallway, Henry wondered what Rufus meant by that foreboding comment.

— CHAPTER 10 —
BON APPÉTIT

*W*ith Penny trotting at his side, Henry kept walking toward the elevators at a leisurely pace. Even though they were equally famished, the excitement of meeting the tailor had not worn off yet; his mind was still racing with questions.

Henry's thoughts were consumed by the most pressing ones. "Why did Barnaby lie to the council last night? And what about the red-haired woman? She sure seemed upset about something when they were arguing on the promenade deck earlier. What was she doing on the *Arthur Broome* anyway?"

On the other hand, Penny appeared to be more concerned about what they would be serving for breakfast. She occasionally licked her lips with eagerness.

Amid Henry's distracting ruminations, he almost lost his balance when they turned the corner and saw the pair of otter brothers waiting by the elevator. Otis and Oscar had been waiting patiently for Henry and his faithful wirehaired dachshund to arrive. The sight of them smiling and standing on their hind legs was more than enough to catch Henry by surprise.

"You two again! I should have known better!" Henry smirked with a laugh. Despite being startled, he was growing fond of the otters. Even Penny had started to warm up to their playful antics. He cheerfully added, "Well, if you're not too busy... Penny and I are headed to the dining hall to get something to eat. You guys coming?"

The otters nodded their heads in synchrony, then took off running toward the elevator. Henry chuckled as they sprinted past Penny and watched in suspense to see who would be the first to push the call button.

When the elevator arrived, Henry and Penny stepped in after the otters. Oscar pushed the buttons *1–8–6–4* on the control panel, and the doors closed immediately. They were whisked away, first moving vertically and then changing directions horizontally.

As the elevator moved throughout the ship, Henry became enamored with his new suit. It almost made him feel like a real Tutori. But underneath the intoxicating smell of his finely cut suit, he knew there was far more to the *APA* than just dressing the part. The nervous excitement beamed from his face. Penny was excited as well, although for entirely different reasons. The majority of which revolved around the impending breakfast feast that supposedly awaited.

The elevator soon came to a stop, prompting Otis and Oscar to take a break from playfully wrestling at Henry's feet. The pair of ebullient otters dashed past the elevator doors once they opened and disappeared out of sight.

"Guess they must be awfully hungry," Henry remarked while following Penny into the hallway. He rounded the corner and looked up in awe upon seeing the grand atrium for the first time; it reminded him of Piccadilly Circus.

The grand atrium spanned four floors high. It had a beautiful chandelier hanging from the ceiling and two winding staircases made of glass leading to the promenade deck where Henry was standing. Tall windows lined both sides of the ship, and natural light from the sunshine outside flooded the room.

This section of the *Arthur Broome* was always bustling with activity during the daytime. There were Tutori eating breakfast in the dining area, Carabinieri officers walking about, and the persistent humming of operators answering radio calls on the floor above. All of that alone wouldn't seem out of the ordinary for a ship of this size, but the plethora of animals running around only added to Henry's amazement.

There were colorful birds flying throughout the atrium, as if it were the Amazon rainforest. At the bottom of the stairs, Henry saw a half-dozen penguins suspiciously waddling past a mountain goat that had a small capuchin monkey riding on its back. Over in the dining room, he saw a Siberian Husky sitting upright at a table, casually eating breakfast with three other Tutori.

Henry had seen Penny do that more than a few times back at home (in spite of Mrs. Fulbright's objections), but he had never seen a small sea lion pup petitioning for some food at the same table. He marveled at the vibrant atmosphere; his eyes jumped from one spot to the next as he tried to take it all in.

"Rufus was right!" Henry mumbled after spotting a snow leopard casually brushing its head against the large bronze statue in the center of the atrium.

It appeared to be a statue of the Koala Prince. The same marsupial Tutori that Henry had encountered back at the tailor's shop was now a sculpture instead of a projection standing before him. The small koala figure in the cloak stood next to an ostrich and a Carabinieri wearing a cape with a raised sword in his hand.

Glancing past the statue, Henry could see Otis and Oscar running from table to table in the dining area. He couldn't help but chuckle after noticing their latest hijinks—Otis was tap dancing while Oscar took grapes and other fruits from the distracted Tutori. "They certainly are incorrigible, aren't they?" he laughed, looking down toward the dachshund at his side. Presuming the otters were otherwise fed daily, he chalked it up to another bout of shenanigans.

Barnaby and Saint-Clair were nowhere to be found. Henry eventually spotted a familiar face, although he had no intention of rushing over to say hello—not after getting a chance to see Roger's kickboxing skills up close yesterday. Still feeling slightly sore and hoping to avoid another bruising encounter with the feisty kangaroo, he looked the other way as Roger gazed out the window.

"*Sweet maple syrup!*" Henry cried out. A panda bear cub had snuck up on him and latched onto his leg. Based on its size, the cub appeared to be around six months old. The surprise of it all and the ship rocking in the rough Atlantic seas were almost enough to send him stumbling to the floor as he tried to maintain his footing.

A familiar voice chimed in, "I see you're making all kinds of friends onboard, huh?" prompting Henry to turn around. Before he could say a word, June bantered, "Rufus did a fine job, indeed... Almost didn't recognize ya without the yellow raincoat."

June teased, brushing his shoulder off with her hand as if she were sweeping away a pile of dust, "Not bad, Kodiak Bay. You clean up nicely!"

Henry's face turned slightly red, and he responded humbly, "Thanks, June! Mr. Robinson took pretty good care of me, eh?" She picked up the small panda bear and asserted, "Yeah, I'm not surprised. I reckon Rufus is the best in the business."

"Indubitably," he agreed. In that instant, a blue macaw swooped down from the top floor of the atrium unexpectedly and flew past both of them, sending Henry ducking for cover.

June didn't even flinch. Unlike Henry, she was used to the animals onboard the ship and wasn't startled in the slightest.

Once Henry sprung to his feet and composed himself, he saw someone wearing a black cowboy hat get off the elevator; it was the same woman sitting next to June at the council meeting yesterday. She had defiance in her eyes and a confident swagger that only a real

Texan could pull off. He assumed the woman was around Barnaby's age, but he couldn't be sure. She had blonde hair that came down to her shoulders, a toned build, and striking blue eyes. The woman was a real Texas belle.

Having developed somewhat of a reputation within the *APA*, she loved proving people wrong and wasn't shy about reminding them afterward. Much to his chagrin, Barnaby had witnessed it more times than he could count.

"Well, well, well... If it ain't *the* Harvey Halifax himself, as I live and breathe," the woman said in a deep southern accent. Henry instantly blushed. He couldn't hide his embarrassment and stammered, "Sorry, it's, um... it's actually Henry, ma'am."

"Oh, my mistake... Well, put 'er there, Kodiak Bay!" the woman fired back as she stuck her hand out to properly greet the nervous Canadian.

"Savannah Sunday from San Antone," she announced confidently while shaking his hand. "Heard we're gonna be working together on that polar bear case." Distracted by her firm handshake, Henry nodded his head in silence. When she finally let go of his hand, it was still throbbing and almost as red as his face.

Savannah didn't even seem to notice and just lifted the panda bear cub out of June's arms. "Don't you worry, Halifax... We'll catch 'em this time. I taught Barnaby everything he knows!" She winked at him and concluded, "Just try not to slow us down, pal," chuckling as she walked away with the panda bear.

Henry wouldn't allow himself to be discouraged so easily and muttered, "It was nice to meet you too." He rebuffed her parting remarks and shrugged. "You know, Canadians are tougher than people think."

Penny growled in support as June laughed. Texans had a unique sense of humor, and June had been around Ms. Sunday long enough to know she meant nothing by it.

A moment later, an unforgettable voice shouted from behind in a heavy British accent, "Oi! So, this is the bloke? The, uh, *captain* of the Kodiak Bay Fire Brigade, was it? What happened, Halifax... Rufus run out of denim?"

Henry spun around—he quickly realized it was the British Tutori and his apprentice from the council meeting last night. They both wore identical gray wool suits and black oxfords. Their attire wasn't exactly the same, though; he noticed that only the older gentleman was wearing the cloak and forest-green necktie. Henry assumed that the boy at his side must have been a Magari because he had on the same black necktie as June.

Fiercely British with square eyeglasses, the older man had short white hair, a cleanly shaven face, brown eyes, and a slightly portly build. He was older than Savannah and Barnaby, although the man looked like he could still hold his own. His Magari partner appeared to be around Henry's age and had brown eyes, brown hair styled in a short Princeton haircut, and a trim physique.

"Technically, I'm only a volunteer for the fire brigade, sir," Henry joked with a half smile. Poking fun seemed to be par for the course amongst the Tutori, but one thing was clear. He would need to toughen up if he wanted to last on this ship.

"Aw, come on, lad... I'm just having a laugh!" the British man chortled. He patted Henry on the back and extended his other arm for a proper handshake. "All kidding aside, I heard what you did. Good on you for chasing Barnaby down. Come on now, give me your hand, mate," he insisted, as his south London accent effortlessly cut through the air. "The name is Albert Blackfriar... but everyone around here calls me Professor Blackfriar."

With a bit of hesitation, Henry shook his hand and responded, "Nice to meet you, sir."

"And don't worry about those cubs, lad. I'm a Londoner through and through. Nobody on this ship knows London Town better than me, and the Frenchman won't get far now that we have a couple Englishmen on the case," Professor Blackfriar remarked confidently. The boy standing across from Henry subtly rolled his eyes as the professor walked off without saying another word.

"Sorry about the professor. He's a good man at heart. Tends to go overboard with the razzing sometimes, though," he said to Henry. The British boy stuck his hand out. "Archibald Ashdown... My friends call me Archie."

"Good to meet you, Archie. I'm Henry... and this is Penny," he warmly replied, shaking Archie's hand. It was a refreshing introduction compared to his experience meeting Ms. Sunday and Professor Blackfriar. June chimed in, "Well, daylight's burnin'... what do y'all say we get some breakfast?" She was feeling quite hungry after waking up early to get some exercise in ahead of the morning sunrise.

They all walked over to the dining area and sat down at the nearest open table. Wondering what they would be serving, Henry looked around for some menus, only to find that there were none on the table. To his surprise, a chef appeared out of nowhere with a wheeled cart that had numerous plates covered in shiny stainless-steel cloches. The chef twirled around the table with dexterity, placing dishes in front of Henry, June, and Archie.

Penny instantly looked up at Henry, grumbling and whining as the scent of food wafted in her direction. He glanced at her and smiled. In the interest of avoiding a tantrum (which didn't take much for this wirehaired dachshund), he leaned over and lifted her onto the empty chair next to his.

Right as Henry was about to ask if there was anything for Penny, he noticed the chef had already vanished. "Where did he go?" he asked. The man disappeared in practically the blink of an eye; it all happened so fast that Henry didn't even get a chance to thank him.

There was now a buffet of plates on the table. Everything from tall stacks of flapjacks to perfectly cooked eggs Benedict and cold glasses of orange juice for everyone—it was quite the spread. Elated about tasting everything in sight, Penny basked in the sweet and savory aromas coming from the neatly arranged dishes.

"Guess he didn't forget about you after all," said Henry after seeing a special plate that had a pyramid of sweet potato puree in the center surrounded by sweet potato sticks. Penny's muffled cries were only loud enough for the table to hear, but he quickly slid the plate within reach to calm her before things escalated.

Henry could certainly empathize with the dramatic dachshund at his side. Despite being in the middle of the ocean and sailing on a ship larger than most buildings in Kodiak Bay, the food looked amazing and smelled even better. There was so much to choose from. Henry ultimately went straight for the eggs Benedict, a familiar dish that made him feel at home after taking the first bite.

About halfway through his meal, June noticed Henry taking another bite of Canadian bacon and asked, "Tastes real, doesn't it?" He froze and replied confusedly, "*Real*? What do you mean by that?"

June responded in a lighthearted tone, "Well, this is the *APA*... Where do you think that Canadian bacon came from?"

Stunned by the question and growing concerned that he was surrounded by people who would sacrifice their lives to protect animals, Henry dropped his fork and answered timidly, "Oh, I, uh... I didn't know..."

"Man, you messed up big time!" June said. "First *APA* test, and ya already failed!" Her demeanor turned more serious as she began scolding him. "Killing animals just so you can have your breakfast? And in front of the Koala Prince, no less! I thought you were better than that, Henry!"

A surreal sense of panic set in. The relaxing and delightful breakfast that Henry was enjoying immediately became overshadowed by a special Texas blend of hostility and vitriol. He kept stammering, unable to utter anything of consequence that would get him out of this mess. In fact, half of what he tried to say was essentially nervous gibberish that even had Penny confused.

None of that seemed to matter, though, because June wasn't finished berating him. "Could've maybe been a Tutori one day too... But it's all over now!"

"Wait 'til the council hears what you did!" she furiously added.

Henry's face turned bright red, and he stammered nervously, trying to defend himself. "Wait, wait, wait... I, uh, I... I didn't..."

Unable to maintain the charade any longer, June burst into laughter. The bewildered look on Henry's face proved to be too much, which compelled Archie to interject, "Alright, alright... Take it easy, mate. She's just pulling your leg!"

"Oh, man, the look on your face was priceless! I'm sorry, Henry... I couldn't help myself!" June admitted. "Just having a little fun with ya!" She turned to her fellow Magari as she concluded, "They do like to have fun on this ship. Ain't that right, Archie?"

Archie sighed with a forced smile, shaking his head. "Yeah, the same kind you would expect watching England at the World Cup." Still confused and unsure if he should continue eating his breakfast, Henry blurted, "Wait, is this real ham or not?" There was a genuine concern peppered in his voice, and he wasn't sure what to think.

Henry had eaten Canadian bacon more times than he could remember. It was a breakfast staple back in Kodiak Bay ever since the town was founded, just like flapjacks and maple syrup. Eating it in the presence of the Tutori onboard the *APA* headquarters was different, though. It gave him a whole new perspective on the savory dish of eggs benedict sitting in front of him. He wondered how many pigs had to give their lives so that he could eat all those plates of ham over the past fifteen years. Henry was overcome with immense guilt just thinking about it.

June laughed and replied, "Don't worry... keep eating. It's ok, I promise!" The last remnants of her laughter dissipated, and she clarified, "You see, everything on this table was made from plants!"

"*Plants*?" Henry asked excitedly, "The eggs? The ham, too? How can that be?" Relieved to know that he didn't break the Tutori code after all, he added, "It looks and tastes just like the ham we eat back home." The befuddlement in Henry's voice was commensurate with the perplexity radiating from his face. He couldn't fathom how this delicious plate of eggs Benedict was made entirely from plants.

Archie piped up, "I suppose you could say the Carabinieri take their duties quite seriously."

"Well, most of it was made from plants," June smiled, proudly explaining, "The meat is actually grown in the kitchen using animal DNA, all without slaughtering any real animals."

Sensing that Henry was on the verge of erupting with a barrage of questions, she carried on, "You see, for years, the Carabinieri Science Regiment struggled to find a balance between feeding the Italian people and protecting the animals that shared their land. And then it all became obvious one day... Eliminate the demand and trust that good people will make the right choice." She took a deep breath. "They started with the three main food groups in Italy... pizza, pasta, and gelato... All delicious, and none of 'em hurt the animals." Penny suddenly stopped eating and looked at June after hearing some of her favorite words.

Henry took another bite of his breakfast as she boasted, "From there, the Carabinieri scientists spent decades experimenting by turning plants into food and creating meat out of thin air."

Archie looked at June with a raised eyebrow, prompting her to further clarify, "Well, technically, they used cells from animals, but most importantly, they always made sure no animals got hurt in the process." She winked at Archie and continued, "They worked tirelessly for the people and animals of Italy until they perfected recipes for the most popular carnivorous dishes. Hamburgers, hotdogs... even ribeye steaks!"

"You name it, and the Carabinieri have a recipe to make it without the need to kill any animals. All guaranteed to have the same taste as the real deal," June affirmed.

"Wow, I had no idea," Henry replied. He was still feeling embarrassed about referring to the Carabinieri in such an ignorant manner when he boarded the ship yesterday, which left him thinking that Valentina deserved another apology.

June chuckled and concluded, "Yeah, everything tasted like cardboard when they first started, but the Carabinieri aren't cowards. They don't give up just because something seems impossible. They put in the hard work and get things done. Period."

Henry was blown away. The Carabinieri were indeed far more than just a police force. He listened intently as June went on and on about the chemistry and science behind all of it. The whole process sounded ingenious, and he agreed that people would probably be less inclined to have that burger or that steak if they had to personally kill all these animals to get it.

By the end of the meal, Henry had a renewed sense of admiration for the Carabinieri and the *APA*. It only fueled his desire to become a bona fide Tutori.

When they all got up from the table after breakfast, Henry grabbed a couple of leftover sweet potato sticks off Penny's plate; he shoved them in the inner pocket of his suit jacket, thinking his beloved dachshund would appreciate a nice snack later in the day. Between Penny's insatiable appetite and the unknown number of animals roaming the *Arthur Broome*, Henry figured it couldn't hurt to carry some extra food on him.

June, Archie, Henry, and Penny walked over to the center of the grand atrium, near the Koala Prince statue. After spotting Roger, Henry anxiously kept his head down. Even though he tried to slip by unnoticed, the sportive kangaroo hopped over to greet them anyway.

Henry hoped for a less eventful encounter this time and was mindful to keep his arms at his side. He didn't want to send any mixed messages to the young kangaroo, especially the kind that Roger might interpret as another invitation to play. But the smell of fresh food stashed in his pocket gave Roger another reason to come closer.

Without any warning, Roger boldly lifted the left side of Henry's suit jacket. The cheeky marsupial lunged for the sweet potato sticks and yanked them out of the inner pocket while Henry watched helplessly.

Happy to see that Roger was more interested in the sweet potato sticks instead of tussling this time around, Henry stared with fascination as the kangaroo gobbled them up. It wasn't exactly the most hospitable reception, but it was certainly less physical than yesterday's confrontation.

Still unsatisfied, the hungry kangaroo inched closer and gawked at Henry in a way that he was all too familiar with; he had seen the same look from Penny many times in the past and knew precisely what Roger wanted. He chuckled and held both of his hands up, announcing, "That's it, Roger. You cleaned me out. I don't have any more, eh?" Henry turned to look at Archie and June for reassurance, but the faint feelings of relief quickly turned into confusion.

Archie had begun to inexplicably mumble under his breath in an overtly jumpy fashion, and his face turned ghastly pale. It was as if he had just witnessed a horrific crime. June didn't say anything, but her anxiety-ridden body language gave Henry the impression that something terrible had happened. Blankly staring down at the floor, she appeared to be afraid of something.

That all seemed less important a second later when Roger became overwhelmed by a violent bout of coughing.

Within moments, the coughing spiraled out of control, and the kangaroo collapsed to the floor, convulsing. The marsupial went completely limp shortly thereafter, sending a wave of terror coursing through Henry's body. It almost felt like he was standing next to a recently ignited forest fire, staring at the arriving fire brigade with a pack of matches in his hand.

Archie and June immediately took a few steps back, leaving Henry and Penny alone right next to the lifeless kangaroo in the center of the grand atrium. An abrupt silence permeated the room. When the bustling noises of the grand atrium fell silent, Henry suddenly felt the eyes of dozens of people and animals staring at him. Even some of the phone operators on the floor above were now peering down at him as they leaned over the railings.

With the motionless kangaroo at his feet, Henry slowly stood up after kneeling down to check on Roger. The panicked expression on his face only grew louder. He had a dozen excuses running through his mind, yet he couldn't find the courage to actually say anything. Penny knew right away that Henry would be facing serious repercussions once Barnaby found out, but she wasn't going to abandon him now. She retreated to a protective stance at his side and proudly held her head high.

The room was eerily silent, and Henry didn't know what to do; some of the bystanders looked terrified, while others seemed disgusted by his very presence.

"Oh, no," Henry gulped when he saw Barnaby stroll in from the hallway near the elevators. He also noticed the Japanese Tutori from last night's council meeting walking by his side, and they appeared to be in a celebratory mood.

Barnaby, holding a birthday cake that had two burning candles planted in the center, carried on laughing while his Japanese colleague told a funny joke.

Their lighthearted demeanor changed the instant they spotted Henry standing over Roger's lifeless body. Barnaby stopped and unwittingly dropped the cake on the floor, sending chunks of icing and baked flour splattering everywhere. Merciless rage began to form in the Australian's eyes.

Henry had never been more scared in his life, and he exclaimed, "I know this looks bad... But I can explain! I, uh, I didn't..."

"Crikey! What's going on here?" Barnaby interjected furiously as he stared down at Roger, who was lying motionless on the floor. "You did this? You killed my best mate?" The whole room could tell he was livid, Henry included. They all heard the unmistakable anger and anguish tangled throughout his thick Australian accent.

"No, no, no, Barnaby... You don't understand! I, um... I didn't mean to!" Henry responded with genuine panic in his voice. "It was an accident! He ate a few sweet potato sticks and just collapsed!"

Barnaby screamed, "Roger is allergic to sweet potatoes, you murderer!"

Henry, frightened and clearly distraught, pleaded, "I'm so sorry, Barnaby! I swear he just took 'em outta my pocket! It wasn't my fault!"

The Japanese Tutori unexpectedly pulled the samurai sword from his scabbard and offered it to Barnaby, who eagerly accepted it. Henry's heart dropped to the floor when he saw the blade come out. He wanted to run back to his cabin, but his legs wouldn't move.

The crowds of bystanders had grown, and their deafening silence only added to the panic. With practically everyone glaring at him, it became clear that nobody was coming to rescue him from this treacherous predicament. A surreal sense of fear set in, and the sound of his heart nearly beating out of his chest overshadowed the absence of empathy in the room.

Barnaby raised the sword in a defensive position and turned to Henry, berating him, "I welcome you into my home! I put clothes on your back! I put food on your table... and this is how you thank me? You poisoned my best mate on his birthday?"

Stammering in fear, Henry inched backward as Barnaby stepped closer.

Otis and Oscar darted over to the grand piano in the corner and started playing a very dramatic-sounding melody. Henry should have been impressed to see a pair of otters playing the piano—or any musical instrument for that matter. But he could only focus on the belligerent Australian approaching slowly.

As the impromptu piano performance by the pair of scampish otters continued, Henry was left to grapple with an enraged, sword-wielding Australian standing just feet away. He apologized profusely, even though Barnaby ignored everything he managed to say.

Barnaby didn't care and wouldn't hear any of it; the incensed Tutori already had his mind made up and refused to stop until he got revenge. Everyone in the atrium could see that his inconsolable rage had robbed him of the ability to reason.

"Mr. Murdoch, I'm so sorry, really! I promise it was an accident! I would never hurt Roger on purpose! Never!" Henry desperately insisted. Barnaby took two steps forward and snapped, "What is it, mate... You think you're bettah than me?"

"Better than you?" Henry repeated, totally bemused by the question and still trembling in fear.

"Are you making fun of me? Is that what you're doing?" Barnaby asked scornfully. The tension in the room commanded everyone's attention, including the slew of animals watching.

Overwhelmed by a sense of shuddering trepidation, Henry's bumbling attempts to shift the blame somewhere else only seemed to make matters worse. The music coming from the piano wasn't helping either. Otis and Oscar kept changing the tempo to sound more and more dramatic with every step that Barnaby took.

Even though Savannah relished the excitement, she could tell that Henry was truly terrified and offered some assistance. As Barnaby continued twirling the sword in a hostile manner, she tossed a sleeve of Tutori throwing darts toward Henry. She shouted a few words of encouragement while the darts sailed through the air. "Show 'em how to tango, Humphrey!"

Henry, blindsided by the improvised toss, frantically tried to catch the sleeve but ended up juggling it between both hands until one of the darts slipped out and pierced his left shoe. Despite the adrenaline coursing through his body, he winced in pain after feeling the dart strike the top part of his foot—it almost felt like a bee sting.

"Oh, this can't be good," Henry mumbled to himself. He looked down at the dart sticking out of his foot and knew he didn't have long before the tranquilizer's effects would start to materialize. With Otis and Oscar still playing the piano and Barnaby only a few steps away, a wave of dizziness washed over his body as he struggled to maintain his footing. He wobbled for a few seconds and then collapsed onto the ground next to Penny, shouting with his last breath, "It was an accident!"

The combination of the dramatic piano music, Penny's aggressive barking, and Savannah's cheering, "Get 'em, Kodiak Bay! Get 'em!" was the last sound Henry would hear before the tranquilizer dart knocked him unconscious.

Eight hours later, Henry was awakened by rough jostling motions, rocking his body back and forth. Struggling to open his eyes, he found himself looking up at the sky as Penny licked his face in a frenzied manner. She snorted and squealed in excitement once he finally woke up.

Henry hugged her with enthusiasm, grateful to see that his best friend hadn't been harmed. The celebration was interrupted, though, after they were jolted backward. In disbelief, he gasped when he realized they were in a lifeboat that was currently being lowered (notch by notch) into the middle of the Atlantic Ocean.

A familiar feeling of panic-induced adrenaline returned when Henry rushed over to the side of the lifeboat. The waves of the Atlantic that were staring back at him confirmed his suspicions. He immediately looked up toward the ship and couldn't believe what he saw. Barnaby was on the promenade deck, pulling the chains on the pulley system as the lifeboat kept inching closer to the rough waves below.

"Barnaby! What are you doing?" Henry shouted with a profound sense of distress in his voice. He felt the lifeboat drop another notch closer to the ocean while the *Arthur Broome* sailed forward at thirty knots toward London—he knew he didn't have much time and had to find a way out of this predicament somehow before it was too late.

Barnaby wrathfully yelled back at him, "You wanna play it soft... We can play it soft. You wanna dance on Roger's grave? We can play hardball then, mate." The irate Australian continued to lower the lifeboat, devoid of any compassion or sympathy.

Henry glanced down at the waves crashing against the *Arthur Broome* once more and cried out, "Mr. Murdoch, please! It was an accident! I swear!"

Not persuaded in the slightest, Barnaby screamed, "You killed my best mate! And now you want my help?" He snickered and warned, "I don't think so, amigo! It's too late for all that now!"

Feeling the lifeboat drop another notch, Henry was worried it would be too late to change Barnaby's mind at this point. The heart-pounding terror of being cast out into the middle of nowhere seemed to intensify with every second that passed. Dangling just a few feet above the unforgiving waters of the Atlantic, the lifeboat was now dangerously close to reaching the end of its rope. Penny's frantic barking got louder and louder each time Barnaby yanked on the pulley.

With the cold ocean mist from the waves pelting Henry's face, he shouted back at him, "You've got this all wrong! I didn't know he would be allergic!"

"Don't do this, Barnaby! I'm truly sorry!" Henry pleaded. The lifeboat dropped another notch and knocked him around like an inflatable beach ball.

"Damn your apologies!" Barnaby hollered back. "Roger is never coming back, and it's always gonna be your fault!"

Absolutely bewildered by what Henry saw next, he mumbled under his breath, "Roger?"

At first, Henry thought he was hallucinating; perhaps he had dreamed up this whole debacle under the guise of the tranquilizer. Penny reinforced his first instincts and barked loudly when she saw the same thing. As another cold spray of ocean water pelted his face, he yelled and pointed with his finger, "Wait, Barnaby! Wait! Roger's standing right behind you!"

Barnaby sighed and threw his hands up in the air emphatically. "Damn it, Roger! I told you to wait for my signal, mate." Roger smirked and instantly bounced out of view as Henry shouted, "Are you kidding me?"

Henry's despair swiftly turned into anger. "Alright, the joke's on me, eh? Real funny. Now, will you pull us up already?"

Even though Roger's early emergence had caused some mild annoyance, Barnaby howled with laughter when Henry figured out what had happened.

Henry grumbled and muttered to himself as Barnaby heaved the chains on the pulley system in the opposite direction. The small boat was hoisted back up toward the promenade deck, where the rest of the lifeboats were stowed.

Once the lifeboat had been retracted and secured into place, Henry immediately grabbed Penny. He climbed back onto the *Arthur Broome*, carefully setting the wirehaired dachshund down on the deck in the process. Fueled by a warranted sense of hostility, he shoved Barnaby furiously and screamed, "What was that about? Are you nuts? You almost gave me a heart attack!"

"Well, well, well... he's got an engine under there after all," Barnaby teased. Surprised by the fury, he felt proud of himself for getting a rise out of the ordinarily polite Canadian lad. He chuckled and added, "Alright, take it easy, mate... Roger and I were just having a little fun."

Before Henry could resume lambasting the cheeky Australian, the red-haired woman he saw yesterday walked out onto the promenade deck and interjected, "When you have finished your muster drills out here, the council would like a word with you, Monsieur Murdoch."

— CHAPTER 11 —
THE PARTNER'S CODE

*H*enry was shocked by the woman's fortuitous arrival, and despite the callous grin shining from Barnaby's face, he wasn't about to let either of them slip away so easily—not without getting some answers first. He rushed over to block Barnaby from taking another step and stood firmly between the two Tutori.

"Not so fast! I want some answers right now, or I'm going straight to the council myself!" Henry demanded. Still fuming from Barnaby's latest shenanigans, he raged, "I deserve to know what the Frenchman is doing here!" Penny let out a few loud barks to let everyone know that she was equally upset.

Barnaby rolled his eyes and snickered. "Alright, take it easy, mate... You can't get fresh hard-shell tacos from just anywhere. This ain't Amsterdam, alright?" Baffled and beyond frustrated, Henry insisted, "What? Can you just tell me what's going on here? You *owe* me that much!"

"I'm not the Frenchman, Monsieur Halifax," the woman interceded.

"See there, mate. She's not the Frenchman, okay? Just a case of mistaken identity," Barnaby nonchalantly proclaimed, hoping Henry would let it go now that he had heard it directly from the red-haired woman.

Henry was speechless at first, but he knew there was more to the story here and refused to give up until he got the *whole* truth. Annoyed by Barnaby's attempt to belittle his concerns and still infuriated from nearly being marooned in the middle of the Atlantic Ocean moments ago, he snarled, "Then, why does she look exactly like Saint-Clair, eh? You're going to tell me this isn't the same woman that walked all over you at the zoo?"

Unexpectedly, the woman giggled at Henry's brazen comments. She was normally a very serious person and rarely laughed, but she couldn't help herself.

Barnaby's face turned red almost immediately. He was clearly embarrassed and tried to downplay the altercation. "Well, hold on a minute now. I'd say it was more of an even-handed tussle for the most part, up until you distracted me and let her get..."

"Tell us the truth!" Henry interrupted, not amused by the absence of any *real* answers.

Barnaby smirked. "Alright, mate. I'm gonna level with ya. The reason she *looks* like Saint-Clair is because... well, she *is* Saint-Clair. I mean, she is... and she isn't." Henry scoffed, "What? You're not making any sense!"

"Patience, my scrappy young Canadian friend. Don't let all that adrenaline and maple syrup cloud your vision." Barnaby laughed and turned his attention to the red-haired woman. "This is *Celine* Saint-Clair... She's a Tutori, mate." Winking at Celine, he fittingly clarified, "One of the best in the business too. We've even worked on a few missions together recently."

Henry stood with his hands on his hips and looked more confused than ever as Barnaby tried to reassure him that he had it all wrong. "She also has a sistah, though. An identical twin sistah that has the same red hair. I've known 'em both for years, and I still can barely tell the two apart. That's right, *Catherine* Saint-Clair and I go way back. We joined the *APA* around the same time. Even went through Magari training together. We were partnahs for years... but things don't always work out the way you think they will."

Mortified that he had overlooked the possibility of Saint-Clair having a twin sister, Henry turned to Celine and attempted to apologize, "I'm so sorry, Ms. Saint-Clair. I didn't mean to accuse you of..."

"It's fine, Monsieur Halifax... really!" Celine interjected before he could finish making amends.

Henry's anger had been replaced by a humbling bout of embarrassment. It never crossed his mind that something as simple as a twin sister could easily explain why a person that resembled the Frenchman would be onboard the same ship as the Tutori. He still wasn't satisfied, though. He glanced at Barnaby and remarked, "Hang on... What about the council? Why didn't you just tell them it was your old partner?"

Barnaby sighed. The painful memories of his old partner were still fresh, and he answered begrudgingly, "Look, mate, there's a lot you don't know. I'm trying to handle this matter delicately. You see, Catherine... or Saint-Clair, as I called her... didn't necessarily leave the *APA* on good terms." He took a deep breath. "She became an extremist. It got to a point where she would only deal in absolutes. You're either with me or you're against me... Ya follow?"

Henry nodded respectfully in silence. He wanted to apologize to Celine again but managed to keep quiet as the Australian carried on explaining, "Well, she took it too far one day... decided there was no place for zoos in this world. She disobeyed direct orders from the Tutori Council, and some innocent bystanders paid the ultimate price." Barnaby shook his head. "There's no coming back from that, mate."

Even though Henry didn't know precisely what happened that day, the pain and anguish in Barnaby's eyes were unmistakable.

"She was expelled from the *APA*, and, oh man, did that make her as cross as a frog in a sock. She's been haunted by a vendetta ever since," Barnaby acknowledged. He looked Henry directly in the eyes and asked sincerely, "Do you know this word? *Vendetta*? It's actually the Italian word for vengeance. It means being totally consumed with inflicting retribution at all costs... All day, every day. And there's nothing more dangerous in this world." The concern in Barnaby's tone was chilling.

"It all makes sense now," Henry thought to himself. He keenly listened as the Australian Tutori concluded, "I imagine she plans to hit every zoo on the map until they're all shut down. Over two thousand out there, and she'll be coming for all of 'em, one by one."

Barnaby exhaled, announcing, "Yeah, it's a tale as old as time."

"A tale as old as time?" Henry murmured. The sudden flood of information drowned out the adrenaline and emotions that were blindly controlling his actions only minutes ago. He was finally thinking clearly again and blurted, "Wait! Why didn't you tell the council about Catherine?"

Barnaby sighed once more and tutted, "It's the partnah's code, mate. Tutori or not, you don't turn your back on your partnah when they've lost their way. One bad chaptah doesn't mean her story is over, alright?" He tried to persuade Henry to see it his way. "If I tell the council, they'll just put a blue notice out on her, and every police department from Byron Bay to Boston will be after her."

"They want those bears recovered safely, and that's exactly what I plan to do tomorrow!" Barnaby exclaimed, trusting his unwavering dedication would instill some confidence.

Henry was conflicted; he knew lying was wrong, but this seemed different. For the first time, he now felt like he understood the wayward Australian. Behind all the jesting and the tomfoolery, Barnaby was willing to put everything on the line to protect someone he truly cared about, even though it meant hiding the truth from the council. If the council found out, it would cost him everything. Barnaby would undoubtedly be expelled, and Henry didn't want to see that happen.

Celine evidently didn't want to see that happen either and added reassuringly, "I don't know what she's planning, Henry, but I do know that Catherine would never hurt those cubs." She admitted, "Still, it's true... My sister broke the Tutori code and got herself kicked out."

"I look just like her, and there's not a day that goes by where the shame she brought upon our family name doesn't follow me around this ship like a ghost. Everywhere, all the time." Celine bemoaned, tears welling up in her eyes. She glanced at the passing Atlantic Ocean and remembered what her father taught her. "Oui, but real sisters do not give up on each other. And I would hate to see her get hurt or locked away in a cage like the animals she seeks to liberate."

Desperate for some compassion, Celine looked at Henry and pleaded, "*S'il vous plaît*, Monsieur Halifax... Please exercise some discretion here and trust that Barnaby will recover those bear cubs. I can assure you that the *APA* will safely return them to the *Kodiak Bay Zoo* as promised."

"Now if you two will excuse me, I must return to the council chambers," Celine said as she walked away and headed back inside. She shouted, "And don't be long, Barnaby! The council still wants to speak to you right away." The door closed behind her, leaving Barnaby alone on the promenade deck with Henry and Penny.

"Alright, mate, time's up. I gotta go change my trousers before I see the council," Barnaby announced while gesturing toward the bottom of his tattered pants.

"Your girl there has some awfully sharp teeth. She almost took my leg off in the midst of carrying you out here to the lifeboat." He winked at Penny and quipped, "I'm really gonna catch hell with Rufus when he finds out about this."

Henry muttered condescendingly, "Serves you right."

"What was that, mate?" Barnaby replied. It prompted Henry to raise a more pressing question, "Hang on! What are you going to do tomorrow when Ms. Sunday and the professor realize we've been chasing Catherine Saint-Clair this whole time? They'll tell the council, won't they?"

The Australian responded confidently, "No worries, pal... You just leave that to *Barnaby Banjo Murdoch*, alright?" He casually walked off the promenade deck toward the elevators, opened the door, and turned to Henry. "In the meantime, you should head on back to your cabin and get some rest, yeah? It's been a long day, and we've got an early start tomorrow."

Carrying Henry from the grand atrium all the way out to the promenade deck like a sack of potatoes had worn Barnaby out, and he yawned at the thought of turning in for the night. "Meet me on the top deck at the aft of the ship... tomorrow morning at seven-thirty," he ordered.

An expression of worry flickered across Henry's face. He still wasn't very familiar with the *Arthur Broome* and asked anxiously, "The top deck? Do I take the elevator?" Barnaby's voice trailed off just as the door was closing. "Follow the ottahs, mate... Just follow the ottahs."

Henry looked around for Otis and Oscar, but they were nowhere to be found. Penny wasn't concerned in the slightest though; she was smiling from ear to ear, thrilled to be back at his side now that he was awake.

"Again, with the otters, he says, eh?" Henry shrugged while gazing at Penny, wondering where the pair of mischievous otters were. He scooped the dachshund into his arms. "Are you alright, girl? Thanks for taking care of me," he whispered, giving her another big hug as she licked his face affectionately.

Now that Barnaby and Celine were inside, it was eerily quiet on the promenade deck.

Henry and Penny both looked out over the railing and marveled at the passing waves of the North Atlantic. There was something about the open ocean that perfectly personified the massive scale and size of the planet. He welcomed the renewed sense of perspective. Regardless of how angry he felt only moments ago, it was always humbling to be reminded of just how small humans really were.

The seas were relatively calm, and there was a beautiful sunset westward, but the dark storm clouds toward the east led Henry to believe another storm was brewing. He loved the thrill of sailing across the world and didn't regret following Barnaby onto the *Arthur Broome*, even in spite of that harrowing stunt with the lifeboat.

With Penny in his arms and having survived Barnaby's antics unscathed, Henry regained his upbeat attitude and took a deep breath as the anger melted away. He smiled and brushed it off as a case of Australian roughhousing. He assumed it was a harmless (yet slightly terrifying) prank for the new guy. "It could have been a lot worse," he thought, sincerely thankful there were no snakes or giant spiders involved.

He still felt somewhat humiliated since so many people had seen him drop the tranquilizer dart on his foot earlier. Practically everyone onboard the ship must've been there, and it wasn't quite the first impression he had hoped for when leaving his cabin this morning.

None of that seemed to matter when Penny licked his nose out of the blue. Henry chuckled and remembered that Penny loved him unconditionally. Grateful to have such a loyal friend, he found solace in her steadfast companionship.

All of a sudden, two massive lightning bolts illuminated the dark, cloudy sky to the east, and the booming sound of thunder that followed triggered Penny's fear of stormy weather. Her cheerful smile had vanished, and she began trembling in his arms.

Henry kneeled and set her down on the deck. Penny ran off so quickly that she was already pawing at the corner of the door by the time he stood up. He rushed over and followed the wirehaired dachshund inside after opening the door.

They turned the corner toward the elevators and stopped abruptly. Henry saw Otis and Oscar standing on their hind legs; their little arms were stretched wide open, signaling for him to come forward. Had it not been for the heart-stopping muster drill he had just experienced, Henry probably would have been startled by their presence. Running into a familiar pair of exuberant otters paled in comparison, though.

Despite the jealous grumbling from Penny, Henry couldn't help but laugh and crouch to accept the apologetic hugs. The pair of mischievous otters winked at the dachshund and raced back over to the elevators. He followed them, watching as Oscar pushed the call button first (narrowly beating his brother).

Otis wasn't pleased. He proceeded to chase Oscar around until the elevator finally arrived. As soon as the doors opened, Otis darted over to the control panel of buttons. He made a point to look his brother in the eyes as he pushed *6–9–9–1* tauntingly.

Henry planted his feet firmly on the floor and tried to maintain his footing while the elevator whisked throughout the *Arthur Broome*, moving vertically and then horizontally again. Otis and Oscar didn't stop wrestling with each other till the elevator reached its destination.

After the bell chimed and the doors opened, Penny followed Henry out onto the sixth floor; they both paused curiously after noticing the otters weren't getting off the elevator. Otis and Oscar waved goodbye as the doors closed, leaving him to presume they were off to turn in for the night.

"Guess we know the way from here, Penny!" Henry shrugged.

Penny trotted closely behind him down the hallway, eager to find out what they would be having for dinner tonight. Between chasing after Barnaby and standing guard at Henry's side all day, she had been thinking about *Don Ciccio's Pizza Window* for hours. The savory smells of food emanating from their cabin only inflamed her voracious appetite.

Henry noticed the lights were on in both June's room and the cabin at the end of the hallway, number *6992*. He wondered who was staying there as he opened his door and switched on the lights.

Surprisingly, the curtains were drawn, and his room had been tidied up. There also appeared to be a new tray of food and drinks on the coffee table in front of the small couch. Judging by the size of the ice cubes in the glass, he could tell the tray of food had just arrived moments ago.

Henry was thankful for another freshly prepared meal, although he found the whole thing boggling. "Who delivered the dinner? And more importantly, how did they know the exact time he would be returning to the cabin?"

Penny didn't seem to care. She was too busy inspecting the tray of food. Her nose sniffed the scents coming from under the cloches as she waited impatiently for Henry to sit down.

Henry opened the balcony curtains and turned his attention toward the tray of food. As he reached for the nearest stainless-steel cloche, the closet next to the bed caught his eye. The door had an envelope taped to it. Despite the rumbling noise coming from his stomach, he slid across the bed like it was the hood of a car, instantly grabbing the envelope off the door.

The typed lettering on the front of the envelope had his name spelled as: *MR. HALIFAX OF KODIAK BAY.* Henry flipped it over, and the seal flap had an embossed symbol of the Tutori that included the following label: *ARTHUR BROOME DEPARTMENT OF TAILORING.* He assumed the envelope must have been left by Rufus.

Henry carefully opened it up and pulled out the small card from inside. The black-colored note was about the size of a business card and included the following message in white lettering: *If you don't believe in yourself, you can't expect anyone else to. Keep your head up and shake it off.*

The message was short, but it meant the world to Henry. He put the note back in the envelope and opened the closet door. Overcome with amazement, he was stunned to find the closet packed with six matching gray wool suits that had navy-blue neckties hanging around the collars (already tied in adjustable Windsor knots). There were also six freshly pressed white button-down shirts and about a dozen pairs of socks on the closet shelf.

Distracted by Henry's new discovery, Penny hurried over and climbed into the closet so that she could give the new wardrobe a proper sniff. It didn't take long before she lost interest and rushed back over to the enticing scents coming from the tray of food on the other side of the room.

Penny's front paws were already on the edge of the coffee table by the time Henry arrived. Her unwavering appetite didn't seem to match the small size of her body. But the dramatic whining mixed in with excited shrieking indicated otherwise.

"I know, I know... I'm hungry too. Let's see what the chef has prepared for us tonight, eh?" Henry exclaimed, walking over to the collection of dishes on the coffee table. He picked up Penny and placed her on the couch. The elation shining from her face was infectious.

Henry smiled at Penny as he lifted the nearest cloche, revealing another beautifully crafted plate of sweet potato puree surrounded by sweet potato sticks. The presentation alone was a work of art in itself and could easily be mistaken for a dish prepared in a world-class restaurant with a seven-course tasting menu. The alluring sight of the sweet potato dish paired perfectly with the savory smells filling Penny's nose. Her cries of excitement only intensified when Henry moved the plate closer.

As Penny devoured the delicious feast of sweet potatoes, Henry lifted the other two cloches. He stared at the enticing plates of poutine and the side of flapjacks covered in pure maple syrup.

"Well played, indeed, Penny," Henry remarked, beaming with approval. It was just what he needed to forgive Barnaby for his questionable sense of humor.

After they finished their meals, Penny climbed onto Henry's lap and immediately plopped down. Her evening wind-down, however, proved to be fleeting; just as she began to relax, her head popped up and suddenly spun around like an owl. A muffled grumble followed as she looked over at the balcony door suspiciously. She thought she heard a strange noise and tensed up even further after something hit the glass.

"What was that?" Henry asked when he saw what appeared to be an ice cube bounce off the sliding glass door and land on his balcony. He carefully set Penny on the floor and heaved the door open, which sent a gust of wind flooding into the cabin. It wasn't raining, but lightning continued to illuminate the sky as he stepped out onto the balcony and whispered, "Hey, who's out there?"

June peered around the balcony divider after tossing a few ice cubes. "Oh, there you are! I was just trying to get your attention."

"Yeah, I think I've had enough attention for one day, eh?" Henry groaned. June smiled and responded comfortingly, "Aw, come on, Henry. Don't worry about Barnaby. He's pulled that prank on just about everyone! Sort of like a rite of passage for new rookies around here."

Feeling the humiliation resurface, Henry replied, "He made a proper fool out of me in front of the entire ship, that's for sure." June fired back, "I wanted to tell you, I swear! But he gave us direct orders!"

"I'm afraid she's correct," Archie chimed in, "and disobeying a direct order made by a senior Tutori is immediate grounds for expulsion from the *APA*." He had peeked around his balcony divider to check on Henry after hearing all the commotion.

"Well, he's got an odd sense of humor, eh?" Henry answered, shaking his head as he smiled. In an admirable attempt to detract from his embarrassment, June interjected, "If it makes ya feel any better, I managed to lasso him good and proper when he pulled that stunt on me. But can't say you're the only one that's been knocked out... Ain't that right, Archie?"

Unamused, Archie's face turned bright red as he tried to clarify, "If you're referring to that day where I fainted, I've told you a hundred times it was a blood sugar thing! You know I get low blood sugar!" Anxious to avoid any further besmirchment to his reputation, he added, "And it was nothing like what happened to Henry... sticking yourself with a tranquilizer dart by accident? Nobody has ever done that before!"

"Alright, take it easy, Arch... I was only trying to cheer Henry up," June teased. She knew it didn't take much to get Archie wound up and couldn't resist pushing his buttons.

Henry appreciated the gesture and spoke up, "Thanks, June. I'm just glad it's all over."

"Don't sweat it, Halifax," June responded compassionately. "And for what it's worth, Barnaby felt bad about the whole dart thing. That part wasn't supposed to happen." As Henry rolled his eyes, she carried on explaining, "No, no, honestly! He actually did a fairly decent job of looking after you during your, um... involuntary slumber. He set you down on the sofa and even placed a pillow under your head to make sure you wouldn't wake up with a sore neck."

Penny let out a few spirited barks, which reminded June to add, "And I personally took care of Penny the whole time. She's a real sweetheart, ya know, but boy was she upset with Barnaby." June tittered and winked at the wirehaired dachshund. "Don't worry though, I stayed by her side until he came back. Then she ran off, chasing Barnaby when he decided to take you outside to get some fresh air."

Archie acknowledged, "It's true, mate. He even had the ship's doctor come and check on you after he cleaned up the birthday cake off the floor for good measure." His tone turned more ominous. "Got to be careful around those Australian blokes... they play by a different set of rules."

"That's for sure, eh?" Henry replied with a shrug. Growing tired of being the center of attention, he asked curiously, "So, how did you two end up on this ship anyway? Aside from Barnaby, working for the *APA* must be a dream come true! Traveling the world... helping animals along the way?"

June chuckled, "Well, to be honest, I never even heard of the *APA* until I met Ms. Sunday. Definitely never dreamed I'd ever be on a ship like this. On the peanut farm in west Texas where I was raised, most people I knew had never even seen the ocean." She recalled her first encounter with the *APA* and sighed in relief, "But I owe it all to Ms. Sunday."

Glancing at the passing waves, she continued, "You see, I got myself into some trouble with the law back home. There was a cattle rancher next door who captured wild horses to keep as his own. Mustangs. They were injuring themselves trying to break out of his stables. The sound of them writhing in pain proved to be too much for me one day... I just couldn't take it anymore. So, I stayed up real late one night and snuck over to his ranch while everyone else was sleeping. Took it upon myself to set 'em free, and oh man, was that rancher furious!"

Henry was captivated. He listened intently as June carried on with the rest of her story. "I figured I might get off with a warning... Turns out I was dead wrong. The sheriff was ready to haul me in to face the magistrate. Can you believe that? I almost got away with it too. Despite his portly condition, the sheriff proved to be faster than I thought. Figured he was all hat and no cattle, if you know what I mean. I didn't make it easy on him, but he caught me running back toward the orphanage, and that was that." She paused to correct herself. "Well, technically, it was a peanut farm... The owners were some of the most generous people you'll ever meet, though. They never had kids of their own and were happy to look after children that had nowhere else to go."

June's cheerful personality vanished as she divulged somberly, "Never planned on ending up there, but that's where they sent me after my parents died in a car wreck on Highway 21." She looked up at the sky and whispered something under her breath in Japanese.

Henry wasn't sure what she murmured, but figured she was taking a moment to remember the happier times with her parents when they were still alive. He knew exactly how she felt and considered himself lucky that Captain Fulbright was there when he needed him most.

Before Henry could say anything to comfort June, her disposition turned more cheerful, and she boasted, "Luck was on my side though, fellas. Turns out, the sheriff picked up a flat tire on the way to the police station. Next thing I know... Mr. Sakamoto and Savannah snuck me out of the backseat while the sheriff was distracted changing the spare tire. It all happened in a flash! I sure was glad they showed up when they did, though."

Archie nodded his head in agreement, while June concluded,

"Yes, sir, Mr. Sakamoto and Savannah really changed my life that night. They brought me back to the farm and gave me a choice. Stay at the orphanage and roll the dice with the sheriff, or follow the path of the Tutori. Not a day goes by where I'm not grateful for the *APA*. They generously offered to help me channel my empathy for animals in a more constructive way that could make a real difference. The following day, I boarded the *Arthur Broome*, and I haven't looked back since."

Henry admired June's courage and replied supportively, "Well, I don't know much about Texas, but the Mounties back home always say... You never put a saddle on a mustang, and I'm sure those horses would agree. You did the right thing in my book, eh?" Wondering how Archie found his way to the *APA*, he asked, "What about you, Archie? How did you end up with this lot?"

"Oh, your royal highness over there?" June interrupted. Henry couldn't believe what he had just heard and repeated, "*Royal highness*?"

June trumpeted, "Well, go on, your majesty... Tell 'em how good you got it over there at Buckingham Palace!" She laughed as Henry assumed he was standing next to the Queen's grandson.

"Here we go again," Archie said, shaking his head. "How many times have I told you that I'm *not* a member of the Royal Family? And you know I've never stepped foot inside Buckingham Palace!" In an attempt to offer some clarity, he added nonchalantly, "My father is the Baron of Cromwell."

"Baron?" Henry blurted out. He wasn't sure if that was some sort of royal title that might be of lesser significance.

Archie replied humbly, "*No*, we are *not* royals. It's more of an aristocratic title." Realizing that Henry could understandably assume he was nothing more than a privileged rich kid without further context, he continued, "Despite my family's affluent background, my father was a Tutori, as was his father before him.

And in keeping with Ashdown family tradition, it's now my turn to serve the *APA*."

"Wait a minute, is the professor your dad?" Henry asked.

Archie laughed, "Professor Blackfriar? Goodness no... He's just my father's old partner. My dad retired after injuring his knee on the job. Professor Blackfriar promised him that he would train me as a Magari. I've been onboard the *Broome* for about a year now, only a few months longer than June."

Henry loved how people of opposite backgrounds could come together in pursuit of a common mission and was thoroughly fascinated by their stories. Even though he could have gone on for hours asking more questions, the weather wasn't cooperating.

Everyone was startled by the sound of booming thunder that followed the latest round of lightning flashes illuminating the night sky. A few seconds later, it started pouring rain, which prompted Henry to shout, "Good grief, we better get inside! I'll see you all tomorrow morning, eh?"

Archie gave him a quick, two-finger salute while June yelled, "See ya later, Halifax!" before disappearing out of sight.

Penny hated the rain and bolted into the cabin the moment she felt the first drop of water hit her back. Drying off a drenched dachshund was no easy feat (especially for those with sharp teeth), and Henry was thankful for her fast reflexes. He rushed inside and hastily closed the sliding glass door behind them.

With Penny hiding under the bed, Henry closed the blinds as the storm intensified and said, "Well, we better turn in early, eh? Got a big day tomorrow!" He kneeled down to pick up Penny and then gently placed her on the bed.

Henry flinched at what he heard next. His attention suddenly turned to the chiming noise broadcasting out of the small speaker built into the ceiling. The delightful ding caught him completely by surprise—he didn't even realize there was a speaker in the ceiling until now.

An older man's voice wrapped in a thick Italian accent poured out of the speaker, "*Buonasera*, signore e signori."

The charming greeting instantly filled the small confines of Henry's cabin. He listened attentively as the Italian gentleman continued the ship-wide announcement by warmly introducing himself.

"This is-a Captain Alfredo Carlucci speaking to you from the bridge. What a wonderful evening of sailing we have ahead of us tonight. No land in sight, and there's nowhere else Captain Carlucci would rather be than sailing the high seas.

"Frankly, I think the *Arthur Broome* is-a one of the best ships out there. Looking back to when she was built, I said you need to build it with solar power. I told Malnati's... I remember talking to them. I said the ship needs to be powered by solar, steam, wind... and recycled garbage. Fossil fuels are not acceptable.

"I said this to Malnati's... You got to have solar and renewable energy for the engines when you build this ship. Why throw the trash out if we can use it for fuel? And now look at what they're doing at Malnati's... Just take a look at what they're doing with Malnati's Shipyard. All the new ships they build are now electric and run on sustainable energy, just like the *Arthur Broome*. Look at the gasoline savings... Take a look at the environment... You got to look at all of it.

"Sì, sì, sì, I talked to Malnati's, and they sent a gift basket to Captain Carlucci as a thank you. You know, frankly, with Malnati's, I think they should have sent a few gift baskets, but that's okay. And there were a few people here who were disappointed with that, but that's okay. Mi scuso, let's talk about the future, though. The past is-a the past, and maybe Malnati's will make it right one day. Sì, it is-a never too late to make things right with a few gift baskets.

"At present, we are steering a course toward London at a current speed of forty knots. Since leaving Kodiak Bay, we have sailed approximately twenty-one hundred nautical kilometers, with a remaining distance of four hundred and fifteen nautical kilometers until we reach London. Our current position is-a *49 degrees, 22 minutes, and 15 seconds north by 17 degrees, 39 minutes, and 30 seconds west.*

"The temperature outside is-a twelve degrees Celsius, and we have northwest wind speeds registering at twenty-six knots. "We are moving into a lingering weather system that will include some heavy rain and thunder.

"And you know, sometimes that happens. But frankly, Captain Carlucci is-a not concerned with the Carabinieri running this ship. Sì, sì, sì, the finest sailors to ever cross the Atlantic, and if I'm speaking candidly here... this ship has been through far worse, let me tell you.

"Now, we should be clear of this treacherous weather by sunrise, but just remember one thing, signore e signori... this is-a the *Arthur Broome*, sì. For Captain Carlucci and the Carabinieri, there is-a no curtain call. Sì, we have the watch, rain or shine, and you can count on us to see you through it all.

"Our expected arrival into the English Channel is-a six o'clock local time tomorrow morning. Aerial disembarkation will begin at seven-thirty... Dockside disembarkation will begin sixty minutes later.

"From all of us on the bridge, *buonanotte...* Sì, sì, sì, *benedici il creatore e tutti quelli che passano per le sue acque.*"

Unsure of what the captain said at the end of his announcement, Henry remarked, "We really need to brush up on that Italian, eh, Penny?" His interpretation of the Italian language quickly became less important after remembering what was said toward the end.

"*Aerial disembarkation*?" he inquired, glancing down at Penny. "Did he say aerial? And disembarkation?" The bewildered expression on the dachshund's face only added to his confusion. He had never heard those two words combined before and wondered if the captain had made a mistake.

"Seven-thirty is the same time we're supposed to meet Barnaby on the top deck." Henry speculated curiously, "Maybe they have a helicopter up there or something?"

Struggling to keep his eyes open and still feeling the drowsy side effects of the tranquilizer dart, he climbed into bed. After flipping the light switch off, he whispered, "Goodnight, my brave girl."

With a soft pillow under his head and the discernable swaying motion of the ship pitching through the rough Atlantic storm, it didn't take long for Henry to fall asleep. Penny rolled on her back and stretched her short legs into the air. She yawned and curled up next to him, shutting her eyes after another adventurous day onboard the *Arthur Broome*.

— CHAPTER 12 —
AERIAL DISEMBARKATION

*T*he next morning, Henry was awakened by a cheerful Penny licking his face. He gave her a big hug and then sprang out of bed to pull the curtains open. Bright sunlight immediately filled the dark cabin.

As Henry gazed at the passenger vessels and cargo ships passing by in the other direction, there was far more to see than just endless ocean waves this morning. For the first time in two days, land was in sight, and he could even see a pod of dolphins flanking the side of the ship; they were occasionally jumping out of the water to make their presence known.

"We must be in the English Channel!" Henry shouted. Penny was still perched on the corner of the bed and barked twice in response.

Despite the harrowing muster drill yesterday, Henry was excited for his first official day working alongside the Tutori. He gave Penny a quick bath and used a towel to dry her off before he jumped in the shower himself. Cleaned up and feeling refreshed, he grabbed one of the pressed gray wool suits out of the closet and swiftly got dressed for the day ahead.

Henry looked down at Penny. "We need to thank Rufus again the next time we see him." The immense pride beaming from his face as he tightened the Windsor knot on his tie had Penny feeling a tad bit envious. She thought he looked quite dashing in his new attire, although she wished Rufus had prepared a matching suit for her as well.

"We better get going, Penny. I don't want to miss anything!" Henry announced. After tying the laces on his new shoes, he grabbed Penny's rucksack. "Guess I should bring this just in case, eh?" Penny smiled and eagerly barked once in agreement.

Henry was afraid that Otis and Oscar were waiting to surprise them again, so he opened the door to his cabin cautiously. Oddly enough, the pair of mischievous brothers were nowhere to be found. "Where are those otters when we need them?" he asked with a hint of panic in his voice.

This wasn't just an ordinary meeting. Henry knew that if he didn't arrive on time, the rest of the Tutori would likely leave without him. With his dreams of shadowing the legendary Tutori at risk of being derailed, he closed his cabin door and headed toward the elevator. Penny trotted blissfully behind, wondering if they were going to the dining hall for breakfast.

"Maybe we should go to the grand atrium and look for help, eh?" Henry asked Penny. He pushed the elevator call button and anxiously waited. His mind was racing and consumed by thoughts about what would happen if he didn't show up on time. The *APA* had very little patience for excuses, and Henry didn't want to get left behind. This could be his only opportunity to prove himself in front of a real Tutori.

Henry stammered, trying to remember the series of numbers the otters pressed yesterday when they rode the elevator together to the grand atrium. The fear and increasing anxiety of being tardy just obscured his memory further.

Moments later, the elevator on the left arrived, and the doors opened as the bell chimed. Henry welcomed the feeling of respite when he saw who was waiting for him, even if it was only temporary.

"The otters! Guys, we need your help!" Henry shouted, rushing into the elevator. Penny followed him warily. She still didn't fully trust Otis and Oscar yet and was mindful to keep her distance from the pair of rambunctious sea otters.

Despite the knowledgeable tour guides now at his disposal, Henry wasn't ready to celebrate just yet. He pleaded, "We need to get to the top deck at the aft of the ship right away!" hoping the otters understood the urgent nature of his quandary.

Otis and Oscar nodded their heads at the same time and then raced each other to the panel of buttons. Oscar managed to get there slightly ahead of his brother. His tiny paws moved fast, but Henry saw him press *1–4–0–1*.

"Good grief, I need to start writing these numbers down, eh?" Henry muttered. He realized that the only series of elevator buttons that he actually remembered was his own cabin number.

Clearly annoyed that Oscar got to push the buttons, Otis spent the rest of the elevator ride chasing his brother around. They darted in between Henry's legs while Penny stood defensively in the corner.

After changing directions a few times, the elevator finally came to a stop, and the doors opened on the top deck platform at the back of the ship.

"You're late!" Barnaby remarked. Savannah and Professor Blackfriar chuckled as June and Archie stood next to them. They didn't say anything, but June's eyes lit up when he arrived.

Henry shrugged and replied confusedly, "Late? It's seven-thirty, just like you said, eh?" Barnaby seemed to ignore his retort and carried on with the preparations to disembark.

Everyone appeared to have some sort of black pack strapped to their backs, almost like Henry's rucksack, but these were no ordinary bags. The black harness straps around their chests and legs left him wondering what was inside the tightly secured packs.

Valentina was also there, standing next to a massive winch system off to the side. She had on her normal Carabinieri uniform and was the only person not wearing a black pack on her back. The list of unanswered questions kept piling up. There was no helicopter in sight, and Henry couldn't fathom how they would be getting off the ship, especially from all the way on the top deck.

Unexpectedly, the *Arthur Broome* picked up speed in a noticeable way as Barnaby suddenly tossed an extra black pack at him. "Put this on, mate."

"What's going on here? Is this... a parachute?" Henry asked, absolutely baffled. Barnaby smirked while Henry held up the black pack by the straps and stuttered, "I, uh, I don't... I thought we were leaving on a helicopter."

Everybody chuckled, except for Archie and Valentina; the first officer of the *Arthur Broome* simply shook her head and sighed. She knew Barnaby all too well. She quickly realized he hadn't prepared Henry for his first aerial disembarkation.

Barnaby responded cheerfully, "What's the mattah, Halifax? You've never been parasailing over there in Kodiak Bay?"

"*Parasailing*? We're jumping off the ship? It's a bit early for the pranks today, no?" Henry said, with a bewildered look on his face. Barnaby stepped forward brazenly and snatched the black pack out of his hands. "Maybe it's best you just wait for us on the ship then. Sounds like you're a little light on experience... and courage too, it seems, huh? No shame in backing out, pal. I wouldn't want to see you break your ankle or something else when you hit the ground."

Before Henry could protest, Barnaby continued trying to discourage the young Canadian further. "No worries, mate. I gave you my word, and I'll have that pair of polar bear cubs back here in no time at all. Why don't you and Penny go relax? Enjoy the breakfast buffet, alright? I heard the chef is serving up a fresh batch of Canada's finest tree sap with the waffles this morning."

"Well, that's awfully kind of you, Mr. Murdoch," Henry jested sarcastically with a forced smile.

Undeterred, he asserted, "But I think I'd rather follow the council's orders. Which, if I recall correctly, meant I was to shadow you wherever you go... starting the moment you step foot off this ship." He boldly quipped, "Only until those bears have been rescued, of course."

Henry could tell that Barnaby assumed he would chicken out the second he saw the parachutes. Even though he considered taking the easy way out as Barnaby suggested, the breakfast buffet would have to wait for now.

"Alright, mate... Suit yourself," Barnaby snickered as he tossed the packed parachute back to Henry. "But don't say I didn't warn ya if you end up in the hospital."

Worried that he could be putting Penny in real danger, a tempting sense of apprehension began to spread throughout Henry's body. He never imagined a parachute would be needed for anything when he boarded the *Arthur Broome* yesterday. He was now dreading the part where he had to actually follow through on the defiant assertions he had made just moments ago.

"Don't worry, Huey! Just hit the ground running, and you should be fine," Savannah advised reassuringly.

Henry noticed Savannah called him by the wrong name once again, but he was too distracted by the trepidation clouding his mind to correct her. It didn't matter if he was terrified about the impending aerial departure—he couldn't back out now, not like this. He might as well put a sign around his neck with the word COWARD written on the front, because that's what everyone would be thinking if he scampered off to breakfast while the others bravely carried out their duties.

Trying his best to remain calm, Henry took a deep breath and stepped forward to put his leg through the parachute straps. The panicked expression painted on his face proved to be too much for June, and she suddenly rushed over. "Okay, stop! Henry can ride tandem with me so that he doesn't get hurt."

Savannah looked over at Barnaby and Professor Blackfriar. They were all equally impressed to see June's intervention in Henry's unwavering stubbornness.

"*Really*? Oh, that would be great! Thank you!" Henry exclaimed, sincerely appreciative of her gracious offer. Penny wasn't quite sure what was going on, but she cheerfully barked twice to reinforce his gratitude.

Valentina immediately walked over to add some more metal clips to the front of June's harness and candidly admitted, "Sì, it is much better this way." She winked at Henry to bolster his confidence as she finished adjusting the clips.

Henry welcomed the encouragement, and for the first time all morning, he remembered that he was capable of doing anything. If another person had already done it, he could do it too. He just had to be brave when it mattered most.

"Alright, let's go over this one more time," Barnaby ordered. "Since Halifax was late to the meeting, we need to recap the game plan here because there's no room for mistakes. We cannot come back empty-handed again."

Henry tilted his head disdainfully as Barnaby continued, "Now, I've already radioed the captain of the *Queen Charlotte*, and she's agreed to let us board before their disembarkation process begins." Somewhat surprised, Henry blurted, "*She?*"

"Yeah, that's right, mate!" Barnaby responded fiercely. His mood soured faster than a cat in a swimming pool. "You got a problem with that, Halifax? Think women can't be ship captains? Maybe she should just stay at home in the kitchen and make you a sandwich with a side of poutine? Is that what you're trying to say?" Henry made an effort to clarify right away. "No... I, uh, I didn't mean..."

"Well, let me tell you something, pal," Barnaby interrupted. "*It's 1962*! I don't know how it works in Canada, but women can do stuff now, alright? You're just gonna have to accept that as fact because last I checked, and I check every single morning, Savannah Sunday here can mop the floor with ya when it comes to anything you think you can do bettah! Say the word right now... Just say the word, and I'll have Archie here bring up some fresh maple syrup from the kitchen. Let's see who can drink the whole bottle quickah!" In a panicked voice, Henry stammered as he tried to explain himself. "No, no, no... You've got it all wrong. I, uh, I didn't mean that at all. I just never..."

Valentina knew he didn't mean anything by it and chimed in, "Would you just stop, Barnabas! Give the kid a break, will you?" She turned to Henry and patted him on the back. "Don't let Murdoch get to you."

"Alright, alright... Take it easy, mate. I was just having a laugh!" Barnaby confessed.

Henry's face was still bright red from being equally embarrassed and irritated by the Australian. He wanted to go a few rounds with Barnaby on the hockey rink (gloves off), but he managed to control his emotions as the Tutori got back to explaining the plan.

"We'll land on the top deck near the bow of the ship. Captain McHugh will be waiting for us at the landing zone. Prior to the passengers disembarking, we will take up positions at the gangway, shipside, and portside. The Frenchman will likely be wearing a disguise, so we need to look for the bag. It's a large black duffle bag, big enough to safely transport two small bear cubs."

Barnaby exhaled and warned, "Be careful out there, though. I've tangled with this maniac far too many times... and the darts don't seem to have any effect. So, watch your back out there, and go straight for the cattle proddah!"

"Oh, that's just bloody beautiful, innit, mate?" Professor Blackfriar chortled. "No matter," he shrugged, "I'm always ready to get my hands dirty... Ain't that right, Arch?"

Archie nodded his head and replied, "Indubitably, sir," while Professor Blackfriar carried on boasting, "Don't worry, Halifax. I have caught far more dangerous characters in my day... Ain't that right, Arch?"

"Course you have, sir," Archie answered right before Valentina announced, "Okay, it's time. Andiamo, Barnaby!"

With the *Arthur Broome* sailing at over twenty-five knots, Barnaby stood by the massive winch as Valentina clipped the cable hook to the front of his harness. Henry watched her intently as she unlocked the crank handle; the anticipation was palpable.

Valentina shouted, "Arrivederci!" as Barnaby yanked the ripcord on the parachute strapped to his back.

A dark-green parachute blasted out of the pack and was snatched by the wind, sending Barnaby flying into the air. He quickly drifted further away from the ship as the towline automatically unwound.

Unable to look away, Henry didn't blink once. His eyes were transfixed on Barnaby, soaring high above the English Channel.

The winch continued to let out just enough slack while Barnaby approached the predetermined height necessary for a safe release. A moment later, the constant clicking sound of the automatic winch ceased, signaling that the towline had been fully extended. Barnaby didn't hesitate and immediately unhooked the cable clipped to the front of his harness. It dropped into the water and dragged behind the ship, prompting Valentina to push the automatic retract button on the side of the winch.

Seeing Barnaby glide effortlessly across the sky gave Henry just enough confidence (in the moment) to think that he could do the same. "That doesn't look so hard," he murmured, watching the Australian pull down on the steering lines to guide his parachute toward the *Queen Charlotte*.

Once the towline had been fully retracted, Valentina turned to Henry and asked, "Andiamo, who's next?" He responded ambivalently, "Uh, maybe we should go over the game plan again?"

Savannah sneered as she brushed past Henry to volunteer. After the cable hook was secured to the front of her harness, Savannah thanked the Carabinieri officer, "Grazie, Valentina!"

The arrogant confidence led Henry to assume that Savannah had done this many times in the past. Still, he admired her temerity and was captivated by the absence of fear on her part. She didn't seem nervous in the slightest. Right before she pulled her ripcord, Savannah howled with laughter and shouted, "You're looking at the game plan, Huxley!" The parachute caught the passing wind instantly and sent her soaring up into the air.

Professor Blackfriar and Archie followed shortly thereafter. Only June, Henry, Penny, and Valentina remained on the top deck of the *Arthur Broome*.

"This is the way. Andiamo, my friends!" Valentina affirmed, looking over at Henry and June.

Henry kneeled down and said, "Alright, let's go, Penny," gesturing for her to climb into the rucksack. She dashed into the bag without hesitation. He put the rucksack on backward, securing it to the front of his chest since he was riding tandem with June.

Penny immediately repositioned herself. She stuck her head out of the top of the rucksack while Valentina finished securing the back of Henry's harness to the front of June's.

Valentina warned, "Last chance if you have a fear of heights!" as she winked at Penny and hooked the towline to the front of Henry's harness. He mumbled, "It's too late to be scared now."

Henry knew his chances of becoming a Tutori would be over if he backed out. He tried to remain calm, although all he could focus on was the sound of his heart racing faster than ever. "Don't worry, Henry. I've done this more than a few times," June whispered in an attempt to dispel his fears. She could feel Henry trembling, which reminded her of the first time she was in this exact situation not long ago.

Once Valentina returned to the winch, she unlocked the crank and shouted, "Buona fortuna!"

June yanked the ripcord fearlessly, and a split second later, they were sent flying into the air, soaring high above the *Arthur Broome*. The parachute whisked up and away, almost like a roller coaster. However, getting off this ride early wasn't an option, and the terror only intensified the moment Henry's feet left the top deck.

Penny retreated into her rucksack, frightened. Clearly not a fan of heights, she decided the juice wasn't worth the squeeze in this instance and was happy to wait until they landed before coming out again.

Henry concentrated all his energy on keeping both eyes sealed shut. Each passing gust of wind that blew through his hair and whooshed past his dangling feet wasn't helping either. Stiff as a board, he didn't open his eyes during the entire ascent. He was worried that any irregular movements would cause the parachute to fall to the ground unexpectedly.

Once they reached the optimum height, June unhooked the towline and used both hands to grab ahold of the parachute steering lines. "You can open your eyes now, Henry. I promise it's safe," she said humorously to reassure him.

Henry finally found the courage to face his fears, slowly squinting until he could see what lay ahead. His first instinct was to panic, and it would have been absolutely warranted after he glanced down at the water below, but a surprising sense of serenity washed over his body. There was something about seeing Barnaby, Savannah, Professor Blackfriar, and Archie gliding through the clouds in front of them that gave him solace. Whatever happened next was out of his control anyway, and he trusted that June would never do anything to jeopardize their safety.

June, on the other hand, was enjoying the ride as only a real Texan could. She took great pride in mastering the art of landing and was determined to impress Henry with her pinpoint accuracy (especially since it was his first time). In fact, she never turned down an opportunity to practice and relished the thrill of it all. She maneuvered their parachute like a professional, using the steering lines to guide them on the same course as the four parachutes ahead of them.

From their high vantage point in the sky, it didn't take long before they spotted the *Queen Charlotte*. Unlike Kodiak Bay, the majestic ocean liner wasn't the largest ship in this part of the world, and it paled in comparison to some of the gargantuan vessels slowly navigating the channel.

The tugboats circling the waterway looked like small toys from the sky above, but it was the enormous livestock carrier vessel docked nearby that grabbed Henry's attention. It was impossible to miss, and he marveled at the sheer size of the gigantic ship parked next to the familiar ocean liner.

As June steered their parachute lower, Barnaby landed on the top deck of the *Queen Charlotte* first.

Henry was impressed by the Australian's landing but gasped when Barnaby detached his parachute. The passing wind sent the dark-green canopy whirling into the air; it billowed aimlessly in the sky like a butterfly floundering in a tornado and suddenly burst into flames a moment later.

The parachute disappeared in that instant, right before Henry's eyes. He was completely astounded by what he had just witnessed.

One by one, Henry stared in astonishment as Savannah,

Professor Blackfriar, and Archie touched down on the main deck. Their parachutes were also swept up by the wind after they released them, catching fire and disintegrating into thin air just like Barnaby's. It closely resembled a small fireworks show, only without the loud crackling and banging that would normally follow.

Henry assumed there must have been a miniature igniter built into the chutes, combined with some sort of controlled chemical reaction. He wasn't sure exactly how it worked, but he thought it was a feat of extraordinary ingenuity all the same.

Penny was anxious by nature (like most dachshunds are), yet she found the nerve to peek her small head out of the rucksack secured to Henry's chest. "It's okay, girl. We're okay... We're okay," he whispered into her ear. Even though she trusted Henry more than anyone else in the world, Penny wasn't entirely convinced and recoiled back into the bag instinctively.

As June and Henry gradually descended, the colossal size of the *Queen Charlotte* became apparent. "Follow my lead and hit the ground running, alright?" June instructed, tugging on the steering lines to bring the parachute into position for the final approach. Henry was desperately afraid of breaking his ankle upon landing and was too distracted to say anything. He merely nodded his head in silence, trying to remain calm.

Barnaby looked up in amusement and grinned when he noticed that Henry had started the running motions far too soon; the young boy's legs were erratically flailing back and forth in the air.

Archie knew the feeling all too well and couldn't help but chuckle at the sight of Henry's comical attempts to run in midair. He recalled his first aerial disembarkation and wasn't ashamed to admit he did the same thing while riding tandem with the professor.

June steered their parachute closer toward the deck. "Here we go, here we go... Get ready!" she warned seconds before their feet touched the deck of the *Queen Charlotte*.

Professor Blackfriar shook his head while Barnaby and Savannah burst into laughter as they all watched June and Henry take a tumble on what proved to be a rough landing. Genuinely concerned that Henry may have injured himself, Archie raced over to check on them. "Are you okay? Is everyone alright?"

Penny leaped out of the rucksack. She continued to frantically lick Henry's face as June unhooked the harness.

"Come on now, Arch. Y'all didn't think I was going to let anything happen to Penny now, did ya?" June shouted confidently. She detached her parachute, which sent it flying into the sky, bursting into flames when a strong gust of wind breezed by. She winked at Henry, sticking her hand out to help him up. "Not bad for your first time, Kodiak Bay!"

Archie patted Henry on the back and added, "Good on you, mate. The first time is always scary, innit? It's in the past now, though! It only gets easier after that!" Feeling grateful to be standing on the deck instead of limping off to the infirmary, Henry replied, "It's harder than it looks... That's for sure, eh?"

The three of them walked over to join Barnaby, Savannah, and Professor Blackfriar, who were now talking to the captain of the *Queen Charlotte*.

"Crikey! How good was the look on his face?" Barnaby joked with the others. He roared with laughter, despite the fact that it was clear the whole experience was quite terrifying for the kid and his furry companion. "Yeah, don't worry, we're fine... Thanks for asking," Henry quipped, shaking his head in response to Barnaby's lack of compassion.

Penny didn't take kindly to the snide comment either, and she let the Australian know with a few raucous barks. She was upset that Barnaby wasn't more concerned, especially considering this was her first aerial disembarkation. Even a fresh sweet potato stick wouldn't have persuaded her to forgive him so easily.

"Well, who is this beautiful little lady?" Captain McHugh said, kneeling to gently pet the top of the wirehaired dachshund's head.

Sniffing the captain's hand defensively, Penny inched backward at first, only to change her mind seconds later. She eventually nestled her head against Captain McHugh's palm.

Henry smiled and answered, "Oh, this is Penny, ma'am. Penny Halifax."

"She is too cute! What a beautiful soul!" the captain remarked as she stood up. Delighted by the young visitors (and Henry's pint-sized sidekick most of all), Captain McHugh smiled and warmly added, "Welcome aboard the *Queen Charlotte*."

— CHAPTER 13 —
THE RMS QUEEN CHARLOTTE

J ane Marie McHugh was a highly accomplished seafarer who spent years climbing the ranks from third mate all the way up to captain of the RMS *Queen Charlotte*.

Always sharply dressed in her uniform, she had brown eyes and long brown hair that went just past her shoulders. It was obvious that she took care of herself with routine exercise.

All she ever wanted to be was the captain of an ocean liner. Despite being one of only a few female captains in the entire world to take control of a ship as large as the *Queen Charlotte*, she commanded respect everywhere she went, from both her crew and other sailors alike. Those who doubted her were quickly embarrassed. She worked harder than anyone else onboard and wasn't afraid to tackle any job on the ship, regardless of the potential dangers that awaited.

Henry could easily sense her empathy and compassion for animals right away. His assumptions were confirmed moments later after Barnaby asked, "So, how's Belle doing anyway?"

"Still the most beautiful Himalayan feline sailing the seven seas," Captain McHugh boasted. She glanced up toward the ship's bridge and added, "Last I saw, she was lounging in my cabin, wrapped up in a soft blanket next to the window."

"Well, please do send her my love, Captain... And we sincerely appreciate your cooperation regarding this matter," he replied cheerfully.

The smile on Barnaby's face vanished, and his demeanor turned far more serious. "Alright, back to business. We know the Frenchman boarded this ship before it left Kodiak Bay, traveling with two stolen polar bear cubs. Captain McHugh has graciously agreed to let us monitor the disembarkation process, where we'll take up positions on each side of the gangway." He exhaled, "Now, just remember one thing... Captain McHugh is in command of this vessel. If any of you spot the duffle bag or the Frenchman on this side of the gangway, ya better run it by her first."

"Don't be a hero, ok? We will handle this matter... but we will handle it discreetly and with respect, agreed?" Barnaby remarked.

Everybody (including Penny) nodded in silence to concur. "Brilliant! Now, if ya don't mind, Professor, I'd like you and Archie to cover the shipside of the gangway. Savannah, June, and Halifax will stay onboard with me to oversee the passenger disembarkation process," he instructed.

Captain McHugh chimed in, "Sounds good to me. Let's find those bears!" She turned around and walked off toward the gangway deck while everyone except Henry followed.

Henry trusted Penny implicitly, but this wasn't the time or place to let her wander around; he bent down and instructed the wirehaired dachshund to climb into the rucksack. He swung the rucksack over his shoulder and raced to catch up with the others. The sound of Penny's nose sniffing the passing breeze reverberated in Henry's ear as he proceeded across the deck toward the stairs. "Okay, my good girl. Let me know if you smell those bears! I know you'll pick up on the scent if we get close enough," he whispered confidently.

Penny licked his ear and smiled. She routinely did this when riding in the rucksack on his back, although this particular instance was meant to confirm her ability to help find the missing polar bears. After all, the rascally dachshund had the most powerful nose in the group.

As Henry, Archie, and June trailed behind the others, June blurted, "So, you saw the Frenchman in Kodiak Bay, right? Did you get a good look at him, Henry?"

There were many things he could do well, but lying wasn't one of them. From the time Henry uttered his first words, Captain Fulbright instilled the importance of integrity. The captain would repeatedly tell him: *"There's nothing more sacred than following through on your word if you shake someone's hand and make a promise."*

In fact, Captain Fulbright never worked with signed contracts or paperwork back on the docks in Kodiak Bay. Every agreement between himself, the fishermen, and anyone else who docked their boat in his harbor was made through a handshake.

Henry desperately wanted to tell his new friends everything, but he knew he couldn't—at least not yet. Keeping Barnaby's secrets was proving to be a full-time job. It put him in a sticky situation, rife with guilt and considerable dubiety.

In a bumbling attempt to steer June away from Barnaby's web of deceit, Henry replied, "Uh, well... the Frenchman was, um... wearing a disguise at the zoo. But I would recognize that black duffle bag anywhere."

Archie interjected, "Never underestimate a hound, June. Penny has over a hundred million scent receptors in that little nose of hers. She was born to hunt, and I'd trust her nose over anyone else's in this whole lot to find those bears." The group rounded the corner at midship and headed down the stairs toward the gangway deck.

With passengers already queued and waiting impatiently to

disembark, Barnaby and Captain McHugh walked to the gangway exit while Henry and everyone else followed. The captain shook hands with the ship's chief of security, a short Indian woman who had emerald-green eyes and black hair, and explained the situation to her at once. The chief of security then introduced herself to Barnaby, Savannah, and Professor Blackfriar.

After a brief discussion, the professor headed down the gangway into the boarding terminal. Archie followed closely behind, though he couldn't shake the feeling that the Frenchman might have already escaped.

"I'm gonna go scan the passenger queue... See if I can spot that black duffle bag in the crowds. You all stay here and mind the gangway," Barnaby ordered. He looked at Savannah and sternly added, "Remember why we're here. We're here for the bears, and the bears only. That's the only priority. Apprehending the Frenchman is a distant second. So, let's handle this quietly, alright?"

"This ain't my first rodeo, hunny... If I were you, I'd be more concerned about catching another beating from this guy," Savannah snickered. Barnaby was overly sensitive sometimes, and in the interest of avoiding a shouting match, she acknowledged, "I got it, I got it... Don't worry. Polar bears first, the French maniac second, okay?" Unamused, Barnaby stormed off to take a closer look at the passengers standing in the queue.

Henry was more interested in the passengers trudging past the chief of security. He watched intently, hoping to come across the black duffle bag as they walked by, one by one. While scanning the area, he could hear Penny's nose sniffing rapidly as she worked to process the mix of scents wafting in her direction.

Thirty minutes quickly passed. June, Savannah, and Henry were growing more doubtful with each passenger that walked by and began to question Barnaby's plan altogether. "Who knows if he's even here?" Savannah bemoaned, "The Frenchman could have already slipped away in a lifeboat by now!"

Henry and June continued watching, undeterred. They looked for any signs of suspicious behavior as more passengers shuffled off the ship. Nothing seemed out of the ordinary until a ship porter pushed a luggage cart to the front of the line. It was packed full; suitcases and bags of all shapes and sizes were overloaded beyond the maximum capacity of the cart. The luggage porter leaned in to talk to the ship's security officer, which obscured his face from Henry's vantage point.

At the same moment, the sound of Penny's sniffing intensified. Henry had a feeling something was wrong and whispered, "What is it, girl?" He felt Penny's long body tense up almost immediately, like she had just picked up on the scent of a passing badger. Muffled growling ensued, capturing June's attention as well.

With his head still hidden behind the luggage, the porter continued pushing the cart onto the gangway once he got the all-clear signal from security. The subtle attempt to slink by undetected only inflamed Penny's suspicions, and her growling had grown loud enough for Savannah to take notice. Savannah, June, Henry, and Penny stared down the gangway like a pack of wrathful hyenas waiting for the right time to pounce.

The older gentleman pushing the luggage cart was wearing a burgundy uniform and seemed awfully strong for a man of his age; there must have been over *one hundred fifty kilograms* of luggage on the cart, and he wasn't even breaking a sweat. Interestingly enough, there was at least one large black bag sticking out of the stacked luggage. From that distance, though, none of them could determine with certainty if it was the duffle bag they were searching for.

When the next passenger stepped up to the security desk, Savannah stuck her arm out to block anyone else from leaving the ship. She looked toward the luggage porter and shouted, "Hey, you!

With the luggage cart! Stop right there!"

Savannah's commands were reinforced by Penny. She viciously barked at least three times before Henry whispered some calming words into her ear.

Still a few steps away from exiting the gangway, the man pushing the luggage cart froze the second he heard Savannah's voice. The porter casually turned around and gazed at the group. Instead of looking flabbergasted, they were confronted with the most evil grin Henry had ever seen—it was the kind of wicked smile that implied something very bad was about to happen.

Without any warning, the man in the burgundy uniform took off in the opposite direction, pushing the luggage cart at full speed in a mad dash to exit the gangway.

"Barnaby! Barnaby! We found him!" Henry shouted frantically while Savannah rushed down the gangway to apprehend the imposter.

Despite her best efforts, the man in the porter's uniform had other plans; he tipped over the luggage cart, causing a wave of commotion as he yanked out a large black duffle bag. The rest of the suitcases toppled over, and Savannah was instantly knocked backward by the mountain of luggage spilling onto the gangway. It was a chaotic mess that completely blocked her path to the exit.

Barnaby heard the clattering ruckus and quickly came running from the passenger queue to find Savannah, June, and Henry tossing luggage to the side as they tried to clear a path on the narrow gangway.

Archie saw the bedlam unfolding and hurried over to block the gangway exit on the terminal side. All those years of playing goalie for his summer football league back home didn't seem to help one bit—he was sent crashing into a nearby pile of *twenty kilogram* flour bags after the luggage porter bulldozed right through him like he was a catcher standing on home plate in Rockford.

Unfortunately for Archie, the ship's crew was in the process of carrying a fresh supply of food onto the ship, and he couldn't get out of the way in time. White flour spread everywhere across the terminal as if it were smoke in a burning building, which just added to the chaos and confusion.

As the luggage porter ran to escape, Professor Blackfriar grabbed him from behind, unsuspectingly.

Working as fast as they could to clear the gangway, Barnaby and Savannah continued heaving luggage while June, Henry, and Penny watched helplessly and tried to stay out of the way. The tussle on the other side of the gangway was only turning more violent in the meantime.

Professor Blackfriar appeared to have the upper hand, but the tables quickly turned when he slammed the man in the burgundy uniform up against the wall. All of a sudden, the professor screamed, "Damn you, Catherine!" Everyone gasped in disbelief when they saw Professor Blackfriar collapsing to the ground with the luggage porter's wig in his hand.

Getting two tranquilizer darts shoved in his leg definitely wasn't part of the plan, but the professor had other reasons for his angry outburst. Slumped over and seconds away from being knocked out entirely by the tranquilizer, he realized there wouldn't be enough time to pay a visit to his favorite chippy in all of London. Professor Blackfriar even skipped breakfast to ensure he could take on a double serving.

With a crucial aspect of her disguise ruined, Catherine's red-flowing hair was now on full display. She slowly peeled the fake white mustache off her upper lip, taunting, "Bonjour, Barnabas! Nice to see you again... And so soon, oui?"

Unable to resist, Catherine winked at Savannah and jeered, "Nice boots, Sunday... très chic. I hope you can run fast in them, cowboy!"

Savannah became enraged. She started chucking pieces of luggage up the gangway toward the ship while Catherine sauntered away in the direction leading to the port terminal exit.

Still covered in white flour, Archie dusted himself off. He rushed over to the professor's motionless body to check on him as Savannah and Barnaby finished clearing the remaining suitcases, finally making it down the gangway.

"Archie, call this in and get the professah back to the ship. Look after 'em, alright, mate?" Barnaby hollered. The British Magari didn't hesitate and obediently replied, "Roger that, sir."

A cloud of white flour continued spreading throughout the terminal hall, making it difficult to see anything beyond a few meters. More concerned about their fellow colleague, June and Henry raced over to see if Archie needed any help.

Barnaby and Savannah paused for a moment, squinting through the haze of flour to see in which direction Catherine had absconded. The crowds of travelers trying to make sense of the unusual downpour of baking ingredients weren't making things any easier.

"What the hell was that about? You knew it was her the whole time?" Savannah yelled. Barnaby knew there were more pressing matters to deal with at the moment and attempted to downplay the allegations. "Alright, take it easy... It's not what ya think. I can..."

"There! That's her!" Savannah interrupted before sprinting away. She spotted Catherine heading for the exit and wasn't interested in hearing any more rash excuses.

"June! Henry! Let's go!" Barnaby commanded, racing to catch up to Savannah. Archie affirmed, "Get after them! We'll be fine!"

Hurrying as fast as they could to chase after Barnaby, June and Henry left Archie to attend to the professor.

Penny was thoroughly enjoying all the excitement (including the powdered flour falling like snowflakes on her tongue) and didn't mind all the jostling. Riding in the rucksack on Henry's back was usually much tamer, but she loved a good chase, even if she was only a spectator.

Barnaby, Henry, and June tore through the passenger terminal, brushing past the crowds of unsuspecting travelers. Once they eventually made it outside, the group came to a screeching halt. Savannah was already in a tense standoff with Catherine, and it didn't look like either of them were going to back down.

Gripping a lasso in her hand, Savannah was secretly hoping Catherine would give her a reason to use it—she loved any chance to show off her lassoing skills, especially on those that tried to escape the relentless wrath of the *APA*. While Barnaby dashed over to help her, June and Henry cautiously stood out of the way.

Henry remembered what happened the last time Catherine got cornered and presumed it was best to keep a safe distance for now. They had veered off toward the freight walkway that ran parallel with the River Thames; it was incredibly noisy due to the hundreds of cattle being unloaded from the livestock carrier docked next to the *Queen Charlotte*.

Barnaby grabbed the electric cattle prod from the holster on his belt and, with a flick of the wrist, the collapsed part instantly expanded into a full-length baton, sending a charge of electricity sparking at the tip. "That's enough, Catherine! It's all ovah!" he shouted in an attempt to diffuse the hostile showdown.

Savannah chuckled and scornfully remarked, "Not so fast, Murdoch! This French scoundrel needs to be taught some manners... and, come hell or high water, she's not going anywhere until I show her how it's done in Texas."

Shaking his head in frustration, Barnaby advised, "Listen, Catherine, just set the bears down and walk away, alright?"

"You ain't getting off that easy!" Savannah chimed in, uninterested in letting Catherine or the bears escape. "Don't matter if ya walk or run for your life. I'm still bringing you in either way. So, give it up while my generous offer is still on the table... 'cause I'm fixin' to embarrass ya in front of these kids if you test my patience any further."

Catherine smiled menacingly. She wasn't intimidated in the slightest, and the defiance in her eyes only became more apparent. "Embarrassed? Moi?" she chuckled, dismissing Savannah's empty threats. Her lighthearted laugh escalated to a sinister cackle before she unleashed a scathing response. "I think it would be impossible to embarrass anyone except for yourself in that ridiculous hat, no?"

Savannah found the unwavering rebelliousness infuriating, and it didn't help matters when Catherine added, "Honestly, I am offended that you would even ask, especially in front of these young Magari. You both know these bears don't belong to the *Animal Protection Authority*... and they don't belong to that zoo either."

"So, I suggest you take the kids and run along now. Maybe go back to the ship to have some milk and cookies with the council before you get hurt. You can tell them I did your job for you... again," Catherine sneered in a daring attempt to persuade them, even though her tone was consumed by a combination of arrogance and insolence.

Disappointed to see that Barnaby had still not holstered his cattle prodder, Catherine's playful demeanor vanished, and she warned, "Or don't... but I'd start working on your excuses now if you want to keep those cloaks, because these bears are coming with me."

In one slick motion, a lighter promptly appeared in Catherine's hand—very much like a magician pulling something from his sleeve in the middle of a trick. She spun around, started to walk away, and in the process, foolishly underestimated Savannah's resolve.

It all happened so quickly. Like a cowboy wrangling a bull, Savannah twirled her lasso up into the air and suddenly flung her arm forward. The rope hurtled toward Catherine, catching her by surprise just when she thought they had given up.

Henry and June watched in astonishment, both speechless and impressed at the same time. June had been to the rodeo more times than she could count back in Texas, but this was her first time witnessing Savannah lasso someone on the job.

After what many would consider to be a perfect throw, Savannah yanked on the rope to tighten the grip. Catherine instantly rolled her eyes in annoyance when her arms became constricted.

Savannah tugged on the rope vigorously, which sent Catherine crashing to the ground, and the lighter fell out of her hand, clanging as it bounced off the concrete.

"Got her! Now, that's how it's done, Barnaby!" Savannah celebrated arrogantly as she and Barnaby walked over toward Catherine. She added, "Yeah, it breaks my heart, 'cause you two steps away from a has-been, Murdoch."

"And that haircut isn't helping," she quipped, referring to Barnaby's insistence on growing his hair out longer than most men his age.

Unbeknownst to the approaching pair of Tutori, Catherine still had another trick up her sleeve. While Savannah blathered on and was distracted with her ego and her insatiable need to prove she was a better Tutori than Barnaby, Catherine managed to pull out a switchblade.

Henry was skeptical that Catherine would give up so easily, and he stuck his arm out to block June when she stepped forward in the same direction. "Hang on a minute," he cautioned instinctively. He remembered the last time Catherine had been cornered back in Kodiak Bay. The incident left his ears ringing for hours and also ended quite poorly for Barnaby.

June brushed off his warranted sense of concern and pronounced, "They got her, Henry. It's safe now! It's all over!" racing to join Savannah and Barnaby, while Henry stayed behind.

The second June took a few steps forward, Penny growled in Henry's ear, and the suspicious dachshund began sniffing the air as if she had just picked up on a familiar scent.

Moments later, the sounds of Savannah's celebratory prattling fell silent when Catherine suddenly stood up; the lasso dropped to the ground with a defeating thud. With a stick of dynamite in her hand, Catherine lit the fuse and jested, "You don't have the time, do you? I've got a train to catch!"

Savannah, Barnaby, and June were instantly transfixed by the sight of the fuse burning. The group was stunned and only had a moment to deal with the repercussions that followed their arrogance.

"Damn you, Catherine!" Barnaby shouted furiously before grabbing June by the arm and retreating back toward Henry.

The disbelief on Savannah's face was ever-present, even as she fled in the same direction to take cover a split second after Barnaby.

Catherine burst into laughter. She relished in delight at the sight of them running for their lives (especially Savannah) and nonchalantly tossed the burning stick of dynamite next to the fence that kept the adjacent cattle from getting out.

Frightened by the unexpected commotion, the sound of mooing intensified among the startled bovines that were shuffling to get away—the hissing and terrifying noise of the sparks showering the ground as the fuse continued to burn was an unwelcome surprise. Henry ran for safety while Barnaby, Savannah, and June frantically tried to catch up.

The sound of exploding dynamite reverberated throughout the freight walkway and could even be heard on the other side of the River Thames. Dirt and debris scattered in every direction, blanketing the area in a cloud of dust.

Disoriented and struggling to get up, everyone appeared to be unharmed, but the damage was done. The huge hole that remained in the cattle holding area left Henry fearing the worst was yet to come.

Five meters of the side fencing had been completely obliterated. The cattle were alarmed, although none of them had actually been injured. Entranced by the sweet sight of freedom, the pack of cows near the opening trudged past the remains of the mangled fence.

Barnaby, Savannah, June, and Henry immediately noticed that Catherine was nowhere to be found. Between the hordes of cattle scrambling to escape the holding area and the clouds of dusty haze drifting down the walkway, it was nearly impossible to see anything. Poor visibility aside, everyone could tell the trouble was far from over when they heard Catherine's wicked cackle echo from a distance.

As the sounds of her maniacal laughter carried further away, Catherine taunted, "Giddy up, cowboy!" (presumably directed at the lasso-wielding Tutori she had just outwitted).

Enraged in a way that June had never seen before, Savannah charged through the thick dust and smoke while the others ran behind her, trying to keep pace. Unsurprisingly, the black duffle bag and the polar cubs were gone. When they finally got a glimpse of Catherine, they could see she had reached the end of the cargo walkway.

Despite Savannah's first instinct to carry on chasing after Catherine, the droves of cattle racing out of the newly created hole in the fence brought them all to an abrupt stop. With a stampede of angry cattle flooding the narrow walkway and hundreds more clamoring to get out of the holding area, Barnaby shouted, "It's too dangerous! We have to take the long way!"

Savannah didn't want to turn around, but she knew Barnaby was right. She pushed him aside in fury and sprinted back toward the passenger terminal exit. June and Barnaby followed, leaving Henry behind.

Henry had become distracted by Penny's incessant squirming

and kneeled to let her out of the rucksack; she was tired of riding on his back and started barking fiercely in his ear the moment Savannah rushed off. Unencumbered and free to stretch her legs, Penny bolted as soon as he set her down. She zipped past Barnaby and June with ease as Henry tried to catch up.

The five of them pushed their way through the crowds of curious travelers meandering about in the terminal. Everyone inside had heard the explosion, and they were still confused as the last remnants of flour settled.

Most of the security guards were preoccupied, doing their best to calm the nervous people congregating near the door by the freight walkway. Henry heard them announce that it was probably just a large cargo container that had accidentally crashed onto the docks, likely dropped by a drowsy crane operator who hadn't sobered up before clocking in for work today. "The same thing happened last week!" the lead security guard asserted. "There's no need to panic. Everything is fine."

After Barnaby, Savannah, June, Henry, and Penny exited the terminal on the other side, they spotted Catherine dancing proudly in the middle of the street near the cargo walkway entrance. She was directing the stampede of angry cattle toward the tourist-laden *Tower Bridge*, and she didn't seem to notice the Tutori watching from afar.

Traffic on the bridge and in the vicinity became gridlocked, which only compounded the chaos unfolding in one of the busiest parts of London. Clearly unamused, irritated Londoners started honking their car horns in frustration.

Savannah was still fuming and loudly cracked her knuckles on both hands before resuming the pursuit. She didn't say a word to Barnaby or the others as she took off running.

Catherine reveled in the calamity. When she eventually noticed Barnaby's black cloak billowing in the passing breeze, it didn't take her long to spot Savannah—the irate Texan was like a bull that had been provoked one too many times, charging ahead blindly and coming straight for the matador. Instead of immediately running away, though, Catherine stuck around (looking Savannah directly in the eyes) to lob another rage-inducing taunt. "You still want these bears, or no?"

The howling laughter that followed was enough to send Barnaby, June, Henry, and Penny racing alongside the stampede of cattle over to the bridge. Catherine didn't want to press her luck and fled once again with the black duffle bag just as another wave of frightened cattle hampered Savannah's pursuit.

Countless livestock were still pouring out of the cargo walkway and onto the bridge. Catching up to Catherine would not be easy, and they struggled to keep pace in the midst of dodging hundreds of panicked cattle flooding the streets.

With car horns honking, cows mooing, and people hysterically shouting, Barnaby, June, Henry, and Penny caught up to Savannah and remained vigilant in their search for any sign of Catherine after crossing the bridge. They watched for any trace of her long, red hair in the sea of pandemonium unfolding around them, swiveling their heads back and forth like a bald eagle hunting for prey.

Flustered and increasingly worried that Catherine had already escaped, Barnaby knew there would be severe consequences if he returned to the council empty-handed again. As the panic in his eyes grew louder, he paced and began murmuring to himself.

Just as their predicament seemed hopeless, Penny's nose pointed the group in the right direction. She erupted in a barrage of raucous barking before suddenly tearing down Tooley Street.

"There she is! That's her! She's headed for the train station!" Barnaby announced when he spotted Catherine's long, red hair amongst the crowds of people on the busy sidewalk. Along with Savannah and June, he chased after the brazen dachshund west on

Tooley Street.

Henry had already started running in that same direction the instant Penny took off. He was more worried about her safety than anything else at this point, and he was furious that she left his side without permission.

As he rounded the corner, Henry spotted Penny standing across from the train station and quickly snatched her up with his arm. "I told you to stick close to me!" he fumed, scolding her like an angry parent who had just witnessed an unsupervised toddler doing something dangerous. She almost darted into oncoming traffic, and if he hadn't intervened, something terrible could have happened.

The anguish sprinkled in Henry's tone gave Penny pause. She was feeling a bit guilty for causing him so much distress and apologized by affectionately licking his face. She knew how to work those puppy-dog eyes better than most, and he couldn't help but smile as the anger melted away. "Please... don't do that to me again, Penny," he whispered into her ear while giving her a big hug.

Feeling relieved and thinking clearly again, Henry rushed across the street, carrying the black wirehaired dachshund in his arms. He barged through the front entrance of *London Bridge Station* and walked to the nearest platform.

Henry set Penny down on the ground and sternly ordered, "Now, behave yourself and don't leave my side, alright?" She agreed begrudgingly with a muffled growl but ultimately obeyed because she knew he was right. This was a train station, after all, and dogs weren't allowed without a leash.

Barnaby, Savannah, and June finally arrived moments later, winded and looking like they could have used a cold glass of water.

"The train to Paris!" June huffed, still panting and out of breath from running down Tooley Street. "Over there!" She pointed at the train parked alongside platform *#4*; it appeared to be on the verge of departing, and there were already quite a few people onboard.

"That's her! Third car from the rear!" Henry blurted out after spotting Catherine's red hair through the windows of the passenger railcar.

Penny growled with contempt. It was a stunning display of restraint for a dachshund that wanted nothing more than to take off running in Catherine's direction. Even Barnaby was impressed that Penny stopped herself in the face of badger-like temptation.

Barnaby laughed and declared, "We've got her now! Let's get refocused back on the mission and finish what we started!" motioning for everyone to follow him toward platform #4. Savannah found his positive attitude irritating. She simply nodded, pursed her lips, and crossed her arms defensively as the others walked ahead.

Without any warning, the brazen Texan dashed forward and grabbed the Australian Tutori by the cloak violently. She used his momentum to throw him up against the wall next to the payphones. It all happened in the blink of an eye and caught everyone by surprise (especially Barnaby).

June and Henry were absolutely stunned and couldn't look away.

Before Barnaby realized what was going on, Savannah pulled out her collapsible cattle prod and flicked her wrist toward the ground in one swift motion to extend the baton. She held him against the wall using her left hand and jammed the cattle prod onto his thigh with her right hand. The intense rage in her eyes was venomous; it felt like she was screaming at him, despite her not saying a word yet.

Henry watched incredulously as Savannah demanded, "Yeah, let's finish this Murdoch! So, aside from never... When were you gonna tell me about Catherine, huh?" She didn't even let Barnaby get a word out and immediately accused him of breaking the Tutori code. "What is it... Are y'all working together now?"

The impromptu interrogation unfolding in front of Henry clearly sent the investigation into a completely different direction.

He was nothing short of astounded and mumbled under his breath to June, "Well, I certainly didn't see this coming, eh?" He wondered if Barnaby's tenure at the *APA* was about to come to an end right here in the train station. All the prevaricating and duplicity had finally caught up to the Australian, and it looked like he was about to pay the price in a very painful way.

Genuinely bemused, Barnaby snickered, "We're a little short on time right now for the Texas two-step," as Savannah furiously cut him off, "Aside from nothing and nobody, what are you gonna have when the council takes your cloak after they find out you've been lyin' to 'em?"

Even though Barnaby enjoyed seeing Savannah all riled up, something about this time seemed different; he was concerned about the precarious positioning of the cattle prodder pressed firmly against his thigh. In a foolish attempt to ease the tension, he relaxed his arms, put his hands up, and remarked, "Well... I'll always have Roger, right?"

"Go on! Admit it!" Savannah carried on with her accusatory line of interrogation, apparently in no mood for his games. "You've been lyin' to the council this whole time!"

Savannah lifted the cattle prodder from Barnaby's leg to press the button on the side. Sparks of electricity poured out of the other end, serving as an overt reminder of the pain waiting if she didn't believe him. She waved the cattle prod in front of his face, getting it just close enough to cause Barnaby to wince, then pulled it back ever so slightly right before making contact.

The pure hostility radiating from Savannah had Henry trembling in fear. It was obvious she wasn't joking around, and he didn't envy Barnaby's current dilemma. June was equally concerned but held her tongue as Savannah released the button and jammed the cattle prod against his upper thigh once more.

Savannah was convinced that Barnaby would just spout another tangled web of highly plausible falsehoods to make her look bad. She preemptively gloated, "Admit it, ya traitor! 'Cause we'd love to see the council rip that cloak off your shoulders."

"Wouldn't we love to see that, June?" Savannah asked, glancing over at her startled Magari partner. Penny spoke up for her and cheerfully barked twice in agreement. The wirehaired dachshund had a memory like an elephant and was still sour about the lifeboat drill yesterday.

Barnaby huffed at the idea as June replied awkwardly, "Uh, well..." and was fortuitously interrupted by the station-wide loudspeaker announcement at that very moment. "Train *3-W-5-6* with nonstop service to Paris, France, will be departing in three minutes... All aboard!"

Savannah released Barnaby but kept the cattle prod out and pointed it at his chest in a threatening manner. "We'll finish this later... But we both know you're not telling me the whole story, Murdoch. Something's going on here, and I'm gonna find out one way or another."

"Now, call it in... before I change my mind!" Savannah demanded, glaring at Barnaby. She pushed the button on the cattle prodder once more to encourage compliance.

Nonchalantly swatting the cattle prodder out of his way, Barnaby warned, "Enough with the dramatics, Sunday. I know what I did and didn't do... And you better choose your next words carefully before you accuse me of betraying the cloak again."

Henry wasn't sure if Barnaby was telling the truth or not, but he was certain that he didn't want to end up on the wrong side of Savannah's cattle prodder.

Confident that the consequences awaiting him upon his return to the *Arthur Broome* would be punishment enough, Savannah holstered her cattle prod as Barnaby picked up the nearest payphone. He dialed a series of numbers, strangely enough, without ever putting any money into the coin slot.

Savannah lifted the left side of her suit jacket to flash a sleeve of tranquilizer darts affixed to her suspenders and insisted, "You best not leave any details out this time either." Barnaby exhaled and mockingly smiled, "No worries, Sunday... I'll be sure to tell 'em what I had for breakfast too, alright?"

They all waited patiently for a few seconds as the line on the other side continued to ring. An operator finally answered, and even though Henry couldn't hear what the operator was saying, he tried to eavesdrop as Barnaby spoke.

"Relay *1–0–0–2–3*," Barnaby said immediately after the operator responded. He confidently stated, "Wishbone. Yeah, that's right... Access numbah *7–4–7–8*, calling from a civilian payphone."

Henry, June, and Savannah listened carefully to ensure they didn't miss anything. Barnaby waited for the operator to stop talking and then replied, "Current status... Still in pursuit of the Frenchman and the bear cubs. Boarding a train to Paris right now with Sunday, her Magari, and the kid from Kodiak Bay. Tell the council we will be at the port of Le Havre rendezvous point later this evening."

For good measure, Savannah put her hand back on the collapsible cattle prod secured to her belt—it was a not-so-subtle bid to discourage him from withholding any additional information. "And what else?" she whispered, sending another look of pure venom in his direction. Barnaby was annoyed and resentfully added, "And one more thing... the Frenchman has been identified as Catherine Saint-Clair." He silently mouthed the words, *"Are you happy now?"* to Savannah, prompting her to smile as she took her hand off the cattle prodder.

"Yeah, that's right... her twin sistah," Barnaby confirmed. His attitude suddenly turned more hostile, and he exclaimed, "Negative, do not send backup!" Irritated by the suggestion that he would need help from anyone, Barnaby snapped at the operator for daring to question him, "Yeah, I'm sure! One thousand percent, okay?"

"Roger that. Ovah and out," Barnaby concluded, abruptly hanging up the phone; he slammed it down so hard that a few coins got knocked loose and spilled out onto the ground.

Henry assumed the council would not be happy to learn that they had been chasing a former member of the Tutori the entire time. He wondered what kind of consequences awaited them when they returned to the ship. It sure sounded like Savannah thought it might cost Barnaby his cloak (which was apparently something she would love to see happen). As far as he knew, Catherine was the only person to ever be expelled from the *Animal Protection Authority*.

"All aboard!" the train conductor yelled from the platform. The sound of the whistle echoed throughout the station, signaling the train was about to depart.

Savannah sneered, "Well done, Murdoch. Now, let's recover those bears before you let her get away again!" Barnaby groaned, too tired to dispel her seemingly baseless allegations.

Henry collected Penny and followed June, Savannah, and Barnaby as they climbed aboard the train, one after another. He never imagined his first trip to Paris would be overshadowed by such animosity, and he remembered that they still needed to actually apprehend Catherine on the way there—something that was much easier said than done.

— CHAPTER 14 —
THE TRAIN TO PARIS

*T*he conductor was the last one to step aboard the train before it started moving; the locomotive accelerated, zooming away toward Paris, while the Tutori searched for the former member of the *APA* who evaded them. Henry assumed Catherine's capture was practically guaranteed since she had nowhere to run. He couldn't fathom how the French thief would be able to escape this time.

Onboard, there was still a line of passengers stowing their luggage and looking for their seats. While the four of them queued in the aisle, Henry placed his rucksack on the open seat next to him. He opened the bag, and Penny immediately hopped in without any grumbling. She was happy to rest her paws following the spirited pursuit through the streets of London.

With Savannah leading in front, Barnaby, June, and Henry followed her in single file, slowly making their way to the front of the train from the caboose. They stepped between the adjoining railcars as the train picked up speed, being careful to mind their balance.

The band of intrepid seafarers looked everywhere for any sign of Catherine, the luggage porter's uniform, or the black duffle bag. They vigilantly assessed each passenger as they walked up the aisleway.

"What if she's wearing a new disguise?" Henry blurted. He

remembered that Catherine had changed her outfit and even her appearance before boarding the *Queen Charlotte* back in Kodiak Bay. To his surprise, Barnaby replied supportively, "Good thinking, mate. Stay on your toes, everyone. Catherine might have another wig, but she can't hide that black duffle bag. So, be on the lookout and let me know if you see anything."

Still annoyed by Barnaby's deceitful antics, Savannah largely ignored his warning. She didn't say a word in response, insulting or otherwise. Like an angry lioness hunting elusive prey, she was laser-focused on finding Catherine; she didn't need Barnaby's help, and as far as she was concerned, he was just another distraction that stood in her way.

As they moved to another railcar, Penny retreated into the comforts of her cashmere-lined rucksack to avoid the gusting wind. There was still no sign of Catherine or her black duffle bag. Henry started to worry that she might have slipped off the train while Savannah and Barnaby were arguing near the payphones. "What if I missed her?" he mumbled to himself.

Henry couldn't deny that Savannah's spontaneous interrogation had been distracting; it would have been the perfect opportunity for Catherine to send them all on a wild goose chase as she stayed behind in London.

Savannah, Barnaby, June, and Henry continued marching forward to the next railcar. Despite trying to stay optimistic, every one of them felt increasingly anxious as they passed each aisle. Catherine was nowhere to be found, and the discouraging sense of defeat grew louder the closer they got to the front of the train.

Another railcar, and still nothing. There was no red hair, no black duffle bag, and nobody who even closely resembled the wily French adversary.

Henry wanted to believe that Catherine was still onboard, but he couldn't shake the notion that she jumped off before the train departed or shortly thereafter. At least, that's what he would have done if he were in her shoes.

The aspiring Magari was careful not to let his frustration turn into blind anger—there was enough of that between Barnaby and Savannah already. Thinking about the potential consequences that loomed if they returned to the ship empty-handed wasn't making it easy to remain calm, though. The immense pressure to emerge on the other side with a win only intensified when Henry remembered that Barnaby didn't even want him there. The tetchy Australian made it abundantly clear from the beginning that he didn't want anyone tagging along, including his fellow Tutori.

Henry suspected Barnaby would put the blame on him if they showed up defeated once again, especially if the man's cloak was on the line.

The lingering fear of getting kicked off the *Arthur Broome* gave Henry plenty of incentive to prove himself when it mattered most. He surmised that Barnaby would probably be happy to leave him (and Penny) stranded at the port in Le Havre with no way to get back home.

As Henry followed June onto the next railcar, he accidentally bumped into her. She had stopped abruptly behind Savannah when the Tutori spotted something of great interest. It all happened so quickly that he didn't even have a chance to apologize to June.

Savannah suddenly spun around after noticing Catherine at the other end of the railcar. "Alright y'all, there she is... at my six o'clock." Henry's whole body tensed up as she instructed, "Now, let's handle this quietly, 'cause we still got seven hours 'til this train arrives in Paris."

Everyone nodded in agreement. Henry's heart began to race, and a surge of adrenaline, mixed with a combination of excitement and nervousness, fell upon him.

There were two pairs of seats facing each other near the door on the far side of the railcar. Catherine was sitting against the wall by the window with a black duffle bag on the seat next to her. The burgundy luggage porter outfit she was previously wearing had been replaced by a train conductor's uniform. And while her new disguise was impressive, the employee cap she had on couldn't hide that red hair, not from Savannah.

The seat in front of Catherine was empty, but there was an older gentleman reading a newspaper directly across from the black duffle bag next to the aisleway. The man was heavyset with horseshoe-pattern baldness, and he wore a double-breasted suit along with thick black glasses.

Savannah turned around and walked briskly toward the front of the railcar. She didn't say a word to Catherine or the bald gentleman when she passed by, though she couldn't resist glaring at them.

Once Savannah reached the exit door, she confidently stood guard and folded her arms in a defensive position. The nasty scowl on her face gave Henry chills. He trusted that nobody was going to get past her, especially not Catherine.

Barnaby strolled up the aisleway, relieved that he had his old partner cornered once again. June and Henry followed him. They both assumed the pursuit that had spanned four continents was coming to an end at last.

The aisle was now blocked in both directions, making it impossible to escape—there was nowhere for Catherine to run this time.

Barnaby sat in the seat across from Catherine and sighed with exhaustion as he plopped down. It was like a leopard that finally caught up to the gazelle he was pursuing, but now he was too tired and exasperated to enjoy the prize. He was exhausted from chasing her all over the world and dodging dynamite explosions at every turn, and his face showed it.

June and Henry stood next to each other to block the aisleway, just in case Catherine tried to slip past Barnaby unexpectedly.

After picking up on the scent of the bear cubs, Penny lifted her head out of the rucksack and began vigorously sniffing. She could also smell the hostility and tension in the air; it consumed the entire front half of the railcar, but she was certain the polar bear cubs were in the bag next to Catherine. The scent was unmistakable.

"Ah... bonjour, bonjour, Barnabas!" Catherine beamed cheerfully. She didn't appear to be tired in the slightest, despite being constantly pursued by the Tutori over the last few weeks. Tilting her head, she teased, "What's wrong, mon ami? Have I been playing too rough for you?"

Catherine took a small sip of her piping hot coffee and then placed the cup on the retractable tray table above her lap. Annoyed by the lack of deference for the *APA*, Barnaby groaned, "This has gone on long enough, Catherine. You need to hand over those bears before someone gets hurt."

Barnaby knew Catherine was never one to listen to reason, but he preferred this approach over the alternative, which involved letting Savannah loose on her like a battery of hungry barracudas in a bathtub.

"Don't you mean... before someone else gets hurt? Honestly, I remember Blackfriar being tougher, no?" Catherine sneered.

Unamused, Barnaby warned, "I'm not messing around, Catherine. The council wants us to hand you over to the police!" He exhaled sharply. "I put my cloak on the line to try and protect you because we were once partnahs... and I'm trying to do right by your sistah, but you have to stop what you're doing, mate. This isn't you."

"No, no, no... this is where you are wrong, Barnabas!" Catherine fired back. "I'm doing exactly what I was meant to do. Exactly what you should be doing if you had a shred of integrity."

The heavyset gentleman sitting next to Barnaby had become uncomfortable with the tone of the conversation. He stood up and tried to excuse himself. "Pardon me, but this sounds like a private matter. Perhaps I should go look for another seat."

Catherine smiled and calmly advised, "I'd stay seated if I were you, Mr. Cooper."

Flabbergasted, the bald man changed his mind and sat back down. The defiance in his eyes had vanished, and a look of dismay followed when Catherine lifted the side of her jacket to reveal a stick of dynamite on her belt.

Equally disturbed by this stranger calling out his name and the not-so-subtle attempt to intimidate him, the older gentleman inquired, "Bloody hell! Who are you? And how do you know my name?"

"Oh, I know everything about you, *Richard Cooper*," Catherine answered villainously. She slowly took another sip of her coffee and set it on the tray table. "I know you live in the posh part of Croydon. I know you leave for work every morning at eight o'clock. And I know you've had a spot of bad luck with the ponies lately, no?"

Catherine glanced over at Barnaby and snickered, "That's right, ol' Richie here couldn't pick a winner even if it was a one-horse race."

"Good grief... here we go again," Barnaby muttered, clearly worried that things were about to escalate. Savannah, June, and Henry just looked at each other in bewilderment, wondering how Catherine knew this random train passenger.

Richard was shocked and replied, "Hang on a minute now, how do you..."

"Do you ever watch humans at the zoo, Richie?" Catherine interrupted. Baffled by the question, Richard mumbled, "What? Humans at the zoo?"

"Come on, Richie... You are the *director of the London Zoo*, no?"

Catherine jeered, grinning from ear to ear, watching him waffle in confusion.

Barnaby took a deep breath and chimed in, "Alright, let's just stay calm here." The shaky trepidation in his voice left Henry feeling worried that this was far more than an innocent question about zoo attendance statistics.

Alarmed that Catherine appeared to know a bit too much for a complete stranger, Richard asked hesitantly, "What's this all about? Who are..."

"You can always tell which ones have empathy by the look in their eyes... The humans who know the difference between *right and wrong*," Catherine proclaimed, interjecting again.

Everyone was flummoxed by Catherine's bizarre tangent and could only wonder how she appeared to know so much about Richard. The more she talked, the less it seemed like this was a coincidence; they were captivated by the mystery of it all and listened as she carried on, "Doesn't matter if it's the mighty elephant locked behind a fence or the flightless penguin confined to a tiny artificial habitat. The anguish and despair can be felt just the same."

Catherine leaned forward, smiling, as she stared at Richard with a piercing look of pure hostility. "Oui, the eyes... They always tell the truth, even when they're lying."

Barnaby sighed. Knowing Catherine all too well, he was worried that the situation was on the verge of spiraling out of control.

The tension in the air was unsettling, to say the least. Between Savannah's unwavering temptation to yank Catherine out of the seat at any moment and Richard's past transgressions piling up, Barnaby desperately hoped to avoid another tussle. He tried reasoning with the stubborn redhead once more. "Well, I'm sure we can all appreciate that lesson in optometry. But let's just handovah that black duffle bag... and we'll all go our separate ways, alright?"

"I'm afraid it's not that simple!" Catherine scoffed, shaking her head emphatically. "You see, Barnabas... When I look into Richie's eyes, the only thing I see is fear." She smiled while staring at the bald Londoner. "Oui, Richie here is nervous as a cat... And his hands are looking awfully dirty from where I'm sitting."

A befuddled Richard glanced at his clean hands and replied, "Have you gone mad? That's what's going on here, innit?"

"Don't worry, Richie," Catherine taunted as her smile disappeared, "I always bring some soap with me for times such as this."

Everyone remained confounded by her banter (everyone except Barnaby). He tensed up and remarked gruffly, "Alright, you made your point, Catherine. It doesn't have to go down like this."

"No, that's where you are *wrong*, Barnabas!" Catherine fiercely corrected him, unconvinced and insulted by the thought of letting Richard off the hook so easily. She took a deep breath and then continued explaining. "You see, Richie here has picked up a nasty little habit... and has gotten himself into quite a precarious situation back in London. The kind that involves a particularly dangerous bookie, I'm afraid. Oui, I suspect our friend Richie is on incredibly thin ice with Mr. Bulford."

Glancing over at Barnaby's watch, Catherine affirmed precisely, "*22 hours, 59 minutes, and 57 seconds*. That's how much time Richie here has left to come up with a small fortune... Otherwise, a severe penalty will be incurred, no?"

Richard winced at the mere mention of the bookmaker's name. It didn't matter that Mr. Bulford was a thousand kilometers away in a completely different country; Henry could tell Richard was terrified of the man.

Catherine relished the look of terror dripping from Richard's face. Even though everyone around her seemed more anxious than a Siamese cat in a swimming pool, she was undeniably enjoying herself.

"Can't say that I approve of his methods," Catherine remarked, "but the man has developed a reputation for getting results... one way or another." Richard couldn't get a word in, and her animosity only intensified as she began berating him, spouting rhetorical questions. "And that's why you're on this train, right, Richie? You don't think I know what you're doing here? You don't think I know who you were planning to meet in Paris?"

"It can't be." Richard's face turned pale as he stammered, "You? You're the... the, the Frenchman?"

Catherine tutted, resentful of the moniker Richard uttered. "You know, I really do hate that name. Oui, je suis français... although I also like to think of myself as an educator, Richie. Personally, I prefer *Le Professeur*... but I'm still tinkering."

Savannah and Barnaby just looked at each other in bemusement as Catherine carried on, "That's right, Richie... There's no greater joy in this world than teaching. I learned that myself years ago from one of the finest public school teachers in all of Philadelphia. Educators like him are one of a kind, working tirelessly to make the world a little less cold and cruel than it needs to be."

"Oui, it's arguably the most underappreciated profession out there, but make no mistake... I don't need your appreciation." Catherine paused to wink at Barnaby and then continued lecturing Richard, "That's not why I do this. My reward is seeing you leave this train a changed man, because that's what teaching is really all about, Richie. I'm here to correct your educational deficiencies. That way you'll think twice the next time you find yourself tempted to participate in such foolish and despicable endeavors."

Henry whispered, "Shh, it's okay, girl," after hearing Penny let out a muffled growl. He didn't realize that she smelled something very worrisome. The scent of perspiration emanating from both Barnaby and Richard had increased considerably.

"Brokering exotic wildlife transactions behind closed doors to pay off your gambling debts doesn't come without its risks, though,"

Catherine warned. Disgusted by Richard's very existence, she continued admonishing him with escalating hostility in her tone. "Working at the zoo, betting on racehorses, selling stolen exotic animals... is there anything you do that doesn't exploit unsuspecting animals?"

Barnaby furtively put his hand on the collapsible cattle prod secured to the side of his belt. Concerned that an outburst of violence was looming, he interjected, "Okay, let's just take it easy here..."

Clearly uninterested in diplomacy or compromise, Catherine shouted over the Australian Tutori, "No need to worry, Richie! I have the two polar bear cubs you ordered... They're right here inside this bag, sleeping peacefully."

Richard nervously wiped the beads of sweat off his forehead using the handkerchief from his jacket pocket. It was obvious he had been set up by Catherine; there was nobody waiting for him in Paris. He had read all about the Frenchman (as well as the missing fishermen) in the newspaper and wondered despairingly if he would ever make it off this train alive.

Showing no signs of backing down, Catherine scolded Richard, "Feeling a bit warm in here, Richie? There's no need to be afraid of a proper education... just like there was no need to kill the mother of these bears. Unless, of course, you selfishly want them for your zoo, no?"

Savannah's patience had run out, and she was tired of Catherine's games. The brash Texan suddenly yanked the cattle prod from her belt, expanding the baton in one swift motion. "I've heard just about enough of this! We're handing both y'all over to the police, and those cubs are coming with me!" Her unwavering tone grew louder as she stepped closer. "Now, get up!"

Catherine replied insouciantly, "Okay, okay."

"Now!" Savannah yelled at the top of her lungs as she pressed the button on the cattle prodder. The sparks of electricity normally encourage compliance, but this time appeared to be different. The French had a unique sense of defiance, rivaled only by the special brand of stubbornness found in the Lone Star state.

In what must have been a fraction of a second, Catherine threw her coffee in Barnaby's face and grabbed Richard by the arm, shoving him into the aisle. His portly body knocked over Savannah, who instantaneously tumbled into June and Henry.

"Crikey!" Barnaby yelled, wiping the coffee from his eyes, while Catherine snatched the black duffle bag from the seat and jumped into the aisleway. With the man's obese body blocking the aisle and Savannah still struggling to get up after being knocked over, Henry was stunned by what happened next.

Catherine stomped on Richard's left hand using all her strength, causing him to instantly cry out in unbearable pain. She blithely pulled a bar of soap from her pocket and tossed it at him. "Stop crying and clean yourself up, Richie!"

Based on the intensity of Richard's screaming, Catherine was certain she had broken all twenty-seven bones in his hand. She usually preferred to avoid violence under normal circumstances. However, in this particular case, she didn't have time to facilitate a proper lesson like she did with the shark fishermen on the *Second Chance*.

Shrieks of panic immediately filled the railcar. It wasn't just Richard either; the other passengers had witnessed the altercation unfolding in the aisle. They rushed to get away, shouting and hollering in fear as they retreated toward the caboose.

Barnaby finally plunged into the aisle once he could see again. He swiped at the coattails of Catherine's latest disguise, only to feel her slip away as she escaped through the door leading to the next railcar.

Savannah managed to get back up and didn't hesitate to charge forward toward the exit door. Her timing proved to be regrettable, though; she accidentally bumped into Barnaby at the same moment he stood up in the aisleway, which only inflamed her fury. Still covered in coffee above the waist, he tried to calm her down. "Easy, Sunday... easy. We're on a train, remembah? She's got nowhere to run."

Glaring at Richard flailing around in agony on the floor, Barnaby shook his head and dismissed the zoo director as he stepped over the man's stout body.

Savannah didn't share Barnaby's sense of compassion. She was fuming after failing to capture Catherine, and in frustration, she pressed her cattle prod against Richard's thigh. He screeched in pain and flailed in the aisle while she held the button on the side.

Despite the rampant anger coursing through her body, Savannah eventually relented once the sound of Barnaby's voice caught her attention. "That's enough, Sunday!" he shouted, waiting impatiently for her by the exit.

June leaped over the man's body, right after Savannah walked over him and intentionally used his chest as a stepping stone in the process. They both followed Barnaby through the door onto the next railcar, leaving Henry and Penny behind.

It would have been all too easy to simply ignore the portly man clenching his hand in pain on the floor, but the inescapable feelings of doubt gave Henry pause. He started to wonder if maybe Catherine was right about a few things. Wrestling with his own hastily constructed assumptions, he realized that he didn't actually know how those polar bear cubs ended up at the *Kodiak Bay Zoo* in the first place. He never thought to stop and think about where any of the zoo animals came from, until now.

The belief that they were doing the right thing seemed irrefutable when he left the *Arthur Broome* this morning, yet the conflicted feelings that surfaced in that instant couldn't be ignored. It was becoming harder for him to know what the bear cubs would really want after listening to Catherine; she had made some compelling points in the midst of all the chaos. The idea of the Tutori being on the wrong side was something he never imagined would be possible.

Henry had a whole new list of questions that only Barnaby could answer. Difficult questions, indeed, but they would have to wait. Carefully jumping over Richard, he rushed to catch up with Barnaby, Savannah, and June.

There was no sight of Catherine in the next railcar—nobody dressed like a *Great Britain Railway* employee either. Worried that she might have already changed into another disguise, Henry ran up the aisle to get to the next door.

"Hit the deck!" Barnaby shouted when Henry entered the adjoining railcar. Catherine had sent the Australian tumbling down the aisle after another brief tussle, and he tried to warn everyone as she launched a volley of throwing darts in the same direction where they were standing.

June and Henry quickly dove into the nearest row of empty seats while Savannah crouched in the aisleway. They all narrowly avoided the tranquilizer darts hurtling toward the back of the railcar.

Before Catherine could grab another sleeve of darts, Savannah jumped up and fearlessly stormed ahead like an angry hippopotamus. She was incensed. Fueled by unbridled rage, she lunged at Catherine, who dodged out of the way and cleverly wrapped the Texan's cloak around a seat headrest nearby. It all happened within the blink of an eye and in stunning acrobatic fashion. The knot was tied with such precision that it prevented Savannah from being able to turn around.

Henry could tell it was a sailor's knot right away. He knew Savannah would be stuck there for at least a few minutes, regardless of how much she struggled to break free—and she was struggling.

She thrashed around and kicked like a bull about to charge a rodeo clown.

Catherine's wicked laugh permeated the railcar. She loved taunting Savannah, but the celebration was swiftly tempered when she noticed Barnaby rushing up the aisle. The sheer fury in his eyes was enough to send her running in the opposite direction.

Barnaby brushed past Savannah, who was still trapped and writhing, as Catherine escaped into the next railcar ahead.

June and Henry darted over to help the beleaguered Tutori. "Just go! I got this!" she shouted. He zipped past them and chased after Barnaby, while she stayed and feverishly tried to untangle the complex knot that pinned Savannah's cloak to the seat headrest.

Henry barreled through the far door and came to an abrupt stop outside, where he found himself teetering less than a foot from the edge. Barnaby was on the railcar in front of him, but it was inching further and further apart with each passing second. He trembled in fear as he glanced down at the rapidly moving train tracks below.

The decoupled train car that Henry was standing on continued coasting as the front half of the train roared ahead toward Paris.

Only seconds before it would be too late, Barnaby screamed, "Jump now, mate! Jump!"

Galvanized by Barnaby's encouragement, Henry felt a sense of bravery wash over him. He yanked down on the rucksack straps, securing the bag tightly to his back, and warned, "Hang on, Penny!" Leaping with all his might, he soared across the gap onto the railcar ahead of him and barely landed on the ledge. He nearly fell onto the tracks, but Barnaby pulled him to safety just in time.

Standing there, gazing at the tracks, Henry watched in disbelief as the back half of the train kept losing momentum.

Barnaby shrieked, "I can't believe that maniac uncoupled the train cars!" while Savannah and June burst through the door onto the ledge of the opposite railcar. Infuriated and still fuming,

Savannah bellowed, "You best not let her get away this time, ya hear! No excuses, Murdoch! Ya hear me?"

The sound of Savannah's voice quickly faded as the back half of the train drifted further away, slowly rolling to a gradual stop.

With the front half of the train speeding toward Paris in the other direction, Barnaby gently grabbed Henry by the arm and said, "You alright, mate? You ready to finish this?" Penny popped her head out of the rucksack, barking twice to confirm she was ready. Henry admired her courage and replied, with a humble smile, "Let's do it, *Banjo*. We didn't come this far to quit now, eh?"

Barnaby chuckled in response and patted the young Canadian on the back. When he turned around, Henry followed him into the next railcar, but they both froze as the door closed behind them.

There she was, relaxing in a seat against the wall at the far end of the railcar; it was Catherine.

Barnaby winked when she locked eyes with him. Finally, he had caught her by surprise instead of the other way around. The annoyed expression staring back at him made all the hassle worth it, and even though it was fleeting, he savored every last second of the modest victory.

Scowling, Catherine got up from her seat and swung the black duffle bag over her shoulder. She forcefully pushed the exit door open, marching forward onto the adjoining railcar.

Fearing that she was about to decouple the train cars again, Barnaby raced up the aisle while Henry mirrored his every step. They burst through the door with bravado, yet came to a halt once Barnaby noticed something alarming ahead—almost like he had seen a ghost. As the two of them stood outside on the ledge, Henry realized the next railcar they were about to enter was unquestionably different.

It definitely wasn't a normal passenger railcar. The door in front of them didn't have a window like the others, and there was a sliding metal crossbar that should have been in place to secure it shut. Henry presumed Catherine had removed the crossbar, leaving it dangling in the wind ominously. But the big red letters painted on the front of the door were far more concerning: *DANGER—DO NOT OPEN!*

Barnaby's black cloak billowed in the passing wind as he looked at Henry and forewarned, "Suspect there's a whole boatload of trouble behind that door, mate. No shame if you want to hang back while I handle Catherine on my own."

Henry nodded apprehensively. "Right behind you, Mr. Murdoch... We can't let her get away now."

The swaying crossbar clattered back and forth while Barnaby turned and cautiously opened the metal door. Despite the howling wind gusting by, Henry could hear Penny sniffing fiercely in his ear; she had picked up on new, unfamiliar scents that came pouring out.

"Ah, très bien! Don't be shy, Barnabas. Come closer... I want you to meet my new friends!" Catherine exclaimed cheerfully as she stood on the other side of the railcar.

Henry followed Barnaby through the door but wished he hadn't once he saw what was waiting to greet them. He found himself overcome with fear. It wasn't Catherine or the large cages on the left side that gave him pause—the three full-grown Bengal tigers did that all on their own. He was drowning in regret for not taking Barnaby's offer to wait outside.

Several bullwhips were hanging on the wall to the right, along with bags of animal feed and costumes that appeared to be from the circus.

Provoked by their new visitors, the only male tiger roared with intensity, triggering the other two females to roar in unison. The thunderous sound from the enraged tigers immediately consumed the railcar, and Henry felt it in his bones. Just by looking at the belligerence in their eyes, he could tell these tigers were wrathful and most likely caught in the wild before being forced into the circus life.

"The wild cat!" Henry mumbled under his breath. He was tempted to turn around and run away out of sheer terror, but instead he kept his feet planted in amazement.

"Don't do it, Catherine!" Barnaby shouted timorously. He slowly took a few steps back and warned, "This isn't a game!"

A surreal sense of apprehension flowed through Henry's body as he watched Catherine rest her palm on the tiger cage door handle. Her chilling laughter echoed throughout the railcar.

Catherine winked at Barnaby and remarked, "Oui, c'est le cas... and I play for the game's own sake." She waited until Barnaby had the proper amount of panic in his eyes, then audaciously swung the cage door open.

It only took her a moment to vanish once again. She bolted out the exit and into the next railcar ahead, while Barnaby and Henry were left to contend with the hungry pack of Bengal tigers that had just been set free.

The sound of the door slamming behind Catherine just startled the tigers further. These animals were clearly malnourished, and now that she had set them loose, their insatiable appetite could no longer be ignored. They were eager to make a meal out of Barnaby since he was closer, though Henry and Penny would have sufficed all the same.

Starving and anxious to stretch their legs, the pack of tigers scrambled out of the cage in a mad dash, coming straight for Barnaby and Henry as if they were a pair of walking T-bone steaks.

Barnaby was uninterested in being on the receiving end of a ravenous, *one hundred and eighty kilogram* Bengal tiger pouncing in his direction. He snatched Henry by the arm and quickly pulled him outside onto the ledge of the railcar. "The lock! Secure the lock!" he yelled frantically, jamming his shoulder up against the door, expecting the pack of tigers to bust through if Henry couldn't lock the door in time.

Henry scrambled to slide the metal crossbar into place and awkwardly fumbled to line it up perfectly. It took him a few seconds, but he finally managed to secure the door.

Barnaby stepped back, grumbling, "Damn that woman!" He wiped the sweat from his forehead and dramatically exhaled while the tigers pounded on the metal door.

"Must be a traveling circus," Henry remarked as the animals roared furiously from the other side. Despite the heart-stopping feline encounter, he wasn't ready to give up just yet. Gesturing toward the step ladder bolted to the outer side of the railcar, he blurted, "We can climb over!"

Barnaby scoffed at the idea. "Let's just calm down, mate." He had just escaped from a pack of wild tigers only moments ago and wasn't ready to trade the sensation of respite for another terrifying round of life-or-death adrenaline. Exasperated, he cautioned, "Not too keen to find out if there's a hoard of bloody snakes waiting for us in the next railcar, alright?"

"But what if Catherine uncouples the cars again?" Henry insisted, "What about your cloak? Those bears will be gone forever!"

"Listen, mate... Uncertainty is our only advantage right now. It's the only thing we've got, you understand?" Barnaby affirmed. Henry didn't fully understand and was having trouble finding the words to match the bewildered look on his face.

Barnaby looked toward the railcar and added, "For all she knows, those tigers tore us to pieces like a pack of crocodiles in North Queensland. We have the element of surprise on our side, and if Catherine spots us now, she is liable to uncouple the cars on us again." Sensing Henry's disappointment, he carried on, "Look kid, I appreciate your enthusiasm... I really do. But this train is moving awfully fast, and I'd hate to see either of us get hurt if you slipped or fell. There ain't no do-ovahs out here, pal."

Penny was beginning to feel excluded and stuck her head out of the rucksack to voice her grievances. Two angry barks pointed in Barnaby's direction gave Henry plenty of reason to reconsider.

"Surely your girl there would rather rest those paws for a bit. What do ya say, Penny? Time for a snack break?" Barnaby asked, slyly pulling a few sweet potato sticks from his jacket pocket.

Henry glanced at Penny (her tongue was watering with anticipation) and reluctantly agreed, "Yeah, I guess that's probably best, eh?"

The adrenaline was starting to fade. There was a part of Henry that wanted nothing more than to chase after Catherine, but not at the expense of breaking his promise to follow Barnaby's lead. He gave his word to Captain Fulbright back in Kodiak Bay and couldn't just toss it away on a whim.

Penny began to cry in excitement at the sight of the sweet potato sticks; the smell alone was enchanting. "Shh, in a minute, my girl. In a minute," Henry whispered as he followed Barnaby back into the passenger railcar.

Barnaby took a window seat in the row closest to the door, while Henry sat down in the aisle seat on the opposite side.

Penny climbed out of the rucksack and jumped into the other window seat directly across from Barnaby. She stared at him with bated breath, waiting patiently for the sweet potato sticks that were promised. Even though he was still sour about letting Catherine slip away again, Barnaby couldn't help but chuckle and happily hand over the sweet treats. Penny's infectious smile had a tendency to lend influence.

Consumed with a renewed sense of curiosity now that his life was no longer in peril, Henry looked at Barnaby and suggested, "Do you ever think we might be in the wrong here?"

Henry felt somewhat tormented by what Catherine said when

she was berating Richard Cooper. Enamored by the sweet potato sticks, Penny devoured them one by one, clearly unaware of the ambivalent sentiments plaguing his thoughts.

Barnaby merely rolled his eyes and dismissed the suggestion that he would ever be wrong about anything.

Worried that the Australian Tutori might have misinterpreted to the point of being insulted, Henry clarified, "I mean... we don't even know where those polar bear cubs came from. They certainly weren't born at the zoo in Kodiak Bay, eh? Those cubs only showed up one day with a big announcement and no short supply of fanfare from the local newspapers to boot."

Barnaby, afraid that Catherine had planted poisonous ideas into Henry's naive mind and hoping to avoid the discussion spiraling into a lengthy debate about whether zoos should exist at all, instinctively deflected. "Look, mate, I've been tasked with recovering those bears and returning them to that zoo. Period. End of story. Whether I personally agree or not is of no consequence." He glanced at his reflection in the window, turned to Henry, and asserted, "Bottom line, if I return to the *Arthur Broome* with anything less than two healthy polar bear cubs, the council is liable to strip me of my cloak. *You got that*?"

Unconvinced, Henry persisted, "But what about..."

"Listen closely, my young friend," Barnaby curtly interrupted. "For some animals, the zoo is all they know. Most of 'em were born into captivity... free from the dangers of the harsh jungle. Free to sleep soundly knowing they won't be another step in the food chain laddah for a biggah, meanah animal hunting in the dead of night. Free from the worry of scavenging for food in the face of starvation. Taken care of by world-class physicians providing round-the-clock healthcare in some cases."

Barnaby clicked his tongue and added, "Years in the unforgiving jungle eventually takes its toll on the best of us." He scoffed, "And putting aside what Catherine said back there, things aren't always so absolute when it comes to zoos. Should they exist? Should they all be shut down?"

"Not for me to say, mate," Barnaby concluded, with a hint of humility peppered into his tone. Henry asked rebelliously, "And what about the *APA*? Isn't it *their* place to say?"

"You've still got lots to learn, kid... But you're asking the wrong person," Barnaby tutted. "The animals will tell ya if they're happy or not. All you have to do is listen. Some probably like the idea of all-inclusive, resort-style living. But I'm sure there are some who would gladly endure the costs of the jungle for their freedom."

Barnaby shrugged and continued, "The price is high... Always has been. But if you're asking for my personal opinion on the mattah, I'd say the sanctuary out there in Alice Springs has got the right idea... Looking after injured and orphaned 'roos from the wild with nowhere else to turn. No cages. No weapons. And the animals are free to leave whenever they please."

Henry wasn't satisfied and badgered him further. "I thought it was your duty as a Tutori to find out where those polar bear cubs actually came from?"

"*My duty*... is to the *APA*, the council of three, and the Tutori commissioner," Barnaby fired back in a snarky tone. "And right now, my orders are to recover those bears and return them to the *Kodiak Bay Zoo*. That's it, mate. Nothing more, nothing less."

Barnaby was growing more irritable with each passing question, and it became clear that he was in no mood for a philosophical debate. Henry decided to abandon his zealous line of inquiry and said respectfully, "I suppose the council knows what's best, eh?"

Absolutely knackered from chasing Catherine all over London and still covered in dried coffee, Barnaby replied, "That's right, kid. Now, if ya don't mind, I'm going to rest my eyes for a bit before we tango with that French hooligan again." He closed his eyes and yawned. "Wake me up when we get to Paris, will ya?"

It didn't take long for the weary Tutori to fall asleep.

Despite the spirited discussion, Henry still had more questions than answers. As he aimlessly stared out the window, he wondered if the *APA* was making the right call when it came to these cubs. He couldn't shake the feelings of doubt cast by Catherine's spontaneous lambasting as he struggled to make sense of it all.

"Maybe they were orphans rescued from the wild... and the zoo was their best chance for survival," he mumbled, trying to convince himself.

Henry desperately wanted to be on the right side, but it was tough to ignore the real possibility that the zoo could have acquired the polar bear cubs from a broker like Richard, a man who buys and sells wild exotic animals as if they were baseball cards.

"Surely the *Animal Protection Authority* wouldn't want to send those cubs back to the *Kodiak Bay Zoo* if that was the case... or would they?" he thought.

Henry only wanted to help. He loved animals and could tell that Catherine seemed to share that same passion. On the other hand, the Tutori clearly thought she had been going about it the wrong way. He remembered that her dangerous antics got someone killed as far as he knew, and it was enough to warrant her expulsion from the *APA*, regardless of how noble her intentions might have been.

Penny had more pressing matters on her mind and was still thinking about *Don Ciccio's Pizza Window*, optimistically hoping the train was headed in that direction. Feeling rather sleepy after her latest snack, the wirehaired dachshund climbed into Henry's lap and curled up to get comfortable; within minutes, she fell into a deep slumber.

Henry tried to stay awake a little longer, but he eventually dozed off as well. He fell asleep with a multitude of questions dancing through his mind. "Where would Catherine turn up next? Would she uncouple the railcars again? Did she change into yet another disguise, making her escape all but certain? What about Barnaby's cloak... Would the council really expel him from the *APA* if he didn't catch her this time?"

— CHAPTER 15 —
FRANKLIN D. ROOSEVELT STATION

*H*enry was awoken hours later, startled by an announcement coming from the train's ceiling-mounted loudspeakers. "Bonsoir, mesdames et messieurs. The train will be arriving at the *Franklin D. Roosevelt Station* in approximately five minutes. Please gather your belongings and prepare for departure. Also, we sincerely apologize for the slight disturbance earlier this afternoon. It looks like there were some technical difficulties with the coupling hooks on one of the railcars, but there's no need to be alarmed. Our engineers have been dispatched to investigate, and we will work diligently to accommodate all impacted passengers. Thank you again for choosing *Great Britain Railway*, and we do hope you enjoy your time in Paris."

Penny felt quite revitalized after her nap and couldn't resist giving Henry a few kisses on the cheek to make sure he was fully awake. He wriggled at first amid the chuckling before finally nestling his head against hers in adoration.

"Nap time is ovah, mate!" Barnaby exclaimed. Stone-faced, he sternly warned, "Now, listen carefully... I'm done playing games with this French maniac. I'm all outta second chances here, and I'll catch hell from the council if I return empty-handed again. So please, just stay outta my way and try not to get yourself hurt, alright?"

"Yes, sir, Mr. Murdoch," Henry obediently replied.

Despite Barnaby's abrasive tone, Henry could tell the Australian was truly worried underneath all the arrogance. He could see the desperation in the man's eyes. If Catherine managed to slip away, it sure sounded like Barnaby's cloak would be in serious jeopardy upon his return to the *Arthur Broome*.

Barnaby turned around and hastily proceeded up the aisleway toward the nearest exit. Henry sprang out of his seat and followed once he finished putting Penny back in the rucksack; she curiously stuck her head out of the top to see where they were headed next.

As they stepped off the railcar, Barnaby and Henry froze in their tracks, tensing up the second they spotted Catherine on the train platform. She was standing there alone. The black duffle bag was hanging over her shoulder, and it looked like she had been waiting for Barnaby to get off the train.

Perhaps it was another not-so-subtle taunt, but it was clear Catherine didn't want to escape just yet; she wanted Barnaby to watch her get away so that he couldn't blame anyone or anything for his failure to rescue the bear cubs. She relished the sight of him losing and wanted to make sure he tasted the defeat in the air before she absconded again, especially now that she knew his cloak was on the line.

Two railcars separated Catherine from Barnaby and Henry. Most of the other passengers were gathered near the front of the train, further up, waiting for their luggage.

The *real* train conductor and some of the *Great Britain Railway* personnel huddled in a circle. They were trying to figure out what happened to the back half of the train as the passengers around them clamored for attention. Nobody seemed happy. The employees kept anxiously flipping through the cargo manifest while turning around to glance at the train tracks in a perplexed manner.

Unbothered by the commotion, Barnaby and Catherine kept

their feet firmly planted. Like a showdown in an old Western film, they just stood there staring at each other, waiting to see who would make the first move.

Neither of them said a word at first. The betrayal in Barnaby's eyes gave Henry the eerie feeling that this was more than just business as usual. It was clearly personal, and the stakes couldn't have been any higher.

All of a sudden, Barnaby yanked the cattle prod from his belt and thrust his arm toward the ground, instantly expanding the full length of the baton in one swift motion, and threatening, "This ends now, Catherine. Right here, right now!"

In spite of the unmistakable hostility, there was a shaky quiver of desperation sprinkled into Barnaby's voice. The losses were piling up left and right. He clearly had a bad feeling that it would cost him everything if he didn't emerge victorious this time around. All that haughtiness wouldn't count for anything otherwise.

"You're a lousy ballroom dancer, Barnabas!" Catherine screamed back in an unapologetically facetious tone. "And your haircut is trash!"

Henry was admittedly impressed by Catherine's unwavering tenacity; she wasn't the least bit intimidated. Yet behind all the bravado, he noticed that she had something clutched in her hand. He was too far away to tell what it might have been, but he assumed it wasn't a white flag.

Knowing that Barnaby was likely to tackle her to the ground at any second, Catherine tossed what appeared to be dozens of dried jerky sticks at his feet the instant he took a step forward. She immediately pulled another handful from the black duffle bag and threw them across the train platform. Henry marveled at the scattered mess of jerky sticks in front of the two circus railcars between them.

Catherine grinned as Barnaby looked fretfully over at the railcars between them—the one with the Bengal tigers inside made him pause, as if it were an unwelcome harbinger. He had been so focused on tangling with his French adversary that he didn't even notice the main sliding door on the side of the railcar closest to him was unlocked and partially cracked open. The opportunity to lock it quickly passed, just as his heart began to beat three times faster than usual. It was too late, and there was nothing he could do once he saw that door rattle.

Enthralled by the scent of dried jerky on the platform, the male tiger stuck his nose through the unlatched door as the mouthwatering smell wafted into the railcar. Henry shuddered and nervously took a few steps back when he saw a large paw slip through the crack.

The hungry tiger pushed the door open effortlessly, lured by the enticing smell of jerky sticks and the promise of freedom outside the dreadful railcar. With nothing in his way, the magnificent tiger let out a deafening roar that echoed throughout the underground rail station while the other two felines emerged from the darkness and stood at his side.

The pair of female tigers couldn't resist the generous window of time they had to fill their stomachs, and the unrestricted freedom that came along with it was too enchanting to pass up.

Virtually all of the other passengers in the train station turned around at the sound of the thunderous disturbance. No one expected to see a wild tiger eagerly looking for his next meal, and seeing three of them at once only terrified the travelers even more.

When the enormous Bengal tiger jumped out of the circus railcar onto the platform below, everyone sprinted toward the exits in a panicked frenzy.

To Henry's surprise, the male tiger didn't pay much attention to the people running for the exits and instead rushed to devour the dozens of jerky sticks in front of the railcar. The smell also tempted Penny, but even she wasn't hungry enough to share a meal with a pack of malnourished tigers.

As Barnaby shuffled backwards to put some distance between himself and the *two hundred kilogram* tiger that was crouching in front of him, he turned to Henry and gravely cautioned, "Careful, Halifax. One swipe from that cat's paw is all it takes to kill someone. Whatever you do... don't make any sudden movements, and try not to look 'em in the eyes, mate. They can smell fear from a mile away."

Henry heeded the sound advice and slowly moved toward the staircase behind him, which led to the exit of the station.

Barnaby stayed put and maintained a defensive stance with the cattle prodder in hand. The other two tigers jumped onto the platform; they casually walked to the nearest pile of jerky sticks, letting the savory smells guide their way.

To make matters worse, a pair of full-grown grizzly bears in the other circus railcar closest to Catherine heard the ruckus unfolding. Its sliding door was unlocked as well, and the bigger bear shoved it open with curiosity. The massive animals briefly looked around before clumsily climbing down onto the train platform. They couldn't resist the aroma of jerky in the station, and it appeared they were just as hungry as the tigers.

At the same time, panicked passengers were frantically screaming and running up the steps to get out of the station as fast as they could.

Henry could only watch helplessly from afar. Uninterested in wrestling a grizzly bear or trying to outrun a pack of famished jungle cats, he felt it was best to stay close to the nearest exit.

Catherine reveled in the chaos unfolding and enthusiastically tossed another round of jerky sticks across the platform. She was cavorting in the foreground, taking great pride in her latest escapade. The frightened passengers scurrying through the terminal didn't share that same sentiment and found her wicked laughter to be less than helpful. Catherine's haunting cackles drowned out the screams of horror that were echoing off the station walls.

Barnaby was madder than a swarm of bees avenging their queen's death and wanted nothing more than to put a stop to Catherine's reign of terror before she did anything else that might get him killed. He fought back the urge to charge forward, though. The hungry animals directly in his path served as a constant reminder of how powerless he was to stop her, and he could tell she loved every second of it. He just stared at her with a revenge-induced scowl while she teased him from a safe distance.

Running short on patience, Barnaby yelled furiously, "You're gonna pay for this, Catherine!" as he rushed to join Henry at the bottom of the staircase. While the remainder of the straggling passengers hurried to exit the train station, Barnaby and Henry watched Catherine cavalierly prance about. The Australian Tutori was incensed and wouldn't take his eyes off her.

The French disguise artist couldn't help but feel confident in her seemingly guaranteed victory. She just frolicked over to the other staircase on the far side of the station.

Henry could feel the radiating anger coming from Barnaby, and he started to worry that Catherine's relentless teasing would only make things worse.

After the circus animals were done devouring the food that was generously given to them, they promptly turned their attention toward the original source of the tasty treats. Catherine was busy scampering up the stairs to get away, but the animals were still hungry. Their rapacious appetites had not yet been fully satisfied, and they wanted more.

The male tiger roared thunderously; the booming noise reverberated off the walls and instantly consumed the entire underground rail station. It was so loud that even Barnaby flinched, nearly dropping his electric cattle prod in the process.

Unexpectedly, Catherine stopped upon hearing the tiger's demand for more food and pulled out another large handful of jerky sticks. Like a trail of breadcrumbs, she scattered the rest of the protein-packed snacks behind her as she ran up the staircase. At the top of the steps, she shouted cheerfully, "Au revoir, Barnabas! Au revoir!" before disappearing onto the street above.

As soon as the male tiger smelled the familiar smell of jerky, he leaped through the air in an obsessive scramble to get to the stairs, easily outrunning the larger grizzly bear that was heading in the same direction. The two female tigers followed suit and climbed the steps with acrobatic agility. They mostly ignored the other brown bear, who had just started awkwardly climbing the stairs in a much less graceful manner.

Even though the circus animals were still feeling quite ravenous, the sweet smell of freedom above ground proved to be far more appealing than another round of appetizers.

Barnaby raced up the staircase on the other side of the station as Henry tried to keep pace without jostling Penny too much in the rucksack on his back. They reached the street and immediately saw hordes of people racing to get away. It was clear that everyone was terrified when the first tiger surfaced from the underground train station below.

Catherine had wittingly scattered another round of jerky sticks in front of the stairs on purpose, which kept the animals preoccupied for a few minutes while everyone else ran for their lives.

"Must be some sort of protest!" Barnaby exclaimed. He couldn't fathom why there were thousands of people flooding the streets this late in the evening—until he saw the army of farm tractors blocking traffic in every direction. It was absolute chaos, even before the menacing circus animals showed up.

Fairly content with the light snack in their bellies and the life-changing sense of freedom in sight, the animals scurried away in opposite directions as Barnaby and Henry watched apprehensively. Having suffered under the hands of humans for years, the wild animals ignored the noisy mob of French protestors and rushed to get away as quickly as possible.

There was no sign of Catherine anywhere. Only protestors packed the streets as far as the eye could see in every direction.

"Damn that woman! We'll nevah find her now!" Barnaby fumed. He kicked over a nearby trash can and yelled, "That French menace just cost me my cloak!"

Undeterred, Henry replied reassuringly, "She's not getting away this time, eh?" The clever Canadian kneeled and let Penny out of his rucksack. After pulling out the last sweet potato stick from his pocket, he looked at her and said, "Alright, let's find those bears, Penny... We need you to lead the way, girl."

The wirehaired dachshund didn't hesitate to devour the delicious treat in nearly one bite; she practically inhaled it. Ready and excited to prove herself, Penny's natural hunting instincts overshadowed everything else. She was eager to embark on the next chase and was determined to find those polar bear cubs.

Penny raised her nose in the air and began sniffing for any sign of Catherine's scent. All of a sudden, she started barking feverishly while her tail wagged back and forth. Before Henry could say anything, she sprinted down Avenue Montaigne toward the Seine River. She zigzagged effortlessly through the crowds with gymnastic precision and lightning speed, like she had just seen a badger.

Henry and Barnaby chased after her, although they struggled to keep pace as the wirehaired dachshund bobbed and weaved around the protestors that filled the streets.

Penny eventually came to a screeching halt when she reached the roundabout in front of *Chez Gastineau's*. With so many pleasant fragrances emanating from the renowned French restaurant behind her, she had to recalibrate her nose to have any chance of finding Catherine's scent again. Henry and Barnaby arrived a few moments later, both of them clearly out of breath and wheezing heavily.

Relieved to see that she was safe, Henry bent over and gave Penny a healthy dose of ear scratches.

Barnaby was less concerned. He needed to find Catherine before it was too late, and he couldn't be bothered to think about anything else. He kept swiveling his head back and forth, looking anxiously for any sign of Catherine's red hair or the black duffle bag.

While Barnaby paced to take his mind off the increasing sense of hopelessness forming in the pit of his stomach, Henry's eyes were drawn to the sky. Having never been to Paris, the boy from Kodiak Bay stared up at the *Eiffel Tower* in utter astonishment.

Even after a hectic train ride and a strange run-in with some very dangerous circus animals, Henry found himself captivated by the larger-than-life work of art in the middle of the city.

"Any sight of her, mate?" Barnaby asked impatiently, which caused Henry to finally break his gaze.

There were protestors everywhere, and Barnaby's frustration was seething. Each passing minute made it harder for him to concentrate. The looming fear of being stripped of his cloak if he returned to the *Arthur Broome* defeated was stressful enough, but the hordes of protestors clamoring around them only made him more upset.

With all the noise and chaos, huge farm tractors blocking every street in sight, and the French Gendarmerie coming toward them in riot gear, it was absolute pandemonium by any measure. The perfect storm of turmoil and French defiance was exactly what Catherine needed to slip away yet again. She had already disappeared into the sea of protestors, and it seemed that Barnaby and Henry were too late.

Penny wasn't ready to quit and barked a few times to get Henry's attention. He instinctively picked her up with both arms to give the wirehaired dachshund a better chance of finding Catherine's trail again. She sniffed fervently, feeling optimistic as a gust of wind filled her nose with a promising mix of new scents.

Barnaby was on the verge of having a full-on meltdown despite Penny's unwavering confidence. The impending consequences of failure were impossible to ignore at this point, and he knew his excuses wouldn't matter this time. Hope was a precious gift that he might never get again if the council expelled him from the *Animal Protection Authority*.

"Forget it! She's gone, mate!" Barnaby cried out in anger. "She's gone... We lost!" The palpable sense of defeat in his voice almost had Henry convinced.

Uninterested in Barnaby's defeatist attitude, Penny suddenly jolted her head in the direction of the *Pont de l'Alma*, which was just past the roundabout ahead. She then let out a ferocious wave of thunderous barks that put her sharp fangs on full display. Even though she was small, Penny's bark implied otherwise; it was both loud and threatening enough to attract the attention of their elusive adversary.

A renewed and welcome sense of confidence washed over Barnaby the instant he heard Henry shout, "There she is! On the left side of the bridge!"

Catherine was standing near the edge of the bridge across the street and inadvertently turned around when she heard the strident barks. As soon as Barnaby saw the train conductor's uniform amid the commotion, he locked eyes with her.

Despite the hundreds of protestors standing between them and Catherine, Henry rashly charged ahead with Penny in his arms anyway. The idea of returning victoriously to the *Arthur Broome* as heroes only fueled his excitement. He was determined to rescue those polar bear cubs and hopefully save Barnaby's cloak in the process. It could be just what he needed to get that highly sought-after invitation from the *APA* council to train as a Magari—something he had been dreaming about since he left Mr. Robinson's tailor shop onboard the ship.

With Penny's deafening bark at his disposal, Henry cut through the crowds of protestors like a great white shark slicing through a school of frightened fish. It was all he needed to clear a path.

Catherine's smug grin promptly turned into a look of frustration when she noticed Henry coming straight for her. As she took off running in the opposite direction, Barnaby screamed, "Wait up, Halifax! Wait for me, mate!"

The thought of anyone taking down Catherine besides himself wasn't something Barnaby could stand for. That's not how Australian rules work. His ego simply wouldn't allow it; he had to be the one to catch her. He brazenly pushed his way through the hundreds of people blocking the roundabout but was unable to keep pace with Henry and Penny as the crowds closed in behind them.

While the Australian struggled to escape the wave of protesters in his way, Henry stopped abruptly at the edge of the bridge and looked around frantically for any sign of Catherine.

Penny began shrieking and flailing uncontrollably in Henry's arms, demanding he set her loose. He reluctantly obliged, fearing her tantrum would undoubtedly escalate in the absence of compliance. She immediately sprinted toward the cobblestone ramp leading toward the riverbank. The hunt would be over when she decided it was over—the lingering scent of those polar bear cubs felt like an itch she couldn't scratch, at least not until she stopped Catherine.

Henry regretted his decision almost right away and chased after his fearless companion.

Penny rounded the corner, and her lengthy body slid in a drift coming off the ramp at too high a speed. Once she got back on her feet, she let out an intimidating combination of vicious growling and barking before charging ahead toward the unsuspecting French bandit.

Catherine was standing under the bridge, feeling overly confident that Barnaby and his new sidekick would never find her. The arrogance that was in the air that evening appeared to be infectious, and nobody was immune. When she saw that Penny was about to stop her escape, though, she scrambled to come up with another hastily concocted diversion.

Refusing to go quietly, Catherine tipped over a full barrel of thick, black oil in a panicked frenzy. The flood of crude oil rushed down the side of the riverbank, rapidly covering everything in its path.

"No, Penny! No!" Henry screamed as he came barreling around the corner too quickly. Blinded by the sight of his beloved dachshund heading straight toward danger, a tidal wave of crude oil instantly knocked him off his feet. He was sent careening into a stack of empty wooden crates next to the riverbank.

Penny tried to leap over the oil but couldn't jump far enough; she ended up landing short and sliding into Catherine's feet unexpectedly.

Henry managed to get a glimpse of Catherine before he slipped, and that split-second revealed far more about her getaway plan than he had initially assumed. She was in the middle of refueling a yellow floatplane under the bridge, using the gasoline pump normally reserved for riverboats. While the dachshund's unwanted arrival had certainly interrupted Catherine's attempt to flee, he knew it wouldn't be enough to stop her.

Already sore, Henry struggled to get back up. The stack of wooden crates had been smashed to pieces, and he knew the bruises that would follow were only going to make the inescapable pain feel worse. None of that seemed to matter when he suddenly heard Catherine cry out in agony, "Damn it, you sassy witch!"

Henry was terrified that something had happened to Penny and was overcome with a surreal sense of panic. Covered in sticky black oil and clambering to get back on his feet, he grabbed the nearest stone pillar and finally hoisted himself up.

Frozen in a state of utter disbelief, Henry looked down the oil-covered riverbank and gasped when he saw Penny mauling the back of Catherine's leg. The wirehaired dachshund had stubbornly clamped onto Catherine's ankle using her sharp fangs, which sent the red-haired woman crashing to the ground. In the midst of wrestling with the fiery dog, Catherine locked eyes with Henry and pulled something from her pocket.

Right as he took one step forward, Henry was yanked backward after Barnaby grabbed him from behind by the collar like an overly protective parent. In the same instant, Catherine ignited the lighter in her hand and tossed the open flame into the pool of oil leading up to Henry's shoes.

It only took seconds for the riverbank to become engulfed in flames—Penny and Catherine vanished behind the wall of fire raging in front of him. The chilling sound that ensued would haunt Henry forever. Penny's ferocious growling turned into a distressed whimper, and then nothing but silence.

Too distraught to care about the burning pool of oil standing between him and his best friend, Henry insisted on charging ahead through the fire but didn't get very far. Barnaby promptly held him back once more.

"Easy, mate! This isn't the way!" Barnaby shouted, trying his best to calm Henry while restraining him from running into the flames. The intense heat caused them both to look away as he exclaimed, "We need to circle 'round to the other side!"

Barnaby's pleas for reconsideration were drowned out by the

sound of the floatplane's engine starting up. Henry recognized that familiar sound at once. He'd heard it countless times while working at the harbor in Kodiak Bay.

Unable to hear any barking, growling, or even crying, Henry knew Penny was in serious trouble, and he didn't have time to wait. Panicked and fearing the worst, he impulsively elbowed Barnaby in the stomach.

Barnaby was completely taken by surprise and immediately hunched over in pain after releasing his grip on Henry's suit jacket. He muttered something in annoyance under his breath, but the tenacious boy was already gone.

Henry dashed forward through the raging inferno without an ounce of hesitation. It didn't matter that his oil-soaked shoes instantly burst into flames. And the intensifying heat from his suit jacket catching fire hadn't slowed him down one bit. He would have done anything to protect Penny, even if it meant charging through broken glass barefoot. There was nothing he wouldn't do to try to save her life.

Unbeknownst to Henry, his suit was made with a special type of synthetic wool that had a reinforced lining designed to prevent injury from knives, sharp teeth, and (in this case) even fire.

As Henry selflessly raced ahead through the towering blaze, Barnaby turned around and retreated back up the cobblestone ramp to cross the bridge on the other side.

Once Henry made it past the pool of burning oil, he quickly realized that Catherine had already absconded. There was no sign of Penny on the riverbank or in the water, either. His suit jacket and shoes were still on fire, though none of that seemed to make a difference when he accepted the agonizing truth. He had lost, and his loyal sidekick was indeed gone.

The terrifying panic only got worse, and it began to dwarf the pain coming from the fresh bruises on his lower back. In the midst of all the dreadful thoughts running through his mind, Henry noticed a pair of tranquilizer darts on the ground—the same type of darts he found at the *Kodiak Bay Zoo*.

The loud noise of the yellow floatplane slowly pulling away gave him a heart-stopping shred of hope, though. He surmised that Penny was headed upriver, and if he didn't do anything about it, there was a real possibility that he would never see her again.

While Barnaby turned the corner onto the riverbank from the other side of the bridge, Henry leaped impetuously into the Seine River.

A cloud of white smoke instantly billowed above Henry as the cold river water extinguished his burning clothes. He raced to catch up to the plane, swimming as fast as his arms and legs could move. After noticing that Barnaby hadn't jumped in after him, the thought of giving up briefly crossed his mind. The daring rescue attempt felt insurmountable once he realized he was on his own.

Even though there was nothing he could do to stop Catherine from taking off, Henry used every last bit of energy in him to keep going anyway, eventually latching onto the plane's pontoon.

"Don't do it, mate! You gotta let go!" Barnaby shouted, watching in dismay as he stood on the riverbank. He was genuinely concerned Henry could get killed if that plane left the water with him still attached to the bottom.

Out of ideas and growing more anxious by the second, Barnaby emptied a full sleeve of throwing darts in Henry's direction. None of the darts managed to strike him, but one came close when it hit the side of the plane's fuselage, narrowly missing his head.

Henry was furious that Barnaby would dare try to put him to sleep at a time like this; it was one thing to stand on the sidelines, but he didn't ask for Barnaby's help once Penny had vanished.

Unscathed by the throwing darts, Henry struggled to tighten his grip as the yellow floatplane picked up speed. His hands were slipping, and it became increasingly challenging to hold on as his legs dragged in the river behind the plane.

"Let go, Halifax! Ya hear me? Just let go!" Barnaby yelled desperately from the riverbanks.

Henry's grip stiffened as he felt the plane lift out of the water while his legs dangled slightly above the river's surface. He knew Barnaby was right but couldn't bring himself to let go. Suddenly, the floatplane started to veer upward after Catherine yanked back on the control column, sending the plane into a rapid ascent.

"Damn it, kid! Let go! Let go now!" Barnaby screamed. He gazed helplessly as Henry clung to the bottom of the plane.

Henry's hands began slipping, and the wind continued dragging him down; he eventually lost his grip and dropped into the Seine River like a bucket full of wet cement.

Barnaby sighed in relief, murmuring, "Man... this kid is nuts!"

With his heart shattered into a million pieces, Henry drifted from the center of the Seine over to the riverbank, where Barnaby was waiting. The boy was truly devastated, consumed by an immeasurable sense of torment and guilt.

Barnaby could see it in his eyes—Henry desperately feared that he would never see his beloved dachshund again.

— CHAPTER 16 —
THE SAMARITAN

*B*arnaby reached down to help Henry climb out of the water and onto the cobblestone riverbank. "I'm sorry, mate. It wasn't supposed to happen like this," he declared somberly as he grabbed the boy's hand.

Buckets of water dripped off Henry's charred suit as he stood up. He was dejected and full of sorrow, too overwhelmed by the loss of his dachshund to say anything. After his seething resentment reached a tipping point, an eruption of rage overshadowed the grief, and he shoved Barnaby into the frigid waters of the Seine River without warning.

The stunned Australian briefly disappeared under the water, only to resurface moments later. "What the hell was that?" he yelled, shocked and annoyed by Henry's temerarious outburst.

"This is all your fault!" Henry cried out in a profoundly contemptuous tone. He had never been so incensed in his entire life.

Henry was a kind spirit that always maintained his composure and would never say a bad word about anyone, but this was different. He wanted answers and just carried on admonishing Barnaby, "How was it supposed to happen then? You knock me out with that sleeve of tranquilizer darts while you let Catherine escape again?"

As Barnaby crawled out of the cold water and onto the riverbank, he laughed at the accusations and misguided attempt to tarnish his good name.

Despite Barnaby's minacious glare, Henry continued berating him, "Savannah was right! You *are* working with that red-haired lunatic for all I know!"

"And now she has Penny too!" he shouted while staring coldly at the Australian.

Barnaby's clothes were drenched, and a puddle from the dripping water had now formed at his feet. If it were anyone else, he would have been absolutely livid. However, the shrill anguish in the boy's voice gave him pause. He exhaled and calmly acknowledged Henry's pain. "It's alright, mate. I'm gonna give ya a pass because I've seen it before."

"You're in shock, but you didn't bring a mirror... and now you're looking for someone to blame." Henry's irate expression turned into a look of shame when Barnaby added, "Anyone except for yourself, right kid?"

Henry's jaw dropped, yet nothing came out. Even though he wanted to scream at Barnaby, he realized the Australian Tutori was right.

It would have been convenient to just put the blame on someone else, and as tempting as it was to take the easy way out, Henry couldn't escape the truth. Underneath all the unbridled anger, there was no denying that Penny was his responsibility and his alone. No matter how he tried to twist it so that he could keep thinking it wasn't entirely his fault, the facts would never change.

After all, Barnaby was the one who insisted he and Penny stay onboard the *Arthur Broome* in the first place. Barnaby was the one who told him to wait before he arrogantly rushed off on his own to face Catherine by himself. Had he listened from the start, none of this would have happened. Instead, Penny was now gone, and Catherine was flying off into the sunset with the missing polar bear cubs.

Overwhelmed by a dangerous combination of rage, sadness, and despair, Henry's eyes watered up. He looked up at Barnaby and responded contritely, "I'm sorry, Mr. Murdoch. You're right... You've been right about everything this whole time."

"I'll do anything to see Penny again. Anything!" He pleaded as tears slowly rolled down the side of his face, "Just help me get her back. Please! Please, sir!"

Henry wiped the tears from his eyes, embarrassed and ashamed that he was now begging for help after blaming Barnaby only moments ago. In spite of his best efforts to stand tough and be courageous, there was a haunting sense of desperation in his voice. The abiding enthusiasm was gone, replaced by a deep despondence that made the Australian Tutori feel sorry for him.

Barnaby looked up at the sky beyond the *Eiffel Tower*. Struggling to come up with a new plan to rescue the polar bear cubs and the missing wirehaired dachshund, he watched as the yellow floatplane flew further and further away. The plane was barely visible at this point, although it appeared to be heading north.

"Wait, I remember the tail number!" Henry blurted. "It was, uh... *S-P-7-1-0-8-1*! Maybe we can track the plane if we radio the nearest air traffic control station?"

Mindful of the boy's renewed sense of hope, Barnaby prudently replied, "We will get it sorted, mate. You have my word... but we can't do anything until we get back to the *Broome*."

Soaking wet and running out of precious time, Henry wasn't sure how they were going to get back to the ship. He didn't even realize that the port of Le Havre was kilometers away on the northern coast of France, much too far from the center of Paris to walk. Naively unaware of this glaring hindrance, he still felt confident they would find a way to get there somehow. His wishful thinking was suddenly interrupted by a clattering noise; it sounded like at least two wooden bats were being dragged along the cobblestone path next to the river.

Barnaby and Henry hastily turned around to find a pack of eight guys approaching. They all wore matching black leather jackets, white t-shirts, blue jeans, and gold chains with pendants that had the number *32* hanging from their necks. Younger than Barnaby but clearly older than Henry, everyone in the group appeared to be in their early twenties.

Henry had no idea who they were or what they wanted, although he knew one thing was clear. These guys were looking for trouble.

A couple of them walked past Henry and Barnaby, dragging their wooden baseball bats balefully against the cobblestone. They didn't say anything at first. The eight of them just grinned and stared maliciously at the Australian.

Within a matter of seconds, the group of French street ruffians had Barnaby and Henry completely surrounded.

Calling out for the police wasn't going to help either—Barnaby presumed they had their hands full dealing with the protestors flooding the streets above. Even though he was admittedly worried about being outnumbered, the brash Tutori refused to show any trace of trepidation. Instead, he greeted them with a smirk (as only an Australian could do when in such peril).

"Well, well, well... if it isn't Soft Tony, Mozzarella Mike, Peppah Jack, and the whole gang! What do ya call yourselves again? *Le Fromage Boys*? Or was it... *Soft-T and the French Fry Crew*?" Barnaby jeered. "How's that hand feeling anyway?"

Henry didn't notice it at first; the ringleader had a lower arm cast bulging under his black leather jacket that came down and wrapped around his hand. It quickly became obvious that Barnaby knew these guys, and their last meeting must have been less than amicable, judging by the baseball bats.

"I'm happy to sign your cast if that's what you're after," Barnaby taunted before glancing at Henry with a confident wink.

The guy standing in the middle wearing the cast didn't care for Barnaby's snide remarks and instantly lost his temper. "It's Bad-T! Bad-T! You got that?" Barnaby couldn't help but laugh as the ringleader screamed like a toddler throwing a tantrum.

One of Bad-T's compatriots unexpectedly chimed in, "Oui, and you better check your tone when you're speaking to the *FDR Boys*!"

Known for causing trouble in all corners of the eighth arrondissement, the *FDR Boys* were a notoriously dangerous street gang in Paris. Nothing more than a pack of wild hooligans, the group frequently hung around the *Franklin D. Roosevelt Train Station*. It was something of a headquarters for them, although their territory extended across the entire neighborhood. Those that had fallen victim to their harassment (tourists and locals alike) started referring to them as the *FDR Boys*, and eventually, the name stuck. Given that their admiration for the American president was the only thing that rivaled their ruthlessness, it was indeed a fitting moniker.

Henry wiped his eyes to make sure there were no tears lingering on his face and immediately tensed up. He clenched his fists as the feeling of adrenaline reignited.

Each minute they wasted talking to these jokers only added to Henry's frustration; his best friend was missing, and he wanted to spend every waking moment searching for her before it was too late. He was determined to get back to the *Arthur Broome* as soon as possible and hoped these French street ruffians wouldn't get in his way.

"Oh, that's right. The *FDR Boys*. How could I forget?" Barnaby snickered as if he were recounting the last time he sneezed. "Now, remind me again... which one of you is illiterate and which one of you doesn't know how to read?"

Bad-T tilted his head in confusion and glanced at his right-hand man for the answer before yelling at Barnaby. "We've been looking everywhere for you!" He pointed emphatically and continued fuming, "Oui, you and the woman with the red hair that broke Bad-T's hand."

Unbeknownst to Henry, Barnaby had a previous run-in with the ringleader a few months ago and ended up breaking all twenty-seven bones in his hand.

It all happened the last time Barnaby was in Paris on an unrelated *APA* investigation. During a routine operation, he encountered the French hooligan, who was callously throwing glass bottles at a pair of stray dogs in an alley. Unable to let that stand, Barnaby figured smashing Bad-T's hand would make it harder for the delinquent to carry on terrorizing the innocent dogs in question. Bad-T was apparently still quite upset and had been looking for the Australian ever since.

Flattered that the posse of *FDR Boys* surrounding him were so eager to have a word, Barnaby replied facetiously in a jovial tone, "Lookin' for *me*? What's the mattah, Soft-T... You need a shortstop to play for your little league team here?" He chortled in amusement. "Isn't it a little past your bedtime?"

"No, uh, I... I can stay up as late as I want!" Bad-T stammered abashedly.

The smile on Barnaby's face faded as his demeanor turned far more threatening. "Yeah, nah... I've got more pressing issues to tend to at the moment. So why don't you clear out of our way before I give you a permanent limp to go along with that mangled hand?"

Bad-T laughed, confident that things would be different this time around now that he had backup. He looked briefly at his fellow *FDR Boys* on both sides and jeered, "Woah, careful, boys! We got a real tough guy here, no?"

"Qu'est-ce que c'est?" one of the *FDR Boys* asked while pointing the tip of his baseball bat toward the Australian's shoulders. Two of the others flipped Barnaby's cloak backward over his head so that it covered his face. "This is a cute cape... *C'est un super-héros*, oui?" The rest of the *FDR Boys* erupted into uncontrollable laughter.

Putting aside Henry's deficiencies in understanding French vocabulary, he was more confused than ever when Barnaby pulled the cloak back to the proper position and joined them in an uproarious round of hilarity. Absolutely bemused, he wasn't sure what to do or why Barnaby thought the disrespect levied at the *APA* warranted such merriment.

In the midst of a patronizing guffaw, Barnaby suddenly sucker punched the nearest hooligan in the throat. The man instantly fell to the ground, gasping for air.

Before the others realized what was happening, Barnaby took off his suit jacket and wrapped it around another guy's head in one swift motion—he forcefully kicked the guy into the pack of unsuspecting *FDR Boys*, sending the entire group crashing to the ground like a set of human bowling pins. It made the *FDR Boys* madder than a French waiter listening to a rude American try to order pancakes for breakfast.

Henry was startled and dismayed by the chaos unfolding in front of him. He just gawked without saying a word as a full-fledged brawl broke out on the riverbank seconds later.

Caught off guard by Barnaby's antics once again, Henry soon found himself tumbling onto the ground after being aggressively pushed by one of the French street ruffians. He didn't want any part of this untimely altercation, but now that they had pulled him into the tussle, he wasn't going to take it lying down.

Still furious about losing Penny and blinded by adrenaline, Henry jumped up and tackled the closest hooligan like an enforcer for the Toronto Maple Barons (*The Wrecker* himself would have been proud).

Barnaby wasn't faring as well, despite having the upper hand in the beginning. The *FDR Boys* had him surrounded as if they were a pack of vultures circling wounded prey in the desert. Outnumbered and stubbornly defiant, he refused to back down even after they all pounced on him at the same time, and the torrent of insults coming from his mouth only seemed to provoke them further.

As the *FDR Boys* continued pummeling Barnaby, Henry dashed over to help. He grabbed the nearest ruffian by the collar, yanked the guy's shirt over his head, and violently flung him into the wall.

Henry had never been in a fight. The occasional bout of teasing at school was one thing, but it never turned physical, not like this. Now that he was left to contend with a slew of French miscreants hellbent on beating Barnaby to a pulp, he remembered the most important lesson learned while watching hockey games with Captain Fulbright: "*You can't back down once the gloves come off.*"

Even with Henry's assistance, Barnaby struggled to turn the tables on the unrelenting bombardment of *FDR Boys* charging from practically every direction. He stomped one guy's foot, only to have another sneak up and grab him from behind. They kept coming at him like starved hyenas surrounding a lion that had been separated from the pride. There were just too many of them.

Hoping to draw their attention away from Barnaby, Henry managed to tackle one of them while fortuitously tripping another in the process. His plan worked a little too well; instead of contending with a few at the same time, nearly half of them shifted their focus to Henry. Two of the *FDR Boys* snatched his arms unexpectedly and held him back so that he couldn't run.

Despite Henry's best efforts to break free, he eventually conceded after noticing the blood dripping from his nose. To make matters worse, he saw that Barnaby had ultimately been overpowered by the rest of the *FDR Boys*. They had him pinned against the wall, diminishing his chances of escaping anytime soon.

"Let the kid go!" Barnaby shouted, prompting Bad-T's top lieutenant to punch the Australian in the stomach without warning. Hysterically laughing in amusement, Bad-T exclaimed, "That's for breaking my hand!"

Henry wrestled to escape their clutches, but he wasn't strong enough to slip away from the pair of *FDR Boys* restraining his arms.

"Who's ready for some batting practice?" Bad-T suggested. One of his fellow compatriots grinned sinisterly and started twirling the baseball bat in front of the Australian's face. It was the same guy that Barnaby had punched in the throat earlier; he was hoping to reciprocate in kind, eagerly stepping up as the first in line to get some payback.

The other guys held Barnaby's hand out against the wall while Bad-T taunted, "What do you say, boys? I'm thinking we break each bone in his hand, one by one. *All twenty-seven of them!*"

Barnaby continued writhing, desperately trying to break loose from the swarm of *FDR Boys* holding him down. No matter how much he wriggled, their grip only seemed to get tighter. Nevertheless, he smirked at Bad-T as if it were all just a big game and sneered, "Are you sure you can count to *twenty-seven* all on your own? I'm worried about you, Soft-T... That's some heavy math for someone who can barely tie his own shoes."

Concerned that Barnaby's spiteful remark might have gone too far, Henry yelled furiously, "Let him go!"

The *FDR Boys* howled with laughter—all of them except for Bad-T. He was in the middle of trying to teach the wayward Australian a lesson and couldn't believe Henry had the audacity to interrupt.

Bad-T marched over and socked Henry right in the nose while Barnaby watched helplessly. The young Canadian instantly hunched over in pain as more blood dripped from his nose onto the ground below.

THE TUTORI'S CLOAK 249

"Leave the kid out of this, ya blundering scoundrel!" Barnaby shouted, powerless to stop them from doling out another beating.

Bad-T blithely scampered over in response, leaning forward until he was face-to-face with the beleaguered Tutori (close enough that Barnaby smelled his rancid breath). The French ruffian gloated, "Maybe we should start with his friend first, no? What do you say, boys?"

He was having trouble deciding which was more fun—taunting Barnaby or whaling on Henry. Bad-T had been dreaming of this moment for a while, waiting patiently for the Australian to return to Paris so that he could personally feed him a cold plate of revenge.

Consumed by unwavering arrogance, Bad-T leaned in again after Barnaby mumbled something under his breath. He asked confusedly, "What did you say?"

Barnaby lurched his head back to signal Bad-T to come even closer, which proved to be a big mistake. Once he was close enough, Barnaby whispered, "Have you ever... had cold soup for breakfast?" No more than a split second had passed before the Australian Tutori unexpectedly thrust his head forward and properly headbutted the hooligan. Bad-T never saw it coming.

The leader of the *FDR Boys* instantly fell backwards onto the cobblestones while everyone watched in disbelief, including Henry.

During all the commotion, Barnaby made another vigorous attempt to break free. Despite contorting his body in every which way, he wasn't strong enough to escape the clutches of the *FDR Boys*, who were grabbing him by the arms.

Blood streamed out of Bad-T's nose like a running faucet. Enraged, he screamed, "Nobody headbutts Bad-T without my permission!" as the group of French troublemakers struggled to contain the unhinged Tutori.

Bad-T snapped his fingers to summon further punishment, and

immediately, one of the new recruits walked over to Henry and punched him square in the stomach. Henry cried out in pain, which only amplified Barnaby's anger. The Australian was incensed after watching the kid take another blow that was meant for him.

In a poor attempt to distract them, Barnaby vehemently shouted, "Come on over here and try that, ya bloody coward! Come on! Let's have a go, mate!" Henry tried to get away, but the older and stronger hooligans who were holding him back didn't budge.

Bad-T cackled in delight; the sight of Barnaby flailing around yet unable to do anything about it was priceless. He signaled his second-in-command with a snap of his fingers, and again, Henry got punched in the stomach as Barnaby looked on in anguish.

Listening to the howling laughter that followed was the last straw. Barnaby had been thoroughly provoked, and he could only take so much. As Henry fell to his knees in pain, the exasperated Tutori stomped on the foot of the nearest French street ruffian and wrestled with the others, using every last ounce of strength he had left in him.

The clouds of despair circling Henry finally started to dissipate once he saw that Barnaby managed to get an arm free. To the chagrin of the *FDR Boys*, the abundance of hope that arrived seconds later caught everyone by surprise. It all happened so quickly.

A blinding spotlight suddenly illuminated the riverbank—the fluorescent light coming from the middle of the Seine River was so bright, it almost felt like the sun itself had shown up, forcing everybody to look away.

Henry welcomed the impromptu distraction but wasn't particularly fond of what transpired next. An insurmountable flood of water crashed onto the riverbank, knocking all of them off their feet. Barnaby, Henry, and the collection of *FDR Boys* were all sent careening to the ground. They struggled to regain their footing and were drenched from the miniature tsunami that seemingly came out of nowhere.

Once most of the water had subsided, Henry noticed a small boat had docked next to the riverbank where they were standing. Without the blinding spotlight in his face, it became obvious that this must have been the same boat behind the aggressive docking maneuver that sent a towering wave of water crashing onto the riverbank. He wondered if perhaps the *APA* had sent reinforcements, courtesy of Savannah Sunday.

While Barnaby and Henry carefully stood up, three of the *FDR Boys* didn't hesitate to walk over and confront the mysterious mariner, who briskly stepped onto the riverbank to greet them.

Bad-T was beyond livid. His leather jacket got completely soaked with water, and he warned, "You just made the biggest mistake of your life, *mon pote*." The impulsive ringleader charged toward the man in a blind rage, totally unaware that he would soon leave with a newfound understanding of what it meant to be humiliated.

Without saying a word, the Samaritan from the boat used Bad-T's forward momentum to toss him effortlessly into the river like he was a bag of trash.

Bad-T's right-hand man challenged the formidable contender next, but he was dealt with just as swiftly. It only took a single smack to the right side of the French hooligan's head (the sound echoed off the cobblestone wall in a chilling manner). He didn't even have time to feel the painful sense of regret that followed; the guy had been knocked out cold after just one slap.

Still not intimidated, the next half-witted street ruffian foolish enough to step forward threw his fists up and brazenly approached. It didn't make a difference, though. He was sent tumbling backward almost instantaneously after being kicked square in the chest.

As Bad-T cowardly swam to the other side of the river, Henry glanced at the pair of incapacitated *FDR Boys* and dashed over to join

Barnaby in case they got up. The five others who were left tried to corner their new adversary. One of them even started swinging a baseball bat around in a threatening manner.

Visibly annoyed, the stranger pulled out a sword from the scabbard on his waist. He was tired of playing games and felt it was time for the rest of the *FDR Boys* to scurry off like the charlatans he knew they were.

Seeing that sharp blade come out was all it took for the wannabe tough guys to start running for their lives. The gang disappeared in a panic, dropping their wooden baseball bats while leaving their two unconscious friends behind.

Barnaby finished putting his suit jacket back on and then walked over to greet the mysterious stranger as Henry stood frozen in wonderment.

Their luck had certainly turned in the face of such a daunting impediment, but Henry was still stunned by the fortuitous arrival of the boat. "Appreciate the assistance, mate... We're truly grateful," Barnaby said, extending his arm to shake the man's hand. There was an unambiguous sense of gratitude peppered throughout his voice.

Now that the scuffle had ended, Henry took a closer look and noticed the sharp-dressed gentleman was actually a member of the Carabinieri. The officer's hat, the white bandolier, the unique cape—he recognized all of it right away when the man stepped into the light. The familiar uniform was a welcome sight, and Henry sighed in relief.

Apparently, the Carabinieri officer saw the trouble unfolding as his boat cruised down the river. He didn't hesitate to break up the tussle when it became clear that the young boy was in danger.

"The Carabinieri? But this is France," Henry quietly blurted with a bewildered look on his face. He couldn't fathom why a Carabinieri patrol boat would be all the way out here on the Seine River. Too befuddled to even thank the man for saving them from the *FDR Boys*, he squinted to see the nametag on the officer's jacket and asked, "Did the *APA* send you? Uh, *Officer D'Acquisto*?"

"*The APA*? Are you alright, son?" Officer D'Acquisto replied confusedly.

"Don't mind him, officer," Barnaby interjected. "He's still a bit shaken up after that little tussle with those rapscallions."

Henry enthusiastically chimed in, "My apologies, sir. I meant to say thank you! We sure are lucky you showed up when you did!"

Officer D'Acquisto nodded, "Sì, sì, there's a young French girl in the hospital nearby who is-a very sick. She desperately needed a transfusion, and one of my fellow Carabinieri offered to donate his blood to help her. It is-a very rare blood type. I just left the hospital and was on my way back to the station when I spotted the boy in trouble."

"We really can't thank you enough, sir," Henry said graciously, sincerely appreciative of this man's selfless act of courage. Officer D'Acquisto looked up to the sky and gestured the sign of the cross with his right hand, thankfully declaring, "Sì, Saint Christopher was looking out for all of us tonight."

Thinking it was best they head back to the ship right away, Barnaby shook the officer's hand once more. "Thanks again, mate. We owe you one, that's for sure."

"Hold on a minute!" Officer D'Acquisto exclaimed, pulling Barnaby closer as they shook hands. A look of suspicion abruptly replaced the smile on his face as the officer curiously inquired, "Your cloak... I know this symbol. I've seen it before. You are... *Tutori*?" Barnaby nodded his head affirmatively.

"I thought it was just legend," the officer dubiously replied, staring at the pendant on the front of Barnaby's cloak. "But it is-a true?"

"Sì. È vero," Barnaby answered modestly.

The Carabinieri standing in front of them looked like he had just seen a ghost. As if he were speaking to a commanding officer, his demeanor turned far more serious. "*Per favore*, are you certain that I can't be of any further assistance?"

Henry interrupted Barnaby (who was about to respectfully decline) and impulsively yelled out, "Yes, please, sir! We need to get back to our ship right away. It's an emergency!" He glanced at Barnaby, adding, "Port Le Havre, right? Isn't that what you said earlier?"

Barnaby sighed heavily in frustration. He felt it was bad form to ask Officer D'Acquisto for a favor after the man had just saved them from a painful encounter with the *FDR Boys*, but it was too late. Henry had already asked, and Barnaby knew the Carabinieri would never turn down an opportunity to help someone in need.

"Sì, this is-a not a problem, young man," Officer D'Acquisto answered. "I know the Seine very well. I can get you there in no time at all."

"Grazie mille, but that really isn't necessary, officer. We can find our own way," Barnaby respectfully interceded. Officer D'Acquisto responded emphatically, "Nonsense! I insist. Per favore." He raised his hand, gesturing toward the Carabinieri patrol boat.

"Thank you, sir. Thank you!" Henry exclaimed. Even though he still didn't know how they were going to find Penny, he was grateful for the man's generous offer.

Barnaby reluctantly followed Henry onto the Carabinieri patrol boat, right behind Officer D'Acquisto.

The sound of the engine firing up gave Henry pause. He glanced over at the incapacitated *FDR Boys* sprawled out on the cobblestone riverbank and wouldn't soon forget that it could have been him knocked unconscious if it weren't for the Carabinieri.

As the patrol boat raced up the Seine River toward the port of Le

Havre, Henry and Barnaby didn't say a word during the entire journey.

Henry was furious with himself for failing Penny when it mattered most. His heart would never be whole again until he found his best friend, and the inescapable feelings of anguish only seemed to get worse with each passing minute. He desperately hoped that she was safe, wherever she was.

Joining the *APA*, rescuing the missing polar bear cubs, and catching Saint-Clair were all Henry could think about less than an hour ago—none of that mattered anymore. He should have just called the Mounties back at the *Crown & Anchor Tavern* when he had the chance. They could have stopped Catherine in Kodiak Bay if it weren't for his selfish choice to follow Barnaby into that zoo.

Henry never stopped to consider the consequences of what it meant to actually be a Tutori. Since stepping off the ship, danger seemed to follow him at every turn.

Enchanted by the legends and tall tales he had heard for years, nothing ever prepared him for the misery of losing his best friend. He would never forgive himself for reciting the Tutori Creed at the docks if something happened to Penny. He tried to stay hopeful, but the despair was getting harder to ignore.

In the midst of all the chaos that unfolded earlier, Henry almost forgot that Barnaby would likely be facing harsh penalties upon his return to the *Arthur Broome*. As troubling as that was, he anxiously wondered if the *APA* council would look past those indiscretions now that Henry needed their help more than ever.

At this point, Henry wasn't sure whose side Barnaby was actually on. It didn't really matter anymore, though. He only wanted to find Penny. Everything else was a distant second, and his stomach was tied up in knots just thinking about her.

Barnaby was feeling equally guilty, although he was distracted trying to come up with a good explanation as to why he would be returning to the council defeated yet again. He knew his cloak was probably on the line, and he figured Savannah had already painted a less-than-flattering picture of today's events when she delivered her report to the council.

Despite his invincible ego and arrogant bravado that normally made him feel confident, Barnaby was worried that his entire life was about to fall apart like a snowflake at a bonfire. Glancing over at Henry didn't help matters either. The guilt was beginning to feel overwhelming. He would never forget the sight of seeing the kid take a beating from the *FDR Boys*—the same beating that was meant for him.

With dried blood all over the bottom half of Henry's face, Barnaby felt solely responsible and could tell the young boy was heartbroken.

It was no secret that he found Henry to be an annoyance at times, but Barnaby never wanted to see the kid get hurt, and he certainly didn't want to see him lose his dog either. There's no doubt that he would burn Paris to the ground if it meant saving Roger from the same fate.

Even though Barnaby tried to convince himself that he was the one who insisted Henry wait for him on the *Arthur Broome*, he couldn't shake the feeling that it was all his fault. He truly felt sorry for the young Canadian lad.

Truth be told, Barnaby didn't think Henry would have the courage to follow him off the top deck this morning and was impressed that the boy proved to be tougher than he first assumed. Catherine was not an adversary to be taken lightly after all. The rest of his colleagues couldn't even manage to keep pace with her, and yet, Henry was still standing. The kid wasn't even a Tutori, but he was willing to put his life in danger to save Penny and those polar bear cubs.

Barnaby figured Catherine would have hit Henry with a few tranquilizer darts back in London (she didn't think twice about doing the same to Professor Blackfriar). He was genuinely surprised to see that Henry had made it this far. That definitely counted for something, and Barnaby decided at that moment that he would do whatever it took to find this kid's dog, cloak or no cloak; he owed Henry that much.

Neither of them noticed the cold wind passing as the Carabinieri patrol boat raced downriver, even though their clothes were still soaking wet from the Seine.

When they reached the port of Le Havre, Barnaby asked Officer D'Acquisto to slow the patrol boat once the *Arthur Broome* was in sight. The Australian Tutori pulled a red stick out of his jacket pocket while they continued to cruise toward the ship. Henry assumed that the water had destroyed it, but he was mistaken.

Barnaby yanked on the white string, and a blue-colored firework was sent flying into the air. The three of them gazed in anticipation, their necks craning toward the night sky above as it exploded. Within just a few seconds, the signal lit up the nearby *APA* ship, giving Officer D'Acquisto his first look at the legendary *Arthur Broome*.

Gesturing toward the massive expedition ship in the distance, Barnaby glanced at the officer and said, "It's that one over there, mate. Much appreciated if you could get us a bit closer."

As the patrol boat approached the starboard side of the *Arthur Broome*, the hidden tender bay door slowly opened. Officer D'Acquisto marveled at the magnificent *APA* vessel. He had never seen a ship that looked so futuristic, and he was astonished at the large retractable door hidden on the side.

Valentina raced out of the tender bay in one of the black zodiacs a second later, circling the Carabinieri patrol boat a few times before pulling alongside it.

Barnaby proclaimed, "Thank you again, officer." He briefly shook the man's hand, gave him a proper salute out of respect, and stepped onto the waiting zodiac.

"Be careful out there, young man," Officer D'Acquisto said as Henry prepared to leap onto the black zodiac after Barnaby.

"Yes, sir," Henry pledged, "and thank you for your help." A matching salute followed right before he clumsily boarded the zodiac, landing far less gracefully than Barnaby.

With the two of them safely onboard, Valentina looked over at the officer on the patrol boat and saluted him as well. Neither of them said a word to each other, but the mutual respect was clear. Officer D'Acquisto just gave Valentina a steady salute and a silent nod as the zodiac zoomed away.

As much as he wanted to tell his fellow Carabinieri upon his return to the station, Officer D'Acquisto nobly decided to keep this encounter out of the official logbooks. It was a night that he would never forget, though.

— CHAPTER 17 —
TANGO-KILO

*V*alentina pulled into the tender bay and quickly stepped onto the rubber dock, while a series of locking mechanisms fastened the hull's watertight seal behind them.

Ruminating about what he was going to say to the council, Henry just stared in a transfixed manner at the saltwater rapidly draining back into the ocean.

Barnaby gazed at the disheartened boy for a moment and said wearily, "Let's go, mate." His tone was more gentle than usual.

Henry stepped off the zodiac and walked toward the elevators in silence. He was so distracted by the thoughts racing through his mind that he nearly lost his balance after being startled by the thundering roar of the Carabinieri's stomping. The booming noise echoed across the great hall the second Barnaby entered the threshold.

There was no gawking this time, though. Henry initially kept his head down, too ashamed of his own failure to look anyone in the eyes. That all changed when he heard a sequence of unusual noises. He eventually glanced up and noticed the guards were doing something different tonight. One by one, they holstered their swords, removed their dragoon helmets, and bowed their heads solemnly as Henry walked by.

Valentina could tell that Barnaby was in a foul mood, which wasn't entirely surprising since she saw that he had returned without the polar bear cubs (for the fourth time in a row). The disheartened look in his eyes made her reconsider teasing him tonight. She kept quiet as they continued walking past the Carabinieri guards lining the hallway.

When Valentina, Barnaby, and Henry reached the elevators, the guards never stomped a second time like they usually did after a Tutori exited the hallway. Henry found it puzzling to say the least, although he had lost that enthusiastic urge to ask Barnaby anything other than how they were going to find Penny.

"The council has ordered me to bring you straight to their chambers... They want to hear your report at once," Valentina declared as she pushed the elevator call button. Barnaby exhaled and replied grimly, "Yeah, I had a feeling they would. I'm sure Sunday will be there too."

Valentina had hoped to let the council ask the tough questions, but she couldn't resist any longer. Henry's charred suit and the copious amount of dried blood under his nose were impossible to ignore. But the absence of the playful dachshund that normally followed him everywhere he went was even more troubling. It made her worry that something horrible might have transpired.

Henry had clearly been roughed up. It looked like a bully had thrown his clothes in a pizza oven while he got knocked around in a bare-knuckle boxing match. Both he and Barnaby were also soaking wet, and yet it was the least of her concerns.

"What happened to Penny? Is she okay, Henry?" Valentina asked dolefully.

The visceral memory of losing Penny washed over Henry as if he were back under the bridge in Paris. Merely hearing the question forced him to relive the moment and feel the vivid pain all over again.

He stammered in a floundering attempt to explain, but the intended words never came out. His eyes just teared up.

Valentina couldn't bring herself to ask him again; she knew instantly that something had gone terribly wrong with their assignment today.

Once the elevator doors opened, Barnaby and Valentina followed Henry inside as he trudged in without answering her.

Barnaby slowly turned to Valentina and remarked, "Don't worry, love. I'll explain everything to the council in short ordah." He looked down at Henry to offer some semblance of reassurance. "We'll find your girl, mate. I don't care how long it takes... I'm gonna make this right."

Valentina pressed *3–6–8–7* while shaking her head in disappointment. She assumed that whatever happened today was probably Barnaby's fault.

An eerie silence fell upon the elevator as it whisked upward and away from the great hall. The direction changed a few times, moving sideways and then back up, until it finally reached the entrance to the council chambers.

When the elevator doors opened, Barnaby suddenly grabbed the sword out of Valentina's scabbard and pushed her from behind as she stepped off the elevator unsuspectingly. She nearly fell over in shock, but luckily managed to maintain her balance.

"Sorry, love! Afraid I need to speak with the doctor first," Barnaby hastily announced. Valentina looked back at him in utter disbelief as he held her sword up in a defensive position. He inched over to the control panel of buttons and quickly pressed *2–1–5–6*.

Henry was absolutely stunned—he couldn't decide if he should bolt out of the elevator or just stay put. His feet remained planted as the indecision intensified.

There was no denying that Henry would have benefited from a

proper examination by the ship's doctor (especially after the slew of injuries he sustained this evening), but not at the expense of keeping the council waiting. He desperately needed their help to find his beloved dachshund and didn't want to give them a reason to kick him off the ship.

The bemused look on Valentina's face curiously turned into a robust grin. She chuckled at Barnaby's futile hijinks and promptly called out for assistance, "Guards!"

Henry backed up nervously when he spotted the pair of Carabinieri guards standing in front of the council chambers leaving their posts; they rushed over right as the elevator doors started to close. For Barnaby's sake, he was lucky they weren't fast enough.

"What are you doing?" Henry frantically asked once the elevator began moving. Barnaby dropped the sword and bellowed, "Do you wanna get Penny back or not?"

Baffled, Henry exclaimed, "Of course! I would do anything. You know that!"

"Then you're just gonna have to trust me, mate. Alright?" Barnaby replied in a resolute manner as they continued their journey across the *Arthur Broome*.

Once the elevator doors opened again, it became apparent that Barnaby was being less than truthful with Valentina—instead of arriving at the doctor's office, they ended up at the ship's bridge. Still bewildered, Henry followed Barnaby as he stepped out to greet the captain.

The captain welcomed them onto the bridge with open arms. "Ah, buonasera, buonasera, Barnabas!"

Dressed in his Carabinieri uniform, Captain Alfredo Carlucci was a short, slightly paunchy man, but still very handsome. The thick white hair underneath his captain's hat reminded Henry of Captain Fulbright; he had the same matching walrus-style mustache (which was a common look among old seafarers).

Captain Carlucci also had a beaming smile that lit up the room in an infectious fashion. Even though Henry felt rather heartbroken, it was the kind of smile that could somehow make you forget you just had the worst day of your life.

"And this must be Signor Henry Halifax, all the way from Kodiak Bay!" the captain added, extending his arm to shake the boy's hand. "Nice to finally meet you, son."

"Good to meet you too, Captain," Henry replied somberly, wishing their first meeting had taken place under better circumstances.

Captain Carlucci sensed that something was wrong immediately. It wasn't only the defeated tone in the young man's voice—his burned clothes and bloodied nose were obviously unsettling. The captain asked, "What happened out there? Is-a everything alright?"

Barnaby and Henry both hesitated to answer. Everything was not okay. Far from it, indeed.

The reluctance in the air gave Captain Carlucci an irresistible opportunity to carry on talking, "Why don't I make you both a nice, warm cappuccino? You know, frankly, I'm more partial to the espresso myself. But, there are a lot of people on this ship that love the cappuccino. And you know, most people don't know this, but a good cup of coffee is-a all about the water. I remember talking to Valentina the other day... I said to her, you don't want to use reverse osmosis water because it has no dissolved minerals. Let me tell you, it is-a not good for coffee. Just ask Valentina... It actually leaches the minerals from the inside of the coffee machine. Can you believe that?"

Captain Carlucci paused for a moment, but it wasn't long enough for Barnaby or Henry to get a word in because he just continued rambling, "If you ask me, I think the real art of espresso as a method of preparation is-a not so much about the bean itself... No, no, no, it is-a really all about the *preparation* of the bean."

Henry didn't even drink coffee, yet there was something enchanting about how the captain could prattle on about practically anything and still make it sound interesting.

"And you know, I'm very close friends with the ship's chief engineer. Sì, sì, sì, Chief Moretti is-a true coffee artist," the captain chortled in the midst of clarifying affably, "well, technically, he is-a just an engineer... although he has also been assigned to carry out other various tasks onboard, including overseeing the coffee. Trust me, I know an artist when I see one. It is-a like watching a ballet each time he makes the coffee. A dance between man and machine, no movement is-a wasted. Now, he prefers the café latte... and you wouldn't believe this, but I promise it is-a true... he makes a little leaf shape at the top when he is-a pouring the foam into the cup. Have you ever seen something like that? Twenty-five milliliters of coffee, made from only seven grams of beans and then about four or five ounces of milk. And honestly..."

"I'm sorry, Captain!" Barnaby finally interjected, feverishly explaining, "You know, I'm really loving this... and I hate to interrupt, but I need your help! We don't have much time here, and I need to run a trace on some beacon darts right now!"

Captain Carlucci replied, "Beacon darts? Is-a everything alright, Barnabas?" He wondered why they were in such a hurry and started to think they might be in some serious trouble; the captain had never seen Barnaby so panicked.

"Not exactly... but it will be, mate. We need to trace my latest sleeve of darts to find the location of the kid's dog," Barnaby answered encouragingly. He glanced at Henry and added, "It's an emergency!"

Henry desperately pleaded, "Please help us, Captain!"

"Sì, sì, sì, no problem," the captain responded. He gestured toward the radar control desk on the other side of the ship's bridge and instructed, "Let's take a look to see if we can lock onto the signal."

Henry was sincerely grateful for the captain's help, even if he felt somewhat embarrassed that his first time meeting the captain would forever be overshadowed by Barnaby's deceit. He was also worried that Valentina could arrive at any moment once she realized they weren't at the doctor's office.

On top of that, Henry remembered that he had accused Barnaby of trying to knock him out with tranquilizer darts back in Paris; he had no idea Barnaby was actually just trying to track the plane the whole time. Regardless of how ashamed he was feeling, Henry knew it wasn't the time or place to apologize. That would have to come later.

"We need to run a trace on some tracking beacon darts for Barnabas and the young Signor Halifax," Captain Carlucci ordered.

Eager and happy to help, the Chief Radarman sitting at the sonar station sprang into action and replied enthusiastically, "Aye, aye, sir... Ready and awaiting the beacon tag numbers."

"Now, I'm not sure which one it was," Barnaby reluctantly warned, "but I know that I emptied the whole sleeve." Visibly frustrated, he wiped the sweat from his forehead and added, "We'll just have to try each one until we get a hit."

The radarman advised, "Roger that, sir. Let's try the first tag ID number."

"Alright, mate... let's give it a go," Barnaby called out, "first tag number is *Tango-Kilo-5-9-6!*"

All Tutori were issued sleeves of throwing darts (tranquilizers and beacon tracers) when needed; they always got marked with a unique set of identification numbers that were in sequential order. Even though Barnaby wasn't sure which dart actually struck the plane's fuselage, he remembered the tag number on the first dart in the sleeve.

Captain Carlucci and Henry watched with nervous excitement as the radarman typed in the beacon tag number and searched for the signal.

"Nothing on that one, Mr. Murdoch," he announced.

Anxiously pacing, Barnaby looked over at the elevator and suggested, "Try *Tango-Kilo-5-9-5*."

Again, the radarman ran the search and confirmed, "No signal, sir."

Barnaby persisted, "What about *Tango-Kilo-5-9-4*?" He apprehensively glanced back and forth between the radar screen and the elevator doors while the radarman typed the tag numbers.

"I'm sorry, sir. Nothing on that one either," the sailor repeated.

Henry's heartbeat was racing. He had a feeling Valentina would be livid if she caught them on the ship's bridge and treated each passing minute as a precious gift. But the despair was only growing louder—another tag number, another dead end. There was still no signal from any of the ones they'd tried to track so far.

Barnaby's demeanor changed abruptly when they all heard the arriving elevator bell chime, and as soon as the doors opened, he yelled, "*Tango-Kilo 5-9-3*! Run that one, mate! *Tango-Kilo-5-9-3*!"

The sudden panic in Barnaby's voice gave the radarman pause, and he couldn't help but turn around to see what all the commotion was about.

Valentina and the two Carabinieri guards from the council chambers stormed off the elevator onto the ship's bridge. The scowling looks smeared on their faces led Henry to believe that Barnaby had run out of second chances.

Flanked by the pair of fuming guards, Valentina marched over to the radar control desk and sternly demanded, "Barnabas Murdoch! Henry Halifax! You are both hereby ordered to follow us to the council chambers. Now!" The Carabinieri guards next to her quickly pulled their swords out at the same time, brandishing them in a threatening manner.

Captain Carlucci didn't appreciate the tumultuous disruption and asked, "Officer Vinciguerra... What is-a going on here? What is-a this all about?"

Surprisingly, Valentina disregarded the captain's questions and shouted, "Right now, Murdoch! Andiamo!" Her tone was laced with hostility, and Henry was scared of what would happen if they didn't comply.

Barnaby brushed off Valentina's commands as if she wasn't even there; he spun around briskly to see if the radarman had any updates. "*Tango-Kilo-5-9-3*! Did you get a hit?"

As much as Henry wanted to find Penny, he could tell by the pure venom coming from Valentina's eyes that any further insubordination would prove to be a big mistake. Whatever patience she had left was completely gone. Even Captain Carlucci, who had seen it all over the years, was surprised by the hostility.

Valentina promptly grabbed Barnaby by the collar and dragged him away toward the elevator before the radarman could answer. Defiant until the end, the Australian Tutori kept shouting along the way, "*5-9-3! 5-9-3*! Run the trace!"

The guards tilted their swords and looked at Henry; he calmly raised his hands to make sure they knew he wasn't going to resist. Hoping to avoid a tussle with the Carabinieri, Henry walked slowly toward the elevators in silence while Barnaby kicked and screamed in protest.

Fueled by her unwavering conviction to carry out the council's orders, Valentina tossed the defiant Australian into the elevator like a bouncer throwing a drunk patron out of the bar. The crew was shocked and gasped in disbelief as Barnaby was sent crashing to the floor.

Valentina didn't have to say anything to Henry; his obedience was all but guaranteed, and he acquiescently stepped into the elevator. The pair of Carabinieri guards stood in front of the doors, blocking anyone from getting on or off.

Captain Carlucci wanted some answers, but even he wasn't daring enough to question Valentina's resolve after witnessing the unexpected outburst. He knew her loyalty to the duties of the Carabinieri was unassailable.

Standing in the elevator, Henry cautiously peered around the guards as Valentina pushed the buttons on the control panel for the council's chambers. He could see the radarman whispering something to Captain Carlucci.

A split-second later, the captain raced over to the elevator when he saw the doors starting to close. "*Deception Island*!" he shouted frantically. "We traced the beacon signal to Deception Island!"

With the elevator now headed straight for the council chambers, Barnaby picked himself up (smiling as if he had just won the lottery) and quipped, "Crikey! Happy to follow you anywhere, love... All you had to do was ask nicely!"

"Oh, I think we are way past holding hands, Barnabas," Valentina remarked irritably. She couldn't believe he would pull a stunt like this. Between checking his cabin, the doctor's office, the grand atrium, and a few other spots onboard, she had practically searched the entire ship to find them. The deafening silence that ensued left Henry wondering what other surprises Barnaby had up his sleeve.

Drenched from the Seine and coming off another failed attempt to rescue the missing polar bear cubs, Barnaby didn't seem worried in the slightest, even though he would be facing some tough questions and possibly the threat of being expelled from the *APA* entirely once the council had their say.

When the rear doors opened, Barnaby and Henry followed Valentina down the hallway toward the council chambers, while the pair of Carabinieri guards trailed closely behind them. Henry's heart felt like it was about to leap out of his chest at any moment.

— CHAPTER 18 —
THE COUNCIL OF THREE

T wo other Carabinieri guards were already standing by the entrance of the council chambers, holding the massive double doors open. Valentina led Barnaby and Henry into the dimly lit auditorium while the pair of guards accompanying them came to an abrupt halt; everyone instantly turned around, glaring at the Australian after the doors slammed shut behind them. A deafening silence fell upon the room.

As Henry continued following Valentina and Barnaby down the aisleway, he felt the eyes of seemingly the entire audience staring back at him. The unnerving sound of whispering grew louder and louder the closer they got to the stage.

There was something different about tonight's proceedings, though. It wasn't just the murmuring gossip or the heart-pounding tension permeating the air—far more Tutori were in attendance this time, all craning to catch a glimpse. By Henry's count, there appeared to be at least three or four dozen Tutori at a minimum. Almost everyone onboard the *Arthur Broome* had shown up to watch, leading Henry to believe that Barnaby was in a considerable amount of trouble.

Even the paintings of the fallen Tutori hanging on the walls seemed to be glaring at Barnaby and Henry in disappointment as they passed by each row.

In spite of the chilling reception, Henry quietly proceeded up the stairs and onto the raised center stage behind Barnaby. Valentina stepped to the side and remained at the bottom of the steps. The muffled chatter only got louder once Barnaby and Henry trudged into the bright stage lights.

A wealth of information could be gleaned simply by looking at them; between Henry's burned suit, the dried blood covering the bottom half of his face, and the squeaky footsteps drawing attention to their drenched attire, it was clear they had failed. Everyone had assumed Barnaby would have triumphantly put the missing polar bear cubs on full display otherwise, but the absence of any animals made it obvious. The look of defeat on the Australian's face just added to the crowd's speculation about the consequences that awaited.

There were a lot of unfamiliar faces in the audience. Some familiar ones stood out, though. Henry managed to spot Savannah and June, Archie and Professor Blackfriar, Celine Saint-Clair, and the Japanese Tutori from the grand atrium; he didn't recognize many of the others.

However, the man sitting alone in the back row caught him by surprise. It was Rufus, the dapper tailor, who subtly nodded when Henry gazed in his direction.

Rufus rarely attended council meetings, but when he did, Barnaby got a little bit more nervous, and it rattled what little confidence the Australian still had remaining.

Despite not having said a word yet, Madam MacDougall was clearly annoyed by Barnaby and his tardiness. The disgruntlement in her voice was evident as she spoke, "Barnabas... how *generous* of you to finally join us!" Hardly the only one irritated by his late arrival, Madam Machado chimed in, "Did you get lost? Or did you just forget that you were supposed to report straight to the council upon boarding this ship?"

Barnaby knew that his charming smile alone wouldn't absolve him of not being able to catch Catherine or recover the missing polar bears. He exhaled deeply and replied, "Honorable council members, I know you're upset, but I can explain..."

"Explain? Explain what?" Madam MacDougall interrupted, still fuming from his insubordination. She carried on scolding him. "Explain why you came back empty-handed again? How the French bandit escaped again... Or that you knew it was Catherine Saint-Clair this *whole* time?"

Madam Cross added, "Please do enlighten us, Mr. Murdoch... because there's been some debate amongst my esteemed colleagues and we're curious to know. When exactly did you start conspiring with your old partner? When did all the lying and treachery actually begin?"

Madam Machado was growing impatient and couldn't resist berating him further. "Go on, Barnabas! Tell us! Where did it happen, Sydney? Tokyo? Kodiak Bay? Your favorite restaurant... The *Crooked Sombrero*? Where were you the moment you decided to betray the *APA*, this council, and every Tutori sitting in this room?"

Barnaby thought he was in for a long night of reprimands, but the three council members' relentless vitriol still surprised him.

Once the bombardment of contemptuous accusations abated, Barnaby arrogantly tried to alleviate their concerns. "It's not what you think... honestly. Now, I don't know what Sunday told you, and frankly, it doesn't mattah, because I'm quite certain that she doesn't know what she's talking about... as usual."

"The hell I don't! He's a damn liar!" Savannah retorted, erupting out of her chair unexpectedly.

Madam MacDougall promptly intervened. "That's enough, Ms.

Sunday! This council will uncover the truth, and we don't need any help!"

The hostile atmosphere was a far cry from the lighthearted criticism levied upon Barnaby the last time they faced the council. It was obvious that whatever Savannah told the council prior to their arrival only seemed to make things worse.

Henry nervously stood on stage in his soggy, charred suit and couldn't help but wonder if the councilwomen would go as far as to expel Barnaby from the *APA*.

Once the irascible Texan took a seat, Madam Cross pressed Barnaby for more details. "Okay, Mr. Murdoch... Let's have it. When did you first realize that it was Catherine Saint-Clair carrying out these attacks against the zoos?"

Madam Machado could see the reluctance building in his eyes and warned, "A word of caution, Barnabas... pride is expensive. Now is not the time to tell us what you think we want to hear. You took an oath, and we expect you to honor every word of it, down to the last period. So, I suggest you pretend like we know more than you and stick to the truth."

"Of course, madam," Barnaby answered respectfully as he looked around the room. "Like all of you, I was astounded to learn that this recent wave of brazen bear heists was orchestrated by my old partner... honestly. And just like my fellow Tutori who participated in today's rescue operation, I only recognized Catherine as the French bandit earlier this morning in London."

He sighed with regret. "Truly, it breaks my heart to see Catherine lose her way, especially like this. She was one of the best we had... Maybe too good, some would say. But I can assure you on my word as a gentleman that I have nevah conspired to help, aid, assist, or support my old partnah in her misguided endeavors in any capacity. In fact, it's quite the opposite. And despite Sunday's deficiencies in keeping pace, I actually managed to track Catherine through the streets of Paris today."

Savannah leaped out of her chair once again and yanked the cattle prod from her belt. "That's it! You and me... outside, right now!" she threatened, sending a look of pure venom in Barnaby's direction.

Professor Blackfriar chuckled in delight. There was a part of him that found their ongoing feud amusing and would have loved to see a scuffle between his two colleagues break out after plenty of close calls in the past.

"Silence, Ms. Sunday!" Madam MacDougall shouted furiously.

Blinded by rage and unable to control her temper, Savannah indignantly hollered, "You're messin' with the wrong Texan, hoss!" She pointed her cattle prod toward Barnaby in an intimidating manner and pressed the button on the side a few times so that he could see the electric sparks from afar.

"Enough!" Madam MacDougall shouted, raising her voice in response to Savannah's blatant disobedience. "One more outburst like that, and we will clear these chambers!"

Thankfully, June intervened before it was too late and tried to instill a sense of calm. She gently grabbed Savannah by the arm, persuading the rowdy Texan to sit down.

With order finally restored in the chamber, Madam Machado urged Barnaby to be more forthcoming. "Señor Murdoch, is there anything further you think this council should be aware of?"

Unable to resist taunting Savannah, he winked at her before admitting, "Certainly, madam. It's true... I don't have the pair of polar bear cubs as promised, but I did not return empty-handed."

A renewed flood of speculative whispers from the audience filled the council chambers.

"After tracking Catherine through the streets of Paris, she escaped in a yellow floatplane... but not before releasing a pack of circus tigers and a pair of grizzly bears at the *FDR Train Station*," he explained.

Fanning the flames of doubt in the audience, Barnaby kept up his unwavering campaign to deflect any responsibility for how today's operation turned out.

"And had I not tagged that floatplane with my last beacon dart, we would have had no idea where she went." He said with a smirk, "No worries, though... We all know that *Barnaby Banjo Murdoch* has impeccable aim, right? I just talked to Captain Carlucci, and he traced the beacon signal to Deception Island."

The three councilwomen looked skeptical as Barnaby added patronizingly, "Now, I'd be happy to alleviate any doubts and dispel these highly egregious, unfounded accusations of this alleged conspiracy. All you have to do is set a course for the northern coast of Norway. Once the ship arrives, I'll personally drag Catherine Saint-Clair in here myself so that she can answer for her crimes."

"I'm thinking Batista, the professor, and, uh... Sakamoto, Raj, and Schumacher should be more than enough to get the job done," Barnaby declared, convinced that he was in no trouble at all. He sensed the reluctance among the council of three and enthusiastically concluded, "We can get the jump on her this time... Go in early and surprise her during breakfast. There's no reason we can't have those polar bear cubs and this Canadian lad back in Kodiak Bay by tomorrow night."

Unimpressed, Madam Cross responded curtly, "Well, thank you, Mr. Murdoch, for that very colorful field report and the unsolicited advice on how to carry out our duties."

Madam Machado shook her head and tutted. "Now, we both know that's not the whole story, is it, Barnabas? What about Penny? Where is she, and why does Señor Halifax look like he's been set on fire?"

Barnaby tried to make light of Henry's rumpled appearance. "Uh, the fire? Oh, right... Yeah, no worries. He's still in one piece, and, um... as for Penny..."

"Silence, Mr. Murdoch!" Madam MacDougall yelled; she was tired of Barnaby's hollow excuses, and the absence of any real details in his report fell short of the deference expected.

Madam Cross looked at Henry and said politely, "Please step forward, Mr. Halifax."

Henry's heart felt like it dropped to the bottom of his stomach as the audience swiftly turned their attention toward him. It was bad enough that he had just lost his best friend—recounting the painful ordeal in front of dozens of Tutori he'd never met only added to the anxiety coursing through his body. He was ashamed to think that none of this would have happened if he had simply listened to Barnaby back in Paris.

Instead of triumphantly returning to the ship as heroes with the missing polar bear cubs, Henry had indeed come back empty-handed. The mercy of the council was his only hope of ever seeing Penny again.

"Tell us, where is your dachshund? What happened to Penny?" Madam MacDougall demanded.

Although he was no longer dripping water onto the floor, Henry's clothes were still noticeably wet from the river, and squeaking noises followed his every step as he plodded over to the center of the stage. He had never been more nervous. Penny's fate rested in the council's hands, and he didn't want to upset them any more than Barnaby already had.

Henry stood quietly for a few seconds; he wasn't sure where to even begin. After glancing at Barnaby for some reassurance, he finally mustered the courage to utter, "I'm, uh... afraid Catherine took her, madam."

Despite the quivering anguish in his voice, Henry managed to carry on explaining, "You see, we were pursuing Catherine near the train station in Paris, and Penny got ahead of me. A tussle ensued, which ultimately led to a fire breaking out below the bridge. I slipped and fell chasing Penny, but I couldn't get up fast enough. Catherine must have knocked her out using a tranquilizer dart because it was the only thing that remained once the yellow floatplane took off."

"I swam after the plane as best I could... It didn't matter, though. I wasn't strong enough to hold on." His eyes teared up while he added remorsefully, "I promise it wasn't Barnaby's fault. He tried to stop me, but I didn't listen."

Sniffling, Henry wiped his eyes as he stared back at the dozens of Tutori sitting in the audience. He tried to cling to what little dignity he had left and refused to crumble after explaining himself to the council. Crying wasn't going to fix anything; crying wasn't going to bring Penny back, regardless of how sad he felt. Henry knew he had to control his emotions in front of the sea of unfamiliar faces, no matter how hard it might be.

"Please believe Mr. Murdoch," he earnestly pleaded, "we need to get to Deception Island right away. I'll go find Penny myself! I just need a ride there!"

Henry sounded like a young man with a broken heart and nothing to lose, a best friend who was willing to risk everything—the kind of desperation that most people never have the chance to experience.

Madam Machado responded compassionately, "I'm sorry to hear about your dachshund, young man. I really am. I can tell how much she means to you. Unfortunately..."

"*Please!*" Henry insisted, unwilling to accept anything less than a plan to rescue Penny. "I don't know what's going on here between Barnaby and Catherine... and I'm truly sorry if I caused any trouble on this ship. But I need your help! My best friend needs your help!"

Another round of haunting silence consumed the room. Everyone, including and especially Henry, waited with bated breath to see if the council would grant his request.

Sensing their hesitancy, Henry's eyes teared up once again as he begged despairingly, "Please, madam. Please."

Madam Cross empathized. She could feel the pain in his heart and politely chimed in, "Well, then... perhaps you can help clear up some confusion for us. You see, we want to believe Barnaby. We really do. However, after four failed recovery operations and facing a serious accusation levied by a fellow Tutori, the burden of trust now falls upon Mr. Murdoch. Unfortunately, I'm sorry to say... he has irrevocably *broken* that trust."

Madam MacDougall wasn't entirely convinced. "If he is conspiring with Catherine Saint-Clair, then this could just be another diversion to send the *APA* to a deserted arctic outpost while she breaks into another zoo on the other side of the world."

Fed up with listening to the flagrant character assassination being carried out against him, Barnaby refused to idly stand by in silence as the council decided his fate. He vehemently pointed at Savannah and shouted furiously, "Crikey! *Eighteen years of loyal service to the APA...* and this is what I get? Baseless accusations from some loudmouth rattlesnake? Maybe you're too scared to say it, but we all know her salsa tastes like it was made in New York City!"

Savannah suddenly jumped out of her seat and raced down the aisle; two of the Carabinieri guards near the front row saw her coming and immediately rushed to block her path.

Incensed and tired of Barnaby's slanderous remarks, Savannah screamed as the pair of guards held her back, "You crossed the damn line! You hear me, Murdoch? Come hell or high water, we're gonna finish this!" Violently struggling to break free in the face of Barnaby's taunting smirk, she bellowed, "And you ain't gonna like how it ends!"

If the Carabinieri guards had not intervened, Henry was convinced that Savannah would have dropped Barnaby like a sack of potatoes the second she got on stage.

Madam MacDougall sprang out of her seat and shouted, "That's enough, Ms. Sunday! It ends now!"

"Guards!" she yelled out. "Please remove Savannah Sunday from these chambers immediately!"

The pair of Carabinieri guards quickly dragged the kicking and screaming Texan up the aisleway toward the exit. After they managed to escort her past the chamber doors, she foolishly darted back inside and hollered at the top of her lungs, "This ain't over, Murdoch! You better watch your back! You hear me?"

The two additional guards standing outside were promptly called in to assist with the removal of the belligerent woman. In the end, it took four guards to actually remove Savannah from the room.

While Barnaby found the whole ordeal to be quite entertaining, Henry was completely shocked and could only watch incredulously as it all went down.

After the huge doors slammed shut with a resounding thud, the gasps of disbelief and incessant chatter finally stopped. The eerie silence that followed left everyone wondering what type of punishment awaited Barnaby. The council was visibly annoyed by Savannah's latest outburst, and nobody doubted that he would be blamed for inflaming the situation.

The gloating grin shining from Barnaby's face wasn't helping matters either (he couldn't resist sneering at the sight of seeing Savannah all riled up as a result of something he said).

Once order was restored, Madam Cross said caustically, "Thank you for that unnecessary contribution, Mr. Murdoch."

"You, *of all people*, should know the rules." She sighed heavily. "One of your fellow Tutori has made a serious accusation against you, and our duty to the *APA* requires a mandatory inquiry."

Turning her attention to Henry, she stated, "However, I'm sure

Mr. Halifax can clear all of this up with the truth. Surely, you know the difference between right and wrong, don't you?"

Barnaby spoke up anxiously, "Okay, that's enough! Leave the kid out of this, alright?"

Madam MacDougall snapped at him, "Silence, Barnabas!" Her tolerance for his audacity had dissipated; she couldn't believe Barnaby had dared to tell the council how to run this hearing in front of nearly every Tutori onboard the ship.

Madam Machado ignored the obvious attempt to distract them from the truth and vociferously asked, "You want our help, Señor Halifax? You want the captain to chart a course for Deception Island?"

Henry's face lit up with excitement at the mere mention of the Norwegian island. But that all changed the moment Madam Machado told him the price that must be paid. "We would be happy to oblige... You just have to answer one simple question."

Apprehensively glancing at Barnaby, Henry wondered what pressing inquiry he could possibly answer that would be enticing enough for them to help him find Penny. The look of bewilderment smeared on his face had many of the Tutori in the audience speculating about the question as well.

Following a few seconds of tense anticipation, Madam Machado asked the one question Henry was dreading the most. "When you first came across Mr. Murdoch in Kodiak Bay... was there any indication that he recognized the French bandit as Catherine Saint-Clair at that time?"

Henry nervously looked toward Barnaby again and struggled to find the courage to respond. The answer itself was simple, though he worried that the consequences of telling the truth could be quite detrimental to Barnaby's position within the *APA*. He stammered, trying to delicately explain, "I, uh... I'm not..."

Feeling powerless to stop the council's ruthless endeavor to expose the truth, Barnaby interjected, "Is all of this really necessary? The kid just lost his best friend! Give it a rest, will ya?"

An infuriated Madam MacDougall shrieked, "Silence, Mr. Murdoch! One more interruption and you'll be removed from these chambers!"

The councilwomen suspected that Henry was about to tell them the same thing Savannah presumed was true, and despite his loyalty to Barnaby, they were confident that he would eventually do the right thing with a bit more encouragement.

Madam Machado tried to reason with him and said, "Look at me, Henry. Barnabas can't help you now, okay?" She warned callously, "You want to go to Deception Island? You want to see your dachshund again?"

Henry hesitantly nodded his head as Madam Machado insisted, "Then all you have to do is tell us the truth... Right here, right now."

Trembling in fear, Henry glanced at Barnaby once again for some reassurance. The look of apprehension staring back at him only amplified the animosity in the air. The temptation to lie for Barnaby's benefit faded when Madam MacDougall began badgering, "Don't look at him. Look at us! Tell us the truth, Mr. Halifax!"

Henry didn't want to betray Barnaby's trust, but he couldn't stand to be without Penny—she was out there all alone, and the mounting guilt was becoming impossible to bear.

Regardless of how much Henry wanted to help Barnaby, it became painfully apparent that the council was in charge. As he stared at the floor and deliberated for a moment, he realized there was no way to escape this impossible predicament unscathed.

Henry turned to Barnaby and lugubriously announced, "I'm sorry, Barnaby. I didn't mean for any of this to happen... I was just..."

"Answer us, Mr. Halifax! Now!" Madam MacDougall yelled before he could finish apologizing to Barnaby.

The council was relentless. They knew it would only be a matter of time before Henry's resolve shattered like a lightbulb rattling inside a toolbox filled with hammers.

Defeated by their unwavering fortitude and desperate to see his beloved dachshund again, the escalating pressure finally got to him. "Yes. Okay? It's true. Barnaby recognized Catherine Saint-Clair in Kodiak Bay... She called out his name from the deck of the *Queen Charlotte*. That's when I realized they must have known each other somehow."

"But I'm not sure if that means they're working together," he added reassuringly in Barnaby's defense, "it could just be a coincidence!"

Barnaby lowered his head and pinched the top part of his nose in frustration, as if to ward off an impending headache. The implications of Henry's admission didn't bode well for his future in the *APA*.

Like most people who break the rules, Barnaby wasn't too keen on facing the consequences, and even though Henry was only onboard as a professional courtesy, the betrayal of the partner's code hurt the most. He was actually starting to like the kid (if only slightly). But that was all over now; Barnaby couldn't even stand to look at him.

Overwhelmed with contrition, Henry asserted, "I promise, that's all I know! I swear!"

"Muchas gracias, Señor Halifax," Madam Machado jauntily replied. The smile beaming from her face didn't make Henry feel any better.

Boisterous chatter erupted amongst the stunned audience as they listened intently. Some called Henry a hero, while others scoffed at his blatant disregard for the inviolability of the partner's code. The rumors and gossip that echoed throughout the chamber halls only compounded his guilt. Henry felt like Barnaby would never forgive him.

Surprisingly, Barnaby remained quiet as he stood on stage under the bright spotlight. His rage was still silently building, though. Grappling with what he considered to be a betrayal of the highest order, he found a tiny bit of solace in Savannah's absence; depriving her of this moment was the only good thing to come out of this council hearing as far as he was concerned.

Madam MacDougall instantly summoned Valentina, "Ms. Vinciguerra... Please tell Captain Carlucci to set a course for Deception Island, full speed ahead."

"Sì, madam," Valentina replied without hesitation. She turned around and briskly left the council chambers to deliver the message to the captain.

Madam MacDougall looked at Barnaby and announced dispassionately, "Mr. Murdoch. In light of the recent evidence that has come before this council, you are hereby suspended from your duties as a Tutori... *effective immediately*."

Madam Machado shouted, "Guards!"

The pair of Carabinieri guards standing on the far side of the stage marched over to Barnaby in a deliberate manner. They quickly pulled out their swords and sliced the front of Barnaby's suit jacket on both sides with pinpoint precision, sending his black cloak falling to the floor.

Along with the cloak, Barnaby saw eighteen years of his life crash down like a house of cards in front of dozens of people he considered to be his family.

Henry felt completely devastated. His immense guilt was becoming unbearable with each passing second and Barnaby's continued stone-cold silence.

Even though the brash Australian could often be disparaging (particularly when talking about Canadians in general), Henry would have happily settled for the familiar snide remarks. Anything would have been better than the heart-pounding silence that he was met with instead.

Henry never wanted to see Barnaby get suspended, especially if it was because of something he said. Right or wrong, he didn't want to be a part of any punishment doled out by the council.

Underneath all the penitence, Henry latched onto the sliver of hope that had eluded him since the riverbank in Paris. On the heels of his confession, he ultimately got what he wanted—the *Arthur Broome* was now headed to Deception Island. And despite the exorbitant cost, Henry promised himself he would eventually try to make things right with Barnaby once Penny was back by his side.

Madam Cross took no pleasure in judiciously carrying out the rest of her duties as a matter of procedure. "A formal expulsion hearing will be scheduled within seventy-two hours. At that time, you will have a final opportunity to submit an appeal to the commissioner."

Barnaby's seething resentment finally erupted upon hearing that he could be expelled from the *Animal Protection Authority*. "You cannot be serious! I'm out here breaking my back for the *APA* every day while you three sit on your thrones playing Monday morning quarterback!"

"The last *three hundred eighty-eight* missions have been perfect, minus the last four!" He arrogantly shouted, "I guarantee you're all gonna regret this come tomorrow morning! Every last one of you!"

Henry shuddered during Barnaby's furious rant. He was still standing right next to him and feared his unbridled rage might spiral out of control.

Madam MacDougall ignored Barnaby's tantrum and simply carried on with the proceedings. "This council will personally oversee tomorrow's rescue operation to recover the missing wirehaired dachshund and the pair of polar bear cubs from Kodiak Bay."

Barnaby was fuming, but he just glared disdainfully at the three councilwomen with resentment. He hoped the pure contempt in his eyes would persuade them to reconsider, albeit to no avail.

Madam MacDougall didn't care in the slightest. "Ms. Sunday, Mr. Zapata, Mr. Sakamoto, Mrs. Gupta, Mr. Schlansky, and Mr. Weathers... you will accompany the council on tomorrow's rescue operation. Please report to the top deck at seven-thirty tomorrow morning for aerial disembarkation."

Henry was stunned to hear the council would be overseeing the rescue mission tomorrow. He had no idea that they occasionally went out into the field to assist with operations that carried an inherently higher degree of risk. As encouraging as that might have been, he knew there were no guarantees they would actually be successful. After all, Catherine had trounced the last team the *APA* sent, and he had the bruises to prove it.

Regardless, Henry was somewhat relieved to know that the *Arthur Broome* was now on route to Deception Island. It would have been nice to hear his name called as well, since he would have certainly preferred to be included in tomorrow's rescue operation, but he welcomed any reprieve from the despair that he could get at this point.

Madam Machado suddenly declared, "Effective immediately, both Señor Halifax and Señor Murdoch are to be added to the cabin restriction list. Neither of you will be permitted to leave your cabins for any reason until further notice. There is a zero-tolerance policy for dishonesty on this ship. *Zero!*"

The look of disbelief that initially washed over Barnaby's face quickly faded; it was promptly replaced by an unsettling scowl. The piercing animosity pouring out of his eyes led Madam MacDougall to presume another outburst was imminent. Before he could utter a single word of protest, she interceded. "At the conclusion of tomorrow's rescue operation, the *Arthur Broome* will set a course for Canada to return Mr. Halifax, the wirehaired dachshund, and the missing polar bear cubs to Kodiak Bay."

"Wait one damn minute!" Barnaby snarled, feeling unfairly characterized as a liar. "It's not what it looks like... Just let me explain what..."

Madam Machado interrupted his objections by merely talking over him, "Guards! See to it that Barnabas Murdoch and Henry Halifax proceed directly to their cabins."

Madam MacDougall swiftly added, "This council has spoken!" Right then, the three thronelike chairs were instantly lowered beneath the floor.

The whispers among the Tutori in the audience only got louder as the Carabinieri guards led Barnaby and Henry up the aisleway toward the exit.

Once they stepped foot outside the council chambers, Barnaby stormed off down the hallway and didn't say a word to Henry or anyone else. A lone Carabinieri guard trailed behind but kept his distance to avoid any further provocation.

Barnaby was clearly too distraught to wait for the elevator, and as far as Henry was concerned, that was probably for the best. There's no telling what would have happened if they were forced to share an elevator together right now. He had just inadvertently gotten Barnaby suspended. Whether it was intentional or not, he assumed the blame would be put on him for this entire mess.

After all, that cloak meant the world to Barnaby. He dedicated his life to the *APA*, and there was no denying that Henry had unwittingly played a role in tonight's proceedings.

The other Carabinieri guard followed silently behind Henry while he trudged over to the elevators and pressed the call button.

When the doors opened, they both stepped in, and Henry apprehensively pushed *6–9–9–1* on the control panel.

As the elevator doors started to close, Henry caught a glimpse of June and Archie exiting the council chambers with the rest of the Tutori. They both looked equally troubled. He could tell that it was undoubtedly out of concern for him and his missing dachshund.

Henry wanted to say something to them once their eyes met, but the elevator doors shut before he could get the words out.

— CHAPTER 19 —
NOTHING TO LOSE

*H*enry wondered what he could have done differently as the elevator whisked away toward the sixth floor. Just this morning, he felt like he had everything figured out. Penny was at his side, and the invitation to join the *APA* seemed all but guaranteed if they managed to recover those missing polar bear cubs. Sailing across the world on the legendary *Arthur Broome*, working alongside the Tutori, meeting all sorts of fascinating people and animals—it was all over now.

The elation and adventure that had followed Henry since he left Kodiak Bay had been replaced with immense feelings of guilt and despair. He couldn't believe how much had changed in less than twenty-four hours. Penny vanished, he got roughed up by a pack of French street hooligans, and now Barnaby was suspended from the *APA*. It felt like the worst day of Henry's life, which was a stark contrast to the exuberance of this morning.

Instead of celebrating after what he had hoped would have been a successful mission, Henry couldn't even leave his cabin, and the one guy he looked up to as a mentor onboard the ship would probably never speak to him again.

On top of that, there was zero chance of him becoming a Magari like June and Archie. The council made that clear tonight. By tomorrow evening, the ship was due to return to Kodiak Bay, and that would most likely be the last time Henry ever saw Barnaby, the Tutori, or the *Arthur Broome* again.

So many things that Henry cared about had been ripped away from him in such a short period of time. None of them compared to losing Penny, but the helplessness that had shadowed him since he left the council chambers this evening hurt the most.

When the elevator came to an unexpected stop, Henry almost got off on the wrong floor. But a familiar pair of otters prevented him from making another untimely mistake despite his distraction from the fallout of the most recent council meeting.

Otis and Oscar dashed into the elevator and raced over to press the buttons as a family of ducks waddled in behind them.

The mischievous otters turned to Henry once the elevator started moving again. They were visibly dismayed. Penny was nowhere to be found, and Henry's charred attire led them to believe that something terrible had transpired. Even the ducks could tell something was wrong.

In fact, the otters were so concerned that their usual routine of playfully chasing each other had ceased entirely. Standing on their hind legs, they stared up at Henry with sorrow in their eyes.

Henry just sighed. He wanted to tell them what happened, but he didn't need to say a word—it was written all over his face. Otis and Oscar exchanged a worried glance of disbelief. They couldn't believe Penny was gone.

When the elevator stopped again, Henry recognized his floor and shuffled out into the hallway.

His Carabinieri escort stayed behind; the guard looked at him and nodded silently, trusting that Henry would go straight to cabin *6991*. Otis and Oscar stood next to the family of ducks and somberly waved their tiny little paws as the elevator doors closed.

Henry trudged down the hallway and turned on the lights after opening the door to his cabin. There was a new tray of food waiting for him on the coffee table in front of the couch, but his stomach was already filled with an unsettling combination of shame and misery. He couldn't think of eating at a time like this.

Looking past the food, Henry noticed the curtains had been closed, and he lumbered over to the other side of the room to pull them open. He went outside and stared up at the moon as the *Arthur Broome* sliced effortlessly through the passing waves; its glowing aura was a welcome flicker of hope amid the dark vastness of the ocean.

It wouldn't be long now before the ship arrived at Deception Island. Yet there were no guarantees that Penny would even be there. Catherine seemed to have an infinite number of tricks up her sleeve, and Henry wondered if she was luring the *APA* into a dangerous trap.

Gazing at the moon's reflection on the ocean waves below, the chilly air passing by reminded Henry that his suit was still uncomfortably damp from swimming in the Seine River earlier. A nasty cold was the last thing he needed right now. He heaved the sliding balcony door shut and decided to jump into the shower.

The hot water and soap instantly provided some semblance of clarity as Henry reflected on the chaos that unfolded throughout the day. Nothing could wash away the agonizing defeat of losing Penny, but the shower gave him a renewed sense of motivation and hope. He was still alive, and that alone meant he was winning. Going after the big prize always starts with one small victory at a time, and washing the dried blood off his face would have to suffice for now after a long day of back-to-back losses.

Feeling somewhat revitalized, Henry walked over to the closet to find some fresh clothes after he finished drying off. He opened the sliding door and saw the collection of gray wool suits that had been delivered yesterday evening. His original pants, sweater, and yellow raincoat were hanging right next to them; they were all freshly cleaned, pressed, and folded, leading him to believe that Rufus must have stopped by sometime today.

This time, there were no special envelopes or encouraging notes, but Henry was surprised by the unique hanger tucked away in the far corner.

Henry pushed the suits out of the way and lunged forward to get a closer look. It wasn't clothing at all. He recognized the black parachute harness almost immediately once it was off the hanger— he had worn one just like it this morning during his first aerial disembarkation with June. Mumbling under his breath, he speculated, "Maybe they put one in everybody's closet?" He wasn't sure how it got there or who delivered it to his room. However, that seemed immeasurably less important at this point.

Placing the parachute on the bed, Henry remembered that he would likely be gone by tomorrow night anyway. Even though he was never officially a Tutori, the council had essentially ousted him from the *Arthur Broome*. He was conflicted and no longer felt right wearing the finely crafted suits that Rufus and the *APA* had given him. As much as he enjoyed getting fitted for his first suit at Rufus' haberdashery shop, he grabbed his oatmeal-colored sweater and dark brown trousers instead.

Henry quickly got dressed, occasionally glancing down at the black parachute harness that was lying on the bed.

Still feeling sore from the sloppy fall on the riverbank in Paris and the violent tussle with the *FDR Boys* that ensued, Henry eventually slumped onto the couch. He stared aimlessly out the sliding glass door as the *Arthur Broome* sailed through the English Channel, desperately wondering if Penny was safe.

The thought of being reunited with his best friend weighed heavily on Henry. It was all so emotionally taxing in a way that he couldn't fathom before today. Combined with the feelings of compounding guilt that stemmed from his culpability in Barnaby's suspension, he was convinced this day couldn't get any worse.

Henry assumed there had to be something he could do to set things right before leaving the *Arthur Broome* for good. There was no denying that he broke the partner's code—the very same partner's code that Barnaby spoke so passionately about. "What would it take to earn Barnaby's forgiveness? What could be done to get Barnaby's suspension lifted?" Every possible answer that popped into his mind seemed to only create more questions.

With his stomach tied in knots, Henry contemplated what he should do next; resting on the couch feeling sorry for himself wasn't going to fix anything.

All of a sudden, the resounding bell chimed from the loudspeaker in the ceiling. The startling interruption jolted Henry forward, and he nearly fell out of his seat. Sitting alone with his thoughts for so long caused him to slip into a light trance. He had completely forgotten about the evening announcements.

The thick Italian accent beaming from the speaker was unmistakable. It immediately wrapped around Henry like a warm blanket.

"*Buonasera*, signore e signori.

"And to all the Tutori that boarded the ship in Le Havre... *bienvenue*!

"This is-a Captain Alfredo Carlucci speaking to you again from the bridge. Sì, now a lot of you probably didn't know this, but I'm fluent in at least twelve languages... Actually, uh, let's call it twelve and a half languages. Still working on that Greek alphabet. Sì, I don't know why they have to use a special alphabet with funny letters. It's almost like they don't want anyone to learn! That's okay, though. It's okay. You all know that won't stop this old sailor from trying.

"At present, we have just departed the port of Le Havre, and the *Arthur Broome* is-a now on route toward Deception Island. Sì, this ship has traveled to many islands in the past, but this particular island is-a right off the coast of Norway.

"You know, you really have to be careful when sailing near Deception Island. Sì, sì, sì, the whole island is-a surrounded by a huge ice field that stretches across the Norwegian Sea for miles. Very dangerous stuff. Those small icebergs can slice through a ship's hull like a warm spoon cuts through soft gelato. Sì, you can trust Captain Carlucci on this. Believe me, I've seen it happen, and everybody knows I love gelato! Probably a little too much!

"Because there were a lot of times where Captain Carlucci was giving advice... many times where I was giving advice and the people weren't listening... And you know, it didn't work out so great for some of those people, let me tell you. No, no, no... it's true. It's true.

"You see, Deception Island looks like a regular island, but it is-a actually an active volcano. Sì, just like the one from Pompeii. There is-a hidden bay in the center, but it is-a only accessible through a narrow entrance on the south side of the island that connects to the Norwegian Sea. It is-a difficult to navigate, even for the most skilled sailors. Molto pericoloso, sì.

"Now, when you look back at the Navy that set up a remote outpost there, I told them... and this is-a true... Captain Carlucci said to them, there are a lot of things that can go wrong with that volcano. I told this to Admiral Bates from the US Navy.

"I said, if you're going to build a remote arctic outpost, there is-a lot of possibility with that... I see a lot of possibilities with a remote arctic outpost. Just look at the success of Antarctica. Look at McMurdo Station... Look at all of it down there. But they made a big mistake picking Deception Island for a research outpost. And it is-a sad because Admiral Bates was a very close friend of Captain Carlucci. He was there when the volcano last erupted, and frankly, it was a mistake for him to be there. Sì, it is-a true. There were a lot of people who were very disappointed with how things ended there.

"And you know, it is-a no surprise that place has been abandoned ever since. I think it's a cursed island if you ask Captain Carlucci, but not to worry, signore e signori... The show goes on. The *Arthur Broome* has a reinforced icebreaker hull. There is-a nothing she can't handle, especially with the Carabinieri at the helm.

"Based on our current speed, the *Arthur Broome* will anchor just north of Deception Island at approximately four-thirty in the early morning hours.

"The current temperature at our destination is-a negative seven degrees Celsius with southwest wind speeds registering at twenty-nine knots. Sì, it is-a very windy out there tonight, and it looks like these weather conditions will carry over into the following day.

"Aerial disembarkation will begin tomorrow morning at seven o'clock.

"From all of us on the bridge, *buonanotte*... Sì, sì, sì, *benedici il creatore e tutti quelli che passano per le sue acque*."

Once the ship-wide announcement ended, Henry glanced at the clock and noticed it was only six hours until their expected arrival time at Deception Island.

As he sat on the couch thinking about Penny, Henry wondered if maybe he should be doing more to rescue her rather than putting his faith in the hands of others. "Twenty-nine knots should be more than enough," he mumbled to himself, peering at the black parachute harness over on the bed. The glinting temerity in his eyes would have definitely made Penny proud.

An unexpected rumbling noise coming from his stomach forced his gaze to the tray of food on the coffee table. Even though he was admittedly starving, Henry couldn't bring himself to eat the delicious-smelling dinner that had been delivered to his cabin earlier.

Looking at food only reminded him of Penny. If she were there, the rascally dachshund would have undoubtedly been clamoring to see what treats awaited under the brass cloches.

Fighting to keep his eyes open, Henry dwelled on the many fond memories that he and Penny shared. Little things. The look of eager anticipation on her tiny face when she heard the sound of the treat drawer sliding open back home, all the times she stubbornly refused to hop into the cashmere-lined rucksack and then instantly changed her mind in exchange for a sweet potato stick, even the incessant barking that wouldn't stop unless he endlessly chased her around for the pure thrill of it—he missed his best friend. Nothing was the same without her, and it never would be until they were together again.

The back-and-forth pitching motions of the *Arthur Broome* traversing the high seas ultimately proved to be too much, though. Henry eventually dozed off, falling asleep on the couch with the lights on.

About six hours later, Henry woke abruptly to the sound of the ship's anchor chain dropping into the water.

What seemed like a matter of minutes turned out to be a rather lengthy nap. Henry was more tired than he thought, but when he opened his eyes, he was feeling quite invigorated. He sprang up and immediately shoved the sliding glass door open that led outside.

To his surprise, there were a few inches of snow covering his balcony. Henry assumed Norway would be cold, although he didn't realize it would be snowing at this time of the year. He peered over his balcony and gaped at the field of sea ice surrounding the *Arthur Broome* as far as the eye could see. Glancing toward the aft of the ship, he could tell that no ordinary vessel could have made the journey—a trail of crushed icebergs floated on either side of the massive wake left behind by the *Arthur Broome*.

Henry noticed something in the distance and hastily grabbed the binoculars lying on the desk inside his cabin. He dashed back out onto the balcony and looked off to the starboard side.

"There it is!" Henry quietly exclaimed under his breath, "Deception Island!"

The entrance leading to the hidden bay that Captain Carlucci mentioned was indeed obscured. It just looked like a mountain dramatically protruding from the depths of the icy Norwegian Sea.

Henry feverishly searched for any signs of activity, his head swiveling back and forth as he adjusted the focus on the binoculars. It only took him a minute to spot the small plume of smoke rising out of the center of the island. His eyes lit up with excitement, and he whispered, "Penny has to be there!"

Despite not knowing if the smoke was a byproduct of the seething volcano, Henry didn't care; he would have happily dodged buckets of cascading lava if it meant there was a chance he could hold Penny in his arms again.

With the excitement building, Henry stepped back into his cabin and closed the balcony door. The lingering doubts tempted him to abandon this treacherous undertaking, but he couldn't give up. Penny was counting on him. That sliver of hope he saw through the binoculars outweighed all the reasons he could think of to stay put and wait for the Tutori to do their job.

After a few moments of anxious pacing, Henry found the courage to look past the potential consequences of disobeying the council's orders. He ran over to the closet and impulsively grabbed his dad's yellow raincoat off the hanger.

Henry rushed to put on a fresh pair of socks and frantically tied his shoes once he finished buttoning up the yellow raincoat. Determined to rescue Penny on his own, he grabbed the black parachute harness off the bed, threw it over his shoulder, and marched over to the front door.

Sitting on his hands, idly waiting for the news of her safe return to the *Arthur Broome*, was no longer an option as far as Henry was concerned.

Clutching the black parachute harness in one hand and the cabin door handle in the other, Henry froze just as he was about to open the door. The feelings of self-doubt had swiftly returned now that he had to step up to the plate. His heartbeat was racing, and the familiar sense of throbbing adrenaline spread to every part of his body. The brazen confidence he once had was immediately met with an unnerving sense of fear; his mind became clouded with everything that might go wrong if he took matters into his own hands and walked through that door.

Even the most experienced Tutori would consider landing in the center of a volcano to be dangerous (and rightfully so). Henry had only ridden tandem with June once, never on his own. If he fell through the ice into the freezing Norwegian Sea below, he wouldn't last more than ten minutes before the hypothermia set in, and since he was sneaking out, nobody would even know to look for him.

Henry thought about turning around. It would have been all too easy and much safer to simply wait for another six or seven hours while the Tutori did their job. They weren't just sending anyone. The council had vowed to personally oversee this rescue mission, and he couldn't ignore the possibility of getting badly injured if he tried to face Catherine alone—the bruises on his back and the remnants of the charred, damp suit crumpled on the floor were proof of that. And of course, that was if he even managed to successfully land at the base of the volcano.

Despite the seemingly insurmountable risks, the indecision was untenable. It was now or never. Henry thought about what Penny would do if the situation was reversed. He knew he owed it to her to at least try, regardless of the danger that awaited.

Eventually setting his fears aside, Henry opened his cabin door and stepped out into the hallway with confidence. He could have sworn he saw Otis and Oscar peeking around the corner near the elevators; he was so distracted by his thoughts that he forgot to catch the door before it slammed shut on its own.

The resounding thud of the door closing behind him didn't exactly invoke the clandestine approach Henry had envisioned, but it did serve as a reminder to pay closer attention so as not to be detected. If even one Carabinieri guard spotted him, this impromptu rescue mission would be over faster than the career of a golf pro who just lost his hand to an unexpected alligator attack.

Apprehensively peering down the empty hallway, Henry wondered if the otters were ever there to begin with. Maybe he was just being paranoid. Nevertheless, the fear of Otis and Oscar potentially running off to alert the captain (or one of the guards) only added to the heart-pounding urgency.

Henry tried to quietly breeze past June's cabin, eager to leave the ship before he got caught. Completely stunned, he froze when her door opened almost immediately after he walked by. Like an angry parent who had just caught their kid sneaking out after curfew, the look of disapproval shining from her face forced him to briefly reconsider taking another step further.

Dressed in her pajamas and looking as if she had just woken up from a terrible night of sleep, June stepped into the hallway and didn't hesitate to confront him. "You don't have to do this, Henry! The Tutori will find Penny, I promise!" She glanced at the black parachute harness dangling from his hand and added gravely, "You could get killed out there on your own! And you don't even know how to land!"

With her hands resting on her hips, June couldn't believe that Henry would dare disobey a direct order from the council. She had never fathomed doing something so perilous and was worried Henry might get hurt, or worse, be cast out into a lifeboat with no way to get home.

Henry briefly heeded her counsel. The palpable concern in her voice matched the chilling warning she imparted, and it certainly gave him pause. Even so, the thought of Penny out there, terrified and alone, couldn't compete with the voice of reason trying to persuade him to stop.

"Maybe. Or maybe they return with nothing... again," Henry replied defiantly. Sure, waiting for the Tutori to save the day all on their own was tempting. It was too late, though; his decision had already been made. He looked at June and affirmed, "I'm sorry... and I appreciate everything you've done for me. I really do. But I can't count on anyone except for myself right now."

"Not at a time like this," he concluded somberly, "not with Penny out there all alone."

Even though June wasn't quite ready to give up yet, her attempt to persuade Henry further was interrupted when Archie suddenly opened his cabin door and waltzed into the hallway.

Unlike June, Archie was fully dressed in his gray wool suit, which was a striking difference compared to her pajamas and disheveled hair. Without the slightest trace of hesitancy or dissuasion, he instantly chimed in, "I would do the same if it were my best friend... No question about it, mate."

Henry subtly nodded his head as an unspoken sign of respect and appreciation for Archie's understanding. It was refreshing to know that Archie felt the same way, especially since everyone else onboard would have likely turned him into the council. He only wished that June could put herself in his shoes; he suspected her attitude would be different if she had lost her best friend.

Afraid of what might happen if they got caught roaming the ship at this hour, June tried to convince Archie to reconsider. "You're not gonna try and stop him?" She said in disbelief, "You know that you could get suspended... or worse, expelled, from the *APA*!"

Archie casually brushed off her concerns and quipped, "Well, that's only if we get caught, right?" He had seen that fretful look on June's face in the past (more times than he could count) and presumed she was about to spout a barrage of reasons to discourage them. The British Magari saw it coming from a mile away and didn't give her the chance, though.

"Besides, my family has been serving under the *APA* for nearly five generations," he added arrogantly, "and I'm willing to risk it for a slap on the wrist."

The Ashdown family was practically *APA* royalty, and his grandfather's father was one of the first to join the Tutori. Archie had never broken the *APA*'s code of conduct, but he was confident the council of three would go easy on him if they did get caught sneaking around the ship.

Not entirely convinced, June frantically pleaded, "But the council! They..."

"Damn the council!" Henry blurted out.

June was stunned. She never imagined that a polite, kind boy like Henry could lose his temper in such a dramatic manner.

Clearly flustered, Henry knew it was wrong to yell at her and immediately apologized, "I'm sorry, June. I didn't mean to snap at you, but please understand... I have to do this. I don't have a choice." Embarrassed that he let his emotions get the best of him, he turned around and marched down the hallway toward the elevators.

Wide-eyed and unable to utter anything of substance, June gaped at Archie as he strolled past her. He was apparently not worried in the slightest and snickered, "Don't worry, Tex. I'll take the heat if we get caught."

June followed and continued trying to talk them both out of going, hysterically pointing out all the bad things that could happen. Despite her frenzied rambling, there was nothing she could have said to stop Henry from leaving. He was more scared about what would happen if he didn't go.

The elevator arrived moments later. Henry and Archie were going with or without her, and they didn't hesitate to leave her in the hallway once the elevator doors opened.

Glancing at Archie to see if he was going to back out, Henry pressed *1–4–0–1* on the elevator control panel. Archie just winked, seemingly to confirm that Henry had correctly remembered the series of numbers that would take them to the top deck.

As the elevator doors closed, Henry gazed at June and remarked ominously, "If I don't see you again... thanks for everything."

— CHAPTER 20 —
DECEPTION ISLAND

*D*espite Archie's unwavering support, Henry couldn't help but ruminate on the slew of potential dangers that June had listed during her yammering pleas to reconsider. He tried to appear calm and confident as the elevator rapidly approached the top deck, though it was impossible for him to ignore her warnings since he was about to cross the point of no return.

Even if Henry managed to safely land at the base of the volcano unscathed and somehow found a way to circumvent Catherine shortly thereafter, he would still be stuck on a remote Norwegian island in the middle of nowhere. The temptation to call the whole thing off and just go back to his cabin before he caused any more trouble seemed more enticing with each passing second.

One way or another, Henry had to end the anxiety-ridden deliberation once those elevator doors opened again. But then he remembered—it didn't matter if he wanted to or not. That's not how friendships work. He knew Penny wouldn't be casually lounging around the cabin if the situation had been reversed, and he would never forgive himself if he didn't at least try to rescue her on his own.

Henry's heart nearly leapt out of his chest when the elevator suddenly stopped and the doors opened. It wasn't just the impending aerial disembarkation; he and Archie were both stunned to see that Barnaby was already on the top deck with Catherine's twin sister, Celine Saint-Clair. Her long, red hair billowed in the wind, and the piercing expression on her face gave Henry chills.

"What the hell are you two doing up here?" Barnaby shouted over the howling wind as he finished clipping the cable hook to the front of his black parachute harness.

Shocked that his furtive attempt to leave the ship had been foiled, Henry stammered, "Well, uh... I was, um..."

Archie was equally surprised (although for a different reason entirely) and confidently intervened, "We could ask you the same thing." He sneered, "Or maybe you just forgot the council placed you under cabin restriction? Effective immediately is what they said, innit?"

"Well, well, well," Barnaby chuckled, "I guess I'm not the only one bending the rules tonight... ain't that right, Arch?" His tone clearly implied that Archie wasn't supposed to be wandering around the ship at this hour, nor was he allowed to be on the top deck without the direct supervision of a tutor.

Henry was grateful for the help, but he didn't want to see Archie get in trouble with the council, not for something that he should have been doing by himself, if at all. In a hasty attempt to avoid tarnishing Archie's unblemished record, Henry chimed in defiantly, "I'm going to find Penny on my own. Archie was just showing me the way to the top deck."

Barnaby and Archie looked at each other in a moment of disbelief, both raising their eyebrows at Henry's renewed sense of conviction.

"Is that right?" Barnaby scoffed. "Well, *I'm going to find Catherine on my own*. And after I recover those bears, I'm gonna haul her in to face the council so that she can clear my name." He pulled out a short sword from the miniature scabbard that was double strapped to his leg and quickly inspected the sharp edge of the blade before carefully holstering it.

The sword wasn't quite as long or intimidating as the one Barnaby borrowed from Mr. Sakamoto in the grand atrium the other day, yet it certainly looked more dangerous than the electric cattle prods the Tutori were known to carry. Even though it was only half the length of a normal-sized samurai sword, it could still do more damage than Savannah's lasso.

"That's right, mate. The council will have no choice but to fully reinstate *Barnaby Banjo Murdoch* once I return with the bear cubs, that overly dramatic dachshund, and my former partnah," he brashly declared. "Hell, they might even throw me a party after I prove Sunday wrong!"

Turning to Celine, Barnaby asked, "You ready?" She nodded silently and unlocked the handle crank in preparation for his departure.

Despite his arrogant bravado, Barnaby promised Celine that he would do everything he could to avoid hurting her sister. It was the only way that he could convince her to assist with this risky endeavor. Without his help, she knew the looming threat of a blue notice would just make things more dangerous for her sister.

Barnaby casually grabbed the ripcord on his harness as Henry and Archie watched incredulously.

Right before he gave Celine the greenlight to release the towline, Barnaby paused for a moment to deliver a dire warning. "This isn't a game, fellas. You understand? You blokes should head on back to your cabins before you both get caught. Let the adults handle this one, alright?" He didn't wait for them to argue or protest.

Barnaby yanked the ripcord a split second later, and as soon as he did, his dark-green parachute caught the gusting wind and sent him flying into the air.

Precisely as Captain Carlucci had predicted, the wind was indeed blowing at twenty-nine knots. It was more than strong enough to facilitate an aerial disembarkation while the *Arthur Broome* remained anchored.

The towline rapidly unwound and continued to automatically let out the perfect amount of slack, forcing Barnaby higher and higher into the sky until he reached the proper height for a safe release. Without a trace of hesitation, he unhooked the cable clipped to the front of his harness and pulled down on the steering lines.

Archie and Henry couldn't take their eyes off the confident Australian as he glided toward Deception Island.

While their necks craned backward, Celine pushed the button on the side of the winch to retract the towline from the icy waters. She glanced at Archie and Henry once the towline was fully retracted and shook her head in disappointment, swiftly pushing the call button for the elevator. The doors opened immediately, and she stepped in without saying anything to them. Only the sound of her sighing could be heard as the doors closed.

The recurring reluctance in Henry's eyes gave Archie another reason to think that maybe Barnaby was right. He put his hand on Henry's shoulder and cautioned, "It's not too late to turn around, Halifax. I suspect you'll be in for a rough landing with this wind kicking up."

The gracious offer to save face was humbling, and Henry considered abandoning his risky plan entirely in that moment, although it became apparent that wasn't going to happen when he rebelliously marched over to the winch. He put on the black parachute harness and secured the cable hook to the front.

Worried about Henry's lack of flight experience, Archie pleaded once more, "Sure you want to go through with this, mate? There's no going back once you pull that ripcord."

Henry was indeed terrified but appreciated Archie's warranted concern. He nodded nonetheless, clutching the ripcord with trepidation. His palms were clammy, and he was sweating profusely, even though it was negative seven degrees Celsius outside.

Archie respected the resolve and decided against trying to talk Henry out of going any further. It was clear this was something Henry had to do on his own, and he needed every last bit of encouragement he could get right now.

Standing in the launch zone, Henry pointed his index finger up to the sky and twisted it in a circular motion to show Archie he was ready for the winch lock to be released. He was far too nervous to say anything at that point.

Henry glanced over at Deception Island and yanked on the ripcord; the gusting wind immediately swept him up into the air.

Archie's mouth gaped as the sound of the winch mechanism releasing the towline incessantly clicked in the background. He was truly surprised and never thought Henry would actually go through with it, especially after Barnaby's warning.

It didn't take long for the clicking noise to abruptly cease—the towline had been fully extended, leaving Henry aimlessly hovering high above the *Arthur Broome*. The wind bounced him around like a marionette, pushing him from side to side.

"Detach! Detach!" Archie shouted urgently from the top deck.

Archie's faint screeching was barely audible over the howling wind, but Henry could see him waving his arms wildly and figured that must have been the sign to let go of the towline. Any lingering doubts were instantly extinguished when the attached towline ran out of slack and jolted Henry forward. Now was the time.

Absolutely terrified as his feet dangled in the air, Henry frantically tried to grab ahold of the hook on the front of his harness. It took him a few desperate attempts on account of his sweaty hands, though. "Finally!" he cried out once he managed to successfully unclip the cable hook.

Henry felt like his heart popped out of his chest and got left behind on the top deck. Watching the towline plummet into the icy Norwegian Sea below served as a horrifying reminder of what would happen if he failed to land on Deception Island.

As the wind carried him further away from the ship, Henry lunged for the steering lines and tried to guide the parachute in the opposite direction toward Deception Island. Without June riding tandem on his back and leading the way, soaring through the air was even more frightening than the last time. He couldn't close his eyes today, and panicking would have only made things worse.

Despite the heart-stopping sensation of being at the mercy of the unrelenting Arctic wind, Henry fixed his gaze on Barnaby's parachute ahead of him. His confidence slowly started to build, and he clumsily steered in the same direction. Seeing someone else do it was all the encouragement he was going to get at this point.

Henry soared past the highest peak of the volcano and noticed that Barnaby was on the verge of landing near the bay of water in the center of the island.

Staring intently, Henry watched as Barnaby gracefully touched down on the ground. The Australian released his parachute in one swift motion a second later; it rapidly billowed up into the sky before catching fire and disintegrating. The miniature fireworks display had become a familiar sight and instantly bolstered Henry's confidence even further. It all seemed so effortless.

Henry was still too high to land himself, but he leveraged his temporary vantage point to survey the surrounding area. "There it is!" he suddenly shrieked. "That's the yellow floatplane from Paris!"

Docked next to a small boat at the edge of the bay, the single-engine propeller plane immediately became a beacon of hope for Henry. He knew Penny had to be somewhere on the island, and he was prepared to search every last inch of the vast caldera to find her.

The bay in the center of the island was surrounded by mountains. It was noticeably calmer and quieter than the choppy Norwegian Sea, a few miles to the southeast.

There were a few metal buildings near the floating dock, most of them dilapidated and deteriorating from years of neglect. The various structures had long since rusted, and the burnt-orange paint scheme on the exterior walls created a drastic contrast to the snow around them. They all appeared to have been abandoned, except for one. The plume of smoke rising from the small building just north of the bay was a dead giveaway.

Henry goggled at the structure with optimism flickering in his eyes; he presumed that Penny had to be nearby. Oddly enough, the metal building appeared to have been recently refurbished. It was located next to a large cave and was the only building that had lights turned on inside.

Barnaby had landed a few hundred yards away, and Henry carefully tugged on the steering lines to glide toward the same spot as best he could. His inexperience was on full display, and the confidence that had been building quickly evaporated once he hit the ground running. The landing proved to be far less graceful than he had anticipated.

Henry's arrival was poorly planned, and everything from the approach to his overall maneuvering was full of mistakes only an amateur would make. Even though he tumbled to the ground and rolled a few times as the parachute wrapped around his body, Barnaby was admittedly impressed (and somewhat surprised) that the kid had enough courage to follow him off the *Arthur Broome*. It was admirable, yet sort of irritating at the same time.

An excruciating feeling of pain surged from Henry's ankle to nearly every part of his body the second he hit the ground. It felt like someone had wacked the side of his lateral malleolus bone with a hockey stick. The insufferable pain dispelled the remnants of arrogance that drove him to leave the ship, but it didn't stop him from getting up off the ground after untangling the parachute. While his ankle didn't appear to be broken, the aching discomfort only intensified upon taking the first step forward.

Fortunately, Henry was finally able to get free of the strings and biodegradable nylon just as the parachute burst into flames and disintegrated in the snow.

Barnaby would have probably burst into laughter if it were under any other circumstances, but he respected Henry's fortitude. The boy's unwavering determination reminded him of his days training as a young Magari. He honestly never thought Henry would be brave enough to come out here all on his own, let alone land a parachute without ending up in the frigid Norwegian Sea.

With Barnaby waving him over, Henry impulsively rushed forward. A sharp pain reverberated up the boy's leg after putting too much pressure on his left foot, and his scampering stride turned into a sluggish limp about halfway there.

Henry certainly wasn't a doctor, although he could tell his ankle was either fractured or badly sprained.

Barnaby spotted the slight limp in Henry's step as the kid got closer and warned, "Look, mate, I appreciate the tenacity. It really is commendable... But it's probably best you sit this one out." He gestured toward the floating dock. "Just wait for me over by the plane, alright? Don't worry about Penny... I'll find her. I promise. You got my word on that."

"No chance, Mr. Murdoch," Henry asserted to Barnaby's surprise. "I'm not turning back now... Not when I'm this close to finding her myself."

Henry didn't care how much his ankle hurt. Penny was his responsibility and his alone; she had to be somewhere on this island, and he wasn't leaving without her.

It's not like Barnaby had the best track record when tangling with Catherine, and Henry wasn't particularly confident in the assurances offered. It was hard to forget that Barnaby had been defeated at least four times since he started chasing the aspiring French educator across the world. Nothing about these failures gave Henry the impression that this time would be any different. He couldn't take that chance with Penny's life.

Barnaby clicked his tongue and cautioned, "Whatever you say, mate. Just stay out of my way and try not to get yourself killed then." He turned around and charged ahead toward the small buildings as Henry trailed behind.

Henry tried his best to keep pace despite the painful limp slowing him down. He could feel the nervous anticipation building with each step, desperately hoping that Catherine and Penny were still on the island.

Moments later, a renewed sense of panic clouded his thoughts. With no sign of his dachshund, the missing polar bears, or the French adversary that had eluded them so many times, he wondered if Catherine had already absconded on a different plane. The floating dock nearby looked like it could accommodate at least three floatplanes and probably about five small boats.

Everything seemed all too easy back when Henry hatched this plan from the comfort of the *Arthur Broome*. But now that he was here, a few seemingly abandoned buildings and a huge, dark cave didn't exactly give him that feeling of guaranteed success he had envisioned. Nevertheless, Henry tried to stay positive and mumbled some familiar words of encouragement as if Captain Fulbright was whispering in his ear: *"You can't win if you're not on the ice."*

As they approached the dimly lit building next to the cave, Henry gasped when the front door suddenly swung open—it was Catherine Saint-Clair.

The train conductor's uniform was gone, but Henry recognized her red hair immediately. Still, her new disguise gave them both pause. Catherine was dressed in a gray wool suit just like Barnaby and the rest of the Tutori, only without the black cloak; she even had the same forest-green necktie that matched. The resemblance to her sister, *Celine*, was uncanny.

Henry couldn't tell if Catherine was simply making fun of Barnaby (taunting him by the way she was dressed) or if she had something more sinister planned that involved impersonating a *real* Tutori for her next caper. Regardless of the true reason, it was clear that Catherine was done hiding. She brazenly walked out and slammed the door behind her, leaving Henry guessing if Penny was actually inside.

Catherine took a few steps forward, smirking menacingly at the sight of Barnaby and Henry. The unquestionable defiance in her eyes implied that Barnaby would have to go through her if he wanted whatever was behind the door.

Barnaby glanced at Henry and ordered, "This is mine, mate. Just hang back and stay out of the way, alright?"

Henry's first instinct was to run into the building and tackle anyone that stood in his way. He didn't care how tough Catherine thought she was, and even though his ankle had been injured, he didn't come all the way out here to sit on the sidelines. The shaky trepidation in Barnaby's voice made Henry think twice, though, and he prudently did as he was instructed.

If Penny was behind that door, it wouldn't do either of them any good if Catherine launched another barrage of tranquilizer darts in their direction. Henry had already seen firsthand how quickly she knocked out the professor in London, so he decided to follow Barnaby's lead, at least for now.

Barnaby marched ahead warily until there was about three meters of space between him and Catherine. They squared off and just looked at each other for a moment in silence until he eventually shouted, "Had a feeling you'd be here!" The hostile tension in the air was thick enough to give Henry goosebumps.

"You never give up, Barnabas... Do you?" Catherine responded, crossing her arms in a defensive position. A vindictive grin washed over her face when she astutely noticed his cloak was missing. Unable to resist toying with him, Barnaby's former partner teased, "Too bad it looks like the *APA* has given up on you, no?"

"Tut-tut," she sighed grimly, "perhaps it is time for you to reconsider your loyalties, mon ami."

The animosity in Barnaby's eyes had only intensified, but that didn't dissuade Catherine from extending a tempting offer in a more joyful tone. "Oui, think of how great we could be together... partners again, just like the old times? Nobody giving us orders! No more *APA* bureaucracy!"

"You've gone too far this time, Catherine!" Barnaby retorted with a hint of desperation in his voice as he pulled the shortened sword out of his scabbard. "Painted me into a cornah, good and propah... but I don't care if things get messy now."

"Oh Barnabas, still the same old dramatic Australian... pretending to be something you're not," Catherine jested. She laughed, not feeling intimidated in the slightest.

"Oui, I know you better than you know yourself," she boasted, "and I have to say... this tough guy, desperado act doesn't suit you well."

"Last chance, Catherine! Just hand ovah the kid's dog and let the polar bear cubs go before this gets ugly," Barnaby yelled in frustration. Unamused by her snickering, he waved the sword back and forth in a threatening manner. "I'm not joking, Catherine. I don't want to, but I will! You know I will!"

Henry tensed up and clenched his fists, fearing he was about to be dragged into another tussle.

"Honestly, I don't know where all this hostility is coming from. You should be on your knees thanking me!" Catherine quipped, casually brushing off Barnaby's threats.

Wondering why anyone from the *APA* would want to thank her for anything, a look of bewilderment briefly replaced the scowl on Henry's face.

"I only did what you should have done on your own." Catherine carried on explaining, "You *and* the council. Although courage isn't exactly abundant onboard the *Arthur Broome* these days... so I can't say that I'm entirely surprised."

Catherine jeered, "If you ask me... they should hang my portrait in the grand atrium after what I've done for these animals, no? Not just a photograph. I'm thinking something like the painting by Monsieur Degas... You know the one, Blue Dancers? A real *French* masterpiece, oui?"

"You can tell the council yourself after I haul you in!" Barnaby shouted furiously.

"Whatever it takes to get your cloak back, right, Barnabas?" Catherine sneered, cackling as Barnaby tightened his grip on the sword.

Henry thought her relentless banter might never end, but he was proven wrong seconds later. Catherine suddenly sprinted toward Barnaby and tackled him to the ground before he had a chance to make the first move.

As Barnaby and Catherine savagely wrestled in the snow, Henry raced up the stairs, and yanked the front door open—he pulled it with such ferocity that the hinge on the bottom nearly broke.

— CHAPTER 21 —
PENNY HALIFAX

*T*he door swiftly closed behind Henry, almost as fast as it had opened. Overcome with an immense sense of relief, Henry just about collapsed upon entering. "Penny! I can't believe it!" he cried out, equally shocked and excited at the sight of his beloved dachshund. She was peacefully sleeping on an overly plush dog bed that was about three times bigger than herself.

Startled by the abrupt entrance, Penny instantly sprang to life and raced across the room to greet Henry after hearing his voice. She was beyond elated and leaped into his arms as he kneeled down to embrace her. The wirehaired dachshund jumped with such force that it knocked Henry backward onto the floor.

"My sweet baby! You alright, girl? Are you okay?" Henry gushed. Penny appeared to be in perfect health. She certainly didn't have any difficulty showering Henry's face with a flurry of ecstatic kisses as she frantically squealed and snorted.

"Yes, I know! I missed you too, eh?" Henry beamed while Penny climbed all over his chest. "It's okay, my good girl! I'm here! I'm here!"

Penny was overjoyed to be reunited with her best friend, although it paled into comparison to the jubilation Henry was feeling—what seemed like only a long nap for her was actually hours of excruciating despair and anguish for him. He was thrilled to be rid of that devastating grief, and it completely overshadowed the throbbing sensation radiating from his ankle. More than anything, he was incredibly thankful that she was safe.

Blissfully staring at her infectious smile, Henry promised himself he would never let anything bad happen to Penny again. He had almost lost her forever, and even though she seemed oblivious to the whole ordeal, it was something he wouldn't soon forget.

As the euphoria faded, Henry eventually noticed Penny's new attire. She was wearing a bespoke black winter jacket lined with soft fleece on the inside. The outfit suited her perfectly. "Where'd you get this nice jacket, eh?" Henry asked as he continued carefully examining her to make sure she hadn't been injured.

"And did someone give you... a bath?" he murmured, puzzled by the absence of any oil or dirt on her body. "Your nails have been buffed too?"

After further inspection, it seemed as if Penny had just returned from the groomers. Her fur was shiny, she smelled like lavender shampoo, and it was obvious that she had been recently cleaned up. Henry's exuberance proved to be fleeting, though. Despite feeling like everything would be okay now that Penny was at his side once again, he remembered the danger was far from over. Barnaby and Catherine were still battling outside.

Henry jumped to his feet and warned, "We're not out of the woods yet, Penny. Stick close to me, and I'll get us out of here, alright?" She sensed the fretful hesitation in his voice and immediately stretched her short legs to prepare for whatever might happen next.

Now would have been the perfect time for Penny to hop into her rucksack, but that wasn't an option—it had been left behind under the bridge in Paris during all the commotion.

Henry darted over to the front door, only to freeze in astonishment as he grabbed the handle. His mouth gaped open when he spotted the black duffle bag resting on the small table nearby. He had been so preoccupied with rescuing Penny that he didn't even notice it when he first entered the building.

Blinded by an unshakable sense of determination to find Penny, Henry had breezed past the bag as if he could just see that beautiful wirehaired dachshund and nothing else. There it was, though, staring back at him—Catherine's black duffle bag, the same bag that everyone from the *APA* was so eager to recover.

Henry marveled at the sight of the one thing in this world that Barnaby would need to get his suspension lifted. He approached warily and noticed the top had already been unzipped.

Peeking inside without actually touching the bag, Henry's face lit up with excitement once he laid eyes on the pair of polar bear cubs inside. The cubs were curled up next to each other in the comfort of their makeshift den, unharmed and sleeping soundlessly. They seemed totally oblivious to the chaotic journey that brought them from Kodiak Bay to this remote Arctic outpost.

"Looks like they are still heavily sedated," he suggested. "Must be something a little stronger than the tranquilizer dart that landed on my foot the other day, eh, Penny?"

Penny beamed with excitement as he zipped the bag halfway shut. She knew Henry would be thrilled to finally catch up with the familiar scent that had eluded them through the streets of Paris.

Convinced that Barnaby's troubles would all be over upon delivering the bear cubs to the council, Henry picked up the bag in a delicate manner and flung the strap over his shoulder. He turned around and paused again as he grabbed the handle on the front door.

"Stay by my side, alright girl?" Henry whispered to Penny. Still smiling with her tongue hanging out, she nodded obediently without hesitation.

Henry slowly cracked the door open, first peering through to find out what awaited them outside. Unable to see or hear much of anything, he opened the door wider and gasped at what he saw—the disturbing spectacle would be etched in his memory forever.

A wave of panic sent chills racing throughout Henry's entire body. It wasn't just what he saw; it was also what he didn't see that terrified him the most. He couldn't even bring himself to step outside.

Barnaby and Catherine were nowhere to be found, but the white snow in front of the building had turned dark red (in the same spot where Barnaby just got tackled a short while ago). Henry assumed the worst, given the copious amount of blood left behind on the ground.

Fearing things had escalated far beyond a spirited tussle, he shuddered at the sight of what appeared to be a fatal encounter.

The red puddle in front of the building served as an ominous warning, and it was clear the stakes were now higher than ever. Regardless of how grateful Henry was to have Penny by his side, there were still no guarantees they would make it off the island alive.

Henry staggered backward into the building and quietly shut the door behind him. He gently set the black duffle back on the ground, hoping not to disturb the polar bear cubs inside.

Frantically searching for anything that could be used for protection, Henry eventually settled for the small hatchet hanging on the wall next to the fireplace. Inside a red box above the only fire extinguisher in the building, the words *BREAK IN CASE OF EMERGENCY* were painted on the thin piece of glass affixed to the front.

"Watch out, Penny!" he ordered. "Move out of the way!"

As soon as he told her, Penny scurried to the other side of the building so she could watch from a safe distance while he used his elbow to break the protective glass.

All it took was one swift hit. Fortunately, Henry's yellow raincoat absorbed most of the impact and left him unscathed. Broken glass came crashing down to the floor as he carefully extracted the small hatchet from the red emergency box. He marched over to the front door while Penny trotted behind him, curious and unaware of the danger awaiting outside.

After picking up the black duffle bag once again, Henry slung the strap over his shoulder and peeked inside the bag to make sure the bears were still sleeping. He gripped the small hatchet in his hand and vigilantly swung the door open all the way this time.

Even though Penny wanted to run ahead of Henry and investigate her new surroundings, she mindfully followed him as he trudged outside. There was still no sign of Barnaby or Catherine (only the grisly pool of blood on the ground).

"No, Penny! Get away from there!" Henry snapped in a soft voice. Her nose had lured her over to the grim trail of blood that led off toward the dark cave nearby.

Penny immediately backed up upon hearing his commands, but she kept sniffing the red snow from a distance after rushing to join him in front of the building.

Henry didn't need a trusty blood spatter analyst to tell him what he already knew—someone had ended up on the wrong side of that sword Barnaby was wielding. The size of the uneven droplets and the sheer amount of overall blood littering the pristine snow made that evident. This was no papercut. He presumed one of them, or possibly both, had been seriously injured.

All of a sudden, Henry heard a clamorous combination of grunts and yelling coming from deep inside the cavern; it sounded like two people brawling. The haunting echoes spewing out of the cave made it impossible to know who was actually winning.

Henry never imagined their latest clash could ultimately end with either Barnaby or Catherine dying. After all, they had been partners for years. Broken bones were one thing, but Henry was worried he could be next if Catherine emerged triumphantly from the cave.

As the eerie sounds of shrieking and groaning continued to pour out of the cave, Henry found himself unable to move. He was transfixed. Overcome by apprehension and pure terror, he couldn't decide if he should run toward the danger to help Barnaby or somehow try to signal the *Arthur Broome* for reinforcements. It felt like he was locked in a prison of indecision, and the key was nowhere to be found.

All Henry could do was stare anxiously at the blood spilled across the snow and wonder who it belonged to as the screams inside the cavern intensified.

In the midst of his panicked deliberations, a jarring thud echoed off the cave's entrance—the sound was only slightly louder than Henry's heart pounding at an alarming rate. That chilling noise alone should have been enough to send him running for his life, yet it was the abrupt silence that immediately followed that scared Henry more than anything.

Henry wasn't sure what happened in that cave, but he wasn't going to wait around any longer to find out. It didn't matter who prevailed. He needed to get off Deception Island right away.

Recklessly charging into the cave would just put Penny in greater danger. And quite frankly, Barnaby's reputation wasn't exactly unblemished when it came to matters of this type; he had failed to capture Catherine at least four times now. The odds were stacked against him the moment he stepped foot off the ship.

To Henry's surprise, nobody had emerged out of the darkness as the clear victor. Nothing, except for ghastly silence, escaped the massive cave. As much as he didn't want to believe it, he couldn't hide from the truth any longer—Barnaby's latest wrestling match with Catherine had most likely turned deadly.

Henry glanced down at Penny with the hatchet still clutched in his hand and declared in a quavering voice, "We have to get out of here!"

Wincing in pain from his injured ankle, Henry limped forward at an urgent pace while Penny trotted along beside him without grumbling or protesting. He was determined to reach the yellow airplane docked nearby and pinned his hopes on alerting the Tutori somehow.

Henry had seen plenty of floatplanes in Kodiak Bay and knew that most pilots always kept an emergency flare to signal for help in the event of a crash landing. Even if the plane was empty, he assumed the keys to the small boat docked next to it were probably still in the ignition.

Fleeing on the boat wasn't his first choice (especially since there was no guarantee it had enough fuel to reach the *Arthur Broome*). But that backup plan would have to suffice for now if it meant he could safely leave the island with Penny and the pair of polar bear cubs.

With Penny at his side, Henry continued marching forward while trying to ignore the overwhelming feelings of trepidation. Keeping the pressure off his left foot was proving to be harder than he expected with a bulky duffle bag on his shoulder and a hatchet in his hand. Despite the small size of the bear cubs, the bag itself had been heavily reinforced, and apparently the padding on the inside wasn't made of lightweight materials.

The burden of it all seemed to get heavier and heavier with each step Henry took. He had trudged through the harsh Kodiak Bay winter snow more times than he could count, although never with an injured ankle. Even so, the relentless Arctic winds weren't helping matters either. If it were anyone else, they probably would have given up by now.

Henry was Canadian, though. He'd had ice running through his veins since the day he was born. Winter wasn't just a season of the year for him—it took on a whole different meaning in the land of maple syrup. The frigid temperatures wouldn't be enough to stop him from carrying on, but that wasn't all that stood between him and the yellow floatplane.

All of a sudden, Henry heard something in the distance and came to an abrupt stop. Even though the rapidly approaching sound kept growing louder, it was tough to see anything through the persistent snow flurries.

Penny knew what was coming almost instantly and charged ahead to protect Henry. She took up a defensive stance in front of him and growled as the distinct scents barreled past them.

Henry carefully placed the black duffle bag on the ground and raised the small hatchet impulsively, clutching it with all his might. His heart felt like it had dropped to the pit of his stomach.

Whatever was headed their way couldn't be good. Penny's resolute snarl quickly extinguished any illusions that their escape from Deception Island wouldn't be riddled with insurmountable obstacles.

Prepared to defend himself and the brave dachshund at his feet, Henry stood his ground nonetheless. It was too late to turn back. He hadn't gotten very far, but there was no way he could run that fast with an injured ankle, let alone with the hefty duffle bag on his shoulder.

As he squinted to see through the snowflakes falling from the sky, Henry's jaw dropped when he finally spotted a pack of six Arctic wolves sprinting in his direction. Despite the compulsion to make a run for it anyway, he knew the wolves were faster than he was. Much faster.

Ready for a fight, Penny exposed her sharp fangs and continued growling viciously with her tail raised. Henry inched forward, hoping to distract the wolves long enough for her to safely run back into the building. Stubborn until the end, there was no way she was leaving his side now, regardless of the imminent confrontation.

What happened next left them both absolutely baffled.

Once they got within striking distance, the pack of Arctic wolves came to a screeching halt unexpectedly. It was bizarre. It was almost like there was an invisible barrier preventing them from pouncing on Henry and Penny.

Henry wasn't sure what to make of it. Perplexed by the sudden bout of self-restraint, he refused to lower the hatchet, especially since the wolves didn't look like they were interested in making new friends. It was quite the opposite, indeed. They just glared at him and Penny, snarling sinisterly with their sharp teeth on full display.

Waving the hatchet back and forth in a threatening manner didn't scare them off either—it only seemed to enrage the wild animals further.

The two wolves in the center of the pack responded with an onslaught of ferocious barking. Penny reciprocated in kind by returning a barrage of deafening barks, leaving the family of Arctic wolves utterly stunned. They were shocked to hear such a thunderous defense coming from an animal of her size; clearly, the unshakable loyalty that this particular breed of dog held for the people they loved was not to be trifled with.

Trusting that the hatchet would serve as a formidable deterrent, Henry was willing to risk everything to prevent any harm from falling upon the cherished dachshund at his side. He didn't want to hurt anyone (and that certainly included animals), but he hadn't come this far to lose his best friend again, not to a pack of blood-thirsty wolves.

It all seemed despairingly inevitable as the wolves slowly started creeping forward—they were tired of waiting to make the first move, and whatever was holding them back no longer mattered.

With adrenaline surging through every part of his body, Henry nearly fainted when he heard someone shouting from behind. "Bonjour, bonjour, Monsieur Halifax!" The hatchet almost slipped out of his hand in disbelief upon hearing the woman's voice. He recognized the French accent almost instantly.

The six wolves immediately crossed the invisible line keeping them at bay and joined Catherine Saint-Clair. Henry was speechless as he turned around. He couldn't believe it. There she was, staring back at him, beaming menacingly as if nothing had happened.

Sure enough, Catherine was proudly holding Barnaby's sword at her side. The blade was covered in blood, and any lingering optimism about his Australian friend vanished at that moment.

Henry knew Barnaby was gone, undoubtedly killed by Catherine in what proved to be their final skirmish. There was no denying it anymore. The blood stains on her gray wool suit made it all painfully obvious. He was on his own now.

— CHAPTER 22 —
CATHERINE SAINT-CLAIR

T oo angry and distraught to say anything, Henry's eyes just teared up—a flood of sorrow, guilt, and rage clouded his thoughts. Running from the truth was no longer an option. He was engulfed by a dangerous torrent of emotions and automatically blamed himself for everything. If he had just stayed in Kodiak Bay, none of this would have ever happened. Penny wouldn't be in this dire predicament, and Barnaby would likely still be alive.

Despite the brash Australian routinely giving him a hard time, Henry had always admired Barnaby. He began to think of him as a friend, even if Barnaby didn't feel the same way. Truth be told, he didn't have many friends back in Kodiak Bay. In fact, he didn't have any friends at all, aside from Penny and the Fulbrights.

Henry still didn't know why Barnaby lied to the council, but regardless of his flaws, he knew Mr. Murdoch was an honorable man with a good heart.

"*Enchanté*!" Catherine exclaimed as the pack of Arctic wolves systematically flanked her on both sides.

Devoid of any remorse or anguish, Catherine seemed to brush off Barnaby's murder like an innocent workplace accident. The blood on his sword wasn't even dry yet, and she was grinning as if it were Christmas morning.

After wiping the tears off his face, Henry tensed up and tightened his grip on the hatchet. He didn't say a word, though—the scowling look smeared on his face let Catherine know that vengeance awaited if she didn't clear out of the way.

Penny kept her gaze focused on the pack of Arctic wolves. She was ready to jump to Henry's defense if any of them took so much as another step forward, confident that her teeth were just as sharp as theirs.

"I have to say, I admire your bravery. Truly. Coming out here all on your own against the council's orders," Catherine smirked, looking down at the seething dachshund next to him. "Oui, I can tell there is probably nothing you wouldn't do to protect that dog."

She playfully twirled Barnaby's sword in the air as a few drops of blood landed on the white snow below and jeered, "Although you probably should have left this one to the adults, young man." Her dispassionate attitude only caused Henry's anger to intensify. The venomous look in his eyes glinted as he mustered the courage to demand curtly, "Step aside and let us pass, Saint-Clair!"

"Have you ever seen an Arctic wolf up close, Henry?" Catherine chuckled, ostensibly ignoring his request. He glanced anxiously at the snarling wolves on either side of her, desperately hoping she wasn't about to set them loose.

A heavy sigh of frustration ensued as she prattled on, "Brilliant creatures if you ask me... But I'm afraid not everyone would agree. You see, wolves have always been treated poorly in fairytales... misrepresented at every turn of the page, and cast unjustly as villains for simply being who they are. Forget the snakes, the crocodiles, or even the tiny mosquitoes that kill more humans each year than the rest of them combined. No, no, no... it's always the wolf they mention first."

"Oui, from an early age, children are taught to fear wolves so they can point and say, that's the bad guy! That's him... The big, bad wolf!" Catherine affirmed. "But they have it all wrong, my young Canadian friend! Just look at these beautiful animals. Look at the loyalty, Henry! Look at the discipline on display here. Honestly, I'm the only thing standing between you and their insatiable appetite."

Henry trembled with apprehension as the wolves continued growling in his direction. The thought of running was becoming more enticing, but he knew acting on that impulse wouldn't get him very far. He was trapped. She could snap her fingers at any moment, and it would all be over in a matter of minutes.

Catherine was enthralled by the panic in Henry's eyes and cried out bombastically, "It's true, mon ami. You see, little Penny may be a descendant of these Arctic wolves, but make no mistake... they are not equals by any measure." She gestured toward the largest wolf at her side, gloating, "Oui, this is the *real* alpha dog here!"

Penny was incensed. She immediately unleashed a bombardment of thunderous barks in rapid succession to dispute Catherine's insufferable remarks.

Catherine cackled in amusement. "*Six hundred eighty kilograms* per square inch of jaw-crushing power with just one bite... versus only a third of that for the overly opinionated hound at your feet."

"They can cut through bone like sponge cake... And with over *two hundred million* scent receptors, these wolves smelled you the second you stepped foot off the *Arthur Broome*!" She warned, "You don't stand a chance, and you never did. They could have ripped you into pieces at any time... and they still can. Like I said, though, you have to admire the level of discipline being exercised here."

Wincing in pain, Henry tottered backward with two panic-induced steps.

Catherine cautioned, "I know what you're thinking... but running away won't do you any good now. No, I'm afraid it is far too late for that, Monsieur Halifax. These wolves *live* for the thrill of the chase. Oui, you would only be doing them a favor."

"That's right, my young friend... They're natural-born hunters, unlike any other." She bragged ruthlessly, "Even when the rest of the animals were on the verge of extinction during the Ice Age, the wolves not only survived ... they flourished in the face of certain death. They laughed in death's face and sent him home crying in tears!"

The pack of wolves erupted into a boisterous round of howling as they pointed their noses up toward the sky. They wanted to make sure there was no confusion; this was their land long before humans arrived, and they had a special way of dealing with trespassers.

In between Catherine's wicked laughter, she let out a few howls of her own out of respect. It merely excited the wolves further, much to Penny's chagrin.

"Oui, the Japanese have a special word for wolves," she sneered. "They call them Ōkami. It means... great spirit."

Henry glared at Catherine as she babbled on, "Don't let the razor-sharp teeth fool you, Henry. These wolves have the power to both kill and heal. It's true. Their saliva has special antiseptic properties that can heal open wounds with only a few licks. Can you..."

"*Enough*! Enough of your games!" Henry suddenly interrupted, shouting scornfully. The shaking anger in his voice even took Penny by surprise.

Henry couldn't fathom how she could keep blathering about wolves as if nothing had happened. She just killed Barnaby, and her suit was still covered in his blood. He thought to himself, "How dare this woman wittingly invoke the help of these wolves to bolster her threats?"

Tired of her senseless gibberish, Henry hastily picked up the duffle bag, planted his feet firmly on the ground, and brandished the hatchet in an intimidating manner. "Now, hear me when I say this..."

"I can throw this hatchet at a speed of *ninety-nine kilometers per hour*," he scathingly warned, pointing the small axe in her direction. "Take a good look because once it leaves my hand, *the two hundred milliseconds* your reflexes will need to activate won't be nearly enough time for you to get out of the way! Not when you're this close!"

Henry yelled furiously, "So, we can all pretend like I haven't spent the past five years competing in Kodiak Bay's annual axe-throwing competition, but just remember one thing... You only have *one hundred fifty fluid ounces* of blood in your body. Lose more than *forty percent* of that, and it wouldn't matter if you had a dozen wolves at your side... None of them will be able to lick that wound fast enough to keep you alive!"

Stunned by his resolve, Catherine's jaw dropped in disbelief. She was admittedly impressed and couldn't believe this kid hadn't given up yet.

"Now, I'm only going to say this once more." Henry demanded with pure hostility in his voice, "Step aside and call off the wolves!"

Catherine exuberantly fired back, "Now, that's what I'm talking about! This is what I have been waiting for... I finally get to meet the *real* Henry Halifax!" She laughed hysterically while twirling the sword in her hand. "Math is fun, isn't it?"

The malevolence in Henry's eyes only grew stronger as he glared back at her—he was absolutely livid that she wasn't taking his warning seriously.

Brushing it off as if he had just asked for directions to the nearest flapjack restaurant, Catherine flippantly disregarded his threat. "Alright, Monsieur Halifax. You win. I'll step aside... All you have to do is drop the black duffle bag, and I will be happy to oblige."

Henry glanced at the pack of wolves flanking Catherine and refused, "I'm sorry, Catherine... I can't do that. These polar bear cubs need to be returned to the *Kodiak Bay Zoo*, where they can be properly cared for."

"The zoo?" she quickly retorted, snickering at the frivolous suggestion. "You mean the jail that I just freed those bears from?"

Catherine's demeanor changed in a blink of the eye, and she protested at the mere thought of taking the bears anywhere. "No, no, no, mon ami. Those bears are happy right here. They don't want to go back to their cages!"

Sensing Henry's reluctance to accept what she thought was an extremely generous offer, she screamed ardently, "We resonate with each other! Like a windowpane upon hearing a certain frequency, vibrating back and forth, those bears and I are resonating!"

Henry could tell she wasn't afraid of him, not even a little bit. That didn't mean he was going to back down, though.

Catherine had a unique ability to rile up just about anyone, and she relished the sight of Henry losing his temper as he shouted, "They're just cubs! These bears will starve to death without their mother!"

Despite the desperation in his voice, Catherine shook her head and sighed with disappointment. "Maybe. Maybe not. But they are better off taking their chances in the wild rather than being locked up in a cage for the rest of their lives. They deserve more than a life of incarceration!"

She suddenly raised her voice and screamed at the top of her lungs, "And who are *you* to say otherwise?"

"I won't abandon these orphaned bears," Henry asserted, stubbornly placing his hand over the duffle bag hanging from his shoulder. "Not out here... not like this!"

With a menacing smile smeared across her face, Catherine threatened, "Let me explain something to you, Monsieur Halifax. If you want those polar bears... you'll need to do far more than just ask nicely. Oui, you're going to have to take them from me, Henry. You'll have to fight me for them. And if you somehow make it off this island alive, you better get used to looking over your shoulder for the rest of your life, because I will hunt you down. I will *burn* Kodiak Bay to the ground. And there's nothing you or anyone else can do to stop me. You understand, mon ami?"

The pack of rowdy wolves flanking her erupted into a rumbustious fit of barking. Their intimidating snarls that followed served as a reminder to Henry of the impending danger if he didn't comply.

As he weighed his dwindling options, Catherine added optimistically, "But not to worry, Henry. I will make this easy for you." She reached into her pants pocket, pulled out a set of keys, and tossed them directly in front of him. Penny cautiously stepped forward to sniff the keys and then retreated into a defensive stance alongside her best friend.

Henry gazed at the keys while Catherine presented a slightly better offer. "There is a small boat docked in the bay with a full tank of fuel. More than double the amount needed to make it to the nearest town, just *twenty kilometers* south of here."

"Drop the bag and take that beautiful dachshund with you before I change my mind," she warned, briefly looking over her shoulder toward the massive pile of blood-stained snow nearby. "Or don't... but either way, those polar bears aren't going anywhere." The Arctic wolves at her side let out another short barrage of deafening barks to encourage him to choose wisely.

Penny couldn't resist snapping at them, and she let out a few resounding barks of her own as the wolves growled in response.

After a moment of deliberation, Henry carefully set the black duffle bag on the ground.

Catherine beamed with enthusiastic satisfaction and cackled triumphantly, like she had just gotten exactly what she wanted. Her impetuous celebration instantly faded once he raised his hatchet in a defensive position.

"I'm sorry... I can't do that, Saint-Clair." Henry gulped and stood firm. "I'm not leaving here without these bears. It's the partner's code."

Accepting the offer would have certainly been the easy way out, especially after learning about the full tank of fuel. There was even a part of him that wanted to take the keys while he still had the opportunity to do so. Running away with Penny in his arms seemed too tempting to pass up, but he remembered what Rufus taught him: "*If you don't believe in yourself, you can't expect anyone else to.*"

Catherine tightened her grip on Barnaby's sword. She tutted with disappointment and quickly brought the dog whistle hanging around her neck up to her mouth.

Henry glanced down at Penny and gave her a reassuring nod. He was willing to put his life on the line to protect her and the pair of polar bears at his feet, no matter how terrified he was at that moment. Even though emerging victorious seemed impossible, it was Captain Fulbright who always told him everything was impossible, *until it wasn't*. Henry knew regret would haunt him forever if he turned his back on Barnaby now.

It felt like Henry's heart plummeted to the ground as Catherine took a deep breath with the dog whistle dangling from her lips. The radiant look of amusement on her face left him fearing the worst.

Right as Catherine was about to exhale, she suddenly froze and gasped in confusion. Her neck craned backward once she caught sight of something neither of them ever expected to see in the sky. A look of pure bewilderment flickered in Henry's eyes as the dog whistle fell from her lips—it was almost like she had just seen a ghost.

Still clutching the hatchet, Henry turned around apprehensively and looked up as well. He couldn't believe what he saw. Utterly astonished and transfixed on the sky above, an overwhelming sense of relief washed over his body. The terror. The panic. The despair. It had all vanished in an instant.

Celine Saint-Clair, Catherine's twin sister, landed on the ground unexpectedly. She had only dropped a few meters behind Henry after detaching her parachute.

The forest-green canopy billowed into the passing wind before catching fire and disintegrating into the sky above them. The sight of the dazzling fireworks display nearly brought Henry to tears. He was beyond surprised and truly grateful for her timely arrival.

Celine stepped forward and stood next to Henry in silence. She pulled the electric cattle prod from her belt and held it up in a defensive position as she glared defiantly at her twin sister.

A renewed feeling of excitement fueled Henry's confidence. He was elated to have Celine on his side. It finally felt like the tables had turned now that he and Penny weren't alone anymore.

"Well, well, well... I have to say, I am genuinely surprised to see you here, sis." Catherine quipped, stunned at the sight of her twin sister, "Oui, she really is as loyal as they come, Henry."

"And to think, it's only been two years since you betrayed me in Kansas City," she facetiously sneered. "Not to worry, though, *Celine*... I left the knife in my back the whole time. Oui, it's been there for over *seven hundred* agonizing days! So, you can drop that little toy in your hand and come pull it out if you're here to apologize."

Henry started to think it might have been better if Professor Blackfriar had shown up instead, or even Savannah. The increasing animosity between the pair of Saint-Clair sisters somehow felt more hostile than anything he had seen over the past few days (and that was putting it lightly).

Celine was visibly upset and shouted, "Just stop, Catherine!" Feeling a sense of rage that could only be triggered by her sister, she huffed and yelled resentfully, "Stop blaming me for your mistakes!

You broke the rules, and you got an innocent person killed! Because of *your* actions... *not mine*!"

Henry trembled as Celine continued lambasting her twin sister, "How many times did I cover for you? How many times did I risk my cloak so that you could keep yours? How many, Catherine?"

"I have been cleaning up your messes since we were children... But we're not kids anymore, and this isn't a game! She shouted in annoyance, "It's time for you to grow up!"

Instead of feeling ashamed or embarrassed, a smug look of immense pride glimmered in Catherine's eyes. She loved watching her sister get all riled up and retorted, "Can you believe this, Henry? She came all the way out here to break my heart all over again!"

There was a faint quiver in Catherine's voice, and Henry could tell that Celine might have gone too far in trying to reason with her sister this time.

"You know, I was told from a very young age that you never turn your back on your sister, Henry. *Never*. You always back her play, no matter what," Catherine somberly remarked as a single tear rolled down her face. "Unless, of course, your Tutori cloak is on the line. Then nothing else matters... Not even family."

The vitriol in the air was foreboding and growing at an alarming rate. Worried that a deadly clash would ensue, Henry tried to reason with Catherine before things spiraled out of control. "Please just listen to your sister. It's time to stop running."

Despite the tears in her eyes, Catherine smiled. "I must admit... I'm a bit jealous of you, Henry. Oui, you should consider yourself lucky that you don't have any siblings. You'll never *really* know how it feels when your sister rips your heart out and stomps on it with every step she takes, like it's a piece of bubblegum stuck to the bottom of her shoe."

"The pain is immeasurable," she earnestly concluded, as a few more tears rolled down her face. "It never really ends, does it?"

Hoping to defuse the tension, Henry tried to persuade her once more. "It's over, Catherine. Drop the sword and call off the wolves before anyone else gets killed." He pleaded desperately, "*Please!*"

Catherine wiped the tears from her eyes, responding fervently, "Here we go again! The young Canadian with the heart of gold, interfering in matters that do not concern him. How gracious of Monsieur Henry Halifax to leave Kodiak Bay for the first time just so that he could come out here and tell me how to live my life." Forcing a smile, she gazed at them and jeered, "You see, this is what you both will never understand... It's impossible to hurt someone who has nothing to lose."

The pack of wolves standing next to her howled in solidarity as Catherine calmly lifted the dog whistle back up to her lips.

Penny growled viciously at the wolves while Henry cocked his arm back as if he were about to throw the small axe as hard as he could. Celine pushed the red button on her cattle prodder to show the wolves what they were up against—electricity sparked out of the tip, sending a clear message to any potential challengers.

They assumed the wolves would be set loose at any moment, eager to attack the second they heard Catherine blow the dog whistle dangling from her mouth. Henry's heart was racing. The anticipation of the impending battle sent beads of sweat rolling down his forehead.

Catherine pointed the sword toward her sister and took a deep breath; that's when everyone froze upon hearing a startling thud.

The astonishment glimmering in Catherine's eyes compelled Henry and Celine to turn around immediately. He nearly dropped the hatchet, shocked by what had caused the commotion. The surprise of it all instantly overshadowed the terrifying feeling of helplessness that had stalked Henry since the moment Catherine called out his name. He eagerly welcomed the sentiments of respite that ensued.

Mr. Sakamoto had just dropped to the ground after releasing his parachute. He calmly pulled the samurai sword out of his scabbard and stepped forward to stand alongside Henry and Celine.

Catherine and Henry gazed up at the sky, completely bemused by the sight of more parachutes gliding through the air. It appeared that Mr. Sakamoto was not alone. They watched incomprehensibly as a swarm of Tutori descended from the sky above. By Henry's count, there must have been a few dozen of them.

Landing one by one, the dawn-lined horizon was illuminated by their parachutes catching fire and disintegrating into thin air, almost like a miniature firework show. It was a magnificent sight to behold.

Even though he didn't recognize everyone, Henry beamed with pride when he spotted June, Archie, Savannah, and Professor Blackfriar in the crowd. The emotional roller coaster ride was finally coming to an end now that he suddenly had the backing of nearly every Tutori on the *Arthur Broome*. He assumed that Catherine's imminent surrender was all but guaranteed at this point.

With at least three dozen Tutori now standing behind him as their black cloaks flapped in the air, Henry turned to Catherine and gloated, "Looks like you chose the wrong side tonight, eh?" Surprisingly, she just cackled in response. Her unwavering arrogance in the face of so many Tutori left him worried that she had at least one more trick up her sleeve.

Henry couldn't comprehend why Catherine was still smirking as if she had won. Totally baffled and genuinely concerned that she was crazy enough to challenge all of them in a fight to the death, a surreal sense of panic set in as he helplessly watched what happened next.

His recent bout of confidence had been shattered into a million pieces, and Henry couldn't believe what he was witnessing. Mr. Sakamoto holstered his sword and marched over to the other side to stand with Catherine.

Unable to blink, Henry stared as dozens of Tutori walked past him, one by one, until all of them (except for Celine) had joined Catherine and her pack of Arctic wolves. The disbelief painted on his face only intensified with each person that walked by him.

Chuckling at the sight of Henry's flustered expression, Catherine warned smugly, "Looks can be deceiving, my young Canadian friend." She winked at him tauntingly and added, "Oui, one must always mind the little details."

Henry had never been more shocked in his life. He refused to believe that the Tutori would ever help someone like Catherine. Not after what she did to Barnaby. "What are you all doing?" he asked, emphatically gesturing toward the large pool of red blood nearby. "She killed Barnaby! She murdered one of your own!"

There was an undeniable sense of panic in his voice. He felt like he was drowning, and everyone was just watching casually from the top deck with life vests around their necks.

"June! Archie... you too?" Henry shouted in denial, unwilling to accept that his new friends would join a murderer like Catherine Saint-Clair. Just when he thought things couldn't get any worse, Celine turned to him and said, "I'm sorry, Henry. I never wanted it to happen like this."

Without saying another word, Celine crossed to the other side, leaving Henry to fend for himself. The unexpected change in sentiment befuddled even Penny.

Abandoned by everyone except for his loyal dachshund, the unbearable hopelessness began to multiply at an untenable rate. He was vastly outnumbered, and his chances of escaping seemed insurmountable at this point.

Overcome by panic and anger, Henry trembled as he held the hatchet in his hand. He never imagined that it would end like this—

not in a tense standoff with Catherine, six Arctic wolves, and three dozen Tutori (some of whom he assumed were friends). The sheer terror left him wondering how he would ever get out of this mess alive.

The Tutori weren't going to blink first. They all just stared back at him in an eerily silent manner, stone-faced and resolute in their bizarre decision to support Catherine.

Henry glared incredulously at their black cloaks billowing in the wind. It felt as if they were attending a solemn funeral, but he wasn't convinced the departed would be limited to Barnaby.

— CHAPTER 23 —
THE TUTORI'S CLOAK

S tarting to regret that he hadn't accepted Catherine's offer to take the boat keys earlier, Henry wondered what he could have done differently. Everything seemed so utterly doomed as he stood there next to Penny.

The panicked deliberations came to an abrupt halt when Henry heard what sounded like someone slowly clapping off in the distance. At first, he thought he was hallucinating, but the faint noise kept gradually getting louder.

Henry just watched in bemusement. One by one, the rows of Tutori casually stepped to the side, clearing an opening down the middle while the tempo of the mysterious applause increased. With his neck frantically craning forward, he tried to catch a glimpse of what was happening beyond the sea of black cloaks.

After the Tutori had finally finished clearing a path, Henry could barely comprehend what he saw—it was Barnaby.

Like the reputed theater ghost of Melbourne, Barnaby emerged from the darkness of the caves that were behind the crowds of Tutori. Despite his seemingly blood-soaked attire, he was beaming with excitement. Henry was frozen in a state of incomparable disbelief and merely gawked at the Australian while the rest of the Tutori stepped back into formation.

Barnaby strolled over blithely, howling with laughter, "Wooooooo! Catherine! You really do put on one *hell* of a show!" He added exuberantly, "I mean, you really had me going there. Honestly! And were those real tears too? Bravo! Bravo, mate!"

Growing more perplexed with each passing second, Henry stammered, "But... but... that can't..." struggling to find the words to match the bewildered look on his face. He was practically speechless.

Catherine bowed gracefully when Barnaby started clapping again. She took a bow in front of Henry before swiftly turning around to bow once more toward the dozens of Tutori standing behind her. Most of the Tutori joined in with the applause as if they were watching a curtain call at the end of a highly regarded stage performance in the theater (some of them even pulled out red roses to toss at her feet).

Once the commotion had settled down, everyone turned their attention back to Henry, who was still mystified by the whole ordeal. An eerie silence fell among the Tutori. They just stared at Henry, waiting for him to piece it all together.

Standing in absolute befuddlement, Henry finally managed to mutter, "You... you really were working with Catherine this whole time, *question mark*?" He was so flabbergasted that he actually said the name of the implied punctuation out loud.

Making sense of how this could all be true seemed unimaginable as Henry gripped the hatchet and asked confusedly, "Wait, all of you were? *Everyone*?"

"But that means... the zoo?" He babbled, more confounded than ever. "The cattle stampede in London? The circus train in Paris?"

Barnaby smirked at the sight of Henry stumbling to uncover the truth while the dozens of Tutori standing behind him didn't say a word. He kept quiet until Henry finally asked the *right* question. "*That was all the APA, this whole time*?"

"Well, hot damn!" Barnaby shouted and suddenly clapped his hands together loudly. "He's scrappier than he looks, right?"

The brash Australian sauntered over and patted Henry on the shoulder reassuringly. "You finally cracked the case, kid! Cracked it wide open!"

Still baffled and feeling like he had infinitely more questions than answers, Henry stuttered. "But... but how..."

"But what, mate?" Barnaby snidely interrupted. He stepped back to join his fellow Tutori, sending a piercing look in Henry's direction. "The *Kodiak Bay Zoo*? The same zoo that purchased these polar bear cubs from an exotic animal dealer after the mother was killed by a pack of *cowards* calling themselves hunters?"

Henry lowered the hatchet, mumbling dubiously, "But, London, the stampede... What about..."

"What about London?" Barnaby interjected, thoroughly amused by Henry's struggle to figure it all out. He snickered, "You mean the hundreds of cattle shipped in abhorrent, outright *heinous* conditions across the ocean? Only to march 'em on down to the slaughterhouse while they wait in line to be killed, *one at a time*? Don't you worry, mate... that's just the tip of the iceberg. There'll be another shipment of cows on those same docks a week from now. And another one the week after that."

The revelations that kept pouring out of Barnaby's mouth seemed inconceivable only days ago. But now, everything Henry thought he knew about the *APA* had been completely turned upside down in a matter of minutes. Still astounded by the idea of an elaborately deceptive spectacle transpiring without even an ounce of suspicion on his part, he continued stammering. "But, that means... the... the train in Paris?"

Barnaby chirped, "The train in Paris?"

"You must be talking about the animals onboard, right?" He sneered vociferously, "The same animals trapped in those tiny cages, forced to perform at the circus? Starved and beaten with whips if they don't comply?"

Absolutely stunned, Henry couldn't find the words to answer Barnaby's barrage of questions. Penny was equally puzzled (albeit for a different reason entirely). She was more concerned about the pack of wolves glaring at her and maintained a defensive stance in case one of them dared to attack.

Barnaby's lighthearted demeanor surprisingly turned hostile, and he screamed at Henry, "*You're damn right it was the Tutori this whole time!*"

Just thinking about the suffering those animals had to endure elicited an incensed passion in Barnaby. He looked Henry directly in the eyes, ruthlessly warning, "The *Animal Protection Authority* doesn't care about the law. And the excuses don't matter either. *We protect those who cannot protect themselves!*"

A silent pause followed, though it proved to be fleeting as Barnaby yelled unexpectedly with all his might, "*For the animals!*" prompting the three dozen Tutori standing behind him to shout in unison, "*All of them!*" The pack of Arctic wolves immediately started a boisterous round of howling after the thunderous chant.

The deafening battle cry left Henry's hands trembling, and he staggered backward as if the booming sound itself had shoved him.

Barnaby didn't even flinch; he just glared at Henry, expecting the young boy to surrender the hatchet at once.

Too befuddled to drop the small axe in his hand, Henry blurted nervously, "The council meetings... Your suspension? None of that was real? It was all just a big show?"

"What is it, mate?" Barnaby scoffed, "You thought you were gonna sashay onto the *Arthur Broome*... join the *APA* and become a Tutori just like that?"

Henry was speechless. He instantly felt humbled and somewhat embarrassed to say anything as Barnaby carried on explaining, "It just don't work that way, mate... You gotta prove that you deserve to wear this cloak if you're expecting an invitation from *Barnabas Banjo Murdoch*. That's right, amigo... Your word alone ain't good enough around here. It takes uncompromising integrity and honor to call yourself a *real* Tutori."

"Guess you could call it a *shadow audition* of sorts," he shrugged. "After all, ya gotta have a taste for the theater like our buddy Bill Shakespeare if you're gonna join the *APA*!"

Barnaby sensed that Henry was in need of a healthy dose of perspective and confidently exclaimed, "But let's not forget... It was *you* that recited the Tutori Creed back in Kodiak Bay! It was *you* that interfered with an official *APA* operation that night!" With a spiteful smirk beaming from his face, he added, "I'm gonna be straight with ya, pal... I took that personally."

Catherine shook her head and chuckled after finally hearing the real reason Barnaby had gone to all this trouble for a new recruit.

"You wanted to see what it was like to be a real Tutori, right?" Barnaby asserted before Henry could answer, "Well, now you know, mate! Kodiak Bay, London, Paris... that was all just business as usual for the *Animal Protection Authority*. No, sir... Don't expect a shred of mercy or sympathy from us if you're in the business of hurting animals!"

Henry had no idea their vetting process could be so rigorous, nor did he ever imagine reciting the Tutori Creed would land him in this much trouble, but Barnaby was far from finished.

With Henry and the dozens of Tutori listening intently, Barnaby clarified, "Decisions have consequences, my young friend. You've gone through *fifteen years* of life making thousands of seemingly inconsequential choices every day. Pancakes or poutine... jean jacket or the yellow raincoat... ice hockey or real sports... and the beat goes on."

"You go to sleep at the end of the day only to wake up and do it all over again. But every now and then, you have to decide which path you're gonna follow in this world. I'm talking about those really important choices that come up... the ones that ultimately change your life forever... the decisions that close one chapter and start the next." He glanced at Penny and winked before ardently concluding, "Well, today is that day for you, kid. It's time to choose between right and wrong... It's time for you to decide if you're gonna go down this road or that road."

Barnaby pulled a duplicate set of keys out of his pocket, dangled them on his finger for a moment, and then tossed the keys at Henry's feet. "You and Penny are free to leave... You can take that boat over there and head to the nearest town right now. It's only about *twenty kilometers* south of here and should be an easy voyage for an experienced sailor like yourself."

"I'll even radio the Royal Canadian Naval patrol ship we passed on the way here. I'm sure they'd be more than happy to take you both back home to Kodiak Bay." He added, "Nobody gets hurt. No hard feelings! Gave Captain Fulbright my word on that, and a Tutori never breaks their word."

The offer was undoubtedly tempting, but Henry never expected Barnaby to extend the enticing invitation that followed. "Or... you can join the *APA*... become a real Magari like you wanted, and prove Sunday wrong."

As Henry gazed down at the keys lying in front of him, still trying to make sense of everything he had just learned, Barnaby cavalierly tossed a fork at his feet.

Catherine raised her sword in a defensive position as Barnaby's tone turned more ominous. "The choice is yours... but it's just like Catherine said," he warned, slyly pulling a tranquilizer dart from his suspenders, "those bear cubs aren't going anywhere either way."

Henry looked timidly at the confused dachshund staring up at him while keeping the hatchet gripped tightly in his hand. As the Tutori awaited his answer, the black duffle bag unexpectedly tipped over by itself before he could announce his decision. The commotion had woken up the pair of polar bear cubs, and their insatiable curiosity had sent them tumbling out of the bag onto the snow.

Growing tired of Henry's indecision, Barnaby demanded, "So, what's it gonna be, kid? Are you with us? Or is it back to Kodiak Bay for the rest of your life?"

Henry peered through the falling snowflakes at the sea of Tutori standing in front of him. Taking a deep breath, he glanced at the polar bears playfully wrestling and quickly raised his arm, clutching the hatchet in the air defiantly. The wolves at Barnaby's side took notice and snarled as if they were about to attack, while gasps of disbelief filled the air.

All of a sudden, Henry flung the axe straight down into the snow next to Catherine's black duffle bag.

Barnaby's eyes followed the small axe to the ground, almost like it was the only thing he could see. His heart skipped a beat in that instant, but when he looked back up, Henry had a hand extended and a huge grin on his face. Once Barnaby realized that Henry had decided to take the offer, he didn't think twice about shaking his hand.

Sincerely grateful for the invitation, Henry announced boldly, "*For the animals!*" Everyone except Barnaby shouted back immediately, "*All of them!*"

The infectious smile painted on Barnaby's face only got bigger as he proudly replied, "Welcome to the *Animal Protection Authority*, mate."

Penny let out three resounding barks to express her acceptance of the invitation as Catherine pulled another whistle out of her pocket. It must have been a special whistle of some sort, because Henry didn't hear a sound despite her blowing quite vigorously. The wolves didn't move an inch either.

Henry stared curiously as the dozens of Tutori standing in front of him stepped off to the side to clear a path again.

Much to Henry's surprise, it wasn't the three council members that emerged from the caves—he was shocked when he saw a full-grown polar bear slowly approaching instead. The massive polar bear stood on her hind legs and let out a booming roar before strutting over to the cubs, who were clumsily playing near his feet. He staggered backward, almost tripping in the process.

The adult polar bear largely ignored him and just nuzzled both of the younger bears with her nose, which left Henry feeling confident that the cubs would be properly looked after by one of their own. Underneath all the deceitfulness, it turned out Catherine was right about more than a few things.

Two of the Arctic wolves suddenly charged toward Barnaby, ecstatic that the charade was now finally over and unable to contain their unbridled excitement any longer. They leaped onto his chest with excitement and a rambunctious familiarity that showed they'd been friends for a long time. He was instantly knocked over by their impromptu greeting, laughing as the wolves showered him with affection. "Alright, calm down, calm down. It's nice to see you too!"

June raced past the crowds of Tutori and rushed over to check on Henry, while Archie chased closely behind. Archie was relieved to see that Henry was safe and chuckled when June emphatically wrapped her arms around him.

As she hugged him tightly, June confessed, "Henry! I'm so happy you're okay!" She was worried that he would be mad at her and frantically tried to explain, "We wanted to tell you this whole time, honestly! But we couldn't! Barnaby gave everyone strict orders to play along. He said it would just be for a few days!"

"Yeah, we're both sorry. Truly," Archie chimed in, adding reassuringly. "But the hard part is over now, right? You made it! *You're in!*"

As June bent down to greet the slightly jealous dachshund at her feet, Henry chortled and extended his arm to shake Archie's hand. Even though it all turned out to be an elaborate display of subterfuge, he would never forget that Archie stepped up to help him when nobody else could. He was honored to call the British Magari his friend and would be forever thankful for the encouragement.

"It's all good. I know you were both just following orders," Henry replied. "I would have done the same thing if I were in your shoes, eh?"

"Yeah, Barnaby lives for the show... that's for sure!" Archie jested, laughing as he carried on explaining. "It doesn't happen often, though. June got by with a few arduous interviews by the council, and I pretty much just had to show up given my father's influence in these matters. Certainly doesn't compare to what you went through!" Henry tilted his head incredulously, smiling while Archie concluded, "With that said, Barnaby is a special kind of bloke... The kind that lives and dies by Australian rules."

Hoping to vindicate herself, June blurted, "I didn't think it was right, but Savannah said to keep quiet and play along. Apparently, each Tutori has the final say on how they audition new recruits, and you managed to find the most, um... theatrical one out of the whole lot."

Catherine walked over and interjected, "And I'm sorry about your dachshund, Henry."

"I never planned to take Penny with me, but she stepped in the oil during that little tussle we had under the bridge," she clarified apologetically. "Her whole backside was covered in it! I couldn't leave her there with that fire burning!"

Henry graciously replied, "Well, I hope Penny wasn't too much trouble! And thank you for taking good care of her... I'm sure she appreciates it very much." Penny barked twice to show her gratitude; she was clearly pleased with the grooming services and her stylish new attire.

Once Barnaby had finished greeting the rest of the Arctic wolves, he marched over to Henry and patted him on the shoulder again. "Not bad for your first run, Kodiak Bay. Not bad at all!" Henry's back was still sore from tumbling into the stack of crates under the bridge in Paris, which reminded him, "Hey, wait a minute... What about the *FDR Boys*? They nearly beat us to a pulp! Was that part of the plan too?"

"The *FDR Boys*?" Catherine asked, evidently baffled to hear they were somehow involved. "You mean that one guy... What's his name? *Tony Lasagna*?"

Barnaby laughed awkwardly. "Yeah... sorry about that, mate. The *FDR Boys* were most definitely *not* part of the show."

"I was truly worried there for a minute," he admitted. "Thought we might both end up in the infirmary after those French hooligans showed up. But we made 'em work for it, right, Halifax?" An exasperated sigh ensued as Barnaby explained, "Caught a few of those cowards terrorizing some stray dogs last time I was in Paris... Had to teach them a lesson before I left. I reckon they've been looking for payback ever since."

"Gotta be careful with those *vendettas*, eh?" Henry shrewdly jested. Barnaby snickered. "Honestly, I thought you would've given up back in London. Never expected you'd even make it off the top deck once you saw those parachutes come out."

Henry huffed, admittedly a bit disappointed (yet not entirely surprised) that Barnaby had underestimated him from the outset. Even though the brazen Tutori struggled to pay him a genuine compliment, it seemed par for the course with Barnaby. Maybe that was just the Australian way.

Nonetheless, Barnaby was feeling a tad bit guilty about the disheartened look on Henry's face and confessed, "Hell, I'd be lying if I didn't say there was a part of me that even wanted to see you get slightly trounced by that cattle stampede, mate. Figured you'd be begging me to take you back to Kodiak Bay after that. I will say, you never gave up... and you had my back even when you thought I was gone for good. That's what really matters. Can't buy that kind of integrity because it has no price."

Even though his back hurt, his nose was bruised, and his ankle was sprained, Henry couldn't help but smile when he finally earned Barnaby's respect.

"Yeah, I guess you could say *it's a tale as old as time*," Barnaby boasted mirthfully. Henry merely shook his head in silence while Archie and June chuckled.

Aside from wondering what kind of library Barnaby was getting his books from, Henry still had about a million unanswered questions and frantically asked, "Hang on a second... I'm still confused. How did you know I would follow you into the zoo that night? How did you know I'd even be there?"

"The truth is... we didn't," Barnaby chortled. "You see, the Tutori can't be seen breaking into zoos and setting wild animals loose in the streets. We *always* operate in the shadows to avoid conflicts with law enforcement... which is why they often look the other way when they see the black cloak." He scoffed, promptly adding, "There's a lot more to it than just helping ducks cross the street. So, don't ever let anyone tell you this job is easy!"

"Catherine Saint-Clair was the decoy that night, and after we saw you, I decided to initiate the stagecraft routine. That's right... propah misdirection to make you, the Mounties, and everyone else think that I was trying to help stop the Frenchman. But like I said, there's always more to the story than you think." Barnaby carried on, "You see, she's my partnah... She always has been. We were working together the whole time."

Henry blurted curiously, "The *stagecraft routine*? But what about everyone else? How did they know about the shadow audition before we even boarded the *Arthur Broome*?"

"Well, look at this guy... He's smartah than the average bear, after all!" Barnaby exclaimed with a grin. "It's all in the signal color, mate. Surely you noticed the firework I launched into the air back on the docks in Kodiak Bay? When Captain Carlucci saw the green-colored signal, he made a ship-wide announcement to let everyone know prior to our arrival. Then we held a secret council meeting once you got to your cabin, and that was that."

In the midst of his long-winded explanation, Savannah marched over and suddenly shoved Barnaby to the ground. "You went too far with that salsa remark, Murdoch!" A few of the Arctic wolves thought he was back to dole out some more ear scratches and eagerly pounced on him once again.

While Barnaby wrestled in the snow with the adolescent wolves vying for his attention, Savannah extended her arm to properly congratulate Henry. He grabbed a hold and firmly shook her hand as she declared, "Canadians are tougher than I thought... You can hang your hat on that, Jack!" Henry smirked, confidently firing back, "Yes, ma'am. The toughest in the business!"

"Brilliant, Halifax! Bloody brilliant!" Professor Blackfriar barged in, sneaking up behind Savannah. "I just wanted to tell you, I've been on the job for nearly *forty years* now, and this was the best damn shadow audition I've ever seen! Almost lost it when she stuck me with those fake darts back in London, but a real Tutori never breaks character, mate. *Never*. I'll admit... it stung a bit, but it was worth the price of admission any day of the week. Yes, sir, that's a show I'll never forget! I still can't believe you did it all without a stitch of denim to boot!"

Henry glanced at him with a slanted smile and raised eyebrows, prompting the professor to throw his hands up dramatically. "Oh, come on, mate, I'm just having a laugh!"

"All kidding aside, you did good, lad... honest," Professor Blackfriar sincerely acknowledged. He shook Henry's hand and said, "The *APA* is lucky to have you onboard!"

As Henry and the rest of the Tutori walked toward the floating dock, he got to meet practically everyone—they kept coming up to him and introducing themselves, all thoroughly impressed with his performance in the show (even though Henry didn't know it had been an elaborate production the entire time). It was a bit overwhelming. But he finally felt like he truly belonged, especially once he realized that most of them were rooting for him to not give up.

With the yellow floatplane and the small boat in sight, a trio of *APA* zodiacs quickly entered the caldera, zipping across the bay. Henry could see Valentina behind the wheel of the boat leading the way and didn't hesitate to jump into her zodiac when it pulled up alongside the dock.

"Buongiorno, Signor Halifax," Valentina announced merrily. "Or should I say, Henry Halifax, *Magari of the Animal Protection Authority*!"

Blushing, Henry quipped, "At your service, Signorina Vinciguerra!" and bowed to let her know the show was indeed over, at least for now. Valentina tittered, "Never doubted you for a second!"

Penny let out two sassy barks, sensing that she wasn't getting the recognition she deserved. Valentina looked toward the wirehaired dachshund and added, "Not with Penny Halifax at your side, of course!"

The ride back to the ship went by so fast that Henry didn't notice he had been smiling the entire way. It was a day to remember, without question. His life had been irrevocably changed, and all he could think about was what sort of adventures awaited in the days to come.

Approaching the *Arthur Broome* definitely felt different this time. He knew his cabin wasn't exactly a mansion, but he was still proud to call it home.

Elated to be back onboard the illustrious ship once again, Henry, Penny, June, and Archie were immediately greeted by Otis and Oscar when the elevator doors in the great hall opened. The pair of playful otters didn't hesitate to crawl up Henry's legs, which sent him tumbling backward onto the ground as Penny and the others watched in amusement.

The otter brothers had grown quite fond of Henry and were pleased to see that he had returned mostly unscathed. They had been worried sick after spotting him leaving his cabin a few hours earlier with the parachute harness in hand. Fortunately for Henry, they had alerted Barnaby out of fear that something terrible could happen.

Despite being exhausted from such a tumultuous excursion to Deception Island, Henry and Penny were famished. They happily agreed to join Archie and June in the dining hall for a stupendous feast, and it was indeed stupendous. The chef had prepared everything imaginable. There were flapjacks, hard-shell tacos, pizzas, pastas, poutine, hamburgers, barbeque, sushi, cannoli, gelato, apple pies, and plenty of sweet potato sticks for Penny.

The rest of the Tutori were also there, and most of them were keenly listening to Barnaby regale the whole room with hilarious stories about all the different times Henry had nearly fainted over the past few days.

Needless to say, Barnaby was very proud of the fact that he had pulled off one of the most elaborate and entertaining shadow auditions in *APA* history.

Amid the occasional outbursts of howling laughter filling the room (Professor Blackfriar was undoubtedly the loudest of them all), Henry took it all in stride, beaming at the sight of Penny and his new friends. And although he didn't realize it at the time, he had become somewhat of a celebrity onboard. His shadow audition had proven to be legendary, setting a high bar for any new recruits who might follow.

Once everyone finished eating, most of the Tutori shuffled out of the grand atrium and went about their day as usual.

Henry noticed the three council members—Madam MacDougall, Madam Cross, and Madam Machado—were curiously absent. He rushed over to stop Barnaby from leaving and asked, "What happened to the council? I thought they were going to personally oversee the rescue mission on Deception Island?"

Barnaby chuckled as the elevator doors opened. Stepping into the departing elevator, he casually quipped, "Afraid they couldn't make it, mate... Ya see, nuns don't work on Tuesdays." And just like that, Barnaby vanished once the doors closed.

With their ravenous appetites now fully satisfied, Henry and Penny spent the rest of the day following June and Archie around the ship. They gave them an official tour, introducing Henry to the ship's doctor and Chief Engineer Moretti down in the engine room (who was in the middle of fiddling with his espresso machine). After meeting virtually everyone onboard, including the librarian, the barber, the chef, and countless others, he even got to chat with some of the Carabinieri guards that had chased him out of the bridge.

Archie went on and on for hours, telling June, Henry, and Penny more about the legendary *APA* and the enthralling missions his father had been a part of years ago—right until the sun started to go down.

Listening to all the stories reminded Henry to ask that they stop by the operators' station near the grand atrium. He was thrilled to finally talk to Captain Fulbright over the ship's radio and enthusiastically told him everything that happened over the past few days.

Mrs. Fulbright was not quite as ecstatic when she heard the chaotic details of what had unfolded. She was absolutely livid that Henry didn't say goodbye before he left, but she calmed down once he agreed to send her a letter every month, no matter what. In between all the fuming and fretful questions, he could tell they were both proud of him.

As the conversation came to an end, Henry promised to return to Kodiak Bay for Christmas in a couple months. Of course, Penny got the last word in with a few joyful barks to say goodbye.

When Henry eventually made it back to his cabin at the end of the day, he couldn't even look at the tray of warm food that had recently been delivered to his cabin for dinner. Even Penny was still full after their gluttonous meal earlier.

As Henry opened the closet door to hang up his yellow raincoat, he instantly noticed the dark-blue neckties hanging inside were now gone—in their place were seven black neckties with an envelope clipped to one of them. He eagerly opened the envelope and pulled out the small card enclosed, smiling as he read the message out loud: *"If your best isn't good enough, real courage is not giving up when doing the right thing isn't the easy thing to do."*

Rufus Robinson's name was signed at the bottom.

Henry's eyes glimmered with pride; he knew right away that it was Rufus who had put the parachute harness in his closet following the last council meeting.

Jealous that she wasn't getting his undivided attention, Penny began to whine at his feet (as only a dachshund could). Henry was surprised that she hadn't fallen asleep by this point and happily kneeled down to pick her up. She showered him with kisses, grateful to be in his arms once again, and affectionately licked every inch of his face.

Henry carried her over to the couch, and they plopped down wearily. He was downright exhausted and could tell that Penny was due for a nap—she could barely keep her eyes open.

With the wirehaired dachshund blissfully resting in his lap, Henry gazed out at the open ocean through the sliding glass door. The throbbing pain from his injuries seemed to just melt away now that Penny was safe. The ship's doctor confirmed that he had sprained his ankle, but she was kind enough to wrap it up for him earlier, using an elastic bandage to stop the swelling.

Nearly thirty minutes later, Henry heard the ceiling-mounted loudspeaker chime just as he was about to doze off. It was Captain Carlucci with a new ship-wide announcement.

"*Buonasera*, signore e signori.

"This is-a Captain Alfredo Carlucci speaking to you from the bridge.

"What a wild shadow audition, courtesy of *Barnabas Banjo Murdoch*! We must all congratulate the newest members of the *APA*, young Signor Henry Halifax and his brave wirehaired dachshund, Penny. Sì, Sì, Sì, all the way from Kodiak Bay, Canada. Benvenuto to the *Animal Protection Authority*. This ship is-a now your home, and there will always be room onboard for all Tutori that seek passage across the high seas. We trust that you will bring honor to those who have worn the cloak before you.

"You know, there were a lot of people out there that thought Henry would fail. Lot of people that I know very well didn't think he would make it. Sì, many doubted him. Even Signor Sakamoto was skeptical. Schlansky too! It's true. But Captain Carlucci told them... I warned every last one of them... this kid is-a tougher than he looks. Personally, I think it is-a the maple syrup. Either way, Signor Halifax is-a pass... Not a fail!

"I will have to say, Signor Murdoch put on quite a show out there, and you know, Captain Carlucci said to him... I said, Barnaby, this is-a risky scheme you cooked up here. I told him... maybe this is-a too much? I remember talking to Barnaby, and I said, my brother in Christ, if you're going to put Henry through a shadow audition, you need to look out for this kid. Frankly speaking, Captain Carlucci tried to warn him that young Henry could really get hurt out there! Just look at what happened with that bloody nose and the *FDR Boys*. Look at the bruises from those crates under the bridge. I mean, just look at the sprained ankle... I think you have to look at all of it. Okay, real bruises!

"And you know, Captain Carlucci is-a very close with Barnaby. And Catherine too. She is-a very close friend of mine... Even though sometimes I confuse her with her sister. It is-a crazy how they look exactly the same! Sì, it can be very hard to tell them apart if you didn't know any better!

"You see, I've watched Barnaby and Catherine work together as partners for years. They eat breakfast together... and you know, most people don't like him, but he is-a wonderful guy. No, no, no, it is-a true. Most people don't like Barnaby at all... Maybe it is-a the Australian accent... but let me tell you, he really is-a wonderful guy.

"I had breakfast with him the other day, and it was delicious. There were a lot of times when I was eating breakfast in the grand atrium, and the chef knew exactly what I wanted.

"And you know, from *1952 to 1959*, Captain Carlucci ate the exact same breakfast every day. Two eggs over medium, two strips of bacon, shredded potatoes, lightly fried, of course, and a tall glass of orange juice. I call it *the signature* around here.

"Now, some of you might have heard this before, but I have to say it again for our French colleagues. The chef here onboard the *Arthur Broome* is-a one of the finest at sea. Have you ever had food made from plants? What about a chicken sandwich grown from animal cells?

"I know, I know... Captain Carlucci would agree that it tasted like cardboard in the very beginning. But that's okay. It's okay. The Carabinieri scientists thrive on doubt.

"And you know, quite frankly, a lot of people doubted the Carabinieri Science Regiment... but never tell an Italian they can't do something. Sì, Sì, Sì, this is-a always a big mistake. This is-a how we got the tower in Pisa. You all know what I'm talking about, right? And honestly, the food tastes better when animals don't have to die for it.

"Captain Carlucci told Barnaby the other day at breakfast... the Carabinieri don't quit when things seem impossible. They're not cowards. Let me tell you... and you know this is-a true... Captain Carlucci wanted to be in the Carabinieri Science Regiment when he was just a young bambino. It is-a true... this is-a true. But when I joined the Carabinieri, I could hear the high seas calling Carlucci's name. Just like my papa and his papa before him. And you know, it could have been a completely different life for Captain Carlucci, but I wouldn't have it any other way. There is-a no place that this old sailor would rather be than with his fellow Carabinieri and the Tutori.

"Now, as I look out from the bridge, we are making good progress since we departed Deception Island hours ago. That Norwegian Sea ice was some nasty stuff, but nothing this ship can't handle. Sì, the *Arthur Broome* is currently sailing at a comfortable thirty-five knots.

"With the assistance of my trusted navigation officer, we have charted a course for Osaka. That is-a Japan for all you Magari onboard. Sì, Sì, Sì, we have received some troubling reports about several Tutori that have gone missing out there. They were investigating an extremely dangerous man that most of us are very familiar with. Now, these Tutori were supposed to check in days ago, but nobody has heard from them. And let me tell you, Captain Carlucci is-a little worried here. Truthfully, I think we should all be a little worried. But rest assured, the Tutori never leaves anyone behind. Sì, the *APA* will get to the bottom of these mysterious disappearances.

"It is-a going to be a long journey, but the *Arthur Broome* should arrive in Osaka in approximately six days. Although, if you think about it, today is-a pretty much over, so we are really only talking about five days if you don't count today. And you know, Captain Carlucci is-a big fan of Japan. Just ask Signor Sakamoto. Have you ever seen the food there? They have these little rolls packed with fare in the center and covered in rice on the outside. And now this is-a true... I've seen it with my own two eyes... They eat them with two wooden sticks instead of a fork.

"Just two sticks! Can you believe that? They make 'em from trees! Sì, it took Captain Carlucci a few tries, but working those sticks is-a harder than it looks. It takes real practice, my friends. And frankly, it takes patience too. You know, I see a lot of possibilities with getting rid of all the forks onboard and just switching to chopsticks. Something for us all to think about.

"Per favore, don't let me keep you up any longer, though. I know it is-a getting late, and some of you must be very tired. But let me tell you, and this goes for everyone... You are always welcome to stop by the bridge anytime if you want to talk about it. Captain Carlucci's door is-a always open.

"From all of us on the bridge, *buonanotte*... Sì, sì, sì, *benedici il creatore e tutti quelli che passano per le sue acque.*"